RETICENT HAWKE

A SECOND GENERATION HAWKE FAMILY
NOVEL

BILLIONAIRES OF NEW ORLEANS: THE HAWKE
FAMILY SECOND GENERATION
BOOK 2

GWYN MCNAMEE

RETICENT HAWKE
© 2023 Gwyn McNamee

Cover Model: Chad

Photographer: Michelle Lancaster

Cover Design: Michelle Johnson at Bluesky Design

Editing: Stephie Walls at Wallflower Edits

To anyone who has ever fought against the demons of their past and never stopped swinging...

HAWKE FAMILY TREE

THE HAWKE FAMILY
Antonia and Sam "The Savage" Hawke

SAVAGE COLLISION

Savage Hawke & Danika Eriksson

Kennedy Hawke

STONE SOBER

Stone Hawke & Nora Eriksson

Isaac Hawke   Coen Hawke

TAINTED SAINT

Solomon "Saint" Clarke & Caroline Brooks

Pope Clarke   Bishop Clarke

TORTURED SKYE

Skye Hawke & Gabe Anderson

Atlas Anderson   Astrid Anderson

BUILDING STORM

Storm Hawke (Matthews) & Landon McCabe

Angelina Matthews   Alessandra McCabe

STEELE RESOLVE

Luca "Steele" Abello & Byron Harris

Jude Harris-Abello (ad)

1

JUDE

Small, soft hands blaze a fiery trail over my collarbone, across my chest, light fingertips searing my skin everywhere they make contact, moving lower, feathering along each ridge of my clenched abs toward the one place I've always wanted her.

I release a deep groan and shift closer to her, relishing her tender, intimate touch, the *only* one I've ever craved.

"Jude..."

My hard cock twitches at that sensual voice, whispering my name in my ear with so much love and desire. Something I never thought I'd hear from her perfect lips. Something I didn't think was possible.

I angle my body toward her again, desperate for more, for *everything* from her. She presses her lips to mine greedily and devours my mouth, her hunger matching my own—raw, carnal, necessary.

The familiar scent of cinnamon and coffee she always carries with her permeates every breath I take, and my mouth waters to taste her. My fingers itch to touch her the same way she does me, to explore and revel in the feel of her smooth skin responding to what I can do to her.

Touch her, Jude.

That's all I want. All I've ever wanted.

"Jude...she wouldn't be doing this if she knew..."

That *other* voice tries to break through, the same one that always ruins these moments, that always shatters the calm and bliss I feel in her arms, but I block it out, concentrating on her loving fingers trailing over my abs and toward my aching cock.

I reach out and grip her wide, soft hips, digging my fingers into the flesh to drag her up against me, my length crushed between us, rubbing against her soft, sweat-slicked skin. She moans into my mouth, her frantic hands sliding between us to stroke me.

"God, yes."

My whispered words are a benediction.

A prayer to my own personal saint.

Because she is my savior.

The only one who has ever been able to do this to me.

The only one who can drag me from the dark depths of my personal hell and out into the light.

The only one I'll ever want to.

"Jude." My name comes more forcefully this time, her voice laced with a frantic need that stirs something deep inside me to give her everything she gives me, a task I fear may be impossible. "Jude, please."

She doesn't need to beg me. Doesn't need to do anything but *look* at me for me to be desperate to give her anything she ever wants.

"Jude!"

Another voice yelling my name jerks me from the dream before it can turn into the nightmare it always does. Before the soft, tender touches become rough, aggressive, and demanding.

The heavy metal loft door slams shut, reverberating through the open space and cutting through the fog still clouding my brain.

"Jude, where are you?"

Fuck.

Allie.

I release my throbbing cock, grab the covers, and tug them over my nude body so she won't see the raging hard-on. Shoving my hand through my hair, I prop myself up on my elbows and try to appear like she didn't just interrupt me having a wet dream like a fucking teenager.

She flings open the bedroom door, two to-go coffee cups balanced precariously in one hand, and raises a dark brow at me, her blue Hawke eyes narrowing on my current state. "What the hell? You're still in bed?"

I groan and drop back onto the pillow, keeping an eye on her to try to gauge if she has any idea what she almost walked in on. "What time is it?"

Too fucking early.

She scowls and glances toward the nightstand, which I could have easily done myself if I weren't so distracted by my aching cock that I can do nothing about now. "It's 7:30 already."

"What?" I blink away the last remnants of my dream, trying to breathe normally to slow my heart thundering against my ribcage. "What are you doing here so late?"

Her focus darts away for a moment toward the shuttered bedroom window she can't see out of anyway.

Odd.

She returns her gaze to me, her lips twisting slightly. "I got a late start this morning."

The longer I watch her, the more she fidgets, shifting from foot to foot, a little muscle near her mouth on the right side twitching the same way it always does when she's lying to me.

What the hell are you up to, Allie?

3

She takes the few steps to the bed and climbs onto it, settling in next to me against the headboard and handing me the coffee while scanning me from the top of my head, over my bare chest, to where the comforter settles over my abdomen. "Late night last night?"

I nod and scrub my hand over the day's-worth of stubble on my face. "Yeah."

She waggles her eyebrows. "Who with? Another hottie from Tinder or Rosalie?"

I chuckle and elbow her playfully. "Wouldn't you like to know?"

She pouts and takes a sip of her coffee. "I would, but you never share any of your sexcapades with me."

Maybe that's because I never have any.

Though, she'll never know that. Letting her believe I spend the nights we're not hanging out together banging random chicks I meet on apps is a lot better than her knowing the truth —a lot better than *anyone* knowing it.

I take a sip of the coffee and swallow the magnificently scalding-hot liquid. Almost immediately, the caffeine coursing through my system helps erase the last lingering fragments of the dream. If Allie had come in a minute later, it would have been too late, and she would have received a very interesting morning wake-up.

"Jude..." She waits for me to turn my head toward her. "Why do you look so out of it this morning?"

The chances of me admitting the reason behind my unusual behavior are slim to none. And I'm a much better liar than Allie thinks I am. "Nothing. I'm fine."

Her dark brow wings up. "Are you, though? Your cheeks are flushed, and you look like you were just going at it with somebody."

Only my fucking hand.

She glances toward the partially closed bathroom door, and

her jaw drops. "Oh, my God. Is someone *here*? Did I walk in on—"

I hold up a hand to stop her because she'll go off on a tangent—that I have no intention of traveling with her—if I don't nip this in the bud pronto. "No. Just a long night, like you said. I can't believe I slept in so late." I elbow her side. "Where were you last night, anyway?"

It isn't like Allie to bail on movie night, especially without telling me she wasn't going to show up. But her disappearances as of late suggest a new beau, one she doesn't want any of us to know about. Not unusual for her to keep her personal life private from the Hawkes, but not from *me*.

She must really like this guy.

Allie averts her gaze again and picks at the edge of the coffee cup like it's suddenly the most interesting thing in the world. "Out."

Evasive much?

"Out *where*?"

One of her slender shoulders rises and falls. "Just out with some of the girls in the Bywater."

I take a sip of my coffee and try to appear disinterested. "Your sister?"

Allie snorts and shakes her head. "Hell, no. I couldn't get Angelina to go out and do anything fun if her life depended on it." She gives me a pointed look. "And *now,* she's fucking pissed at me for coming in so late this morning and then immediately running over here to bring this to you."

I smirk, picturing Angelina's soft skin flaming in her anger with her sister. "Well, tell her I'll leave a bigger tip next time."

Allie's elbow hits me in the ribs, and she chuckles. "You haven't paid for a drink once since Angelina opened the place. I don't think she'll believe you're going to start now, let alone tipping."

I groan and drop my head back against the headboard,

letting my eyes drift closed, the draw of the incredible dream making me want to crawl under the covers completely and fall back asleep instead of chugging this drink to get wired and start my day. "You know I feel bad about that, and I'm going to keep offering even though you both keep saying no."

The *tsking* noise fills my ears, and Allie shifts beside me. "I'm not going to let you pay for your drinks, Jude. You're *family*."

I cringe at her words, the guilt automatically carving away at my chest from the inside out.

To most people, being considered a Hawke—even if not by blood—would be a good thing. It would mean acceptance into one of the most prominent families in New Orleans. Money and power. Prestige. Anything you could possibly want at your fingertips. But being a Hawke has its drawbacks—one very big one, in particular...

I incline my head toward the café across the street. "Shouldn't you get going before your sister tears you a new one?"

Her phone buzzes in her back pocket, vibrating against the mattress, and she lifts her ass to reach back and grab it, then stares at it, scowling. "Perfect timing, as always."

She flips the phone toward me so I can read it.

ANG

Where the hell are you? Give him his coffee
and get back here. We're busy.

Allie rolls her eyes and shoves her phone back into her pocket as she scoots off the end of the bed. "You better appreciate how much I love you, that I'll take that kind of attitude from her just to bring you your coffee fix every morning."

I lay my hand against my bare chest, directly over my heart. "You're a true hero."

"Yeah, yeah." She waves me off. "You just writing today?"

I chuckle and run my hand through my hair to get it out of my eyes. "Do I ever do anything else?"

She stops at the door and looks at me for a moment, her eyes softening as if she wants to ask me about something or make a comment, but she doesn't. "I don't know what it is you do all day, to be honest. You won't let me read anything you write, not even before you submitted it to that publisher."

I squeeze my eyes closed and shake my head. "I'm sorry, Al. I just can't. I feel..."

Jesus. What's the right word?

Embarrassed. Angry. Panicked.

Deceptive...

Because you're trying to hide from her what you know she would see if she read what you're currently writing. What you haven't been able to get out of your head until you finally started writing it down...

The thing you never thought you'd put on paper.

"Maybe one day."

Of course, nothing prevents her from picking up my first book and reading it at any time—except my request that she doesn't. The same request I made of all the Hawkes.

She scowls and takes a sip of her coffee, then points an accusatory finger at me. "That sounds like a copout, buddy. But one of these days, you're going to leave that computer open and I'm going to dig right in and email myself a copy of whatever it is you're working on."

"That would be theft."

She smirks. "So, sue me. I'm sure Isaac would love to represent me on a frivolous case like that."

I bark out a laugh. "And I'm sure Stone would love to beat Isaac's ass on *my* behalf."

Her lips twitch again, but her smile falters quickly. "You sure you're okay?"

Have I ever been?

7

A huge part of me, the part that has always seen Allie as my other half, no different than if we had been in the same womb and shared our parents, wants to come clean with her, wants to unload everything I've been carrying around on my shoulders for the last few years. But the bigger part, the part that was always called weak, that feared the repercussions of failing, refuses to let anyone see that, to know what lives and breathes inside of me.

I force a smile. "I'm good."

You just gave me blue balls, but it's the least of my problems.

"Okay. I'll call you later." Her brows rise. "Are we hanging out tonight?"

"Yeah. Unless you ditch me again..."

Guilt finally appears in her blue gaze. "Yeah, sorry about that. Really. I meant to text but got caught up with—" She stops herself. "Anyway, I'll see you later." She takes a step toward the front door, then turns back. "And hey, if you're *that* tired, whatever you're working on must be really good. I'm sorry if I interrupted one of your sessions or something."

I wince.

One of my sessions.

She meant brainstorming and writing, not stroking my cock while I dreamed about the one woman in the world I can never have.

I wait until the sound of the heavy exterior door slamming closed hits my ears before I release a disgruntled groan, take another sip of my drink, and climb from the bed. My semi-hard cock still aches between my legs, and I step into the bathroom and glance at myself in the mirror.

Al was right. My disheveled blond hair falls over my eyes. Pink still highlights my cheeks. It certainly looks like someone who was just getting it on.

Hell.

The simple thought of the dream makes my cock stir fully to life again, and I take it in my hand and wince.

Don't do it, Jude.

It's the same thing I tell myself every time, but I know I will, despite knowing how wrong it is. Because it's an addiction—one I acquired the moment I saw her fifteen years ago—that's only grown stronger as I've spent more time with her, seen who she really is at her core, watched her pain and drive and witnessed how deeply she cares for everyone around her and protects them.

She's an addiction I'll never shake, no matter how many reasons there might be to try.

I make my way out of the bedroom into the main loft space and slowly inch toward the window overlooking the street. Standing in the shadowed corner, no one can see me, but I can see *her*.

Shining, thick, dark hair spills down over her shoulders, bouncing and swinging with each step she takes. Perfect pink lips turn up into a genuine smile for every customer. Her ass sways almost rhythmically as she walks around Hawke's Daily Grind, her curves shown off in the skin-tight jeans and white T-shirt with a plunging neckline.

"Fuck."

I stroke my cock a few times, and that's all it takes for the low tingle to start at the base of my spine. It's always the same. Every day. Watching. Knowing I can never have her. Can never touch her. Wanting.

I have to turn away before my orgasm, filled with relief, frustration, and guilt, finally hits me.

———

ANGELINA

THE BELLS above the door jingle over me, and I step out into the early morning light, balancing the tray with a coffee and a breakfast sandwich on it. I use my free hand to block the sun from my eyes and step over to the small bistro table where Damon sits, reading his usual morning paper.

"Here you go, Damon. Sorry about the delay." I force a tight smile at the handsome older man with silver hair. "I'm here alone this morning."

He glances up, and his lips curl into a warm grin. "No problem at all. Where's your sister today?"

I fight the desire to unleash my anger toward her at one of my best customers. "Running late, apparently."

Though, I wouldn't fucking know since she ran in, made their drinks while I was with a customer, and then bailed again.

The same annoyance I've felt all morning tightens my skin, and I set down his drink and sandwich, itching to get back to the other customers who need attention inside since I'm juggling everything by myself.

But I never let customers see that. I can't. No matter how annoyed I may be at Allie. "Anything else I can get for you?"

"No, thank you, and I do hope your day gets better."

It's impossible *not* to return a genuine smile at his kind words. Since he started coming around the Grind over the last few months, he's always been one of the nicest customers—and most loyal. Every day, without fail, at 7:30, this is his *spot*. The kind of customer who keeps Hawke's Daily Grind thriving.

That isn't anything to complain about and is precisely what I've always wanted—if I don't drop dead from sheer exhaustion. "Me, too."

Because I could fucking use a break.

Which I will never get if Allie doesn't tear herself away from Jude long enough to do her damn job.

I look up at the windows, and there aren't any signs of them.

The door across the street that leads to the stairs up to Jude's loft opens, and Allie steps out, nose buried in her phone, as always. She makes it to the curb, then glances up and down the street for traffic before she bolts across it, avoiding eye contact with me.

She hits the curb on our side of the street and waves to Damon. "Morning, Damon."

Damon nods at her. "Morning, Alessandra."

Her name rolls off his tongue with a perfect Italian accent, something he usually manages to hide. He gives me a knowing grin as I head into the café, hot on her heels, empty tray in hand.

"Where the *hell* have you been?" I do my best to whisper, but several of the customers sitting at the tables just inside the door look our way.

Shit.

Forcing a smile at them, I follow her to the kitchen at the back. As soon as the swinging door closes behind us, I grab her arm and turn her to face me.

"Seriously. You can't stay at Jude's condo all night, not even come home in the morning, then show up here, grab his drink, and go right back to him an hour and a half after you're supposed to be here to *work*."

Allie cringes slightly, then shakes her arm free. "I'm sorry. All right? I just overslept."

I narrow my eyes at her. The little twitch at the corner of her mouth gives away her lie. She's been telling a lot of them lately, but with Allie, you never really can tell what the hell is going on. The girl lives and loves recklessly and hard. It's one of her best qualities, but it also gets her into trouble more often than not.

That's what makes this situation so impossible.

I shove the empty tray at her. "Get to work. A bunch of tables need to be bussed, and I'm busy as hell at the counter. I need you here at 6:00 every morning unless you'd rather come in at 4:30 like I do to bake."

She offers me an annoyed glance, setting her purse on the small desk I keep as an "office" in the corner of the kitchen. "You know I can't bake."

"You damn well *can* bake. Nana and Mom taught both of us the same damn thing. So don't pretend you don't know how. You just don't *want* to."

She scowls, but before we can get into the same old argument about her role here or her unwillingness to use the skills she's been taught, I duck back out into the main space to keep an eye on the customers.

Three more stand in line at the counter, waiting to be helped, glancing around, looking for someone to assist them.

Shit.

I hustle back to the register and take the first order, peeking at the door every few seconds to watch for her to finally come out and get to work. "I'll get that going for you right away."

Allie reappears from the back, looking properly chastised as she quickly clears the three empty tables to make room for the new customers.

Whatever the hell has gotten into her had better get the hell out.

I can't run this place by myself, and with Pam and Betsy only here part-time in the afternoons, that leaves me with Allie to run it during the busiest times. And she's becoming more and more unreliable the older she gets.

Isn't it supposed to be the other way around?

If she weren't my own damn sister, I'd fire her.

I must curb my annoyance, or I'll never get through this day. It's times like these I really see the effect the age difference between us has created. The twelve years I have on her have always put me firmly in the "caretaker" role over Allie, and as she gets older, she seems to resent it more and more. If there were anything I could do to tamp that down, I would, but until the girl is more reliable, I have to ride her ass, or the café suffers.

Something I can *never* allow.

Not when this place is my entire life.

I get to work on the drink and watch the man who just ordered it head back outside to settle in at one of the tables on the sidewalk. More tables mean more customers, but having to run in and out a dozen times every hour I'm here takes its toll. My feet and back already ache, and I've only been here a few hours.

Who would have thought I would feel geriatric at thirty-seven?

This stuff isn't supposed to happen until I'm in my fifties. Though, some days, I feel like I might as well be eighty.

The old spinster living with her sister...

All I need is a few dozen cats, a fraying knit sweater, and a pair of horn-rimmed bifocals...

That complete picture sends a shiver through me as I pour the customer's black coffee, add two creams per his request, and nod to the next customer in line. "I'll be right back. I promise. Sorry."

There's nothing worse than leaving someone standing in line, waiting to give you their money, but Allie's inability to get here on time has left me in a position where I never want to find myself again. Precisely why I try to never rely on anyone for anything, because in the end, people either fail you or leave you.

I walk around the counter and out the front door to set the drink at the table, and a flash of movement in the window of Jude's place catches my attention, just like everything the man does always has.

That same dark, recessive corner that always draws my eye does so again, hoping to catch a glimpse of the most reticent and enigmatic Hawke. The beautiful, damaged boy who turned into such a fiercely private man.

13

Almost as if he can feel me looking, he takes a step forward out of the shadow, only his upper torso visible—the tattoos on his lean, muscular chest and arms standing out clearly in the morning light.

His pale-blue eyes blaze even from across the street, and he lifts his coffee cup to his lips and takes a sip before he inclines it toward me and nods a thanks.

I force a smile at him and give a little wave, but I'm not feeling so friendly toward the man who seems to be monopolizing Allie and keeping her from coming to work.

As if it isn't enough, those two have been attached at the hip since they were ten years old when he showed up at Nana's house with Luca and Byron. Now, he's actually keeping her from doing her damn job. But a quick glance in the front window finds her behind the counter, taking orders, so I can take a breath for a second.

I make my way back inside, checking each table before I finally manage a moment to lean back against the counter and take a deep breath of the coffee and bakery-scented air.

"Angelina, did you hear me?"

"Huh?" I turn toward Allie, shaking my head. "Sorry. What?"

"Can I get two medium skim-milk lattes with sugar-free vanilla syrup?"

"Yes, of course."

The more I work, the less I think, and the less I think, the better I feel.

It may not be the healthiest way to deal with all the trauma in my life, but that's what's gotten me through every day of my life since Dad died, the thing that will continue to get me through—not relying on anyone else for my own happiness and comfort.

I make the lattes quickly, steaming the milk and making the espresso without even having to think about how to do it. Pure muscle memory at work. I slide them across the counter toward Allie.

She raises a brow at me and hands the drinks to the customer. "Are you all right?"

"Yeah. Why?"

Her gaze darts around the café at the customers eating and drinking and paying us no attention at all. "I'm really sorry about this morning."

An apology?

I never anticipated she would actually take any responsibility for what she did today, but it doesn't solve one of the major problems. "Please, just tell Jude that he needs to come to get his own coffee from now on."

Allie tenses and shakes her head. "I can't do that."

"Why the hell not?"

It's not that I don't know that Jude is a bit antisocial. The man hasn't set foot in the Grind in years, even though he lives right across the street. But his addiction to my quad-shot lattes has persisted enough to make Allie run one over every morning, rain or shine.

Instead of answering my question, Allie just squares her shoulders, as if she's readying herself for a fight. "I'll make sure I'm here early enough to get it to him without interfering with the work schedule."

I sigh. "Don't make promises you can't keep, Al. You only let people down when you do that."

She has the audacity to look hurt by the comment. "That's not fair."

"Isn't it? You missed the last three Sunday dinners at Nana's, and I can't even remember the last time Jude went. The two of you are so attached at the hip that you're letting it interfere with real-life obligations."

"Nana understands why Jude and I aren't there."

"Does she?" I raise a brow at her. "Because she sure seemed pretty upset yesterday."

Allie winces.

"I don't know what you're doing, but you need to get your shit together. Stop upsetting Nana and be here on time and work, or...I'm going to fire you."

She gapes and glances at the customers milling around, then takes a step closer. "You can't fire me."

"Yes, I can. The Grind might be under the Hawke Enterprises umbrella, but I'm listed as the owner. That makes me your boss, whether you like it or not. Even if you're my sister, I can still fire you if you're not doing your job, and lately, you haven't been."

Unshed tears shimmer in her eyes for a second.

Shit.

Allie blinks them away and turns her back to me. "It won't happen again."

She hustles off before I can say another word. As much as I'd like to believe her, I don't. Something's been going on with her for months, and all she does is come up with excuses and tell me half-truths or flat-out lies.

Maybe I'd have better luck with Jude.

I glance out the floor-to-ceiling windows at the front of the café and over toward the condo, but his window is empty. A strange mix of relief and concern settles in my stomach, but a massive cement truck rolls by, followed by several other work trucks.

Leaving Allie at the counter, I head outside, blocking the sun with my hand again to stare down the street. Dozens of construction workers mill around outside a storefront two blocks down—one of the only ones we don't own on this end of the street, a few doors from The Hawke's Nest.

"What the hell is going on down there?"

"Oh, I heard Barb and Pete finally sold." The familiar voice from behind me makes me turn toward it.

"Oh, Nancy! I'm sorry. I didn't even realize you came in and ordered." I glance down at the two lattes I just made sitting on the table in front of her. "What did you say about Barb and Pete?"

She smiles. "I used to go into their shop all the time for little things, but yesterday, when I went, it was all locked up and empty. Like it had been cleared out over the weekend."

"You're kidding me." I glance back down toward the work happening. "We've been trying to buy that storefront for years."

Nancy offers a kind smile. "I know. Your Uncle Savage is an old high school friend of mine, and I know the family owns almost the whole street. I was always kind of surprised they never sold to you."

"Do you know who they sold to, who the new owner is?"

She shakes her head and takes a sip of one of the drinks. "No, I don't." Her gaze flicks over my shoulder, and she smiles. "Oh, you made it!"

A crisp, light scent wafts over me as a well-built man with copper-colored hair in an immaculate suit stops next to me and flashes me a grin, his green eyes sparkling. "Excuse me. Do you mind?"

He points to the empty chair at Nancy's table I'm currently standing in the way of.

"Oh, I'm sorry." I step back to allow him to take the open seat.

Nancy waves it off. "Oh, don't worry about it, Angelina. This is my lawyer, Cassius Whitaker."

My spine stiffens, and ice instantly floods my veins, washing away any warmth from the morning sun. I narrow a glare at the man who has caused so many problems for the Hawkes. "I know the name."

He gives me that same lopsided grin that probably melts

the panties off any woman he throws it at and takes a sip of the drink, crossing his ankle over his knee and leaning back casually. "I'm sure you do. Tell your cousin, Isaac, hello for me and that I look forward to our next battle in court."

Motherfucker.

As if my day isn't bad enough, now I have the enemy drinking my coffee.

2

JUDE

The second hand ticks one more notch. Then another. Another. A deliberate, controlled, snail-like pace moves it around the clockface, but time doesn't seem to advance between each check of its progress.

My chest tightens, and I rub at it absently, pacing the old, wooden loft floors, alternating between worrying about both Allie and my lack of progress on the book and trying to keep myself from going to the window to watch the life I want and can never have pass by on the street below.

This tension tightening my entire body only builds the later the minute hand advances and the more the sun streams in through the floor-to-ceiling windows.

Allie should have been here an hour ago with my coffee. That's two days in a row she hasn't shown at her usual time.

Something's definitely up.

It isn't like her to keep secrets from me. That has the acid churning in my stomach as much as the lack of food so far today does.

I have to do something to burn through this anxious energy, but no matter how many words I put down on paper, they're not the right ones. Hours and hours of staring at the screen, typing and deleting. Cursing myself out for not being able to properly get out what's bottled up inside me.

Even the aggressive workout in my makeshift gym in the corner wasn't enough to clear my head. Brutalizing my body with lifting and cardio usually helps me release the constant tension that keeps me on edge, but the burn of my muscles from an hour of weights and a five-mile run before the sun even came up hasn't helped at all.

Something's wrong with Allie, and on top of that, if I don't make some headway on this book, that fat advance sitting in my bank account will end up right back with the publisher.

I finally allow myself to walk to the window and glance down at the still-dark café. Which means Angelina is in the kitchen baking and Allie hasn't arrived to start prepping the front of the house like she should have.

Fuck.

If I didn't think I had a caffeine addiction before, I'm confident I do now. The first day in two years that she doesn't show up with my drink, and I'm literally shaking for it. Combined with all the anxiety of her strange behavior, it will kill me if I don't do something about it quickly.

I tug out my phone and pull up Allie's text chain.

JUDE

Where the hell are you? Are you okay?

Usually, the three little dots indicating she's responding pop up immediately, but not today.

Radio silence.

Fuck.

I scroll to Angelina's name and pause with my finger hovered over it. Just like I have millions of times over the years.

When there were so many things I wanted to say. Things I needed to. Things she needed to hear but never did. Things I've held back and forced deep inside rather than overstep my place.

Just fucking text her already.

I pull it up and look at the last message she sent me a few months ago when Isaac brought Jack and Viviana to meet the entire family. The same rock sits in my gut reading it again.

ANG

You're really missing Sunday dinner again?
When Isaac is bringing his daughter to meet
everyone for the first time?

I didn't respond to her then, unable to come up with a valid excuse I haven't used the almost hundred times I've failed to show at Nana's for our weekly "family" dinner over the last two years.

Which makes it even more awkward to be texting her now, seeing that massive gap in time I let hang between us, but this isn't the time to let my own guilt get in the way of what needs to happen.

I let my fingers fly over the keys.

JUDE

Any sign of Allie this morning? I'm worried.

Waiting for a response, I lean my bare shoulder against the glass and watch the café, hoping to catch a glimpse of her.

Three little dots pop up on my screen, and I hold my breath, waiting.

ANG

Nope, I assumed she was with you.

Shit. That means she didn't go home last night.

And that Ang is probably pissed at me, thinking I'm keeping Allie from coming to work on time.

JUDE

She didn't sleep here last night. I haven't seen her since she left around midnight after we watched a movie.

ANG

She didn't come home last night. I even slept on the couch so I could talk to her when she did, and she isn't responding to me this morning.

JUDE

Me, either.

A half-dozen messages unanswered.

Shit, shit, shit.

I shove a hand through my hair and return to pacing, the only thing I *can* do when I'm caged in here like a wild animal. My bare feet slapping against the wood floors echo through the high ceilings and off the metal rafters.

Angie and I need to figure out what's going on with Allie before this goes any further.

JUDE

We need to talk. Any chance I can get you to bring me my coffee while I try to find her, and we can try to come up with a game plan?

Talk.

Such a simple word. Such a simple concept. Two people together. Sharing with each other. But as soon as I get in Angelina's orbit, my brain short-circuits, and I lose my ability to speak.

It's been almost two years since I've been in the same room as the woman who has such a chokehold on me, and my palms sweat merely anticipating the possibility she might come over.

ANG

Are you fucking kidding me? You can't make your own coffee there?

JUDE

It isn't as good as yours. And we really need to talk about Allie.

Maybe the compliment will help ease the sting of my selfish request, but without my daily intake of caffeine, I won't be able to concentrate on the situation or be able to figure out what Alessandra McCabe is up to.

I can almost see Angelina rolling her Caribbean-blue Hawke eyes at my response. The way her annoyance always wrinkles the skin around them and twists her perfect bow lips.

It shouldn't be so damn cute, but everything about her is.

ANG

Fine. As soon as I have a break, I'll be over.

Almost immediately, the reality that Angelina will be coming into my place hits me like a Mack truck.

Angie...

Here...

A cold sweat breaks out over my skin, and I scan the condo as I shove my phone back into the pocket of my gray sweatpants, still damp with the sweat from my earlier workout.

Even though I just cleaned, everything still appears dirty, unkempt, in disarray, the same way I am. The stacks of books along the wall next to the window make me look like some psychotic Hemingway-ish reclusive shut-in, which isn't too far from the truth.

But it isn't the way I want Ang to see me for the first time face to face in so long.

Maybe I should have showered before I asked her to come over, but she could be here any second, and I wouldn't want to miss her and piss her off even more because I don't answer the door.

Unlike Allie, Angelina doesn't have a key and free rein to my place. She just holds the reins to my heart. Always has and always will.

The eldest Hawke may not know the stranglehold she has on me, but every move she makes, every smile, every laugh, every word—even those said with snark and sass—it all only further cements that woman in my soul.

And she's about to walk in here and see me like this. I check myself in the mirror, running my hand through my too-long hair to try to keep it out of my face. But it's a lost cause, always has been.

"You look like Flopsy, the rabbit."

Mom's voice rings in my ears, bringing with it the same stab of pain it always does. The memory of her warm, gentle hand brushing it away from my face and trying to tuck it behind my ear, and it falling right back over my eyes. Her tilting up my chin and looking at me with so much love I can still feel it warming my chest twenty years later.

"You're a good kid, Jude. Don't ever let your father convince you otherwise."

I squeeze my eyes closed against the agonizing assault of memories, then shove away from the counter and return into the loft to pace, glancing out the window every time I reach that side of the room. Back to counting the seconds ticking by on the clock, this time, waiting for the other sister.

The café door opens, and her familiar dark head of hair appears. I immediately freeze, my body tense, already anticipating having her so close.

She glances up at the window as she crosses the street, her

24

eyes locking with mine. A familiar energy crackles over my skin, and I swallow thickly as heat spreads through me.

Why does she do this to me?

Every fucking time that woman looks at me, it's like she sees right through me, straight past everything I let the world see to the darkest parts I keep hidden even from Allie.

From the very first time my eyes met hers...

Fifteen years hasn't changed a damn thing.

Except maybe made me love her more.

She hits the sidewalk under my window, and I jog over to the wall panel to buzz her in downstairs and unlock the metal loft door so she can come in.

I lean against the wall and wait, my knee bouncing incessantly.

It was stupid to ask her to bring over the coffee.

I'm a wreck this morning with Allie MIA. I should have just called Angie, tried to discuss this over the phone instead of having to be so close to her, knowing what her presence does to me. This isn't how I want her to see me—for *anyone* to see me.

A hard pounding comes from the door. I jerk away from the wall and tug it open with my heart in my throat. After almost two years of watching her every day from that window, she's finally *here*.

Annoyance twists her lips, and the low-cut V-neck T-shirt exposes the soft swell of her perfect breasts, heaving slightly with each breath she takes. I let my eyes rake over the tight jeans hugging every curve below her waist, and my cock twitches.

Fuck.

Her gaze travels over my bare torso, down across my sweat-pants that likely aren't doing a good job concealing my reaction to her presence, and she clears her throat awkwardly and holds out the coffee. "You really don't know where my sister is?"

Forcing my eyes to meet hers, I reach out to take the drink. My fingers brush hers, and that same little jolt passes through my arm that I felt the first time she touched me, when she laid her hand on my knee and gave me a gentle squeeze. It was meant to be a simple reassurance then, a promise that I was safe and would remain that way, but in reality, it was so much more.

The first time in years I had truly *felt* safe with an adult. The first time someone said something to me that seemed completely genuine. Someone who offered something freely, without judgment, without expectation of anything in return.

That was fifteen years ago, but that moment lives in my mind as vividly as the dark ones of my past.

I shake my head and pull my hand away, bringing the cup to my lips to take a sip in order to give myself a moment to regain composure. "No, we watched a movie, and she left. I assumed she was going home."

Angelina runs her hand through her hair. The thick strands fall right back into place as she releases a heavy sigh. "That's two nights in a row."

I freeze. "She didn't come home the night before, either?"

She shakes her head, pressing her lips together firmly. "No, and given your reaction, I assume she wasn't here."

I shake my head. "Your parents?"

"No. If she had gone to Mom and Landon's house, I am sure I would've heard about it."

"Shit."

So, I was right about the guy...

There isn't any other reason Allie would be disappearing and spending nights out without coming home or checking in with anyone. She's caught in a dick trap somewhere, and apparently, she's having trouble getting out of it and coming up for air.

I lean against the door and try to appear casual, but that's impossible with the woman of my literal dreams, the one who saves me from the nightmares, the one I can never have, standing right in front of me, and my best friend MIA.

She squeezes her eyes closed for a moment and shakes her head. "I have to get back over there. Betsy came in early to help cover Allie's shift since I can't get ahold of her. But I can't leave her there alone."

I hold up the coffee. "Thank you for this. Really. I'm going to contact everyone to see if anyone else might have heard from her. I'll text you to let you know what I find out."

With as busy as Hawke's Daily Grind always is, there's no way she'll be able to make the calls we need to in order to track down Allie. One of the Hawkes *must* know something. Someone *always* does.

Her gaze softens slightly, some of her earlier annoyance melting away, replaced by the soft, welcoming look she usually gives me. "Thank you. I appreciate it."

We stare at each other. Tension thickens the air between us. A familiar one I'm sure she's felt as much as I have over the years. Like something's building, like it *has* been building, and we're reaching some sort of point of no return. Even after two years, it hasn't changed, hasn't dissipated. If anything, it's only gotten stronger.

Her gaze darts away from mine abruptly, and she turns and hustles down the short hall toward the stairwell. That perfect round ass of hers sways in the tight denim, and my cock stirs against the soft fabric of my sweatpants.

Fucking hell.

I step away from the door and let it slam closed before I lean back against it and close my eyes.

My best friend is missing, and her older sister is torturing me.

————

27

ANGELINA

KENNEDY BLOWS into the café like a hurricane coming off the gulf, pale-blond hair flowing behind her, her perfect red lips screwed down to a scowl. She marches toward the counter, sets her Valentino bag on it, and releases an annoyed huff, drumming her manicured nails against the marble. "I fucking hate Cassius Whitaker."

I chuckle and pour her a black coffee, the only way she ever drinks it, though I don't know how she hasn't destroyed her stomach with how much she consumes daily. She grabs it from me and takes a giant gulp of the scalding liquid, wincing slightly.

"Why don't you ever wait for that to cool down?"

She focuses her Hawke-blue eyes on me, a slight grin curling her lips. "I like it the temperature of the surface of the sun."

I chuckle again and shake my head. "I don't know how you do it."

She grins. "My dad says I have a nuclear mouth."

My barked laugh draws the attention of a couple of customers, and I slap my hand over my mouth to try to silence myself.

"*Sorry.*" I mouth to a few of them. "So, what did Cass do this time?"

After he showed up here unexpectedly yesterday and sat outside, drinking coffee with Nancy, I knew something had to be up. That man always seems to have his hands in something that will negatively affect one of our businesses, like his recent failed attempt to stop the groundbreaking on The Hawke Hotel.

In a few weeks, we'll be able to shove it up his handsome, pompous ass when the first bulldozer starts clearing the land.

Kennedy scowls. "What *hasn't* he done?"

The bell jingles above the door, and we both turn toward Isaac as he approaches, wearing a matching scowl on his face.

"Oh, God." I return my focus to the CFO of Hawke Enterprises. "Can I assume you two are here about the same thing?"

Isaac stops next to our cousin and leans a hip against the counter in his perfectly tailored suit. "You tell her about Cass yet?"

Kennedy shakes her head. "I was just about to. Would you like to do the honors?"

He huffs as acid churns in my stomach.

"Shit." I glance between the two of them, the powerhouses of the second generation of Hawke Enterprises—our legal "fixer" and the woman who plans to take over from Savage and Gabe when the time comes. "If this requires both of you to break the news, it can't be good."

Isaac gives me an apologetic look. "I did some digging after you texted to say he was having coffee here with Nancy Abner yesterday. I thought it was a little suspicious, him being here and him being with *her*."

I narrow my eyes on him. "Why would it be odd for him to have coffee with a client?"

"Because she isn't just *any* client." His gaze darts to Kennedy, then back to me. "Do you know what Nancy does?"

I shake my head. "No. She's been coming in here for years, several times a week, but I don't think she and I ever talked about that."

Kennedy's lips purse like she just tasted something sour. "She manages all the building inspectors for Orleans Parish."

Flashes of the work crew I saw down the street float through my brain. "Oh, God..."

Before the words even leave Isaac's lips, I close my eyes to wait for the impact. With everything else going on, it seems like another blow I'll just have to take and try not to let it knock me out completely.

"Falco Enterprises bought the empty space from Pete and Barb."

His voice echoes in my head, bouncing off my skull like some dark, foreboding warning of what's coming. I open my eyes, locking them with his. "And what are they putting in there?"

Kennedy and Isaac exchange a look, and Kennedy's hand finally stops the incessant drumming on the granite.

Her normally warm blue gaze turns icy. "A coffee shop."

I stumble back a step until my ass hits the counter behind me where the espresso machine stands, and my hands immediately curl around the edge, giving me something to cling to while my legs start to tremble. "You're joking."

Isaac shakes his head. "We need to talk."

Talk?

The word barely registers through the cloud of panic settling over me, and I scan the café for Betsy and find her cleaning a table in the corner. I motion for her to come over.

"I need to talk to my cousins. Can you handle everything for a couple of minutes?"

She nods, either missing my distress or intentionally not mentioning it when she passes me. I lead Isaac and Kennedy out front onto the sidewalk, which is—thankfully—empty at the moment. The mid-afternoon summer heat keeps everyone inside, and it gives us some much-needed privacy to discuss the new threat.

All three of us immediately turn to look down the street toward where the vigorous construction signals a rush to complete the renovation of the small mom-and-pop general store into a coffee shop that will put Hawke's Daily Grind right out of business.

"A fucking coffee shop?" I rest my ass on one of the bistro tables. "Are you kidding me?"

Kennedy lowers her hand on my arm and squeezes gently.

"It'll be okay, Angelina. You've been here for a long time. Your customers aren't going anywhere just because a new place opens up."

"You don't know that."

Isaac steps in front of me to direct my attention to him instead of the impending doom only a few blocks down. "I'm not going to let them do this to you. To us."

I shake my head as tears start to burn in my eyes. "You can't stop them. You and Uncle Stone have been trying for years, and you haven't made any headway."

His jaw tightens, the dark stubble there barely hiding the tic of the muscle that always happens when he's pissed. "That's not true. We got the ruling from Judge Cramer."

"Yeah, and that was what, four months ago? Then Whitaker lost his opposition to the hotel groundbreaking. And even after that, they're right back at it again." My anger hardens my words, though I'm not mad at Isaac. He and Uncle Stone have gone to war with Falco Enterprises and their mouthpiece, Cassius Whitaker, to try to protect the Hawke investments. They've done all they can. It just isn't working. "What was it you said Cass told you?"

Kennedy scowls. "That he gets paid whether he wins or loses, and he enjoys the challenge Isaac gives him in court. Such a smug bastard."

Smug is right.

The way his lips tilted when I realized who he was flashes through my head. "Good-looking, too."

Her head whips toward me. "Excuse me."

"Sorry. I didn't mean to compliment the enemy. But..." I shrug. "I'd be lying if I said he wasn't."

She huffs and crosses her arms over her chest, tapping her Louboutin-clad toe against the sidewalk as she glares down the street toward the workers. "I swear to God, if that man and I are ever in the same room, I'm going to gouge out his eyes with my heel or maybe just drive one into his balls."

Isaac chokes on his own breath with a laugh. "Shit, Kennedy. I don't ever want you mad at me."

Her eyes flick to our cousin, and she scowls at him. "I'm pretty sure I beat you up enough over the last thirty years that you know not to cross me."

He chuckles and mirrors her stance with his arms crossed over his chest. "That was because you were older and bigger than me—for a while. You took advantage. And it was all well before I started training heavily with Atlas. I could take you now."

She takes a step toward him defiantly, her lips twitching, fighting a smile. "Oh, you think so? I've spent some time sparring with Atlas, too, you know. I bet—"

I press a hand against both of their chests to push them away from each other. "Will you two stop the pissing contest? We have bigger problems right now." I nod toward the workers down the street. "What are we going to do about that besides filing a lawsuit that's probably going to go nowhere?"

Kennedy sighs. "If I had my way, I'd march right down to Cass' office, steal his files, and dig through them until I find out who owns Falco Enterprises."

I turn to Isaac. "You guys really can't figure it out?"

He releases a disgruntled little noise in the back of his throat. "Trust me. Dad and I have been working nonstop and have every private investigator and every other avenue we can think of on it. But whoever it is has covered their tracks well." His eyes harden. "That's what worries me."

A little shiver rolls through my spine, and Kennedy rubs my arm as goosebumps pebble on it.

"It'll be okay. Don't look so nervous. We'll figure it out."

"What if it's..." I can't even say the words, afraid if I voice them out loud, it might make them true.

With so many things left uncertain after the fallout with Satriano and Roselli when Jack and Viviana appeared in our lives, my mind can't help but immediately go to the man who controls New Orleans with a quick trigger finger.

Isaac sneers. "If it's the Rosellis, we'll connect it, eventually."

The last time Roselli showed up here and threatened the Hawkes, Isaac and Uncle Gabe had to shoot up a damn church to rescue Jack from Satriano. I don't want to even think about what might happen if we have to face another threat like that from someone so close.

As it stands, we've all been on edge, wondering if someone from the Satriano family will show up from Italy, seeking revenge for what they did to save Jack. Cutter and Valentina may have done their best to wipe out what was left of the Satriano crew, but there are always those who linger in the shadows. Those are the people we need to be afraid of, the ones who could pose a threat to any of us.

Another shiver rolls through me. "Have either of you heard from Allie?"

They exchange a look, and Isaac narrows his eyes on me. "No, why?"

I press my hands to my temples, fighting the sudden headache hammering against my skull. "Never mind. Don't worry about it." There isn't any reason to panic *yet*. This isn't unusual for Allie, just bad fucking timing. "Tell her I'm looking for her if you do."

Kennedy offers what I'm sure she thinks is a reassuring smile, her eyes darting to the empty space across the street beneath Jude's loft. "You know, maybe if we had a big grand opening at the same time or right before they do, we could draw attention away from them."

Isaac follows her gaze, his eyes flicking up to Jude's windows. I follow his focus, searching the huge panes of glass the same way I almost always do when I come out here, but the most mysterious Hawke isn't anywhere in sight.

The fixer for the entire Hawke family releases a despondent sigh, something akin to defeat—something I would never expect from Isaac. "If you think you're going to get Jude to open his bookstore that quickly, you're fucking crazy, Ken."

She shakes her head. "I wasn't thinking about the bookstore."

I flick my gaze between them, trying to unravel whatever's going on. "What am I missing here?"

Isaac rubs at the back of his neck and glances down at his shoes before his eyes meet mine again. "Since we were all here and we made the announcement that Jack is pregnant, I've been talking with Luca and Byron about using the space as a studio and art gallery for her."

"Really?"

He nods slowly. "But they bought it for Jude."

Kennedy looks up to his window. "And he hasn't done anything with it for the three years he's lived there. So, we have a dusty, empty spot in prime real estate. If he's not ever going to do anything with it, then it makes sense that one of us does."

Jack's expanding belly, that I rubbed at dinner only two days ago, comes to mind immediately. "Can she even paint right now?"

The corner of Isaac's lips twitches, his disgusting obsession with her shining through. "There are some types of paints, paint thinner, stuff like that she obviously can't handle, but she's been doing a lot of pencil and chalk drawings, and there are some styles of paints she can use. She's still working, and right now, she's working out of the corner of my theater room because I don't have anywhere else to put her in the condo. She needs the space, and she's good enough that we could sell her stuff."

Kennedy nods. "She really is talented."

I try to picture what a studio and gallery would look like across the street instead of the bookshop I've been anticipating since Byron and Luca announced they had purchased it for Jude when he graduated college and was starting his master's program. "Actually. It's a good idea."

Isaac nods. "I know."

But it being a good idea doesn't mean anything. "And what did Byron and Luca say?"

He looks up at Jude's place again just as Jude appears in the window and stares down at all of us. He doesn't wave, just allows his icy eyes to drift over the three of us, scrutinizing and examining us like he's trying to determine what we're discussing rather than just coming down to join in.

Kennedy smiles and waves at him, and he finally inclines his head.

Isaac turns back to us. "They said they'd talk to him."

I release a heavy sigh. "Somehow, I don't think that's going to solve the problem. I don't anticipate he's going to be very receptive to the idea."

Almost instantly, Isaac slips from cousin mode into family attorney mode, crossing his arms over his chest, his back stiffening. "Well, at some point, if he isn't going to do anything with it, someone has to. It could be exactly what we need to shove it to Falco until we can take them down for good."

Kennedy offers a hopeful smile. "Well, let's hope he *is* receptive to the idea."

Something tells me he won't be.

Even though I've barely spoken to him other than a few text messages and hadn't seen him in person for what feels like forever until today, I can't see him giving up his dream. "And if he isn't?"

Isaac's eyes harden in a way I learned from a very young age to be leery of. "Then I'll go have a talk with him."

3

JUDE

The buzzer sounds through the loft, breaking the minimal concentration I somehow managed to find tonight, and I jerk my fingers back from the keyboard and squeeze my eyes closed. After staring at the bright screen for hours in the otherwise dark space, the blinding white flashes against my lids make me wince.

Buzz! Buzz! Buzz!

"Fucking hell..."

I set my laptop on the floor in the corner where I sit to write, push to my feet, with a cringe at the protestation of my back muscles, and glance out the window down to the street.

Luca takes a step back from the door and looks up at me.

Shit.

Just what I need tonight.

I scrub my hands over my face and make my way over to buzz him in, then unlock the door while I wait for the man who became one of my adoptive fathers to head up the steps. A minute later, the knob twists, and he pushes his way inside as I pull a beer from the fridge and pop off the top.

His dark eyes immediately dart to me in the kitchen to the right of the entry. "Get me one of those, too, *piccolo guaio.*"

Ignoring the nickname he's used with me since the first time we met, I hand him the beer and reach for another. He settles onto one of the stools at the kitchen island with a slight groan that I'm sure he wishes I didn't hear.

He watches me for a minute, his heavy brows furrowing deeply over dark eyes that can be hard as granite. But right now, they soften with concern, the same way they did when he found me, as if he could instantly see I needed help and that he was the only one who could give it to me. "You look like shit."

Snorting, I angle my beer toward him. "Thanks."

"I'm serious, Jude." He glances over his shoulder toward my work corner. "How long have you been working today?"

I groan and glance at my watch. "I don't know, twelve hours?"

His eyes widen, and his lips turn down. "That's a long time to sit and stare at a screen."

I snort and take a swig of my beer. "What would you know about it? You've never sat behind a computer in your fucking life."

Luca scowls at me and tightens his hand on the beer, the Abello family crest on the ring on his right hand glinting in the pendant lights hanging above him.

Okay, maybe that was a step too far.

He prefers to keep his former life as the head of the Abello crime family in his past, but it doesn't make what I said untrue. The things he did didn't require him to sit at a computer day in, day out. He spent most of his time with a gun in his hand or ordering those who had them to maintain control over one of the most powerful mob organizations in the U.S.

Instead of getting angry at my frankness, Luca simply releases a heavy sigh. "True, at least in my early years." He glances up at me. "But I've been spending a lot more time behind the desk the last thirty years, and you know it."

I don't bother coming up with a response because it doesn't require one. We've reached the spot we always find ourselves in —a stalemate. Staring each other down, waiting for the other to say something. Even after fifteen years, connecting with Luca seems impossible, not when I purposely keep him and everyone else at arm's length.

Finally, after two more sips, I raise a brow. "Is there a reason you came by other than to tell me how shitty I look?"

He leans back on the stool, running a hand through his dark hair that's graying at the temples—one of the very few physical signs that the man is human and aging. "I need to talk to you."

This can't be good.

Whenever Luca Abello wants to "talk," it usually ends with one of us pissed off. Me because he's asking me to do things I can't, or him because he thinks I'm a selfish prick who just doesn't *want* to.

"About what?"

"A couple of things, really." He picks at the label on his beer bottle. "Like why you haven't been coming to Sunday dinner. Nana asked again. It's impossible for her not to take it personally. Are you pissed at us for some reason?"

I squeeze my eyes closed and shake my head. "No."

Far from it.

The Hawkes are the most generous people I've ever met in my life, the type of family everyone wants to be part of, and here I am, pushing all of them away at every opportunity and making them believe they've somehow done something *wrong* when all they've ever done is save me.

I thought Luca understood, that they all did, that none of it is *personal.*

I can't believe he's going to make me say this.

"I can't, Luca." Even after all these years, after everything he and Byron have done for me, after they brought me into their family and gave me a home, I can't bring myself to call either of them *Dad.* "You know why."

He nods slowly and picks at the label on his beer, peeling it away. "There's something else I need to talk to you about."

And he looks more nervous about this than he did talking about not going to Nana's house. That settles a heavy stone of dread in my stomach.

"What's that?"

"The bookstore."

I freeze with the bottle halfway to my mouth, then set it down and swallow thickly. "What about it?"

Why the hell haven't you opened it?

It's the question all the Hawkes have been asking since I moved in here three years ago, since Byron and Luca bought this building specifically so I could have a place to live and operate my own bookstore beneath it while I worked on my master's and wrote.

That was the dream. The one that lived in my head since the moment they first brought me into a bookstore at age ten. It opened a thousand new worlds to me. Places where magic and happily ever afters existed. Where people had families and unconditional love surrounding them. Where orphans found where they belonged and felt safe.

I thought I had found that, but it all changed in the blink of an eye. The "safe" world the Hawkes created for me, the life they allowed me to lead, it all vanished in an instant, and I can't even tell them why.

Luca watches me carefully, as if he's afraid to ask but knows he has to. "Are you prepared to open it *now*?"

I grab my beer and take a long drink, mostly to avoid answering the question, but it isn't one I can ignore for long. "I'm thinking about it."

It's the same answer I've given him and Byron for years, but we both know I won't do it. He stares me down with an intensity that reminds me of who he really is, of what he was before Byron made him leave that life.

Some of the most powerful and vicious men in the world crumbled under Luca Abello's hard stare, but I stand firm, refusing to give in when he doesn't really want to hear what I have to say, anyway.

Finally, he drains his beer and slams the empty bottle onto the counter hard enough to make me wince. "Well, the time has come to make a decision in that regard."

Make a decision?

I wasn't aware there was any decision *to* be made. That space is mine to do what I want, and at this moment, that means leaving it empty.

"What do you mean?"

"Isaac's girlfriend, Jack, who you've never met"—he gives me a pointed look—"is an artist, and she'd like to use the space as a studio and art gallery."

"No." I grip the counter with my free hand, my fingers burning with the pressure I'm putting on them in my annoyance. "It's going to be a bookstore."

Luca pushes up from the stool, the metal legs scraping against the wood. He plants his hands flat on the counter, leaning over it slightly toward me. "Is it? Because, right now, it looks like a goddamn empty dust box. It isn't a good look for our street, and now, more than ever, we need something in that space."

"Why now more than ever?"

He presses his lips together in a firm line and shoves off the counter, marching over to the windows. Even dressed in casual linen pants and a button-down white shirt, Luca still carries himself like the mafia don he once was—broad, muscular shoulders back, spine straight, powerful hands fisted at his sides.

Stopping at the floor-to-ceiling windows, he points down and to the left. "Maybe you spend too much time watching Allie at the café to pay attention to what's happening down the street, but Pete and Barb sold."

"What? I thought we'd been trying to get that property for years, and they wouldn't sell. What changed their minds?"

He turns back to me and crosses his arms over his chest. "We have been. And I don't have a fucking clue what changed their minds because they didn't sell to *us*."

"Who the hell did they sell to?"

His eyes go almost black, and he sneers. "Falco Enterprises."

"Shit." I rub at the back of my neck and take another drink, wishing it were something stronger than beer. "When did all this happen?"

"The last few days. Isaac, Stone, and Savage went and spoke with them not even two weeks ago, and they said they weren't prepared to sell, that they enjoyed running their shop, and weren't ready to retire yet. But they assured us that when they were, they would come to us first."

"Well, that didn't happen."

He releases an incredulous sigh. "No, it sure as hell didn't. And now, they're opening a coffee shop."

An icy chill spreads over my skin. "They're what?"

Luca nods slowly as the seriousness of the situation dawns on me.

I open and close my mouth a few times, trying to come up with the right words. "But, Angelina and Allie..."

"Exactly. Competition setting up two blocks away isn't a random occurrence. Falco Enterprises has been after us for a long time. I don't know what their game is, but right now, it appears to be to hurt the girls."

"Shit."

He walks back over to the counter and leans across it again. "I know you love Allie, and you'd do anything for her..."

I lift my head slowly to let my eyes meet his. He has no idea how true those words are, but he means them in completely the wrong context, misunderstands what lies at the core of my relationship with her. "I would."

She's my best friend. My other half. The one member of this family who has never asked me for anything I can't give and never expects anything in return for the love and kindness she shows me because she knows I have no way to give it back.

Luca's gaze softens. "Then do this to make sure she and her sister don't lose their livelihood. What are people going to want to do, sit at Hawke's Daily Grind, staring at an empty space across the street filled with dust or one with beautiful art hanging on the walls? Or, hell, even beautiful books."

He says the last few words gently, in that tone he used with me the first time we met when he wrapped his large hand around my scrawny arm and tugged me off the concrete from behind the dumpster outside The Steele Hawke Cage. The one that seemed so out of place coming from a man like him. The one that always tugs at my heart slightly because I know he cares. And even more because I know I'm incapable of giving him what he wants from me.

I set my beer down on the counter behind me and release a heavy sigh. "Give me some time to think about it. A few days, at least."

A muscle in his tightened jaw tics. "I'm not sure what's going on with you, *piccolo guaio*. I know things have always been"—he thinks about it and picks his words carefully—"difficult since you came to live with us, but I thought we were all headed in the right direction. You graduated. You seemed to be enjoying your master's program. You got your book deal. And then, you just"—he holds out his hands absently—"disappeared. You haven't been coming to Sunday dinners. No birthday parties. None of the openings for any of the new businesses. Hell, you haven't even been to one of Atlas' matches in over two years. And I'm not the only one who has noticed your absence. I know you've gotten a few calls from Nana. You're breaking the old woman's heart."

The knife that slices through my chest anytime anyone mentions Nana takes another swipe, and I absently reach up and rub at the spot through my T-shirt.

Antonia Hawke is a fucking saint who raised five kids on her own after Sam died, and she's one of the strongest and most loving women I've ever met in my life. The kind of grandmother I always wanted and never had. But then, once I did have her, I couldn't handle it. Couldn't bear her touch when she tried to hug me. Couldn't stand all the *life* in her home. The chatter of everyone around me. The back-and-forth, good-natured ribbing that, in my head, always turned into angry arguments that led to horrible consequences...

I drop my head and let it hang for a moment.

Luca wants me to open the bookstore, and he's using Jack's request as an excuse to push me. He just doesn't understand how far he's asking me to go.

"A couple of days to think about it. Please."

"That's all I can give you, *piccolo guaio*. I'm sorry it can't be more, but we've given you as much time as we can."

I nod my understanding and watch him walk toward the door.

He pauses with his hand on the knob and looks over at me again, true affection in his gaze. "We miss you. All of us. I hope you know that."

With that, he opens the door, steps out, and lets it slam

closed behind him. The sound reverberates through the loft like a gunshot going off, signaling the end of my ability to do this any longer.

Every time Luca or Byron come over, they tell me the same thing, but tonight, it went even further. I've reached the point of no return, where I might not be able to keep the truth from them anymore. Where I might be faced with revealing the thing I've kept hidden for so damn long from everyone, even Allie.

I pull out my phone and glance down at it again, but she still hasn't returned any of my messages. My chest tightens, and I dial her number again. It goes straight to her voicemail, just like it has all damn day.

"Alessandra McCabe, if you don't call me back within thirty minutes, I'm sending the goddamn cavalry after you, and trust me, you don't want Gabe, Saint, and Bishop hunting you down because they'll be harder on you than even I will be. *Call. Me. Back.*"

I end the message, text the same one to her, and slip my phone back into my pocket as I grab my beer and make my way over to the window to lean against the cool glass and stare down at the café.

Angelina bustles around, moving the bistro tables up against the outer brick wall as the day ends and she gets ready to shut down for the night.

The sun setting behind the buildings on the west side of the street casts long shadows across the asphalt, but I can still make her out clearly.

Even if I couldn't see her, I would know every curve. The way her body moves. The fall of her hair. The way she always takes a moment to stand outside the Grind and stare at it before she goes back in for at least another hour of cleaning and getting things ready for the morning.

She'll be back at 4:30, and I'll be here waiting.

ANGELINA

THE WORDS SCRAWLED across the cover of the heavy book in my hand reach something deep in my soul I've kept locked in there for fifteen years since the first time I saw him at Nana's that Christmas morning—the knowledge that the boy I was looking at was so lost, he might not be able to be found.

I knew it when I was twenty-two staring at a ten-year-old terrified Jude, and the last fifteen years have only confirmed it. Seeing him today cemented it. I had hoped things would have changed since the last time we stood face to face, that perhaps, the time he's spent locked away, working on his manuscript would have opened him up, but that same stony, impenetrable wall he's always had up stood firmly in place the moment he opened the door to me.

That same look he carried then still lies deep in his gaze, that fear of everything, the belief that anything could pose a threat. Including the Hawkes.

Even me.

Jude will never be able to accept what he's been brought into. He will never truly be a Hawke, no matter how hard anyone tries to pull him in. I never realized how much that was true until I saw that intentional distance in his gaze. The same lost boy, just grown now.

My eyes drift to his name scrawled on the bottom of the book cover, and I drag my fingers over it slowly—one letter at a time.

In the year since it was published, I haven't been able to bring myself to open it—partly because he asked all of us not to read it but mostly because something keeps telling me it might break my heart and reveal things I will never be able to forget.

And I'm already haunted by too many things to take on the demons of the blond boy with the sad blue eyes.

Despite the words, "A work of fiction," underneath the title, what I do know about Jude's history before he came to live with Luca and Byron makes me question how much of it might actually be based on things he experienced while he was living on the streets.

I take a sip of my wine and stare at the book for what feels like an eternity.

Why did you even take it out tonight?

It was safe in its space on the bookshelf, the same place it's occupied since release day. *I* was safe, not knowing its contents. But something made me pull it out the moment I walked in the door tonight.

Maybe my continued concern over Allie's strange behavior and needing a distraction. Or maybe because I saw Jude face to face for the first time in two years without the wall of glass and two stories between us. Because I felt that same pull to him, the draw that has always made me want to take him in my arms when I know he won't allow anyone to do that.

I lean back against the armrest on the couch, rest the book on my thighs, and take a sip of my wine. The deeply acidic tannins coat my tongue, and I swallow the heavy liquid and release a sigh, flipping open the cover to the dedication page.

To the one who always made me feel at home.

My phone dings with an incoming message before I can even make it to the first chapter.

JUDE

I left her a voicemail and a text telling her I was going to send Gabe, Saint, and Bishop to look for her if she doesn't respond in thirty minutes.

> Good. I was going to do the same thing if I didn't hear from her in the next hour. I'll let you know if she contacts me.

I stare at the closed door of her room, tempted to go back in there again and rifle through all her personal belongings to find an answer to where she might be disappearing to lately, but I fight that urge.

Allie has always been a free spirit. She loves hard and falls fast, and I can't even count the number of boyfriends she's gone through in her short twenty-five years on this planet. Far more than me with another twelve years on her.

I'm sure she's holed up with some super-hot bad boy who will end up breaking her heart in a few days, or weeks, if she's lucky...

The hard knock at the door makes me jump and almost spill my wine, but I set it on the coffee table, drop the book and my phone onto the couch, and make my way to answer it.

I look through the peephole, take off the security latch, and tug open the door. "Byron, what are you doing here?"

He offers me a kind smile, steps in, and presses a kiss to my cheek. "I'm actually looking for your sister."

"Huh, that makes two of us."

His brow furrows, rising to his graying hair. "What do you mean?"

I wave a hand toward the couch and close the door as he walks over to it and slowly lowers himself. "Do you want a glass of wine? I have a bottle open."

He offers me a smooth grin. "I've never been one to turn down a drink from a beautiful lady."

I smirk as I pour another glass.

"Now, what do you mean you don't know where Allie is?"

Releasing a heavy sigh, I drop onto the couch, hand him the

drink, and grab my own from the coffee table. "She's been acting weird lately. She was late yesterday morning and lied about where she was."

"With Jude?"

I shake my head. "No, I don't know where. Promised me it would never happen again, and now, she's been MIA all day today, not even responding to messages."

Byron stiffens. "Jesus. Do your parents know? Did you call Savage and Gabe or Saint?"

I glance at the clock, trying to tamp down the growing panic his questions seem to be inducing. "She hasn't even been gone a full day. This isn't the first time she's disappeared on us; it's just been a while. She always turns up, and I don't want to start any unnecessary drama."

He shakes his head. "Your sister missing is not unnecessary drama."

I take a sip of my wine. "Jude just left her a message and a text saying that if she doesn't call him in thirty minutes, he was going to alert the cavalry."

Byron smiles and takes a sip of his wine. "Good. You need to find her tonight, even if it means getting everyone out looking for her."

"Why were *you* looking for her, anyway?"

He leans back on the couch and releases a sigh. "I heard about your new neighbor."

I scowl and glare at him, even though he isn't the one I'm so pissed at. "Those fuckers."

He chuckles low, his eyes lighting with humor despite the situation. "My thoughts exactly."

"What does Allie have to do with that?"

"Well"—he offers a guilty look—"Luca went over to talk to Jude tonight."

"Oh, I see." I point at him. "You got the easy job, and he got to go busting some kneecaps so that he felt like his old self again."

Byron releases a deep laugh, his head dropping back. "Something like that. I thought I should talk to her, see if she could speak with Jude, get him to see why it's so important that we get something in that space immediately, whether it be the bookstore or an art studio for Jack."

"I'd love both." I shrug and take a drink. "Either one would be a great complement to the café."

"I know." He nods slowly, swirling his wine and staring down into it like it holds the answers he's looking for. "When we bought that place, I really thought Jude was going to do it..."

He trails off, the pain in his voice making my stomach churn slightly.

I try to see what he does in my wine, but the longer I stare into it, the more it looks like blood and becomes unappetizing. "Me, too. I remember how excited he was. It was the happiest I've ever seen him. He would spend hours down there measuring things, drawing up plans. I could see him through the front window, but I don't think he's been in the space in a long time."

Byron shakes his head. "He hasn't been."

"How do you know?"

"The dust—no footprints."

"Jesus...what's going on with him?"

He abruptly stopped coming to the Grind for his morning coffee and to work, claiming he couldn't concentrate in the public space anymore, but I never truly bought that excuse. After seeing him today, I'm more confident than ever that there's more to it.

Byron's hand tightens on his drink. He pushes to his feet and makes his way over to the window overlooking the water. He rests his shoulder against the wall and stares out at the boats and the city lights along the shore. "We don't know."

My gaze immediately darts down to the book on the cushion beside me. "Could this have anything to do with his childhood?"

Byron glances back at me, and his eyes shift to the book. "Did you read that?"

I shake my head. "Not yet. I was actually wondering..." I rest my hand on top of it.

One of his brows rises. "How much of it is true?"

I nod.

He releases a heavy sigh and takes a drink of his wine before swirling it and staring down into it again. "I wish I could say none of it is, but the truth is that what's in there pales in comparison to what he really went through. He fictionalized parts of his life, but the real story...he could never put on paper."

The real story...

"I don't even think Luca and I know the full extent. I don't know if we want to know."

Shit.

That makes me feel like a real asshole for giving him a hard time about the coffee this morning...and every morning. And for missing dinners with Nana. And for how standoffish he's always been with everyone except Allie.

"Anyway"—Byron pushes off from the wall and approaches —"do you want me to stay until you hear from your sister?"

I shake my head. "No. I'm sure if she doesn't turn up soon, you'll hear about it."

"Undoubtedly." He sets the half-empty glass on the kitchen counter, then approaches and leans down to press a kiss on my cheek. "Please text me updates."

"I will, and I'll see you at Sunday dinner, if not before."

"Yep. I wouldn't miss it." He pauses at the door and turns back to me. "You know, when I first moved to New Orleans, I didn't have anything. No friends. No family. No money.

51

Nowhere to call home. Your uncles...they gave me a job, helped me find a place to live. They trusted me with their business and made me feel like I was part of this family. I've never doubted I was a Hawke, even though I don't have the last name or the blood." He stares at the wall absently, shaking his head. "I think that's Jude's problem. No matter how much Luca and I tell him he's part of this family, he'll never believe it."

Tears start to pool in my eyes, and I take a sip of the wine. I no longer want to try to keep myself from releasing some sort of sobbing sound.

My emotions are all over the place tonight. Too many things happening at once. Allie missing, my business in jeopardy, and now this with Jude and Jack that could cause drama when no one needs it.

"Do you think there's anything any of us can do? I mean, I'll be honest, I haven't always been understanding about the fact that he's never at any of the family stuff."

Byron nods. "No one has. The Hawkes have a lot of expectations that maybe aren't fair in all circumstances. It took me a long time to figure out that they're there for a reason, and it's only because they love you and they want you to be involved in everything."

"But if you don't want to be?"

He offers a shrug. "I'm not sure there's anything we'll ever be able to say or do to get him to want to be part of this family."

I offer him a sad smile. "I'm really sorry you and Luca have to deal with this. I know how much you guys love him."

Byron swallows thickly, his eyes shimmering. "We do, as if he were our own son. It doesn't matter where he spent the first ten years of his life. We love him the same way Landon loves you."

I flinch at his words, and he offers me a sad smile, steps out the door, and closes it behind him.

It isn't anything I haven't heard from others before—

Landon himself a thousand times. He's been in my life since before I turned six, rescued Mom from the depths of her despair when Dad died, helped her build a new life. He's been a wonderful father figure to me, but he isn't Dad, and he never will be.

So, maybe I understand a little bit of what Jude's going through, just the tiniest bit.

And maybe this will help me understand a little bit more.

CHAPTER ONE: THE DARKNESS

The complete darkness has a life of its own. Every slight wisp of air, its breath. Each creak of a floorboard, its voice—

My phone buzzes next to me, and I almost drop the damn book.

Fuck.

I press my hand over my racing heart and grab my cell.

ALLIE

> I'm FINE! You and Jude need to calm down. DO NOT CALL ANYONE. I'm with a friend and didn't feel good, so I slept almost all day and just woke up to this flurry of damn messages like the world was ending. I'm okay.

I glare at the message. Leave it to Allie to disappear, make Jude and me worry, and then be *mad* that we actually care about what's happening with her.

Was I so difficult at her age?

Doubtful.

ANG

> GIRL. YOU ARE IN SO MUCH TROUBLE! YOU CAN'T JUST DISAPPEAR ON US! DON'T EVER DO THIS TO ME AGAIN!

ALLIE

I'm SORRY! But I'm OKAY! Proof of life!!!

The photo comes through of her smiling at the camera, but there's something off about it. Something missing from her eyes.

Something is definitely wrong.

4

ANGELINA

My phone buzzes next to me on the counter, and I glance over at it, lifting my flour-covered hands from the dough.

ALLIE

I'm still not feeling well. Not making it in today.

You have to be fucking kidding me.

As if it isn't bad enough that she made all of us worry yesterday, now she's bailing on me.

Again.

At least she had the decency to text this time. I check the time—05:03. Early enough that I might be able to get Betsy or Pam to come in and cover for her. But this is it, the final straw. Whatever's going on with her needs to be dealt with.

Now.

It's worth it, Angelina.

This is what you've always wanted.

I keep telling myself that, that all the time and effort I put into this place to make it my own, to make it successful, is worth all the physical pain and the annoyances of being a business owner. But on days like this, it's really hard for me to believe it.

These are the times I wish I had just accepted one of the dozens of jobs that Hawke Enterprises could have offered me after college instead of going out on my own with this place.

Even under the protection of the family umbrella, sometimes, when it rains, it pours. And today is an epic deluge waiting to happen. I can see it on the horizon as surely as the hurricanes that will soon start threatening the city again.

I wash my hands, grab my phone, and dial Betsy.

"Hello?" She answers so groggily that I wince.

"I hate to do this again."

Betsy groans. "She's not coming in?"

"No. And I know you were just here yesterday for an extra shift, but—"

"No, no, it's fine. I'll be there in half an hour."

The slightest bit of my anxiety over what I need to get done before opening releases. "Thank you. You're a lifesaver."

"Just remember that when I ask for a raise."

My laugh fills the kitchen, but there really isn't any humor in it. Not when Falco Enterprises is breathing down our necks and my assistant manager keeps disappearing.

My phone buzzes.

JUDE

Did she just text you to tell you she's sick?

ANG

Yes. She's not coming in again.

JUDE

Do you believe her?

56

It's a valid question. Though I'm not sure I have the answer.

Alessandra was born a crappy liar. Mom always saw right through her attempts at misdirection or to assign blame my way for something she did. Of anyone, Jude and I are probably best at reading her these days, but it's impossible to tell what's really going on if she won't get into the same room with any of us—which is likely why she's been avoiding that.

ANG

I don't know. I think we need to have a talk with her in person.

JUDE

An intervention?

ANG

Yeah, something like that.

JUDE

My place tonight?

His place...

How is it that he's lived there for three years and I've never set foot in there?

I know the answer.

Because you avoid being alone with Jude.

At first, it was because he wouldn't go anywhere without Allie, but as he got older, matured, grew from that boy to a man, things shifted in a way that constantly left me feeling off-kilter.

The strange energy that always crackles between us. The intensity in his penetrating gaze every time he looked at me. My inability to look away anytime our eyes met.

It unnerved me more than I'd ever admit to anyone, let alone myself, and even a two-year hiatus hasn't changed it one bit. But I can't let the weirdness with Jude interfere with what's important here—getting to the bottom of what's happening with Allie.

ANG

> Okay. Your place tonight. You get her there
> and don't tell her I'm coming.

JUDE

> All right.

The three little bubbles pop up, then disappear, like Jude's revising whatever he intends to send.

JUDE

> Can you bring me my coffee today?

Annoyance immediately flares at his request, thinking about all the things I have to get done before Betsy gets here. That, combined with avoiding his intensity today when I'm already on edge, decides my answer for me.

ANG

> Not today. You can cross the street and
> come get it. I can have it ready in five
> minutes.

The three little dots don't pop up like I'm expecting them to, and I frown at my phone, then make my way toward the café window to look up at his. He stands in front of it, staring down at his phone.

Even from across the street, I can see the strange look on his face, the return of the confused little boy he once was for a brief moment. Then suddenly, his hands move and the three little dots pick up.

JUDE

> I'll just make some coffee here.

I glance back up at him, but he's gone from the window.

58

My stomach twists slightly—guilt eating away at me from the inside out.

Though I only got through the first twenty pages of his book last night before I was too exhausted to keep my eyes open anymore, it was enough for me to understand that I might not want to know everything about Jude Abello-Harris. That if I did, I wouldn't be able to go on day to day, knowing what he suffered.

You could have brought him a damn coffee.

Maybe, but right now, I have seven other things to bake before we open.

I cast one last quick glance at his window, then over at the empty space beneath it before I head back to the kitchen and return to work. But all the whisking and mixing and baking can't keep my mind off what's happening. When the final cookies go into the oven, I grab my phone and head out front to call the one person who might be able to get the truth out of Allie if Jude and I can't tonight.

"Angelina? What's wrong?"

I sigh at Mom's melodramatic tone. "Does something have to be wrong for me to call you?"

She laughs lightly. "It does when it's not even 06:00 in the morning."

True.

Storm Hawke McCabe is well aware of how busy our mornings are here...and that I *never* would call while trying to get the café open.

"I'm worried about Alessandra."

"Why? What happened?" The panic in her voice rekindles old memories of another call she received so many years ago.

Even at five, I knew something was wrong, that something was happening that would change my life. I just didn't know how much that call and the fallout would shape my future, alter the way I saw everything and everyone.

"I'm not sure. She came in late two days ago, then missed work yesterday and today. She said she's not feeling well and is staying at a friend's."

"She hasn't been home?"

"No." I lean against the glass and stare out at the street. The trail of construction workers making their way to the site just down it stiffens my back. "I need her here, Mom."

She releases a heavy sigh. "I know, and I understand it's difficult when she's not as invested in the business as you are."

"Mom, she doesn't give a shit. I can't have her here anymore if she's not going to show up and work. You know I'd do anything for her, but at this point, I've reached my limit of understanding. Uncle Savage can find her a different job. Maybe she can work at the gym or one of the restaurants. Or, I don't know, be Kennedy's assistant or something. Get her coffee and do her dry cleaning."

Mom snorts. "Oh yeah, I'm sure Allie would love taking orders from Kennedy all day."

I have to smile at that. If she thinks I'm demanding, she'll never survive the feisty blonde mirror image of Aunt Danika.

"I don't know. She just needs to do something other than get my blood pressure up. Jude and I are going to try to talk to her tonight."

"You think that will help?"

"I don't know." I chew on my lip, trying not to anticipate the worst when I already know Allie is likely to react badly to any attempts to intervene. "She's been dodging him, too."

"Really?" The concern returns to Mom's voice. "If she isn't telling him..."

"I know."

"Call me after you talk to her, and I'll try to reach out, too. I'll let you know if I speak with her. We may need to get the others involved."

Exactly my worry.

Once we sic the whole Hawke crew on someone, it becomes one against two dozen and it's impossible to go into those situations without some anger directed at the mob.

I end the call and press my face against the glass as the sun finally peeks over the edge of the buildings on Jude's side and hits the street.

It's going to be hot again today, which means the tensions will only rise.

Hopefully, we'll survive it and get to the bottom of what's going on with Allie.

———

JUDE

MY HAND SHAKES as I reach for the doorknob, and I pause for a moment with it there, concentrating on the cool metal against my palm, trying to ignore the sound of it rattling slightly.

Jesus. Get a grip.

I inhale deeply, squeeze my eyes closed, and turn it.

Every day, I open this door for the deliveries that keep me alive in here—food, laundry, books, toiletries, and everything else, but today, the door seems heavier, solid, more like the protective wall it has literally become.

The massive, thick piece of metal swings back into the loft, and I force my eyes open to stare at the short hallway that leads to the stairs down to the street. It might as well be a thousand miles long in my tunnel vision.

No.

Ten feet.

Fifteen at the most.

Maybe fifty steps to the stairs.

Two flights down.

Three feet of sidewalk.

Two lanes of road.

Three more feet of sidewalk to the café door.

Maybe another eight to ten feet to the counter.

Just thinking about it tightens my chest so much that I can't suck in any air. I rub at the ache, gripping the knob with my other hand so tightly it feels like the metal might crush.

You can do it.

One step at a time.

Count them.

It's right across the street.

Blood whooshes in my ears, and bright spots dance in my vision. I try to take another deep breath to slow my heart's thundering against my ribs, but it comes more like a gasp and does nothing to help calm my rising panic.

I visualize each step.

One foot in front of the other.

The top of the stairs...

Though, I haven't seen them in so long that I can barely remember what they look like.

Each tread down.

A slow descent with my hand gripping the railing.

Pushing through the glass door at the bottom of the stairs.

The street I look at every day.

The same cracks on the sidewalk I have memorized.

Man the fuck up and do it.

I take another deep breath and let it out slowly. It releases the tiniest bit of tension from my chest, but my phone buzzes in my pocket before I can use my renewed determination to advance.

Fuck.

I pull it out, still clutching the knob and staring down the hallway.

ALLIE: Can't tonight. Not feeling well.

Fuck.

She's already trying to get out of coming over to talk to me. Even though I tried to make it sound casual, like we were just hanging out, she has to know I would've confronted her about what's going on.

> If you aren't here tomorrow morning, I will send EVERYONE to get you and drag you from wherever you are, kicking and screaming if I have to.

It isn't an empty threat. There are any number of people I can get to do it. Gabe, Saint, Bishop, Atlas, even Luca. If any of them knew what's been happening the last few days, they'd have her locked up at Nana's house or somewhere else so fast that it would leave her head spinning.

I've tried to give her a little space to sort through whatever the hell is going on, but I've reached the end of my rope.

Go get your drink, Jude. You'll feel better.

Yeah, keep telling yourself that's the reason you're so fucked up.

Lack of caffeine.

I shove the phone into my pocket, take a half-step forward, let the door slam behind me, and wipe my sweaty hands on my jeans.

One.

Two.

Three.

My chest starts to tighten again.

Breathe.

Four.

Five.

Six.

I don't even make it to ten before the pain is too strong, the burn in my lungs so severe that I realize I'm holding my breath.

Fuck.

Panic smashes into me like a massive tidal wave brought in by another summer storm, washing over me, drowning me, making me stagger backward toward the condo, hand against the wall.

I throw open the door to stumble back inside.

It slams shut behind me, and I make it halfway across the room before I collapse onto my knees, gasping for breath, my chest tightening more and more.

Fuck.

I crawl to the wall and sit back against it. Dropping my head between my knees, trying to regain any semblance of control over my body.

What the fuck are you doing, Jude?

I scrub my hands over my face and twine them in my hair, tugging hard on the strands. The pain prickling across my scalp helps pull my focus away from the crippling anxiety threatening to suffocate me.

My phone buzzes again in my pocket.

No, it'll only make it worse if you keep reading Allie's excuses.

It buzzes a second time.

Fuck.

I manage to pull it out.

ANG

I'm bringing you your coffee.

Buzz me in.

Hell.

The buzzer sounds through the loft, and I get to my feet on shaking legs, using the wall to steady myself. They tremble so badly that I can barely make it across the loft without tumbling forward.

I lunge toward the door and grip the knob, willing it to keep me upright as I reach up and push the buzzer to let her in downstairs.

She can't see me like this.

Can't know.

I press my back to the heavy steel separating me from the hallway, sucking in deep breaths, shoving my hair back from my face.

How the fuck do I open the door for her without her seeing what a fucking mess I am?

The knock sounds directly at my back, vibrating through my shoulders.

Angelina...

I can't ignore her, can't pretend she's just outside. Even through the door, I can feel her presence, picture her waiting, just as frustrated and concerned with the Allie situation as I am.

There isn't any way out of this but to face it head-on. I push myself off the thick metal, grip the knob again, and open it slowly.

Her eyes immediately narrow on my face. "Are you okay?"

"What?"

She holds up the drink. "I felt bad about not just bringing this over to you, and now, I feel even worse. Are you sick? Do you have whatever Allie has? Is she not totally full of shit?"

Fuck. I must really look like fucking hell.

"Tired." I shove hair away from my face. "Been writing a lot."

Her cheeks flush slightly, and she averts her gaze.

What the fuck is that about?

She clears her throat. "Oh, I hope it's going well, your new book."

Not really, but I'm not about to tell her about it.

Angelina extends the coffee to me. "Here."

I reach out and grab it, careful not to let my fingers brush against hers the way they did yesterday. Afraid of what that might do to me in my current condition. But when I start to pull away, she wraps her hand around my forearm, leaning in close enough for her sweet scent to surround me.

Heat spreads from where our bodies connect, up through my arm and out into every fiber of my being, immediately releasing all the anxiety from my body as if a valve has been switched open.

"Don't work too hard. You need to take care of yourself." Her lips curl into a sad smile. "I worry about you."

Fuck. Just what I need, her pity.

"I'm fine." I tug my hand from her hold, and she lets hers fall to her side. "Allie isn't coming tonight, by the way. She just texted me to say she still isn't feeling well."

"Hell." She rolls her eyes, then presses her lips together, hands propped on her hips. "Well, I talked to my mom. She was going to try to get her to come home. I'll let her know Allie is bailing on our planned talk."

"Good." I take a sip of my coffee, seeking anything that might distract me from the buzz of energy still coursing through my body from her touch. "Something needs to happen...and fast. If she doesn't show at your parents' house tonight, we won't have a choice but to do something more...aggressive."

She presses her lips together and issues a low little hum of agreement. The sound goes straight to my cock, making it twitch against my jeans. Of all the times to get a hard-on...

Angie rubs the heels of her palms into her eyes and sighs. "If she isn't back tomorrow, I'll bring you your coffee again."

"You don't have to do that."

I don't trust myself so close to her, what I might do or say when she's right here in front of me, touching me, giving me everything I need without her even knowing it.

Ang lowers her hands and offers me a half-smile. "Yes, I do. You're family."

Fucking hell.

It's the last thing I ever want to hear out of Angelina's mouth, confirmation that she'll always see that little boy I was in that closet and not the fully grown man standing before her.

Sometimes, I really hate being a Hawke.

5

FIFTEEN YEARS AGO

JUDE

The most beautiful house I've ever seen rises in front of me, practically a mansion. Nothing like the crappy apartments and motels where Dad and I stay. This place doesn't have rats and roaches...or any of the other things that keep me awake at night.

Luca squeezes my shoulder, and I flinch, taking a step to the side and watching him carefully. I still haven't figured out what the man wants from me, why he's doing this, but I will.

Everyone always wants something...

He jerks his hand back apologetically. "Sorry. Don't worry. The Hawkes will love you. They love everybody." The corner of his mouth quirks up. "Even me and that can be really fucking hard sometimes."

What does that even mean?

Ever since he found me, he's been making weird comments like that, saying things that don't make any sense. But I won't ever ask. I keep my mouth shut as much as possible around

Luca and Byron. There isn't anything to say. Nothing I would ever want them to know.

Luca motions toward the front door, and I glance behind me at Byron, who offers me an encouraging smile.

Byron steps up next to me, keeping his hands clasped together in front of him, far away from me, like he can tell I might run if he touches me. "Let's go in."

In there?

It's like something out of a fairy tale. Christmas lights hang from every eave and twinkle in the darkness settling around us. A sleigh with nine tiny reindeer sits in the middle of the yard, a Santa waving to the cars passing by, the mechanical "ho, ho, ho" cutting through the silent, chilly air.

We never had a sleigh. Never had a Santa. Never had a lawn or anywhere to hang lights. Not even a tree...

This isn't where I belong. These people. This house...

I retreat a step, but Byron inclines his head toward the flickering holiday lights, encouraging me forward.

"We don't need to stay long if you don't want to." He squats in front of me, putting his eyes on my level. "We'll just get some of Nana's great food and then head back home."

Home.

He said the word so easily, like the beautiful condo they brought me to yesterday has suddenly become that for me. But it can't be that simple.

Luca slowly walks up the path to the front door, then peers over his shoulder to ensure I'm following. I take one small step at a time, running my shaking hand over the unfamiliar crisp fabric of the button-down shirt they gave me.

He knocks but doesn't wait for anyone to answer, just opens the door inward and motions for me to enter. The most magnificent scent hits me—something warm, rich, and spicy that makes my mouth water and my stomach rumble even though they ensured I ate breakfast and lunch, far more than I have eaten in a long time.

Christmas music plays from speakers I can't see, and I scan the small entryway that branches off on either side into larger, open rooms. At least a dozen people sit and stand around a living room immediately to the right, chatting and laughing, a few even playing some sort of board game at a table in the corner.

None of them even look our way as Luca closes the door behind us.

He squats in front of me, his dark eyes soft. "Just remember, you have every right to be here."

Can he read my thoughts?

Something sour climbs my throat, and I swallow it back so I don't puke on these people's beautiful floors.

Does he know?

That thought, that Luca and Byron might know what I was doing outside the club...

Don't embarrass them.

I squeeze my eyes closed and force myself to breathe before I open them again.

Byron motions to the left toward a dining room where a long table is set immaculately with red tablecloths, fancy plates, and more silverware per person than I've ever seen in my life. "That's where we'll eat."

Jesus, these people are loaded.

I look down at myself again, at the shirt and new dark jeans Luca and Byron bought for me—the first clothes I've ever had that came with tags still on them.

They feel weird.

Too tight.

Too clean.

Too new.

Luca raises his hand to rest it on my shoulder again but

pulls it back before he makes contact and smiles. "You look good. Let's see if we can find you a friend."

A friend.

That's what they said—that they were *friends*. That they wouldn't hurt me. That they only wanted to help.

Others have promised that, too.

But they always want something.

My stomach turns, and I try to hide my instinct to gag.

That pretty blonde doctor from last night said I was okay, that I wasn't sick at all, but I don't feel right. My skin too tight. My chest weighed down by something sitting on it. My hands sweaty and shaking.

Luca pushes to his feet, his black pants falling perfectly into place again, and motions for me to follow him in. I don't have a choice.

Where would I go if I left? If I ran?

We walk past the living room and dining room. Several people stop their conversation and watch us, their eyes wide or narrowed curiously. The blond doctor stands near a fireplace. She smiles and gives me a little wave.

I lower my head, hiding behind the hair that always falls over my eyes. Byron's voice behind me makes me glance back, and I find him stopped, talking to a group in the living room. Maybe trying to explain why this strange little boy is in their home.

When I definitely shouldn't be...

The instinct to turn and bolt out that front door, run and not stop until I find a familiar street and Dad, hits me so hard that I drop my eyes to the floor to check for any obstructions between me and my escape.

You can't go back...

Somehow, my feet keep moving me forward, following Luca into a kitchen where he embraces an older woman with gray-ish-white hair and an apron over her green and red dress. He whispers something to her, and her eyes dart to me, widening slightly, still vibrant even in her old age.

She pulls away from Luca and approaches, bending down to me. "Hi, Jude. You can call me 'Nana.'"

I stare, unable to pull my eyes from hers, and she stares right back at me, as if she can see straight into me and every dirty secret I hold there.

The corner of her mouth curls slightly. "I think I should introduce you to some of the grandkids."

How many of these people are there?

Too many.

The sounds of dozens of people mix with the music, filling my ears, making it impossible to think. I wipe my sweaty hands on my jeans and continue to stare at the woman as she waits for a response from me that I can't give her.

She pushes to her full height and offers me her hand. When I don't slip mine into hers, she gives me another smile. "Come on."

I glance up at Luca, and he nods his approval.

"Go with her."

All the noise. The lights. The laughter. My head starts to pound as my chest tightens.

The woman who insisted I call her "Nana" leads me down a hallway with several open doors on either side. "Here's the bathroom if you need it. These are the bedrooms. Most of the older kids are out back since the chillier weather doesn't seem to faze them. Playing poker or something else they shouldn't be." She makes a *tsking* sound with her tongue and shakes her head, but her lips curl playfully. "I think Alessandra, Isaac, and Pope, who are closer to your age, are back here."

Who?

She drops names like I should know who they are. Maybe she has no idea that I've only been with Luca and Byron for twenty-four hours and barely know *their* names.

We reach an open door at the end of the hall, and she steps through it. Three heads pop up from where they sit together in the middle of the bed. My eyes dart over the two boys quickly, but when they reach the girl, my breath catches.

Long dark hair spills around her face and down her back, and piercing blue eyes meet mine. "Who's this, Nana?"

The two boys watch me suspiciously.

Nana motions to me. "Pope, Isaac, Alessandra, this is Jude. He came with Luca and Byron."

The three kids exchange confused looks, then the girl slides from the bed and holds out her hand.

She grins at me expectantly. "Allie."

I stare down at it until she finally pulls it back and shrugs.

"Okay, we were going to play *Uno*." She points to the cards piled on the mattress. "You want to play?"

Uno?

Allie's brow furrows, waiting for my response, and Nana squeezes her shoulder.

The older woman nods toward me. "Why don't you just let Jude watch until he understands the game?"

"Okay." Allie runs back to the bed and climbs onto it, grinning at the two boys as Nana retreats from the room with an encouraging smile. "Watch me decimate both of them."

The dark-haired boy with blue eyes Nana introduced as Isaac scowls. "You wish."

Allie elbows him as she deals the cards. "You two are about to get *killed*."

I recoil and squeeze my eyes closed, all the air rushing from my lungs in one whoosh. Something heavy pushes against my chest, my vision blurring. I press my hand over my heart, trying to breathe, but all that comes is short, shallow breaths that won't fill my lungs.

"Jude?"

My name comes from far away, as if somebody's saying it

from a different part of the house. I try to open my eyes, but the room spins around me. I stagger back toward the open door and into the hallway. Running my hand along the wall, I move forward until it hits the jamb of the next door.

Tumbling into the room to my knees, I try not to pass out like I have so many times before, fighting the darkness, scanning ahead of me with blurry vision.

An open closet.

I crawl into it, past some clothes, and into the back corner. Sitting with my knees pulled against my chest, I drop my head on them, trying to block out the memories racing through my mind.

Blood.

So much blood.

Pain.

Screams.

The clothes to my left move slightly, and I jerk my head up and press myself even farther into the corner.

Allie's blue eyes meet mine, and she offers me a little half-smile as she pulls the closet doors shut behind her, leaving one cracked just enough that a tiny sliver of light filters in.

What is she doing?

She slips in and sits next to me. Her shoulder brushes mine, and she pulls her knees up to her chest, wrapping her arms around them, mirroring me. Without a word, she drops her cheek against her knee so she's facing me and gives me a tiny smile, barely visible in the darkness.

Silence settles around us—the noise from all the people and music muffled by the walls and clothes. Her steady breathing fills the air. Slowly, I'm able to take a breath again, then another.

Everything stops spinning.

The red that filled my vision disappears, and my shoulders relax on a heavy sigh.

For the first time in forever, for one second, I *almost* feel safe.

———

ANGELINA

I TUG OPEN the sliding glass door, but a chorus of grumbling sounds from behind me, making me turn back toward the table I just vacated. Kennedy, Atlas, and Astrid all glare at Bishop, who wears a smug grin on her face as she rakes all the money from the central pot toward her.

She points a finger at each of them. "You are all *sore* losers."

They should be used to it by now. That girl is a damn shark.

Coen watches from his chair, his eyes on her pile, far too young to play with the older cousins but intent on being part of the action any way he can. I ignore their bickering and step into Nana's house, beelining for the kitchen where Mom, Aunt Skye, and Nana are working on dinner and likely approaching the time they'll need more hands. "Mom, you ready for my help?"

She glances up from whatever she's mixing and nods. "Yes. I need you to make the salad and start bringing some things to the table. Can you please grab your sister and have her come help, too?"

"Got it." I lean to try to see into the living room, where just about everyone has gathered for pre-dinner drinks and games. "Where is she?"

She nods toward the back hallway. "One of the bedrooms, with the boys."

As usual.

They're like three little peas in a pod. Practically inseparable. Except when Isaac and Pope get annoyed with Allie beating them at whatever game they're playing.

"All right." I make my way down the hall toward the sound

of Pope and Isaac bickering in the back bedroom. Leaning against the doorjamb, I watch them shove a stack of cards around, debating who said *Uno* first. "Where's my sister?"

They both shrug absently, and Pope motions toward the hall.

His dark-bourbon eyes flash toward me for a moment. "I don't know. She disappeared after Jude."

"Who the hell is Jude?"

Isaac and Pope exchange an awkward look, and Isaac shrugs, finally wrangling the cards from Pope.

Pope scowls at Isaac and leans back on his elbows on the mattress. "I don't know. Apparently, he showed up with Byron and Luca. Looks like he's about our age."

"Huh..."

Where the hell did Luca and Byron pick up a kid?

I'm confident there's a story there. There always is when Luca is involved, and I'm sure we'll all hear about it later. Right now, I need to find Allie. "Any idea where they went?"

They both shake their heads and return to their card game, apparently unconcerned with the new arrival or Alessandra vanishing with him.

Though, they can't have gone far.

I stick my head into each bedroom on my way down the short corridor, scanning for any sign of them, but I come up empty.

Where the hell did they go?

Nana's house isn't *that* big, and with everyone here, there shouldn't be anywhere to hide where someone wouldn't see them. Even if they tried to sneak outside, the adults in the living room or the guys at the table on the back patio would have seen them.

I wander out into the living room where Byron, Luca, and pretty much the entire Hawke clan sit or stand around, talking and laughing, the colorful lights on the Christmas tree in the corner reflecting off the glasses of whatever they're indulging in tonight—likely some of Uncle Savage's favorite Barolo.

Uncle Savage turns his head away from his conversation with Luca and Byron and raises an eyebrow. "You need something?"

"Have you guys seen Allie?"

He shakes his head. "No, why?"

Savage *always* knows what's happening with everyone, which means wherever they are, they're being careful to hide it. I sigh and run a hand through my hair. "Isaac and Pope said she went after Jude."

Luca and Byron exchange a look, and Savage drums his fingers on his knee, his brow furrowed.

Byron climbs from his seat. "We'll help you find him."

He steps up to Luca and whispers something in his ear. Luca nods and gives me a tight smile, his already-dark eyes darkening even more than normal.

Unease starts to coil around the base of my spine.

They're not telling me something...

Not that it's unusual, especially when they're discussing business. But this isn't business.

What could they possibly be hiding about this kid?

That question lingers in my head as they follow me from the room toward the hallway.

Savage motions down toward the bedrooms. "Angelina and I will check the house." His gaze darts to Luca and Byron. "You two check outside and ask the other kids out there if anyone has seen them."

Everyone nods their agreement, and Bryon and Luca beeline for the front and back doors while Savage follows me down the hall toward the bedrooms.

I pop my head into Mom's old room, now used mostly for storage unless someone has to crash here for some reason. My gaze bounces over the small space, and I start to leave when the slightly cracked closet door makes me pause.

When I was in here earlier to grab a jacket for Bishop to wear outside, I swear I left it open...

I take a few steps toward the closet, listening for any signs that Allie might be in there with this mysterious Jude, but the only thing filling my ears is the Christmas music Nana has piped through the house and the occasional raucous laughter from the living room.

What would Allie be doing in the closet with a boy she doesn't even know?

Crap.

She's only ten, and that was a *long* time ago for me, but I remember getting that first crush on a boy and wanting that first kiss. It would be just like her to rush for it with someone she had just met, too.

I pull the doors open all the way, exposing two sets of shoes in the corner, then tug the clothes off to the side to catch them in the act.

Better me than Mom or Landon, or God forbid, Uncle Savage...

Allie lifts her head from her knee and turns toward me, then shoots her hand out to my arm quickly before I say anything, her eyes wide with warning.

My gaze darts to the blond boy beside her, huddled in the darkest corner of the closet. The most brilliant Nordic-blue eyes I've ever seen stare back at me, brimming with so much fear in them that my heart instantly shatters.

What happened to this boy?

Allie squeezes my arm. "Ang, this is Jude. Jude, this is my sister, Angelina. She's cool. You can trust her."

Trust me?

It's an odd choice of words for a ten-year-old, but seeing the petrified look in Jude's eyes stops me from questioning it. Wherever he came from, however he got to Luca and Byron, it was a horrible road—one that's left him scared and scarred. Anyone could see that with one glance at the kid.

I swallow past the emotion clogging my throat and offer him a little half-smile. "Hi, Jude."

He doesn't respond, just continues to stare at me as if he doesn't quite understand what he's looking at. I shake Allie's hand free and slowly reach in and set my palm on his forearm where he has it draped over his knees. A little spark jumps where our bodies connect, but he doesn't flinch away from my touch like I expect; he just stares at my hand on him for a few seconds before he glances up at me.

"It's okay to be overwhelmed by all this." I wave my free hand absently, then squeeze him gently. "I've been a part of this family for twenty-two years, and even I can't handle it all the time."

Allie glances between us, watching both Jude and me. "Our family is a little..." She struggles for the word. "Um...complicated?"

Exactly.

I nod my agreement and glance around the closet Nana uses to store all her extra clothes. "This is a good hiding spot. Quiet. Away from the fray. If you want to stay in here the whole time, I can bring you food when it's ready and make sure nobody bothers you."

A second of silence hangs in the tight space, then Jude releases a massive rush of air, as if he's been holding it in his lungs the entire time, and gives a sharp nod.

Smiling, I squeeze his arm again. "Don't worry. You'll be okay, kiddo." I wink at him, then push to my feet. "I got you."

"Allie, Mom and Nana need help in the kitchen, but why don't you stay here with Jude and keep him company unless he'd rather be alone?"

He glances at Allie and back at me, shaking his head. "I want her to stay."

His words come softly, like he's afraid to even speak them or what might happen if he does. The reality of what could have made him so timid and fearful makes tears burn in my eyes.

Allie beams at him, then places her hand on his knee, interlocking their fingers. "We'll be okay. Will you bring me a plate, too?"

I nod, then retreat and close the doors, sealing them back into the space that seems to make that beautiful, broken boy feel safe.

What have Luca and Byron gotten themselves into?

Closing the bedroom door, I lean back against it, squeezing my eyes closed. Heavy footsteps make me finally look to the right, and Luca approaches, concern knitting his brow.

"Did you find them?"

I nod and motion toward the living room to ensure we're out of earshot of the kids. He narrows his eyes but follows me from the hallway, and I pull him toward the small alcove outside the kitchen.

Scanning around to make sure no one is listening, I lean in closer to him. "He's in the closet with Allie."

His eyebrows rise to his hairline. "In the closet?"

"Not what you think." That boy's face flashes through my head, an image I doubt I'll ever be able to forget. "He looked terrified, Luca, like he thought..."

I can't even put into words what I saw in those blue eyes.

Luca sighs and runs his hand through his dark hair just starting to grow gray at the temples. "I'm worried about him. Do you think we should leave? Bring him back to our place?" He glances around at everyone bustling to get dinner ready. "Maybe this was too much on only his first full day with us."

I rest my hand on his arm, giving him a gentle squeeze. For all the horrible things Luca Abello has done in his life, he has a good heart. Otherwise, he never would've been forgiven. He never would've been let into this family. He never would've gained our trust, and he certainly wouldn't be with Byron. He's trying to do the right thing with that boy back there—whatever that might be.

"I think he's okay with Allie. He seems to like her."

The corner of his lip twitches. "Well, that's easy to do. She's a good kid."

I chuckle and pull my hand away. "Are we talking about the same Alessandra, the one who keeps stealing my makeup and clothes, even though they're way too big for her?"

He grins at me. "You're lucky you have a sister. I was an only child, and my father wasn't exactly Dad of the Year."

I flinch at his reference to Dom Abello, the man who caused so much agony for our family and so many others. If Luca hadn't been raised away from his father for so long, I doubt he would have ended up even half the human being he is today.

A long sigh slips from Luca's lips. "I don't know what I'm doing with that kid, Ang."

The uncertainty in his eyes, the worry for both that boy and for himself and Byron, renews my faith that he *can* do it. He cares too much not to.

"You and Byron will be okay. Is he going to stay with you for long?"

"I don't know." He rubs a hand against the dark stubble on his jaw. "This is all very new. We need to take some time to figure out what's going to happen and what we need to do to make sure he stays safe."

"Safe?" There's that word again. "Safe from what?"

Luca glances around, then back down the hall toward the door to Mom's room. "From the man who calls himself his father."

6

ANGELINA

Allie's car pulls into Mom and Landon's driveway, and I let the curtain fall back into place over the window and turn back to the living room and the people waiting in it.

Like staring at a jury about to decide someone's fate.

I motion toward the front of the house. "She's here."

Landon runs a hand through his sandy-blond hair, his mouth pressed in a firm line as he paces. "Are we sure this is necessary?"

Mom glowers at him. "Of course, it is. She's been MIA for days. We have no idea what's going on with her, and she's left Angelina hanging. We can't let this go on any longer."

The fact that Mom got Allie to agree to come here tonight in the first place when she's been avoiding Jude and me only confirms my suspicions—Allie thinks Landon is going to believe her bullshit and help convince Mom to lay off her. Jude and I would never do that. She's picking what she *thinks* is the easier road. Daddy's little girl, hoping he's going to jump in and protect her when the rest of us will push for answers.

Landon looks over at Aunt Nora in the corner of the living room. "And remind me again why Nora's here."

Nora crosses her arms over her chest and leans against the wall. "Because if she's on something, I'll be able to tell."

The thought that Allie might have someone gotten herself wrapped up in something like that makes my stomach churn, and I turn away from them to hide the tears starting to form in my eyes. I need to wipe them away and get control of myself before Allie comes in, or I'll spook her.

That's the last thing we want.

"You don't think..." Landon inhales sharply. "I just can't see her using drugs. I mean, we've told her about what happened with Stone. She's too smart to get involved with that."

Nora sighs. "I know, but she's young—"

The front door opens, and everybody falls silent. Allie steps in, her eyes widening and darting around the room at everyone.

Mom approaches, arms open to embrace her, but she stops short, pressing a hand to her chest as she examines her daughter. "Honey, are you okay?"

She's right.

Allie looks like shit.

Her normally bright eyes appear dull. Red and puffy. Her usually perfect skin pale and splotchy.

Maybe she is on something.

She did say she wasn't feeling well the last few days, but I assumed it was a bullshit excuse for her to hole up with some guy for a while.

Maybe it was more than that.

Allie accepts Mom's hug, her gaze darting to mine apologetically. "I haven't been feeling well."

"Come in. Come in." Mom pulls away and holds her at arm's length. "Do you want something to drink?"

The mention makes Allie turn green, and she shakes her head. "No, I'm okay."

Mom walks her over to the couch, and she takes a seat beside her. Immediately, Mom pulls one of Allie's hands between her own, clutching it to her like she's afraid if she lets go that Allie might run out of here before we get answers.

Landon approaches and presses a kiss on Allie's cheek. "Are you sure you're all right, sweetheart?"

Nothing about this is all right. I've never seen Allie looks so...out of it. Jude was right to be worried. This seems like a lot more than just not feeling well, and as soon as I find out what's going on, I'll text him to let him know how the meeting went.

Allie looks up at her dad. "Yes. I've just been staying at a friend's house." She looks over her shoulder. "Hi, Aunt Nora."

Nora gives her a hard smile. "You okay, kiddo?"

Lips pressed firmly together, Allie scans all our faces. "Why does everybody keep asking me that?"

I take the chair facing her across the coffee table. "Because you've left me in a lurch three days in a row. Because you're being secretive. You're not even telling *Jude* what's going on, and you tell him *everything*. Everyone's worried about you."

She glances around at us again. Landon at her side. Mom sitting next to her. Aunt Nora in the corner. Her eyes fly open wide, her jaw dropping. "Oh my God. Is this an *intervention*?"

And here go the hysterics...

This would have gone so much better if it had just been Jude and me at his place, but she's too smart for that. If she has something to hide, it wouldn't stay hidden with the two of us going at her, and if she knew I would be here tonight, she probably never would have agreed to come.

I simultaneously want to hug her and scream at her for making us all worry, especially when I have Falco Enterprises trying to fuck with me, but if I don't calm her down, she'll go completely off the rails and nothing will get resolved tonight.

An emotional Allie never thinks clearly. I need to get her to rein herself in long enough to talk through this rationally.

I hold up a hand. "No, nothing like that."

"It is." She gapes. "Holy shit. You guys think I'm on *drugs*?"

I lower my face into my palms and release a frustrated groan. "I didn't say that. I just...I'm worried about you. We all are, and if there's something major going on and you need some time away from the café, I need to know that so I can plan accordingly, maybe get Astrid or Coen to come help for a while until you're back."

She shakes her head, her eyes watering. "I can't believe this. I can't believe you guys would actually think that. I told you...I wasn't feeling well."

"But you also didn't respond to me for entire days at a time —or Jude. He's freaking the fuck out."

Allie ghosting *him* might be the most concerning part of all of this. Since the day he arrived into this mess we call a family, Jude has relied on Allie and their friendship like a life raft in a storm. Always together. Always whispering conspiratorially. She's the only one he ever lets in, and now, she's pushing *him* out.

She winces, the tears finally spilling over and down her cheeks. "I'm sorry."

Mom releases Allie's hand and wraps her arm around her shoulders, squeezing her close. "What's wrong? Fever? Stomach?"

Aunt Nora approaches and squats in front of her, her keen, scrutinizing doctor's gaze darting all over. "What are your symptoms?"

Allie avoids looking directly at Nora, instead staring at where her hands rest on her lap. She swallows thickly. "I'm okay, really. I drank too much a few nights ago, and"—her head snaps up—"no, I don't have a drinking problem. Then, I didn't get enough sleep and didn't eat well. But I'm feeling much better now. I'll be back to work tomorrow."

Her reassurance doesn't lift the dread from my stomach. "Are you sure?"

She nods a little too vigorously. "I am."

No.

Something about her behavior is still off, and everyone in the room knows she's keeping something from us. Maybe she won't say whatever it is in front of Mom and Landon, but I *will* get the truth out of her tonight.

Nora glances at Mom and Landon, then over her shoulder at me. "Allie, Angie, come with me. I'm going to do a quick exam."

Eyes wide, Allie shakes her head. "It's really not necessary. I'm fine."

Rising and propping her hands on her hips, Nora gives her a *don't fuck with me* look. "Do you want me to drag you down to the hospital?"

I climb to my feet. "You know she'll do it, Al."

Aunt Nora is nothing if not thorough. No one can get anything past her. She's probably the last person Allie wants to see right now, but it's better than the alternative. If I had called Pope to come check on her, all hell would have broken loose.

"Fine." Allie slips from under Mom's arm and pushes to her feet. "If it will make you feel better."

Landon pulls her in for a hug while Nora grabs her medical bag from the corner and motions for us to follow her. Allie casts a few furtive glances back at me, and Nora leads us into Allie's old room and closes the door behind us.

Sealing our fates?

Something ominous settles over the room, and Nora offers Allie a tight smile. "I got the impression there were some things you didn't want to say in front of your parents out there."

Allie looks at me, her eyes filled with fear I hadn't seen

there before, that she somehow managed to hide beneath a mask of anger at us.

Oh, no. Something's very wrong.

I rush forward and wrap my arms around her. "Oh, my God. Are you okay?"

Bursting into tears, she buries her face against my neck. "I don't know. I've just felt like crap the last couple of days. I'm exhausted...but I can't sleep. I'm hungry...but I can't eat. I've been an emotional wreck, crying all the damn time."

"Where have you been?"

Allie sniffles and pulls back, looking away from me. "A friend's house."

"Does this *friend* have a name?"

She peeks up at me. "He does, but I'm not giving it to you."

Shit.

I fucking knew it.

The only time she does shit like this is when she has her heart wrapped up in something—or someone—usually bad for her. Allie's ability to see the good in people blinds her to the bad, to the things that will burn her in the end.

No doubt, whoever she's been with the last few days falls firmly under that *bad for her* category.

I try my best to hide the disdain for the man I haven't even met from my next question. "Did he at least take care of you the last couple of days?"

She pulls out of my hug and wraps her arms around herself protectively. "He was busy."

Exactly.

Another deadbeat piece of shit who only cares about banging her and disappears when she's sick.

Nora and I exchange a look, and she motions for Allie to sit on the edge of the bed.

"I want you to understand something right now, Al. I'm your doctor. Whatever you tell me, I can't say a word to your mother or father, and if you want Angie to leave the room, too, she will."

I start to object, but Nora gives me a dirty look that tells me I better not open my fucking mouth.

Allie glances between us. "No. I want her to stay."

Nora nods and rubs Allie's leg gently. "I'm worried if you've been sick, you might be dehydrated. You may need an IV, potentially antibiotics or antivirals. But I need you to answer something first."

One of Allie's brows rises slowly. "What?"

"Is there any chance you're pregnant?"

Allie stiffens, a tear slipping from her eye. "I..." She shakes her head like she's trying to remove the question from her brain as even a possibility. "I don't think so."

"Well"—Nora gives her a hard look—"are you sexually active?"

"Christ..." Allie's cheeks redden, and she buries her face in her hands. "This is not a conversation I want to be having with you, Aunt Nora."

She offers her a kind smile. "I'm sorry, but I have to ask it. Would you rather Pope was the one here asking these questions?"

Allie goes stock still and shakes her head. "God, no."

Nora rubs her arm gently. "So, is it possible you're pregnant?"

"I really don't think so."

Thank God...

Of all the possible reasons for Allie's behavior, it never *once* crossed my mind that she might have herself in *this* kind of situation. We don't *talk* about our sex lives—or my lack thereof —but Allie has always been *smart* about that aspect of her life.

At least, I thought so.

Nora tosses me a look, pressing her lips together. "I'm going to draw blood and run it anyway, just to be safe. Are you really feeling better, or did you just say that to get all of us off your back out there?"

Allie releases a deep breath. "I am feeling better. Not so dizzy or nauseous as the last few days."

I slide onto the bed beside her and wrap my arm around her shoulders. "Can she just come home with me?"

It's been so weird not having her there the last few nights but not because she wasn't in her bed. It isn't unusual for her to crash with some random guy she's hooking up with or at Jude's on a fairly regular basis. But something felt different this time. Each minute she was gone felt like it was ticking closer to something catastrophic.

Nora eyes both of us, then sighs. "Let me run a quick exam, and as long as I don't find anything concerning, she can go home with you. But you will call me *immediately* if anything changes."

We both nod our agreement, and Nora opens her bag and starts grabbing whatever she needs to conduct her exam. Allie shakes next to me, her entire body trembling so badly the mattress beneath us vibrates.

Whatever's going on with her runs far deeper than just her being sick the last few days. Something has her shaken, off-kilter. But if she won't own up to me, maybe she will for Jude.

―――――

JUDE

WHEN ANGELINA TOLD me their mom had convinced Allie to go there after she ditched me tonight, hope bloomed deep in my chest that all of this would be resolved. That some sort of answer would finally be found and we could go back to how it all was before she started acting so strangely. But the simple text from Angie a few minutes ago alerted me that things had not gone as planned.

I read it again, back to pacing the same path I always fall into.

ANGIE

I'm bringing her to you.

Relief mixes with a sense of foreboding.

She'll finally be here in front of me, but whatever is going on, it wasn't something a conversation at her parents' house tonight solved.

A key sliding into the lock stops my pacing, and I hold my breath, waiting for the door to push open. Allie steps in slowly and lets the door close behind her.

The dim light from the oven hood casts a vague silhouette of her small frame against the wall, but even from here, I can see her trembling.

I rush over to her and tug her against me. "Al, where the hell have you been?"

She wraps her arms around me and buries her face in my chest. Her heavy sob makes my stomach clench, and I rub up and down her back, burying my face in her hair.

"Al, what's wrong?"

A million horrific possibilities race through my head. The kinds of things I wouldn't wish on my worst enemy. The things I know all too well. And if she doesn't start talking soon and telling me what's happening, I may lose my fucking mind.

Her tears soak my T-shirt, and I finally drag her back from me, grasping her chin to force her to look up at me. Red, puffy eyes meet mine, and her bottom lip trembles.

"What's going on, Al? Where have you been? Are you all right?"

Just a few of a million questions, and the worry I thought would dissipate as soon as I saw her has only grown worse.

Allie isn't the crying, blubbering type.

Not ever.

She makes mistakes. She deals with the consequences. Sometimes she fights back against the judgment pushed on her by the rest of the family. But she never backs down. She never crumbles under the weight of it.

Until now...

"Come on, Al."

I lead her into the bedroom, climb on tothe bed, and pat a spot next to me, where she normally sits every morning when she brings me my coffee. She climbs up with me, still sniffling, then settles next to me and lowers her head to my lap, looking away toward the opposing wall and the TV hanging there.

She won't even look at me...

What are you doing, Al?

I run my fingers through her hair, waiting for her to say something, to offer any explanation for what the hell has been going on, but all she does is release a heavy sigh.

For the first time in fifteen years, her silence makes unease fill my gut. I always appreciated her ability to just *sit* with me, how she never forced me to talk or offer any explanations for what I needed in those moments when I became overwhelmed by everything. But now, knowing something is *very* wrong, I can't stand the air empty of words.

I twirl a silky, dark strand around my finger. "You know how worried I've been about you?"

She nods and squeezes my leg. "I'm sorry. I didn't mean to worry you."

"You could have called me back or texted more than bullshit non-responses."

If I were a stronger person, I would have gone out looking for her that first morning she didn't show. I would have tracked her down, *made* her talk to me. I shouldn't have let it go on for days...

92

Allie sniffles. "I was sick."

Something about the way she says it doesn't sit right, leaves acid burning in my throat. "Were you really?"

She nods again, playing absently with my sweatpants, fingering the fabric and brushing it across her cheek. "I felt like shit, and I didn't keep my phone plugged in. I was watching movies and sleeping. It drained the battery."

I wish I could believe her, but I know Allie McCabe better than anyone, and she's holding something back. "This all sounds like bullshit to me."

My words come out a little harsher than I intend them, and Allie stiffens and glances back at me, tears trickling down her cheek.

"I swear, Jude. I was just lying in bed, trying desperately not to throw up again."

Staring into her eyes, I can see it's true, but something else lies in their depths. A darkness lurking behind the bright blue, something she doesn't want me to know, doesn't want to have to say.

A sob slips from her trembling lips, and she presses her hand over her mouth. "I think I'm pregnant."

It takes a second for her words to register, and it's my turn to stiffen. She turns onto her other side to face me, the kind of fear I've only ever seen in my own reflection staring back at me now.

"Jesus, Al. Are you serious?"

She nods.

"Who's the father?"

Instead of offering me the answer, she bites her bottom lip.

I raise a brow. "You don't know?"

"I do." Allie turns her head down, burying her face against my stomach. "I just..."

"Aren't going to tell me?" I tilt her chin up, forcing her to meet my gaze. "What the fuck, Allie? We tell each other everything."

Well, almost everything.

Maybe it's a dick move to be so self-righteous about it when I've been keeping something so major from her for so long. But this is different. *So, so* different. This is life-altering shit, not something she can stick her head in the sand over and pretend isn't happening the way I so often do with my own shit.

I tamp down my distress, not wanting to amp hers up even more. This isn't about me being angry with her; it's about what happens going forward. "Does the guy know?"

She shakes her head. "No."

"Have you been at his place the last few days?"

Allie nods, but she doesn't say anything else, just trembles against me, biting into her bottom lip so hard I'm afraid she'll break right through the skin.

"Al, you *have* to talk to me. You *have* to tell me more about what's going on."

It takes her a moment, but she finally pulls out of my hold and sits up, facing me, tucking her legs under her. Sitting like that, so scared and fragile, Allie doesn't look twenty-five. She's back to that ten-year-old girl who joined me in the closet and offered me the first true friendship I'd ever known.

"This guy is..." She sighs, the corner of her lips twitching. "I really like him, Jude, like a lot. And the sex is..."

I can't help but smile at her trailing off. "Well, at least he wasn't a two-pump chump who knocked you up."

"God, don't say that." She squeezes her eyes closed. "Please don't joke about it."

"Are you sure you're pregnant?"

She shakes her head. "No. But as soon as Aunt Nora asked, I just...I don't know. It felt like maybe she was right. She drew blood and says she'll know tomorrow."

So, no one will be getting any sleep tonight.

The possibility that Allie might be pregnant never crossed my mind for even a second over the last few days, but now that it's out there, I have to ask the question.

"What if you are?"

"Oh, God..." Allie leans forward and buries her face against my chest, allowing me to drag her onto my lap and up against me. "What am I going to do, Jude? I can't be a mother. I can't even fucking take care of myself."

I chuckle softly, even though it *really* isn't funny, and rub her back. "You'll be fine. It's not like you don't have two dozen other people who will help you with the baby."

"That's not my point." She releases another sob. "*You're* pissed at me. *Angie's* pissed at me. *Mom and Dad* are pissed at me. I can't do *anything* right, and I'm supposed to bring a baby into this world?"

Her fear seizes my heart, tightening a vise around it, and I pull her back and hold her face between my palms. "Don't panic until you know there's something to panic about."

She scowls at me. "Funny, coming from you."

Ouch.

That one slices straight at my gut, and I flinch.

Her gaze immediately softens. "Shit, I'm sorry. I didn't mean that."

I press my lips together and inhale deeply through my nose, trying to quell my anger. "No, it's true." Dropping my head back against the headboard, I release a sigh and let my hands fall from her face. "Maybe I am a hypocrite, but Al, you're probably the strongest person I've ever met in my life. You never back down from anything. You take on any challenge head-on." I return my gaze to hers. "Even me being so fucked up when we met fifteen years ago didn't faze you. You came and sat with me in that closet, ate Christmas dinner in there with me, a total stranger, like it was no big deal. You gave me exactly what I needed in that moment. Someone to just sit with me. You never said a word, not a fucking word, because you knew that was what I needed. So, I need you to tell me what *you* need now. What do you need me to do for you?"

Tears stream down her face, her distress tearing me apart from the inside, and she releases another sob. "I don't know."

"Are you going to stay here tonight?"

We've slept in the same bed so many times together that I've lost count, but it's like having my sister beside me. And after the last few days, it's the kind of comfort we both need. Now, if it were *her* sister, that would be a different story.

She shakes her head. "I can't. I told Angie and my parents that I'd go back to our place. Ang wants me there."

Can't blame her for that.

Angelina was just as worried as I was about Allie's disappearance. She needs the security of knowing she's under the same roof.

Leaning forward, I press a kiss to Allie's forehead, then pull her against my chest again. She releases a contented sigh and lets me hold her.

I drag my fingers through her hair again. "You know, having a baby wouldn't be the worst thing in the world."

She barks out a laugh. "Yeah, it would. I mean, I'm barely with this guy. I live in an apartment with my much-older sister. I work at *her* coffee shop. I can't even remember if I've ever held a baby. I'm not exactly mother material."

"You have a lot of amazing role models in this family." I drop my head back against the headboard again. "My mom was…"

Allie stiffens.

Shit.

I can't let this moment with her lead to me unloading truths I've managed to keep locked away for so long. Biting back what I was about to say, I shake my head. "Not great, but she did love me. I knew that. But you, God, I always envied what you had.

Storm's a wonderful mom. And Landon is like the perfect dad. Plus, you've got all your aunts and uncles and your nana, plus your sister. Angelina would never let anything happen to you. She would never let you fail."

She pulls her head back and looks up at me. "What if I do, though?"

Locking my gaze with hers, I shake my head. "No one will let you fail at this. I promise."

"How can you be so sure?"

I think back through the last fifteen years to all the trials and tribulations the Hawkes have faced, of all the things I've gone through, yet they've continued to stand by my side. Not because they have to. Not because they were under any sort of obligation. But because they *wanted* to.

They took a wounded, terrified kid under their wings and nurtured me like I was one of their own, even when I pushed everyone away with all the power I had in me.

I do my best not to dwell on it too much because if I did, the guilt of my own failures would crush me, but the reality of who the Hawkes are can't be ignored in times like this. "Because I know your family, Al, and they'll do anything for you, for any of us."

"You really believe that?"

I shake my head. "No. I *know* it. You'll be okay, kiddo."

She grins at me. "Isn't that what Angie said to you on Christmas?"

"Yep."

And that's the way she'll always see me, as that small, broken boy in the closet.

7

JUDE

The dark bruise and swelling around her eye make it hard to tell if she's still crying or if she's finally managed to calm herself down. It would be better for both of us if she did.

He hates when she cries.

So do I.

Crying only makes him angrier, only drags out the attacks and makes them worse. But if she can calm down, if she can stop crying, he might just leave.

She glances over at where I cower in the corner and mouths to me, "I'm okay."

But she isn't.

Not this time.

Blood trickles from her split lip and the gash at the corner of her temple and drips to the floor.

Dad moves in toward her again, blocking my view of her sprawled on the couch. His broad shoulders tense even more, his hands fisting at his sides, knuckles already ripped open. He leans *forward and grips her chin, cranking her head to the side so I can see her face again.*

Her eyes dart to me, then back up to him, the fear in them unmistakable. Not when I see it so often.

He snarls in her face. "I hope you understand what you did, why I had to do this." ,

She nods vigorously.

"Don't ever steal from me again."

Don't do it, Mom.

I know she wants to say it wasn't her, that she didn't steal anything. That he used the money last night to buy more drugs and just forgot. It isn't in her nature to hold back, but she keeps her mouth shut this time and just nods again.

Dad releases her and takes a step back, shoving his crimson-stained hand through his hair. He turns and looks at me. "What the fuck are you doing in here? Get the fuck out."

I don't want to leave her, but I know what will happen if I don't.

My whole body trembles as I climb up from the hard, worn floor and slip out of the room, pressing my back against the wall just outside to listen.

Something rustles.

He whispers something to her I can't make out that makes her issue a sob.

His heavy footsteps move toward the apartment door.

I bolt down the hallway and into my room before he can see me. The front door opens and slams closed loudly, echoing down to me, and I release the breath I've been holding since the moment I got in here.

Mom's soft footsteps approach, the familiar creak of the floorboard halfway down the hall announcing her presence. She slowly enters my room and lowers herself to the bed, waiting for me to join her.

I hesitate for a minute, too stunned by her appearance to move. She swipes at the blood, trying to stop it from dripping, and I finally

rush to the closet and grab a towel for her, even though it won't do much good.

She'll need stitches this time.

But it isn't the worst he's done.

Not by far.

I press the towel against the cut on her head, and she drags me against her and holds me tightly.

"I'm okay, Jude. Just a little blood."

Mom grabs my chin and tips my face up to her, smiling, even though her split lip bleeds more. "Sometimes you're the windshield, and sometimes you're the bug. Today, I'm the bug, but it won't always be that way."

It sure feels like it.

"Don't let life make you the bug all the time, Jude."

The door to the apartment opens and slams shut again, and we both jerk upright and turn toward the sound. His heavy footsteps approach.

He shouldn't be back so soon, unless he isn't done with her—

BAM. BAM. BAM.

Pounding on the condo door jerks me awake from what I wish was only a nightmare instead of a very graphic memory. Sweat drenches me. The sheet clings to my skin, my chest heaving as tears stream down my face.

"Fuck..."

Gasping, I struggle to find my breath, hand pressed over my bare chest where my heart thunders against my ribcage.

Here I thought I had outrun that dream, that it might actually stay away for good. It's been months since *that* particular memory came back so violently and vividly.

I never would have believed that I would prefer the *other* nightmare material, but I can't do this again.

I can't watch that again.

Not again.

Fuck.

I scrub my hands over my face, wiping away the hot tears and trying to stop more from falling. Apparently, the possibility that Allie could become a mother has brought the memories of my own rushing back in the worst way possible.

That's what I get for mentioning her last night, for opening that door. Now, I might not be able to close it again.

BAM. BAM. BAM.

Who the fuck could that be?

"Jude?"

Even through the heavy metal door, Angie's voice stiffens my spine.

How the hell did she get up?

I toss back the damp covers and rummage around on the floor for a pair of sweatpants to tug on because I highly doubt she'd want me to open the door in the nude.

Things are already weird enough between us without me flashing her so early in the damn morning.

She pounds again; the sound echoes through the lofted ceiling. "Jude?"

"I'm coming."

The deep, painful fog of the dream still clouds my head, but I stumble toward the door, running my hands through my hair. Any other time, Angelina standing outside my door would bring up a whole different type of panic, but after that nightmare, I can't worry about what she'll see when I open this.

I unlock the door and tug it open, rubbing my eyes to try to wake up fully. When I drop my hands from my face, Angie stares back at me, her Caribbean-blue eyes wide, pink lips parted slightly.

Her gaze travels from my face down over my exposed chest and abs to my sweatpants, then jerks back up. A pink flush spreads across her cheeks, like she's just been caught doing something she shouldn't, and she clears her throat. "Did I-did I wake you up?"

Thank God she did.

Because I know what happens if that dream keeps going.

It always ends the same.

I avert my gaze, concentrating on the coffee cup in her hand so I don't fall down the dark hole of that memory. "Yeah, kind of."

"Shit, I'm sorry." She holds out the disposable travel cup to me. "I thought Allie always brought this around six."

"How did you get into the building?"

Besides me, only Allie, Luca, and Byron have that key. It's the way I've always wanted it, offering another layer of protection I so desperately need.

Her cheeks darken, and she ducks her head slightly, eyes dipping to my feet. "Allie gave me the key this morning."

"Is she at work?"

After how distraught she was last night, I can't imagine she got up at five a.m. to get ready and head to the café to make coffee while she's waiting for her fate to be determined.

Angelina shakes her head, her dark hair piled on the top of her head barely moving. "She's at home. Still didn't feel well. Waiting for the results..."

She looks away, likely thinking the exact same thing I am.

Allie's life—*all our lives*—will change with the results of that test.

I'd give anything to be able to be with Allie, to reassure her that no matter what, I have her back. We *all* have her back.

The Hawkes don't let each other fail. Which is precisely why none of them can ever know what's really going on inside my head. Especially Angelina.

The woman who always twisted me in knots at the same time she's offered me the only true sense of peace I've ever experienced stands just outside the door, shifting from foot to foot, waiting for me to grab the coffee.

I slowly reach out to take it from her. Our fingers brush

again, and goosebumps break out across my skin. She jerks her hand back, trying to hide her reaction by running it through her hair, but her hand lodges in the messy bun, and she mutters a curse under her breath.

I'd love to believe she felt it, too. That every time we touch, she has the same visceral reaction to me that I do with her. That I've *always* had since that fateful Christmas. But that would be wishful thinking. And even if it were true, it wouldn't mean anything. It can't.

Not when she's Allie's sister.

Not when she's a Hawke.

Instead of acknowledging the strange chemistry, I take a sip of my coffee and give her a tight smile. "Do you know when she'll find out?"

She shakes her head and glances behind me into the apartment, fidgeting with her hands, her lips twisting like she has something to say that she can't manage to get out.

"Do you...want to come in?"

In the three years I've lived here, Angelina has never set foot inside my place, but it isn't curiosity that's making her uneasy now. It's the uncertainty of what's happening with Allie. The one I share. And we can't talk about it with anyone else but each other without betraying Allie.

She peeks back down the short hallway toward the stairs, then at her watch. "Astrid is coming to help me this morning, so I have a couple of minutes."

Hell.

Angelina Hawke is in my personal space.

This was a bad idea.

But it's too late to come up with an excuse to keep her out. She walks past me, and the scent of freshly baked croissants and coffee fills my nose, making my cock twitch against the soft fabric of my sweatpants.

Fuck.

That damn smell.

The one that is just *Angie* since the day she opened the Grind, back when I actually went in, when I would spend hours there with my laptop, studying or writing, watching her work and move. Back when I *could* still do that.

I let the door close, then wait a few seconds to try to regain my composure before I follow her into the loft space.

Angie glances at the workout equipment, over to the kitchen, then to the front wall of windows overlooking the street and the corner where I always do my best work. "Did she tell you who the guy is?"

I step behind the kitchen counter to put something between us and lean forward onto my elbow, shaking my head. "No. You?"

She chews on the corner of her lip and shakes her head. "No." Turning to face me, she screws her brows down. "It's weird, isn't it? I mean, I know we aren't always super receptive to her boyfriends, but for her to not tell either of us anything about this guy..."

"I know. It worries me, too, but you must have dated some guys you knew the family wouldn't be thrilled about."

Even thinking about it sours the coffee in my stomach, and the faces of all the guys I've seen her with over the years taunt me from deep in my memories where I tried to bury them.

She rolls her eyes and gives an incredulous laugh. "Maybe in high school. But it's been a *looong* time."

Her emphasis on the word makes me freeze with the coffee cup halfway to my mouth.

How is that even possible?

Angelina Matthews is the most stunning woman I've seen in my entire life. Beautiful, driven, talented, thoughtful, and kind. She's everything a man could want.

She went on dates, flirted with men out on the sidewalk, where I'm forced to watch it. Yet, that coffee shop has become her constant companion instead of someone who might actually be able to give her what she needs and make her happy.

I didn't know it until this exact moment, but she's given up. She's resigned herself fully to committing her life to that business and everything else she does for everyone else in the family rather than seeking her own happiness.

Classic selfless Angelina.

She returns her gaze to mine and blushes again. "Sorry, that's probably too much information."

Given what Allie thinks, that I've spent the last few years fucking around with random women and holing myself up in here just to write rather than going to family events, Angelina probably believes the same.

It's better than the alternative—anyone knowing the truth.

I twist the cup between my hands, staring down at it as if it might offer me the answer to my question. "What do you think she'll do if she is pregnant?"

Angie sighs and tugs the hair tie from her bun, letting her thick, dark strands free to fan around her face. "I don't know."

"I told her you wouldn't let her fail."

Her brow furrows. "What?"

I stare at my coffee cup, suddenly embarrassed to be revealing what I said about her last night. "I told her you wouldn't let her fail. That you care too much, that you always take care of her, and that you wouldn't let her be a bad mom."

Her silence makes me look back up at her.

She stares back, her brow knitted. "I don't know if I should be thanking you for the compliment or insulted that you think that."

"What?" I jerk upright. "What do you mean, insulted?"

"I mean, you basically just implied that I'm a glorified adult babysitter for Allie because she can't get her life together. Just because I'm twelve years older than her and have no life doesn't mean I'm going to take over raising her kid for her."

Oh, hell.

I hold up a hand apologetically. "No, that's not what I meant."

Not at all.

Angie stalks past me toward the door. "I get it. At thirty-seven, I'm already a spinster, right?" She stops with her hand on the knob and closes her eyes, shaking her head. "I devoted my entire life to helping Uncle Savage and Gabe with the various businesses. I worked at the bars and restaurants, helped them hire staff and get them up and running, and when I finally opened that café, I felt like I had something of my own. But now, it's *all* I have, right?"

"It doesn't have to be."

She doesn't even look back at me, just pulls open the door. "Yes, it does."

It closes behind her with a final click that seems to cement her words even heavier on my heart.

Angelina thinks she can't have a life outside those walls.

She understands what it feels like to be trapped; we're just trapped by different things.

———

ANGELINA

A CAR WHIZZES past me on the street, the driver blaring the horn and shaking his fist. I jerk back onto the curb so I don't step right in its path, slapping my hand over my heart before it climbs into my throat.

"Holy shit."

I almost killed myself—all because I wasn't paying attention, too distracted by how pissed off I am at Jude and what he just said. With everything else going on, the last thing I need is *that* man throwing hard truths in my face.

Asshole.

He isn't wrong, though.

What do I have besides the café and keeping an eye on Allie?

No love life.

No *sex* life.

No anything but up before dawn and home after dark. Day in and day out. Over and over again. Anything it takes to keep this place successful.

And all that could be in jeopardy now.

The work continues on the building just down the street, and I try not to focus on it too much as I cross the two lanes of traffic—safely this time—and hustle to the Grind, jerking open the door a little harder than I intend.

Astrid glances up from where she stands behind the counter. She tucks a hunk of blond hair behind her ear and narrows her eyes on me. "What's wrong?"

I force a smile. "What makes you think anything's wrong?"

"Well"—she drums her nails on the granite—"first, you were over there a little too long to have just dropped off coffee. And second, you look like somebody pissed in your Cheerios."

I try not to let my mouth twist into a scowl, but it happens anyway. "Jude just..." Making my way around the counter to join her, I try to wave it off before she drags me into a conversation I don't want to have. "Never mind."

Astrid shakes her head and pulls her hair up into a ponytail, giving me a keep-going look. "Jude *what*?"

Pissed me the fuck off.

Told me something I didn't want to hear.

Was spot-on in his assessment of my current life situation...

I glance toward his place, but his windows stand empty. "He made it clear why he's a professional with words. He sure knew what to say to get under my skin." I cross my arms over my chest with a huff. "I mean, he basically said I have no life."

She barks out a laugh and glances out the front window

toward his place. "I mean, that's kind of funny coming from him, right?"

I smirk at her. "I know he spends most of his time at his condo and avoids family functions, but Allie swears he has a bustling social life with hot chicks he picks up on apps."

Astrid continues to stare out the window, drumming her nails on the counter again. "I'm not so sure about that."

"What do you mean?"

She offers a little half-shrug. "I don't know. He just never struck me as the banging-random-chicks type." Her gaze cuts to me. "He doesn't even let any of *us* touch him, so how is some rando he swipes left with gonna do it?"

He lets me *touch him...*

Though, given the way I seem to react every time we touch, maybe we shouldn't. And Astrid does have a point, something I hadn't even considered.

I pour a cup of coffee and take a sip, even though I don't need anything else to get me more wired this morning. "I guess he's not." The more I think about it, I've never seen him with *any* girl except Allie, not even when he was in high school or college with raging hormones and that sad beauty that could have landed him any babe he wanted. "But that's what Allie said."

And why would she lie about that?

Astrid raises her pale brows. "Why were you two talking about your sex life, anyway?"

I almost choke on my coffee. "We weren't talking about my sex life or the lack thereof, per se."

Shit.

No one else knows that Allie might be pregnant except me, Jude, and Aunt Nora.

I can't tell Astrid.

But even without the potential baby situation, she understands how Allie can be at times. She can definitely weigh in on what Jude said about my relationship with my baby sister.

"Jude just commented about Allie being unreliable and me kind of mothering her."

Astrid barks out a laugh. "And you got mad at that?"

"Well, *yeah*."

She reaches out and pats my arm. "Honey, it's true. You're the oldest...by *far*." A fact that makes her lips pull into a grin. "Inevitably, you became kind of a second mother to most of us, especially her. I mean, by the time she came along, you were what, twelve or thirteen?"

I nod. "Almost thirteen."

"You were the permanent babysitter for her, Pope, Isaac, and Coen, then Jude when he came into the picture until they were all old enough to handle themselves."

"True. Though, by the time Jude joined the crew, it was less babysitting and more wrangling them and making sure they didn't burn down the house."

She smirks. "And who helped teach Allie to read?"

"Me."

"Helped her with her homework when your mom and Landon weren't home?"

"Me."

"Who lives with her and does all the cooking and cleaning at the apartment?"

I scowl at her. "Okay, I get your point."

She holds up her hands. "I'm just saying. Jude didn't exactly comment on something that isn't right out there in plain sight."

If she weren't one of my best friends *and* my cousin, I might actually be pissed at her for pointing that out. But as it stands, annoyance tightens my grip on my mug. "Oh, now you're taking his side."

"No sides. Seriously." Her shoulders rise and fall. "All I'm saying is maybe you spend a little too much time here and focus a little too much attention on Allie's life rather than your own."

"Yeah. What life?"

She jabs a finger into my chest. "Exactly my point. But maybe you'll meet someone tonight. It should be busy."

The insanity music nights always bring also means making bank tonight, and with smooth-voiced, easy-on-the-eyes Dan Roe performing, it's sure to be a packed house—but not a crowd full of eligible bachelors. More likely, a bunch of single women looking to catch the eye of the sexy singer.

All it will mean for me is a ton of extra work today preparing for the rush of the crowd in the evening.

The perfect time for Allie to be gone...

No one knows this place—or the customers—better than she does.

For all her faults, she's excellent at her job.

Cheerful. Friendly. Great with the customers. Easy with a smile or compliment to make their day better.

People will be looking for her, asking about her, wondering if she's all right.

And I have no idea how to answer that.

The door opens, and the bells above it jingle. I turn away from Astrid, toward whoever entered, and freeze with my coffee cup halfway to my lips. Cassius Whitaker walks toward the counter slowly, his gray suit hanging immaculately over lean muscles.

A sly grin spreads across his lips, and Astrid spins to face him head-on at the counter, plastering on her professional smile, ready to take his order. She clearly has no idea who stands across from her.

He sets his hand on the counter, an expensive watch glinting under the overhead light. "Angelina, what a pleasure to see you again."

The smug bastard offers me a smirk that might actually affect me if I didn't hate him so damn much.

I scowl at him, still annoyed he had the balls to come in—again. "Cass, what are you doing here?"

Astrid's eyes dart between us. "This is Cass? *The* Cass, as in Cassius Whitaker?"

He extends a hand to her, his green eyes lighting. "And who might you be?" His gaze rakes over her appreciatively. "Must be one of the Hawkes. Astrid, perhaps?"

She jerks her hand out of his. "How do you know that?"

Another grin tilts his lips. "I know quite a bit about your family."

Astrid gives him a saccharine-sweet smile. "Then you should know you're not welcome here."

His eyes widen slightly as he glances at me. "Is that any way to treat a paying customer?" He *tsks* and shakes his head, offering a slight shrug. "And here I thought I was going to get a nice cup of coffee this morning before I check on the progress down the street."

Anger floods my veins as I set my coffee cup next to me so I don't throw the scalding-hot liquid in the bastard's face. "I know what you're doing."

His eyes widen. "Trying to buy a cup of coffee?"

I step forward and nudge Astrid out of the way. "No, what you're doing down the street."

"*I'm* not doing anything down the street." He shrugs again. "Falco Enterprises is."

"Yeah, but they're *your* clients, and you are the one acting on their behalf."

"So, that's why all your ire is directed at me?" One of his brows rises slowly. "Because I'm doing my *job*?"

His false incredulous tone makes me contemplate the coffee toss again, but that would only give him more ammunition and lead to criminal charges and a civil lawsuit against Hawke's Daily Grind. All things we can't afford right now.

This is a place of business, and I have to act like it, even when the customer is trying to put me *out* of business. But it doesn't mean I can't point out his serious mistake.

I force a smile. "Your veiled threats aren't so veiled anymore, Mr. Whitaker. This is the most clear attack your clients have made against us, and Isaac and Stone are going to stop you."

He drops his head back and releases a laugh that fills the still-empty café. "Oh, ladies, you sure have given me some entertainment this morning, but what about that coffee?"

Astrid looks at me, brow raised, drumming her fingers on the counter while I contemplate whether it's worth it to shove it up his ass and tell him to go fuck himself when I could just as easily pour a simple cup of coffee and send him on his way back to our enemies.

Be the bigger person, Angelina.

Dad's voice echoes in my head so clearly it freezes me in place. Even after over thirty years without him, I can never forget those little things he said, the wisdom he imparted. The warmth and love he gave Mom and me.

It instantly quells my rage toward Whitaker, and I smile at him, spreading my hand toward the menu like Vanna White. "What would you like to order?"

A satisfied grin pulls at his mouth again. "I would love a large quad latte, please, with skim milk."

Before I even have to ask her, Astrid sets to work making it, glancing at me out of the corner of her eye as I ring him up and accept his payment. I'd much rather burn it, but turning down any paying customers with the competition looming wouldn't be bright.

He leans against the counter while he waits for his drink, never taking his eyes off me. "I am going to need a lot of coffee over the next couple of weeks while we finish up down the block. Can I expect the same type of icy reception from you every morning?"

I plaster on another fake smile. "I'm sure you have some $10,000 Italian espresso machine at your house. Why don't you just use that?"

He smirks. "I do. But I much prefer yours. It's made with love."

I scowl at him. "You really are a prick. You know that?"

The corners of his perfect mouth twitch. "So I've been told, mostly by your family."

I shouldn't push it. I should leave it to Isaac and Stone to deal with Cass Whitaker and whatever the mysterious owners of Falco Enterprises are up to, but I can't bite it back. Not when my livelihood is at stake and they're undoubtedly planning something even bigger.

"Why do you hate us so much?"

"Hate you?" Cass pushes off from the counter, straightening his tie. "You've got it all wrong, Angelina. I don't hate anyone. I just do my job, whoever pays me."

I cross my arms over my chest. "I don't believe that for a second."

"Don't you?" A smile crosses his face. "Well, I'd love to gain your trust. Perhaps you'd allow me to take you out on a date."

Something clatters behind me, and I glance over at Astrid, eyes wide on me, the dropped spoon on the floor near her feet.

I clear my throat. "A date?"

He grins. "Yes. You know, where two people who enjoy each other's company go out, perhaps have some food, scintillating conversation." He leans across the counter, palms flat, getting far too close for someone who isn't romantically involved. "And if things go well, I'll make you an espresso at home in the morning."

I press my hands against the counter and mirror his stance, leaning forward. "Over. My. Dead. Body."

He chuckles and steps back, offering a shrug. "Your loss."

"You are going to be the one who loses, Whitaker. Isaac and Stone don't fail. Ever."

Astrid slides his drink across the counter, and he grabs it, tipping it toward her in thanks.

"They might not, but you will once the competition opens down the street. And that Hawke Hotel of yours everyone's so excited about? It might have some competition soon, too."

He offers a wink and slips out the door, leaving me speechless.

Astrid grabs my arm. "What the fuck did he just say about the hotel?"

I slide my phone out of my back pocket. "I don't know, but I need to call Isaac and Uncle Stone so they can find out."

8

JUDE

The lively guitar music, smooth vocals, and constant excited chatter of all the people hanging around Hawke's Daily Grind fill the condo, seeping in through the cracked windows along with the humid, warm summer air.

These types of quintessential New Orleans nights emanate a vibe that lives on the breeze. Without setting foot in there, the energy vibrates out, across the street, through my bones, and tingling across my skin.

I can't see the stage tucked into the back corner of the Grind from here, but I know this sound. Their artist tonight has been there before, strumming at his guitar and singing covers of popular songs to throngs of women willing to throw themselves at him.

Dan something?

The crowd he always draws must make bank for Angelina. Customers spill out onto the sidewalk at the small bistro tables and cram into every spare inch of the café.

These evening music nights are always busy, but something seems different tonight.

A buzz.

An energy I can feel vibrating through me as I stand in front of the window and watch Astrid and Angie bustle around, refilling drinks, taking orders, with Betsy at the register. But there still isn't any sign of Allie, despite her insistence that she would make an appearance tonight.

I check our messages again, rereading the ones from earlier today.

> JUDE
>
> Did you get the results from Aunt Nora?

> ALLIE
>
> Yes, but I haven't looked yet. I just can't.

> JUDE
>
> Come do it over here with me.

> ALLIE
>
> Tomorrow. I just need one more day before my world potentially implodes.

> JUDE
>
> Okay. Whatever you need. You'll come by tonight anyway after the café closes?

> ALLIE
>
> Of course.

But she hasn't shown up yet, even though the music has been going for well over an hour already.

Maybe she won't come.

Maybe she checked the results and is having a total breakdown alone at her place...and I can't even go to her to help.

Fucking hell.

The music stops, quickly replaced by something on the radio piped through the speakers. I use the singer's break to grab another beer from the fridge, then wander back to the window and sit on the ledge, staring out, waiting for another glimpse of the woman who has had me twisted in knots of regret since this morning.

Why did I say that to her?

Of course, she took it the wrong way. She's already on edge because of what Falco is doing down the street and this shock with Allie. What was meant as a compliment about how incredibly kind and giving she is only seemed like a criticism.

Which has left me watching her all day, hoping for any acknowledgment from her that she doesn't hate my guts permanently—one I have yet to receive.

I take a swig of my beer as Angelina steps out from the Grind onto the sidewalk. The summer breeze rushes down the street, fluttering her hair around her face, and she brushes it behind her ear, laughing at something a customer near the door says.

But she doesn't look up like she normally would. Like she *always* does.

She's really pissed.

Maybe rightfully so.

I should have kept my mouth shut about her relationship with Allie. Al may be my best friend, but it isn't my place to comment on their dynamic—not to Angelina.

It isn't my place to say anything to *anyone* about how they live their lives, really. Not when I don't see anyone outside these four walls and haven't been an active member of the family for going on two years. And even then, I held back so much. It wouldn't be fair to act like I was in any way involved with the inner workings of the Hawkes.

And watching Angie now, it feels like I never will be.

She scans the street like she's searching for someone or something. Her shoulders fall, disappointment written all over her face as she starts to head back inside. But Allie comes around the corner, rushing toward the café, and Angie stops and waits for her near the door.

There you are.

Allie approaches her, and Angie pulls her in for a hug and whispers something in her ear. I can't hear them from up here, but they both glance up at me. Allie waves and offers me a sad smile.

Good to see you, Allie Cat.

Work might not be the best place to be when she's attempting to process what's happening in her life, but maybe it will help take her mind off the potential bomb ticking and waiting for her to look at it.

Losing myself in work certainly helps me avoid facing other things.

When I don't have major writer's block...

I stare at my computer on the floor. The cursor still flashes in the exact same spot it did when Angie came this morning. Taunting me. Making tension build in the back of my neck so tightly it feels like it might snap.

Or maybe I will.

I rub at it as I take a sip of the beer and watch the girls on the street, laughing and chatting with some of their regulars—the same people I see coming and going, day in and day out. The people who keep the Grind going.

A dark-haired guy steps out of the Grind and approaches them, guitar slung over his shoulder, a smug grin on his face as he takes in everyone gathered at the bistro tables.

He moves toward Angelina and Allie and stops in front of them, leaning in to whisper something over the music still playing over the speakers. Whatever he says makes Angie laugh, tipping her head back, the sound carrying across the street and up through the window straight to my cock.

It hardens almost instantly, and at the same time, jealousy tightens my hand around the glass bottle.

What the fuck is going on between those two?

She reaches over and lays her hand on his tattooed arm, leaning toward him as she says something that earns her a grin from the musician. My blood heats, my body tensing as I watch the exchange. He nods his agreement to whatever she said and turns to Allie, dropping his head low to hers to relay something that makes her laugh.

Before I can stop myself, I pull out my phone and fire off a text.

JUDE

What's going on with Angie and that guy?

Allie reaches into her purse and pulls out her phone, reads the message, then immediately jerks her head up to look at me, narrowing her eyes. Angie continues to talk to him, her head tipped toward his in a conspiratorial, all-too-familiar way that doesn't exactly scream *business* relationship.

ALLIE

WHAT DO YOU CARE?

Shit. Why do I care?

Angelina is an adult.

She can do whatever she wants with whomever she wants.

There isn't any good reason for me to be asking the question. I even *told* her to go out and get a damn life today, yet here I am, jealous as fuck when she flirts with someone.

JUDE

Just need to know if it's someone I need to look out for.

That seems reasonable, doesn't it?

The girls know I always keep an eye on them and the Grind. It helps everyone feel a little safer about them closing up late at night by themselves when they know I can see them and everything that happens inside and on the street.

Allie reads my message, then glances back up at me, her annoyance cutting through me even from across the street.

ALLIE

> You have absolutely nothing to worry about
> where Dan Roe is concerned.

Dan Roe. Now I have a last name.

And apparently...absolutely no self-control when it comes to Angelina Matthews.

I pull up every social media platform I can think of on my phone and search like a teenager stalking his damn crush. Dozens of profiles show up, but only one with a handsome, dark-haired man with sultry bourbon eyes holding a guitar and singing like he belongs on *America's Got Talent*.

Very talented.

Very flirty.

Very single, according to his profiles.

Fuck.

My knee bounces rapidly as I watch Angie and Allie talk with him. Whatever he's saying has Angie's full attention, and the way she keeps leaning toward him and touching his arm makes me want to chuck the bottle across the room against the goddamn bricks.

It wouldn't be the first time I did that—completely lost my shit, watching something happen to Angelina. Every minute. Every day. Every week. Every year. Every *moment* we've spent together, all I've ever wanted is to protect her from everything in this world, to be the one who gave her the things she thought she couldn't have.

Not *that* douche.

You don't have any right to be jealous.

None.

That very true fact doesn't make me feel any better, though. It doesn't make me worry about her any less. It can't stop this burning need inside me for that woman.

Most of the time, I can handle being here, watching life pass me by in a world I don't want any part of. But missing out on things with Allie, with the rest of the Hawkes, knowing what they all must think about me because of it—knowing what *Angelina* must think—crushes me today.

I've never wanted to be outside this glass more than I do in this moment, watching her. After what I said to her this morning, maybe she's finally trying to do what I insinuated—find a life outside the café. It's almost like it's intentional, a show put on for my benefit to prove a point she doesn't need to make to me.

Why the hell did I ever suggest it?

Apparently, to torture myself...

And it's working.

ANGELINA

FORCING myself to stay focused on tonight's talent rather than the broody blond across the street, I lean toward Dan so he can hear me over the chatter outside and the music floating through the speakers. "Can I get you anything before you go back on? A drink? Something to eat?"

Dan gives me a half-cocked grin and shakes his head. "Nah, I'm good."

His gaze roves over to a table of women clearly checking him out, and he smirks and winks at them, eliciting exactly the response I'm sure he's anticipating.

I was right about women throwing themselves at him all night, and he's eating it up. Whether he's inside on the stage, guitar in hand, or standing out here, taking a break from his performance, the man oozes a confidence that borders on cocky.

Though seeing all the women falling all over him all night, he clearly has his pick of women and takes advantage of that to get laid plenty.

Certainly *not* the kind of guy I had hoped might appear when Astrid joked about me potentially meeting someone tonight.

Of their own accord, my eyes drift away from Dan and across the street to Jude's window. I've done my best to avoid acknowledging him, to keep my focus on work and preparing for tonight rather than on what he said and how every time I go over there, I'm off-kilter the rest of the damn day.

But it's a battle I'll never win.

I've never been able to take my eyes off Jude Abello-Harris, and that isn't about to stop now just because I'm pissed at something he said.

He stares down at us, beer in hand, his blue eyes blazing with something I either haven't noticed before or have tried to ignore—the green tint of jealousy.

I should let go of my anger from earlier, let Jude stand and watch Allie flirting with Dan and stay out of it. But I can't stop myself from reaching out to rest my palm against Dan's bulging bicep, squeezing gently as a fuck you to the guy who made me feel like such an idiot this morning.

"You let me know if you do need anything. Everything's on the house. You're doing a great show tonight."

He smiles and settles his hand over mine. "Thank you, Ang."

Allie slips her phone back into her purse, casting an annoyed look at Jude. "I'm glad I was able to make it for the second part of it."

Dan grins at her and motions for her to enter the Grind in

front of him, placing his hand on her lower back and leaning in to whisper something that makes her laugh and swat at his shoulder playfully.

Shameless flirt.

But is that such a bad thing?

Jude's words from this morning won't stop ringing in my ears, making me question everything that seemed so clear only yesterday. Maybe I always will be alone, but only because that's the way I've always wanted it, the way it has to be.

I slip back into the bustling café. Dan weaves through the crowded tables and returns to the stage, adjusting the mic as he settles on the stool and rests his guitar on his knee.

Allie makes her way over to the table in the corner where Isaac, Jack, Pope, Bishop, and Atlas sit, sliding in next to Jack and as far away from Pope as possible.

I roll my eyes and head toward the counter to help Astrid. Those two have to get over whatever little tiff they had. I'm sick of having to dance around the fact that they don't want to be in the same room anymore. There's already enough family drama without having to handle them with kid gloves.

Dan leans into the mic and smiles. "This is one of my favorite songs. I hope you guys enjoy it."

He strums the first few chords, and I can't fight my grin or the tears welling in my eyes.

"Hotel California" was Dad's favorite song. The vivid memory of riding with him in his car, the windows rolled down, him singing it at the top of his lungs, hits me so hard that my steps falter.

My eyes burn, tears threatening to fall with each note he plays.

Shit, I can't cry in here.

I swipe at my eyes and try to concentrate on checking all the tables for anyone who might need refills, making my way from the back toward the front again, intending to head out onto the sidewalk for another sweep outside.

A black sedan pulls up on the street and comes to a stop right in front of the door, double-parking and apparently not caring that it's blocking traffic.

Who the hell is this?

The passenger door opens, and a burly man in a black suit steps out and makes his way to the rear door to open it.

Shit.

Expensive Italian loafers appear below the door, and the man stands and smooths his hand over his suit coat.

You have to be fucking kidding me.

The same panic that seized me when he was here the first time rushes through my veins, freezing me in place for a second before I turn and race toward the back, weaving through the tables until I hit the one in the far corner where Astrid stands, talking to everyone.

I slide to a halt beside her, and they all glance up at me, eyes wide at my abrupt appearance.

Isaac's face shifts instantly into hard, unyielding lawyer mode. "Ang, what's wrong?"

"Roselli just pulled up outside."

"What?" He glances at Jack, who rests her hand over her growing belly protectively, fear already flashing in her eyes. "You go in the back. You, too, Astrid, Allie."

They all scowl at him, but he, Atlas, and Pope push to their feet and follow me out toward the front. Roselli hits the sidewalk and moves toward the door, and Isaac grabs my arm and tugs me back a step.

"You go back there with them, too."

"What? No." I jerk my arm free from his hold, setting my shoulders back. "This is my place and—"

"And it seems you have a very bustling crowd tonight, Ms.

Matthews." Roselli's cool voice rolls over me, leaving goosebumps on my skin and a chill in my blood.

Too late for me to run now.

I turn toward him slowly, and Isaac and Atlas put themselves in front of me protectively, with Pope directly at my back.

Isaac straightens his shoulders, stepping closer to the man he had a similar showdown with in the café only a few months ago. "What are you doing here, Roselli? I thought we made it very clear that you weren't welcome the last time you dropped by."

He offers a smug grin, unaffected by the animosity in Isaac's tone or the clear tension his appearance has created. The two goons who stand behind him scan the crowd suspiciously, watching for any dangers.

Hilarious, considering he's the biggest one I know.

Roselli spreads his hands wide. "I enjoy live music. And with such good company, how could I resist?"

Atlas takes a step forward, squaring his shoulders, his hands fisted at his sides, prepared for a physical battle if Isaac doesn't win the verbal one. If Roselli has any idea what Atlas "the Hurricane" Anderson is capable of, he'll tuck tail and run before those fists start flying.

The dark eyes filled with intelligence and distrust roam over Atlas, and Roselli flicks his gaze to meet Atlas' icy-blue one. "You must be the boxer."

A sneer twists Atlas' lips. "And you must be the asshole."

Roselli tips his head back with a laugh, looking at his two men over his shoulder. "He's also a comedian."

Isaac shifts forward until he is right in Roselli's face, so he can be heard well over the music and no doubt for the intimidation factor since he has several inches and at least twenty pounds of muscle on the man. "You need to leave before I make you."

The air around us stills, heavy with a tension I can feel in every breath.

Isaac is going to start a war with threats like that.

Roselli's eyes harden and darken to an almost onyx, any trace of humanity evaporating from his face. "And here I thought we'd become friends after the Satriano situation."

Isaac's spine stiffens, and he swallows thickly, the only outward clues to his concern over the situation. "Satriano was unfortunate. It had to happen. But it hardly makes us *friends*."

The contempt with which he spits out the word makes me wince and swallow back the bile rising in my throat.

Roselli raises an eyebrow. "Taking out the head of one of the most powerful families in Italy in my territory *had* to happen?" He chuckles softly, the sound lacking any real humor. "It's cute that you think it wouldn't have consequences."

That sure gets Isaac's attention. He shifts slightly, an almost imperceptible half-inch retreat. "What do you mean, *consequences*?"

The relative quiet we've enjoyed recently shatters with that single word. All the things I've lost, that the *Hawkes* have lost because of men like Roselli and Satriano, rush through my head in a constant stream of despair.

Roselli reaches into his pocket and pulls out a cigar, then turns back to one of his men, who hands him a lighter. He flicks it, leans into the flame, and lights his cigar, puffing away at it and blowing the smoke up into the dark night. "Your actions and those of the Marconis have rustled up a lot of interest in the Hawke family and in what they're doing here in New Orleans. I hear you're opening a hotel."

Isaac sneers at him. "Again, none of your fucking business."

"Isn't it now?" Roselli's dark brows arch menacingly. "I let you take out the head of a rival family in my territory. That makes everything you do my business."

Shit.

We should have known this was all too easy, that he wasn't going to simply let it go just because he was the one who warned us the Satrianos could cause trouble.

That was no altruistic move. He wanted them gone before they threatened him, and he wanted leverage against *us*.

He releases a ring of smoke and motions inside. "I would love to stay and enjoy the music this evening, but if you're uncomfortable with my presence, perhaps we should schedule a time when I can sit down with you"—he points his cigar at Isaac—"your father, your uncles, and the pretty blonde. What's her name? Kennedy?"

Oh, God.

Pope threads his muscular arm around Atlas' waist to hold him back, but Isaac can't be stopped. He steps forward until his chest brushes against Roselli's.

His two men behind him reach for their weapons. If they pull them out here, it's going to cause absolute chaos. Several customers are already paying attention to our conversation, and it isn't as if Roselli is inconspicuous. Anyone local will know who he is. And now that he's been seen here twice, the rumors are going to start, rumors we don't want, that we're somehow connected to them.

The Hawkes have spent a long time distancing themselves from organized crime after what happened with Dom Abello. A Roselli complication forced upon us because of what Isaac had to do to save his family would destroy us again.

Stepping forward, I press my hand against Isaac's shoulder, pushing him back as I smile at Roselli, who takes a puff from his cigar, seemingly unconcerned by Isaac's proximity or the postured threat of Atlas. "Mr. Roselli, while I appreciate your patronage, I'm going to have to ask you to leave this evening. We've already reached maximum capacity, as you can see."

A slow grin spreads across his face, and he inclines his head slightly. "I do see that you're quite full." He stops for a few seconds and listens. "But your musician is quite good. I can understand why." He offers a little half-bow. "Until we meet again."

Fuck.

This isn't going away. *He* isn't going away, no matter how hard we might try. He turns back to the car, still parked near the curb, and his man opens the back door and lets him in.

Pope releases Atlas, who rushes toward the car as it pulls away. "You stay the fuck away from us."

His threat hangs in the night air, and I glance up and see Jude watching intently, his eyes wide, lips twisted.

He just saw everything.

9

JUDE

Luca's car screeches to a halt on the street, blocking traffic, but he doesn't give a shit. He throws on the flashers and jumps out while Byron climbs from the passenger seat immediately after him.

What the fuck is going on?

It's the same question I've been asking for the last fifteen minutes while I pace in front of the window, firing off text after text to everyone who was just out on the street, waiting for any one of them to respond to me and tell me what just happened.

Who the hell was that guy?

Nobody good, given the way Atlas postured and looked ready to punch him out. Even Isaac appeared on the edge of losing control, and he always prides himself on remaining calm and presenting a polished face for Hawke Enterprises. If *he* was rattled, it means something is going down. Something that involves Angelina...

Fuck.

I shove a hand back through my hair and watch the Grind.

People start to file out, and I glance at my watch. They don't close for another hour, which means whatever just went down is bad enough that Angelina is shutting down early.

Fuck, fuck, fuck.

I fire off another text to Isaac and send the same to Luca and Byron. Maybe since they're here now, they'll clue me in before I have a damn aneurysm.

JUDE

What the fuck just happened? Who the hell was that?

Given the look of the two muscly men who climbed out of the car with him, I certainly have my guesses. But with his back to me and the vehicle blocking my view, all I can do is speculate until somebody fucking answers me.

I text Allie next.

JUDE

Al!! What the hell is going on? Are you okay?

I send the same to Angelina and pace.

Back and forth.

Back and forth.

Pulling on my hair so damn much that I probably won't have any left by the end of the night. But I don't even care about that or that anybody who looks at my windows will see me acting like a fucking lunatic up here.

Somebody fucking answer me already.

The overwhelming helplessness crushes me. Sweat breaks out over my skin, and the longer my phone remains silent, the harder it becomes to keep myself calm.

That was a *threat.*

Plain and simple.

A threat to *Angie.*

I look at the door for the hundredth time, my fingers itching at the thought of opening it. My chest tightening, imagining rushing down that hall and taking the stairs two at a time to go find out what just happened.

If there were any time to do it, it would be now. Tonight. When I'm stuck without answers and a thousand horrible possibilities racing through my head. But I can't make myself move away from the window toward the door, no matter how badly I want to.

People continue to clear out of the café until only the Hawke crew remains inside. Another car pulls up outside behind Luca's, and Gabe, Stone, and Savage join the others.

Holy shit.

They're bringing in the big guns.

This time, I try Pope again, desperate for any information that might stop my rising panic.

JUDE

Can you tell me what the fuck is going on?

Finally, the three little dots pop up, letting me know he's replying.

POPE

That was Roselli.

"Fuck..."

The name alone sends icy dread through my entire body. That man doesn't show up without a purpose. And nothing he does can ever be good for the Hawkes.

This is the second time he's come to the Grind. The second time he's posed a danger to the girls. The second time I've had to watch and do nothing.

JUDE

What did he say?

He made some vague threats. Angelina seems
a little shaken.

A vise tightens around my chest. After everything the
Hawkes have been through, how Angelina suffered as a child
with the loss of her father, a threat, no matter how vague, from
a man like Roselli isn't anything to take lightly.

She's probably freaking the fuck out.

And I'm stuck over here, watching all of it unfold from
twenty-five feet away behind a wall of glass meant to keep
things out that I use to trap myself in.

It doesn't matter that the Hawkes always band together to
address any danger or that she has any number of people to
support her...*I* want to be the one comforting her, assuring her
and Allie that it will be okay.

The two most important people in the world to me are
suffering, and I can't do a damn thing about it.

I fire off another text to both of them.

JUDE

Come over when you're done with the family
meeting.

Seconds tick by, and the more I watch the clock, the slower
it seems to move. By the time the café door opens and the
Hawkes start to file out, I must have walked ten miles back and
forth in front of the windows.

My phone buzzes.

ALLIE

I'm exhausted. I'm going home.

JUDE

Are you all right?

That releases a tiny bit of the pressure crushing my lungs.

Bishop will not let anything happen, and I watch Isaac walk Allie around the building to the parking lot while the rest of the Hawkes disperse.

Angie, Astrid, and Bishop move around the café, cleaning tables, stocking, and getting what they can ready for tomorrow. The lights start to click off one by one, which means they'll all head home soon, and I'll be left agonizing all night, wondering if Angie is okay.

I stare at my last message to her, and even though I know I shouldn't, I send another.

Angie stops in front of the window and pulls her phone from her back pocket. She reads my message, glances over at me, then back to Bishop and Astrid.

She says something to them, and then all three file out the front door and Angie locks it. Bishop and Astrid head off down the street to wherever they parked while Angie stares up at me, a single pane of glass separating us. Even from here, I can see how tense she is, how what just went down with Roselli has shaken her.

"Come on."

Do you really want her to come over?

It feels like a horrible idea, but the need to pull her into my arms, to assure her that she'll be safe, that everything will be all right, outweighs any concern over what she might see when she does come.

Angie stares at me for a few more moments, as if she's

135

debating what she's going to do as much as I have been what I should do, but she sets off across the street toward me.

My breath catches, and I watch until she hits my building, pulls out a key, and slips it into the lock. I swallow thickly and move toward the loft door, unlocking it so she doesn't have to when she gets up.

I open it before she even reaches halfway down the hallway, and she freezes, her red-rimmed eyes locking with mine. Thick black lashes, clinging together with tears, open and close rapidly as she tries to blink them away.

The look in her eyes says she's ready to bolt, but I got her this far.

Swallowing past my reservations, I take a half-step toward her, holding the door open behind me. "Are you okay?"

It's a stupid question, given what just went down, but I can't help thinking about how badly this could all end, about everything Angie's already been through.

She considers me for a moment, almost like she might turn around and walk right back out. Maybe she should. Every time I talk to her, I seem to fuck it up somehow. It might be better if she just went home, comforted Allie, and forgot all about the idiot across the street. But I won't sleep without knowing, without a confirmation from her perfect pink lips.

"Please, Angie." I start to take another step toward her but stop myself. "I need to know what's going on. I need to know you and Allie are okay."

It might be a simple ask, but each step she takes toward me seems hard for her, like she has to force herself to take them. She pauses in front of me, her terrified eyes meeting mine, offering me no answers. Only questions linger there. Ones I can't decipher.

She slips past me into the condo. That damn bakery and coffee scent hangs over her and fills my lungs, and I let the door close behind me and follow her into the living room.

Chewing on her nails, she goes to stand in front of the windows, staring out from the same place I just watched all that unfold.

"Roselli, did he threaten you?"

She stiffens and glances over her shoulder. "With those types of people, isn't everything a threat?"

Fair enough.

"What did Luca say?"

If there's an expert on the fucking mob in New Orleans, it's the former head of it. He may have left that life behind decades ago, but he still carries weight in that world. And I know from experience he isn't afraid to use it when he wants to accomplish something.

"He's going to call him, make a stink about how he never should've been here."

I move closer, needing the comfort of knowing she's all right. Her body starts to tremble, and she wraps her arms around herself, still facing the window.

Stopping halfway across the room, I force myself to stay back. "What did he say, *exactly*?"

"He made it very clear that what Isaac did to rescue Jack has created a problem for him."

"Shit." I run a hand along my jaw. "I mean, we knew it could, right?"

She nods. "I'm not sure what we're going to do." She turns her head slightly and glances back at me, a tear sliding down her cheek slowly. "I'm already freaking out about this new coffee shop going in down the street, then this stuff with Allie. Now we have to worry about the mob? *Again.*"

It's a lot.

More than a lot.

"You need a drink."

A tiny laugh falls from her lips. "I could probably use one."

"I could, too."

Having to stand here, watching all that unfold without being able to go help her, I truly felt more like a fucking useless piece of shit than I ever have in my entire life. And having her here now, not being able to comfort her at all, not being *allowed* to, is even worse.

I move into the kitchen and grab a bottle of wine from the fridge and two glasses from the cabinet. The sounds of her moving around the open space behind me fill my ears, and I glance back to find her checking out the books stacked along the wall where I normally sit to watch the real world go by outside and write.

All my favorites.

The worlds I've lost myself in over the last fifteen years rather than get bogged down in my own memories, the ones that seem to want to come back so strongly all of a sudden.

My back to her, I pour my wine and immediately take a massive drink, hoping the alcohol might stop me from shaking. "Did Allie tell you she got the results?"

"She doesn't want to look until tomorrow."

I pour her a glass, wiping the few drops I spilled because my hands won't stop trembling. "Can't you call Nora?"

"She won't tell me anything. Doctor-patient privilege."

As frustrating as it is not to have the answer about Allie, it's probably a good thing Nora is bound to keep quiet. Given everything she knows about me, I wouldn't want anyone finding out any of it, especially not Angelina.

I grab the glasses and turn back toward her, almost dropping them when I find her with my open laptop in her hand, eyes locked on the words on the screen.

Fuck.

———

ANGELINA

He waited, and he watched. Just like he did every day. For the door to open. For the sunshine to light her face. For the breeze to blow through her midnight hair. For her blue eyes to light up the world around her. For her to smile. For her to laugh. For her to forge ahead and embrace life fully despite all the reasons she shouldn't.
But mostly, he waited for her to look up.
For her to acknowledge him. For her to see what waited behind the glass without the distortion it provided.
All he wanted was to be seen.

O*h, my God.*

Every nerve in my body tingles, my stomach flipping wildly.

It's the ultimate intrusion into Jude's head. An assault on his intimate thoughts. Something I was never meant to see.

Each word spills onto the page like poetry. A love song from someone who has spent years watching the woman he loves. Who has memorized every detail. A plea from a man who believes he can never have her.

I shouldn't be reading this...

His footsteps behind me make me jump, and I glance over my shoulder at him. He stands in the center of the loft space near the couch and coffee table, holding two glasses of wine, his face a blank mask as his eyes move from the screen to my face.

"I..." I open and close my mouth, struggling to find the right thing to say. "I'm sorry."

I set his laptop back on the floor next to the books—where I should have left it instead of being nosy—and take a half-step back from it, the words replaying in my head over and over again.

My eyes naturally drift to the windows, down to the café, from precisely where he stands every day, trying to imagine what he sees.

His best friend...

The only person he's ever connected with in the fifteen years since Byron and Luca took him in...

The girl who might be pregnant with another man's child...

My heart aches for him, for what it must be like to see her every day, to know he can't be with her. I turn back toward where he still stands motionless, frozen in place by my asshole intrusion. "Does she know?"

His blond brows rise slowly. "What?"

I twist back to look at the café. "Does Allie know you're in love with her?"

It's so obvious; anyone could see it.

Hell, everyone has seen it.

The entire family has assumed the two of them have been together for years and have just been hiding their relationship for fear of how we might all react. We all grew up together, are "family" for all intents and purposes, even if we don't share blood. That complicates things beyond belief.

But if they *have* been together, it would explain why she's been so secretive about her boyfriends.

Oh, my God.

I whirl back to face him. "Jesus, Jude. Are you the father?"

We don't even know if she *is* pregnant yet, but the possibility that it could be Jude's has my mind spinning.

His eyes widen, and he sets the wine on the coffee table. "Fuck. No." He shakes his head, taking a step toward me. "Allie and I aren't like that."

The tiniest bit of pressure releases from my ribcage at his insistence, though I don't have any time to explore why it would matter to me if they *were* involved that way.

A bigger issue looms over us, and I motion toward the computer. "But does she *know*? Does she know you're *in love* with her?"

My question hangs in the air, growing heavier with each passing second, weighing on us like the thick, July New Orleans air. Jude squeezes his eyes closed as if my words physically pain him.

It shouldn't be a hard question to answer, and there isn't any point in him trying to hide it after I read *that*. Anyone could see he wrote it about Allie and that only someone madly, obsessively in love could create such beautiful words. Could *feel* so completely and love so utterly.

He takes a step toward me.

Then another.

Another.

Until he's so close, he could reach out and touch me, keeping his eyes clamped shut the whole time. When he finally stops his slow advance, he opens them again, and the soft sky blue, the same eyes I saw on that little boy the first time we met, stare back at me with something I've never seen in them before.

A new kind of fear...and something else.

"It *isn't* about Allie."

"What? But..."

The words replay in my head. The description of her dark hair. Her blue eyes. Watching her from...

Oh, God.

Jude reaches out and slides his hand to my cheek, tilting my face up toward him. That same buzz of electricity pulses between us. The heat from his palm radiates through me, warming me deep in my soul, making me want to lean into his touch when I should be pulling out of it. But the intensity of his gaze holds me steady, refuses to release me from its magnetic grip.

This is why I've avoided Jude, why I've never sought him out, why I've never allowed myself to think about the way I feel around him. Because if I did, I somehow knew I'd fall down this hole and never be able to get out of it.

His thumb moves across my cheek softly. "It's always been you, Angelina. Always."

"Wh-what?" I slip away from him, stepping back toward the windows, needing to put some distance between us so I can try to process what I must somehow be misunderstanding. "No, that's not..." I squeeze my eyes closed. "This is so not what I thought was going to happen when I came over here tonight. I just needed..."

I don't know what I needed.

Maybe to talk to somebody who's been through the type of things most of my cousins have never experienced. Someone who understands fear. I've seen it in Jude's eyes his whole life, that constant tension, like he's always ready to run from whatever demons chase him. And now, he's staring at me with the same look because he's afraid of what he just said.

"Please, don't say that, Jude."

He shouldn't.

He can't.

It's too much.

Too complicated.

Too wrong.

I stumble back until my shoulders hit the window, trying to find any way to get him to take the words back, the ones that will change everything in a way that we can never go back from. "You don't mean it. It's just adrenaline. The situation." I motion behind me toward the street. "You saw everything. You're just—"

He takes a step forward, then another, but I don't have anywhere to go. His left hand flattens against the glass beside me, pinning me between his hard, lean chest and the window.

No. This can't happen.

"You're not thinking clearly, Jude."

His warm breath flutters over me, his body so close that the heat radiating from him seeps into my bones. The crisp, fresh scent of his aftershave or cologne fills my nose with each breath.

This is the closest I've ever been to Jude, the closest I've ever seen *anyone* get to him, and the intensity may crumple my knees.

He stares directly into my eyes, a confidence exuding in his that he hasn't held before. "Yes, I am thinking clearly. I'm not a little boy anymore, Angie. I haven't been for a long time. I know how I feel, how I've felt for, fuck, what seems like forever." He lifts his right hand and feathers his fingers over my cheek. "And it's you. From the day my eyes locked with yours in that fucking closet, it's *always* been you."

I squeeze my eyes closed because I can't look at him anymore, not when his words are cutting into me so deeply, not when they're dredging up things I've kept locked away so tightly.

The way my heart stopped when I saw him that day. The immediate pull I felt to the beautiful boy, who looked so lost and terrified. How I wanted to pull him into my arms and hold him, comfort him in a way it appeared no one ever had. How badly I wanted to *help* him. So he could break free of the demons that sent him scrambling in there in the first place.

All I wanted that day was for him to understand he was *safe* with us and always would be. But I'd be lying if I said that didn't change. That I never noticed the looks he's given me over the years. That I didn't see the way he intentionally put space between us whenever we were in a room together but watched me intently, like he was memorizing every move I made.

And I'd be lying if I said his looks didn't affect me...

How could I have been so stupid? How could I not have seen?
You did.

You just pretended not to because it was easier than seeing the truth.

I can't hide behind my closed lids forever, not when his fingers brush over my cheek, not when his body is so close I can feel the tension vibrating off him.

There isn't any way to ignore it now, to pretend there isn't something more between us that I've been running from and he's been hiding from.

You can't pretend anymore, Ang.

I reopen my eyes, and he's so close that all he would have to do is lean forward to press his lips to mine. So close that I can smell the wine on his breath and almost taste the sharp tang of the tannins it must contain.

Jude doesn't look away from me, doesn't even blink, just stares into my eyes with an intensity that sends a shiver through me. "I've sat here every day for the last three years and watched you, Ang. I *see* you." He squeezes my chin between his fingers. "And I know you see me, too. Even when you pretend you don't."

All the times I've forced myself not to look up, only for him to flash through my head anyway...

The hundreds of times I have looked because I couldn't stop myself.

Yet, I never came over.

Not once.

Because I was afraid.

Afraid of him and what I always felt whenever we were in each other's orbit.

Afraid of what I knew was wrong, that no one would understand.

He slowly dips his head, telegraphing his intent, giving me every chance to say no, to push him away, but I can't or won't. His lips brush over mine.

Softly. Gently. Reverently. Like he's trying to savor it and make it last forever. Like he's worshipping me rather than taking from me.

Despite all the reasons to say no, to shove at his hard chest and force him away, I clutch at his shirt, and a tiny moan slips from my throat into his mouth.

He ghosts his lips across mine a few more times, then pulls away, and the fire burning across his eyes ignites something deep inside me that I'm not ready to admit.

"I..." I release his shirt. "I have to go."

I slip out from between his arms and run toward the door, half expecting him to chase after me. But it slams closed behind me, and I make it across the street before I finally look back.

He stands in exactly the same spot as always, watching, only this time, I don't force myself to see that little boy anymore.

10

ANGELINA

The second I step into my apartment, I let the door slam behind me, then lean back against it, squeezing my eyes closed as if doing that will somehow erase what just happened with Jude.

But my body won't let me forget.

Not during the drive home. Not during my climb up the stairs to our door. Not now that I'm inside, willing his words to stop racing through my head.

It isn't about Allie.

It's always been you.

Allie's bedroom door creaks open, and she steps out, rubbing her eyes. "Ang?"

Shit, I hadn't meant to wake her.

I don't want her to see me like this—so off balance. So...confused.

"Go back to bed, Al."

She yawns and runs her hair back through her disheveled

hair, looking even more exhausted than she did tonight at the café. "Are you okay?"

I nod. "Yep, I'm just going to shower off the day and then climb into bed. Were you able to get any sleep?"

God knows I won't be able to.

Not after Jude just left me utterly speechless and questioning everything I thought I knew about myself. Forget Falco Enterprises trying to put me out of business and Roselli's little impromptu visit, the way Jude looked at me tonight, those words I read on the page, *that* is what will keep me awake, wondering what it all means and what the *hell* I'm supposed to do with it.

Twisting her hands in the giant T-shirt she's sleeping in, Allie glances away. "Not really. I don't know that I will."

The hint of separation, like she's balancing on the edge of completely losing her shit, draws me off the door and over to her. I pull her into my arms. She trembles, and I squeeze her tighter, her body somehow feeling even smaller and more vulnerable than it normally does.

"Why don't we look at the results? You'll feel better, knowing one way or the other." I pull back and hold her shoulders. "Really, not knowing has to be worse."

Allie shakes her head. "I'm not ready to know. I'll do it tomorrow."

It's there in her eyes. The truth. She doesn't *have* to look.

She already knows the answer, just like I do deep in the pit of my stomach—Allie's going to have a baby she's absolutely not ready for. And me forcing anything will only make her try to cut me out.

Allie has to do this *her* way, just like she's done everything else in her life.

She leans forward and presses a kiss to my cheek. "Goodnight."

"Goodnight."

Part of me wants to follow her into her bedroom, climb into bed with her like we used to when we were little, and hold her to me all night, ensuring her everything will be okay. But we aren't kids anymore. Pretty damn far from it. And no matter how much I want to be there for her, she seems to want to do *this* part of it on her own.

I release a heavy sigh and trudge to the bathroom, feeling every hour I've been on my feet ten-fold and stripping off my clothes as I go.

What a fucking day.

Who would have thought being threatened by a mob boss would be the least surprising part of the last twenty-four hours?

Jude's pale-blue eyes pierce my mind, and I suck in a sharp breath, reaching in to crank on the shower and wait for it to get up to temp.

Steam starts to fill the bathroom within minutes, and I step under the water and close the shower door, sealing myself in. The hot spray hits my chest, and I turn my face up into it, letting it wash away everything it can.

But I can't get rid of the memory of what Jude said or the way he kissed me.

Fuck, Jude kissed me.

And I can feel it all over again.

His soft lips moving easily against mine. The way he cradled my face. His warmth permeating every part of me. The desire, the need he poured into the simple action. How much I didn't want him to stop.

Heat rushes through my body, and my clit throbs for attention I haven't been giving it—that no one has in a long time.

This is Jude we're talking about.

JUDE!

There are too many reasons to count why this is wrong. Why it can't *ever* be possible. Why we both need to pretend

149

tonight never happened. But my body doesn't seem to care. And in this moment, neither can I.

I let my hand slide down my stomach and between my legs. A low moan slips from my lips with the simple brush of my fingers over my slick core, already wet from a simple kiss from a man I absolutely should not be interested in.

You're going to hell, Angelina.

I've spent most of my life terrified of fire, of what flames can take so quickly, without warning or apology. I've avoided anything that might scorch me, anyone who might reach deep enough inside me to ignite that part of me that could make me combust, but one kiss from Jude was enough to set me aflame and make me want to *burn.*

My pussy aches, and I slip a finger inside, clenching around it, knowing it won't be enough. Grinding my palm against my clit, I thrust into myself, seeking release from the tension of the day, of the impossible situations coming at me from all sides. But it won't come because I *can't.*

"Shit."

I tug my hand away, yank open the shower door, and lean out to rummage in the counter drawer until I get to the small, discrete box at the bottom.

If I think about what I'm doing and why, the guilt will creep in and ruin my ability to relax enough to actually find the release I need so badly. Pushing away the reasons it's so wrong is the only way I can do this.

I tug out the miniature vibrator I keep hidden in here and slide the door back into place. Cranking on the waterproof device, I press it between my legs, angling the small, round head against my clit in exactly the right way.

"Fuck..."

My entire body jerks, and I rest my free hand against the slick tile to keep myself upright.

Hot water beats down my back as the vision of the way Jude

looked at me flashes against my closed lids. The memories of every time we've touched over the years follow quickly after it.

That little electric spark I've never wanted to acknowledge.

The way I've avoided it, avoided *him*, because that current between us always tried to draw me too close to the man who never let anyone near him.

It's *always* been there.

Too powerful to ignore anymore.

My body starts to tense as I switch the angle of the vibrator and suck in a sharp breath. The orgasm hits me so fast that my vision goes black, my knees failing under me.

I sag back against the wall, using it to keep me upright as wave after wave of pleasure courses through me, that all-consuming conflagration I was seeking until I finally can't handle it and jerk the vibrator away.

Shit.

Muscles twitch.

Breaths come heavy.

I turn it off and let it fall toward the drain.

My legs sag, and I allow myself to slide down until my ass hits the tile. I bury my face in my hands, the water hitting me keeping me warm, even as a shiver rolls through me.

All the adrenaline surging through my system from the events of the day finally dissipates, leaving me shaking on the floor. A sob escapes my throat, and I clamp my hand over it, afraid to wake Allie and let her find me like this.

I'd love to blame it on everything that happened today. The mad rush at work. Roselli's threat. Not knowing Allie's fate. But Jude's words—on the page and what he said—shook me more than I would ever admit.

I see you.

That's the last thing I wanted.

I could have had any job I wanted in the Hawke empire. I could be running it all as CFO with Savage and Gabe instead of

Kennedy. As the eldest, it's my birthright to take over what they've built, what we've *all* helped build, and they offered it to me more than once.

But that's never what I wanted.

It wasn't my dream.

I wanted to blend into the background. To live my life and have my coffee shop and be content to just *be*. I never wanted a spotlight pointed at me, never wanted anyone to focus their passion on me when I know I can't return it fully.

Being seen, being *wanted* by Jude Abello-Harris is far too dangerous and precisely the kind of thing I can't have.

Not if I want to survive.

JUDE

Sweat pours down my face and chest, soaking into the waistband of my athletic shorts, but I just keep running, mile after mile, my feet pounding on the treadmill as I stare at the white wall in front of it. My lungs and muscles burn in protest, but I keep pushing, refusing to stop even when my brain screams at me to relent.

I have to do something to work off this tension that's tightened my body since the moment Angelina walked out of here earlier. If I don't relieve it somehow, I'll snap in half.

Keep going.

Keep running.

Away from something or toward it?

That's the question I can't seem to find an answer to, no matter how many miles tick by on the digital counter.

Six miles.

Six damn miles and I still can't stop thinking about the way she smelled. The way she tasted. Exactly how I always imagined she would. Sweet. Sinful. Perfect. Her lips moving hungrily against mine and that little moan that slipped from her mouth into mine before I forced myself to pull away.

Fuck.

My cock stirs against the fabric of my shorts, an affliction I'm sure to suffer from even more now.

I slam my hand against the stop button. The machine immediately jerks to a halt, and I grip the handrails, gasping and heaving, sweat pouring down onto the tread.

What the hell was I thinking?

Saying that to her...

Kissing her...

The simple answer is...I wasn't.

All this shit with Allie, with Luca and Byron wanting me to do the bookstore and make a decision, with the Falco fucks threatening the Grind, with Roselli showing up and then Angie finding the book, it pushed me to a point where I couldn't control myself anymore, where I couldn't hold back what's been bottled up since I was old enough to know what want and need meant, old enough to understand how much I loved her and why I couldn't have her.

Fifteen years of wanting that woman, and I finally had a taste.

It will never be enough.

It never *could* be.

But what the fuck am I going to do about it?

I climb off the treadmill and sway on unsteady legs to the bathroom, purposely avoiding looking in the mirror on my way to the shower.

I'm the last person I want to look at right now.

If I did, all I would be able to see are my failures, my weaknesses, and what a mess I've made of everything so damn quickly.

She ran.

I kissed her and she fucking ran.

"Goddammit…"

I crank on the shower, shuck my shorts, and step under the cold spray. The icy drops pelt my skin, stinging it until my entire body burns, but it's exactly what I need. Something to snap me out of whatever altered state I must have been in to do something so stupid and reckless.

But even the freezing jets of water hitting my hard cock can't bring it down.

Fucking hell, Angelina.

Why does it have to be her?

The woman who witnessed me at my worst. Who watched me collapse under the weight of everything that happened to me before Luca and Byron found me. Who saw me as a lost, broken child and likely always will.

Of all the people who have come into my life over the last fifteen years, all the women who tried and failed to keep my attention, the only one who ever held any piece of my heart is the one who can see right through me and always could.

I wrap my hand around my cock, stroking it slowly, the contact on the sensitive flesh instantly making me flinch. "Fucking hell…"

My strangled words echo off the tile, and I grit my teeth as my cock jumps in my hand. Long, slow strokes lead me toward the liberation of my tension. Smooth palm against hard flesh. The wintery waterfall cascading around me, not holding me back at all.

I won't last long like this, with all this pent-up frustration and energy, with the feel of her lips against mine stuck so vibrantly in my head.

Angelina Matthews is the most dangerous thing I've ever experienced in my life. Wanting her. Needing her the way I do will be the end of me. I've survived so many things that would have crushed someone else, that should have destroyed me. But in the end, it will be my love for that woman that is my undoing.

I tug harder, twisting my palm against the head over and over again, my increased pace doing nothing to help calm the wild anguish blasting through my veins.

You can't have her.

Even if I wasn't fucked up beyond belief, she's Allie's sister, practically family. It could never happen. It can never work. Besides, if she knew the truth...

That thought sobers me for a second.

Tell her. Tell her the truth, and you'll be free.

Once she knows, she won't even be able to look at me again.

It'll make things easier for her and for me.

She can forget this ever happened. Pretend she never read those words. That I never kissed her. That I never told her the crazy things that fell from my lips so freely when I should have bitten them back.

Even knowing the truth would disgust her and send her running from me doesn't kill my erection. The throbbing desire to be buried inside her, to feel her moving under me, all around me. To experience her kiss on my lips again, her soft, warm touch, her nails scouring my back. All of it is too much.

"Fuck, fuck, fuck."

I increase my pace, tugging and jerking at my flesh until the low burn finally starts at the base of my spine. It sears through me like a tidal wave of shame and hate, and I come on a wild cry that echoes off the tile, hot spurts shooting across the floor to swirl down the drain with the water.

The shower may have washed away the sweat, but I haven't eradicated my need for her. The only way that'll ever happen is if she knows the truth, if I tell her enough to *make* her stay away.

"Fuck."

Slapping my palms flat against the tile, I hang my head,

then reach out and crank the water to hot. It takes a while to build up to temperature, but once the heat hits my neck and shoulders, I release a relieved sigh, some of the tension melting away slightly.

I stand like that until the water starts to go cold again, so long that my entire body starts to sag.

It's late. So much has fucking happened in the last few days, yet I know I won't sleep tonight. Not even after running six fucking miles. I can't. Not now that I've fucked up everything with her and complicated things with Allie even more.

Jesus.

Allie.

What the hell is she going to think? What is she going to say if Angelina tells her what I did?

She won't understand.

No one will.

It's a betrayal of everything the Hawkes have ever done for me to think I can feel this way about her, that I had the audacity to touch her and kiss her when she just went through a horribly traumatic confrontation with a man who is a serious threat to them all.

What the hell is wrong with me?

The same question has looped in my head for years, since well before Luca and Byron found me and gave me this new life. And it's only hammered more incessantly against my skull recently. The longer I stay here and lie to everyone, pretend everything is fine, the louder it gets, demanding an answer I can never find.

And now I've offered it more ammunition.

I finally stand fully and force myself to wash my hair and soap off. No matter how long I stand under the scalding spray, it won't be long enough to fully wash myself clean.

Not after what I just did.

Angelina must hate me now. Maybe that's a good thing, and

once she knows the truth, I can finally be rid of my desire for her. No one could understand, could accept the scars and taint that permanently mars me. Keeping it all a secret was meant to protect me, but perhaps it's the way to ensure she stays protected *from* me.

It might be the way out.

Keep telling yourself that.

It's been fifteen years, and nothing has changed how I feel. I'm struggling to find any way to remedy this, to salvage the quagmire I've created.

But I've just sealed my fate with one fucking kiss.

11

JUDE

Not once...

Angelina hasn't looked up once since I woke from a restless sleep at 4:00 AM and started staring out the window, hoping to catch a glimpse of her.

Watching her arrive and unlock the front door...

Seeing her move around the Grind and outside on the patio, getting the tables set up and ready...

Looking every bit as fucking beautiful as she always does.

Dark hair piled up on the top of her head to get it out of the way while she bakes. Ass firmly encased in jeans that stretch with her every step. Her soft, pink lips moving as she talks to herself or sings her way through all the tedious things she has to accomplish on her own each morning.

She never stops working. Never stops pushing herself. But now that she's gone through her entire daily routine without a single glance my way, it makes me wish I had stayed in bed, where there might be a chance of pretending I didn't fuck up everything last night.

Or that things didn't get ten times worse this morning.

I glance at my phone for the hundredth time and reread the message I found waiting for me the moment I opened my eyes.

ALLIE

You're going to be an uncle.

Great fucking time to drop a bomb, like the fact that I'm in love with her sister...

The woman who won't even *look* at me today.

I have to see her face to face.

I have to talk to her.

I have to know if she told Allie what happened last night.

This isn't the time to be throwing something like this at Al, so if she hasn't said anything, then I have to convince her not to. We can both pretend this was some bad dream instead of me being stupid.

It doesn't matter how hard it is—I have to go.

I push away from the window and walk to the door, mustering up all the willpower I have.

It's just across the street.

It's just across the street.

You used to do this all the time.

You used to sit there for hours, working, drinking coffee, talking with them.

The memories of that time, when things were so *easy*, when it didn't feel like the world was crushing me under it, assault my brain, taunting me with how it used to be—*before.*

I wince at the onslaught, then tug open the door and step out into the hall.

Deep breaths. Keep moving.

One. Two. Three. Four. Five. Six. Seven. Eight. Nine. Ten. Eleven. Twelve. Thirteen. Fourteen. Fifteen. Sixteen. Seventeen...

I was wrong about the number of steps to the stairs. They

descend in front of me, metal treads I used to climb up and down so easily, two at a time, without even thinking about it. Now, I stare down them and have to slap my hand against the wall when the whole hallway starts to spin around me like some violent theme park ride.

No.

Two flights.

One step at a time.

I take a deep breath and hold it, then step down the first one, my hand clutching the railing so tightly my knuckles whiten. Second step, third, fourth. By the time I reach the landing, my entire body trembles.

You used to do this every day, multiple times a day. You used to go to the Grind. You used to go to classes. You used to go to Nana's for dinner. You used to...you used to...you used to...

I repeat the words over and over with every step I take.

You'll be fine.

There isn't any option not to be. I can't let my mistake with Angelina derail things for Allie. She needs both of us right now, uncomplicated by some bad decision I made in a moment of weakness.

Her life is about to change dramatically, and it could send her spiraling. Allie loves too hard and feels too much all the time. She needs Angelina and me to be strong, to be her rocks, to support her fully without the distraction of some unrequited obsession making things awkward.

Allie can't ever know.

She can't find out.

I hit the bottom step and scan the foyer I haven't seen in two years. The door to my left that leads into the empty space that would've been my bookstore stands locked, just like it has been this entire time.

My dream now relegated to collecting dust.

It's all I ever wanted, my own store where I could sell all the books I love so much and share the worlds I discovered when my own was such a horrible place to live in.

Yet, my own fucked-up head has stopped me.

I'm going to make it to the café today, though.

I refuse to give in to this.

You just have to cross the street, Jude.

The glass door out onto the sidewalk looms in front of me, one final barrier between me and the world I shut off and locked myself away from. I step forward, twist the lock, and push it open.

A wall of hot, fresh air hits me, and I pull it deep into my lungs. The scent of the ocean and the coffee from across the street swirl around me on a light summer breeze. All it does is make me think of her, of how *she* smells, of how she felt...

Shit.

If she saw me like this, if she knew how fucked up I am, things would be so different. And just like last night, I can't decide if that's what I want or want to avoid at all costs.

Do I tell her so she knows and she'll stay away, or do I hide it so there might be a fucking chance?

I focus my narrowing vision across the street to the Grind. Several customers sit at the small bistro tables on the sidewalk, chatting, enjoying their drinks and food, completely oblivious to the panic engulfing the man standing on the sidewalk across the two lanes of traffic from them.

Remember to breathe.

I inhale and look both ways, then step out onto the cracked sidewalk I see every day, where I watch people walking by, going about their lives completely oblivious to the dangers around them, to how easily things can do a one-eighty and shatter the peace in their world.

One step, two, three, four. My toes hit the curb, and I stare down at the asphalt. Maybe twenty-five steps across, then another five to the door.

You can do that.

One—I step out onto the road.

Two, three—I scan both ways again as my vision starts to blur.

Four, five—someone honks, and I see a car approaching through the fog.

Six, seven—my chest starts to tighten.

Eight, nine—a horn blares again, and a car swerves around me to go past.

Ten, eleven, twelve—I can't get in air.

Thirteen, fourteen, fifteen—darkness starts to creep in at the edge of my vision.

Sixteen, seventeen, eighteen—I stumble on the opposite curb, my knees hitting the sidewalk.

Fuck.

I struggle to get my feet back under me, but I only make it another foot before that darkness creeps in so far that I can't see anything at all.

Total blackness engulfs me.

The whoosh of blood in my ears drowns out the noises on the street.

Everything spins.

My skin starts to crawl.

No, no, no, not now.

Not like this.

I shouldn't have tried, but now it's too late.

Have to get back, get home.

I take a step back and stumble. My hip slams into one of the small bistro tables.

"Hey, are you all right?" The voice sounds like it's coming at me through a long tunnel, echoey and so far away.

Even though my eyes are open, all I see is a pinpoint of bright light surrounded by thick, inky blackness.

Shit.

I know this feeling. It's happened before. That day, the last time I was out here. When I realized the world is still such a dangerous place. When everything I worked for disappeared in a single, agonizing instant.

This doesn't lead anywhere good.

I can't let it happen again.

I'm going to pass out.

ANGELINA

A FLASH of movement in the floor-to-ceiling windows at the front of the café catches my attention, and I glance toward it and do a double-take as Jude crosses the street, heading straight for the Grind.

Shit.

I should have known he would show up when I didn't bring his coffee this morning, especially if Allie gave him the news.

I'm going to be an aunt.

Allie's having a baby.

The reality hasn't quite sunk in yet—for her or for me.

I've never seen such a haunted look in her eyes as when she came into my room and told me while I was getting ready to come in this morning. In an instant, she went from being my twenty-five-year-old sister to the tiny baby Mom and Landon brought home from the hospital on that rainy morning.

Delicate. Fragile. Needing comfort and support and care.

That has to be my focus now, not the fact that Jude Abello-Harris kissed me last night and said things he never should have.

"Can I get another sugar in there?"

I drag my attention from the sexy blond man approaching the

Grind and back to Damon, who I've rudely ignored. If he weren't a regular and so casually chill about everything, I would worry more about it, but Jude's approach makes it impossible to think about anything else. "Sure. Do you want to put it in yourself?"

"No." He flashes a grin. "You can."

I tear open the packet with trembling hands and dump it in, stirring a little too vigorously as I wait for the bells to jingle above the door, marking Jude's entrance.

What do I say to him?

It would be so much easier if I knew how I felt about the whole situation, but my head has been a jumbled mess since the moment I realized the words he had on the page weren't about Allie.

This is *Jude* we're talking about. The boy Luca and Byron saved from something so vile that they can't even talk about it. The boy I helped hide in a closet rather than interact with the family. The boy I watched grow and mature into an intelligent, enigmatic man.

Because he *definitely* isn't a boy anymore.

I pop the lid on the coffee and slide it across the counter, intentionally not looking toward the door, trying to avoid the inevitable. "There you go."

Damon grins and tilts the cup toward me. "Thank you. I'm sorry I have to take this to go today."

He steps away from the counter and, without a line behind him, there isn't anything to keep me from looking for Jude. I let my gaze drift toward the door, expecting to see those Nordic-blue eyes searing into me the same way they did last night—filled with so many questions I absolutely can't answer right now—but he isn't there.

Where did he go?

A loud scraping noise, like one of the iron bistro tables moving, comes from outside, followed by a massive clank.

Several customers jump from their seats, visibly shaken even from my limited view through the windows.

What the hell is going on out there?

I rush around the counter toward the door and throw it open to find Jude on his knees on the sidewalk, head dropped low, hand pressed to his chest like he can't breathe.

Oh, my God...

"Jude?" I kneel in front of him and grab his shoulder, trying to get him to look up at me. "Jude, can you hear me? What's wrong?"

Slowly, his eyes drift up to meet mine, and the panic there seizes my heart in my chest. "Can't. Breathe."

Shit.

"Are you having an allergic reaction?" I shift my hand to his neck to check his pulse, even though I don't have a clue what I should be looking for. His pulse thunders under his clammy skin, beating against my fingertips too fast to count. "Should I call an ambulance? Do you need an EpiPen? What?"

He shakes his head, squeezes his eyes closed, and motions toward his place. "Home."

Fuck. What the hell's going on?

I grab his arm and help him to his feet while several people around us stand, watching the incident, whispering amongst themselves. "Jude, tell me what's happening. Are you okay?"

He sags like dead weight against me, and I wrap my arm around his waist and lead him to the curb. Each step seems labored, his normally strong body not functioning properly.

Leaning against me, his eyes moving in and out of focus. "I shouldn't have..."

"Shouldn't have what?"

I check the street both ways, then usher him across the street, holding out a hand to oncoming traffic and annoyed drivers who blare their horns. He stumbles a few times, unsteady in a way I've never seen him before.

We make it over the other curb and to the locked door, and he fumbles in his pocket for the key. I pull his hand away and fish for it until my fingers close around his keychain.

"I got it." I unlock the door, throw it open, and help him to the steps. "Can you do the stairs?"

He looks at me with unfocused eyes, then squeezes them closed and nods. "Yes."

His answer lacks confidence I share. In all the years I've known Jude, I've never seen him like this—not unless I count that first day.

We ascend agonizingly slowly, with Jude leaning on me heavily, his other hand gripping the handrail tightly until we finally make it to the top. I move us down the hallway to his door, try the knob, and shove it open, urging him inside.

He stumbles in and slips out of my hold, dropping to his knees.

"Jude." I grab his shoulder and try to get him to turn toward me. "Jude, look at me."

Ignoring me, his eyes closed, he slowly crawls to the closest corner, dropping onto his ass and pressing his back to the wall. He rests his elbows on his knees and lowers his head, burying his face in his hands.

Shit.

I've seen this position before. I've seen *him* like this...fifteen fucking years ago in that closet.

Is all of this because of what happened last night?

He said, "*I shouldn't have...*" That could mean so many things—he shouldn't have written what he did, he shouldn't have told me how he felt, he shouldn't have kissed me.

I pull out my phone and text Allie. She may be dealing with her own major issues right now, but Jude is her best friend. If anyone knows how to handle this, it's her.

Something's wrong with Jude. Can you come over?

Almost immediately, the three little bubbles pop back up.

ALLIE

I'll be there in 20 minutes. Is he okay?

ANG

I don't know.

Slipping my phone back into my pocket, I lower myself to my knees in front of him, the hardwood floors unyielding. "Jude, I don't know what I'm supposed to do." I set my hand on his arm, and he doesn't pull it away. Doesn't flinch the way he does when anyone else touches him. "Jude, what do you need me to do?"

When this happened before, Allie just *sat* with him.

I can do that.

I can sit.

But what if I'm wrong.

What if this is something I can't handle on my own?

This would be far better handled by someone with some damn medical training—Nora or Pope or even Skye. Any of them would know what to do, how to approach him without making whatever is happening ten times worse.

"Do-do you want me to call Aunt Nora?"

He shakes his head, gasping slightly, like he's still trying to find his breath. "No. God, no."

"Skye? Pope?"

Without a second of hesitation, he shakes his head again. "No, I'll be okay."

His tone doesn't instill much confidence in that. Nor does

the fact that he can't look at me and still struggles like he can't get enough air.

"What do you need me to do?"

"I need..."—he inhales a shaky breath—"shower. I need to get in the shower."

"Okay." That I can do. That's simple. "I'll go turn it on."

I pull my hand from his arm, rush into his bathroom, and crank on the shower.

Hot or cold? Shit. We'll go with hot.

A cold shower seems cruel, given whatever is happening out there, but maybe it would snap him out of it. Help him get back here with me.

I hurry back and find him in the same position, unmoved. "It's on."

He slowly lifts his head, and his eyes meet mine. That same fear that was there the first time we met stares back at me. "I need you to stay."

"I'm not going anywhere, Jude."

"No." He winces, shaking his head, his long blond locks falling back over his face. "I need you to stay in the bathroom with me to make sure I don't scrub off my skin."

Shit.

He's serious.

This has happened before, and not just when he was ten years old. That truth slams into me so hard it rocks me back on my feet as all my interactions with him over the last few years come flooding back.

Allie always brings Jude his coffee. Jude never comes to any of the family gatherings anymore. Luca and Byron are always saying we should cut him some slack.

This has nothing to do with what happened between Jude and me last night. He can't leave the loft without having a panic attack.

12

ANGELINA

I hold out a hand that feels like a woefully inadequate gesture, given the situation. Jude stares at it for a minute, like he isn't sure he wants to take it. The blue of his eyes shifts through a dozen shades and a million emotions before he eventually slides his palm against mine, and I tug as he pushes himself up off the floor.

We stand, facing each other, our gazes locked, neither of us looking away for a few moments. A shudder rolls through him, breaking the trance, and I walk with him into the bathroom, keeping a close eye on his body language to ensure things are moving in the right direction.

He leans against the counter, taking several deep breaths, his eyes squeezed closed. His lips move rapidly, as if he's talking to himself, hyping himself up to do something. He takes a deep inhale and grasps the hem of his T-shirt to pull it off, lifting it to expose his rock-hard abs and chest.

Shit.

I back out of the bathroom and turn to head back to the

living room to give him some privacy, but a single word stops me in my tracks.

"No." The strain in his voice pulls at the pain I always carry with me. "I need you to stay in here. Just"—he closes his eyes again—"turn around or something."

"Okay."

Jesus, I don't know what to do here.

It's like being thrown into the deep end to save someone drowning without having any idea how to swim yourself. I've spent thirty years treading water, barely keeping my head above the choppy, deadly sea. Each storm that hits drags me back under, and each time I have to fight my way back to the surface, it gets harder and harder. More weighing me down. And now Jude is the one going under, and I have no idea how to rescue him.

He tugs his shirt over his head, fully exposing his perfectly chiseled body.

I may want to still see that little boy who sat in the closet so terrified on Christmas Day, but Jude is far from a child. And I definitely shouldn't be looking at him like this.

Turning my back to him, I lean against the doorjamb, listening to the sound of his clothes hitting the floor. The shower door slides open and clicks closed, and I shift back and lean against the counter where he just was, trying hard not to let my gaze wander to the left into the steamy shower stall.

Crack.

Something falls against the tile, and I jump, my head whipping in that direction.

Jude stands under the spray, his hands pressed against the wall in front of him. Even from here, I can see his body shaking the way it did out in the living room. With his head dropped low, he looks so...destroyed.

Everything in me screams to go to him, to help him, but I don't know how.

How do I help him when I don't even understand what's going on?

Only one thing comes to mind.

The single thing I can think of that I might want if I were in his position.

It's a huge gamble because Jude isn't like everyone else. He doesn't crave social interaction and despises when people invade his personal space—even more when they try to touch him.

But I can't stand by and watch him suffer without at least trying to help.

I grab the hem of my own shirt.

What the hell are you doing, Angelina?

Probably something I shouldn't.

I pull the soft fabric over my head, let it fall to the floor, then slide off my jeans, leaving me in my bra and thong.

My hands shake as I slide open the shower door. His head jerks up at the sound, and he glances back at me, his eyes an ocean of pain and fear.

A bar of soap rests near the drain between his feet and must have been what I heard him drop. The way his entire body trembles so violently, he probably can't even keep his hand around it.

I bend down and pick it up, then take two steps toward him until the spray off him starts to hit me. He continues to watch me, his body frozen stock-still, the water pounding down on his neck and upper back.

He doesn't say a word. Doesn't tell me to stop. Doesn't automatically shift away the way he usually does when someone approaches.

I close the distance between us and wrap my arms around him, tightening them against his heaving stomach and pressing my cheek between his muscular shoulders.

Almost instantly, his body relaxes, sagging forward slightly

173

as if a giant weight's been lifted from him with my simple touch. The hot water drenches me, soaking my bra and panties.

But I just hold him.

The only thing that matters is that he's okay.

When his breathing returns to normal, I pull my cheek from his wet skin and wait for him to say something, but he doesn't move, doesn't react. I tentatively slide the soap along across his muscled back, over every ridge and valley, then down his legs and reach around him to clean his tattooed arms still bracing him off the wall.

I slip my hands around him again and glide over his strong chest and work my way down toward his rippling abs, but his hand lashes out and tightens around my wrist, stopping me.

What the hell *am I doing?*

He pulls his other hand from the wall and takes the soap from me, then gently squeezes my wrist again. It's all he needs to do for me to know that I need to get out, that I need to get away from him.

For both our sakes.

I take a few steps back and watch as he keeps his back to me and continues to wash himself over and over, scrubbing at his skin until it's bright red.

"I need you to stay in the bathroom with me to make sure I don't scrub my skin off."

"Jude..." My voice sounds strange coming back at me off the tile. "You need to stop."

He stiffens, then lets the soap fall to the tile again. It swirls in the water and settles against the drain. He releases a heavy sigh, then shifts slightly under the water to tilt his face up into it.

One thing is abundantly clear—I shouldn't be watching. But I can't tear my eyes away from the way the water trickles over the muscles of his shoulders and back, how when he raises his arms to run them through his wet hair, it sends a rush down over his perfectly formed ass and thick thighs.

Jesus, I have to get out of here.

I grab the shower door, slide it open, step out, and snatch one of the towels hanging on the rack right outside, wrapping it around myself. The soft, fluffy material settles against my skin, and the image of his—raw and red—flashes through my head.

Maybe I shouldn't leave him alone...

I turn back toward him, but he still has his face turned into the water. "You should get out, Jude."

He nods, then reaches forward and turns off the water. But he doesn't move, just stands there, staring at the tile in front of him.

Clearing my throat, I snatch my shirt and jeans from the floor. "I'm, uh, going to go get my clothes back on."

I hustle out to the kitchen to grab a Ziploc bag to put my wet underwear and bra into.

This clearly wasn't a well-thought-out plan because I have nothing else to put on under my clothes. Instead, I towel off the best I can, drop my wet undergarments into a bag I fish out of one of the drawers, and tug on my jeans and T-shirt.

My nipples pebble immediately against the soft material. "Shit."

I press my palms against the granite and drop my head, trying to get some sense of what just happened.

My phone buzzes in my back pocket, and I pull it out and find a dozen missed calls and five frantic texts.

ASTRID

Where the hell are you? You just disappeared.

Was that Jude?

Answer me.

Where are you?

> I'm calling my dad if you don't respond to
> me!!!!

Fuck, fuck, fuck. I totally forgot about Astrid.

She came out of the kitchen to find me gone without any explanation.

I'm a fucking asshole.

I fire off a text.

ANG

> I'm so sorry. Jude needed help with something urgent. I'll be back as soon as I can.

But I can't leave him like this—not until I know he's okay.

The man was worried he was going to tear off his own skin, and seeing him like that, I can see how it would happen. But now that I've witnessed all this, it puts so much into a different perspective.

God, I've been a fucking asshole.

I should've seen it, should've known.

He's never been comfortable at family functions, never really interacting with anyone but Allie, always off in a corner by himself. He never really went anywhere but our events and school…

Those were signs, right? That I should have seen?

Does anyone else even know?

Allie must.

How could she not, given how much time they spend together?

Fuck.

I catch movement out of the corner of my eye and find Jude stepping from his bedroom, a pair of jeans and a white T-shirt now covering his pinkened skin.

His eyes meet mine, filled with so much shame.

Jude isn't ungrateful for what the Hawkes have done for him.

176

He isn't angry.

He's fucking broken.

———

JUDE

THE WAR I'm already fighting in my mind and against my own body only gets more intense the moment I see my worst nightmare in the kitchen.

Why didn't she leave?

I wanted her gone when I came back out. Didn't want her to see me like this anymore. Couldn't let her witness the aftermath of my epic spiral. I wanted to be able to pretend it didn't happen. Act like she never experienced me in this state. That I didn't just reveal that broken, helpless part of myself to the woman I've loved for as long as I can remember.

But that desire to hide this part of me from her battles with every fiber of my being, *wanting* her to be here for me. Waiting to take me in her arms again, to hold me and give me that same feeling I had for those brief moments in the shower when I could forget how fucked up I am and relish in having her touch against my bare skin.

It's always a damn battle where Angelina is concerned—between what I know is wrong and what my heart can't live without.

And seeing her standing at the kitchen counter, her hair soaked, T-shirt clinging to her bare breasts after she removed her wet bra, nipples practically poking out through the thin fabric, knowing she doesn't have any underwear on under those jeans, a whole new battle begins.

Fucking hell.

I scrape my hands over my face and slink off toward the couch without a word, willing my body to stay in control.

What do I even say to her?

There isn't any way to explain what just happened without embarrassing myself even more, without making it impossible ever to look her in the eye again.

I slowly lower myself onto the leather cushion and drop my head back to stare at the metal beams on the lofted ceiling.

Minutes tick by with an awkward silence hanging in the air, and I wait for the slam of the door closing as she leaves to go back across the street. Where she *should* be. Doing her *job*. Running her damn business. Not babysitting me the same way she did when Allie and I were ten.

Only it doesn't come. Instead, the soft sound of her bare feet padding across the wood floor tentatively move closer.

My entire body tenses, my hands fisting at my sides. I let my eyes drift closed, like that will someone erase the last hour.

Do I tell her to leave or stay?

The one person I *never* wanted to see me like this is the one who got me through it. I can't pretend it didn't happen, that she doesn't *know* now.

Fuck.

I sense her in front of me, that warm cinnamon and coffee scent somehow still clinging to her, even after being in the shower. It wafts over me, and I inhale deeply, taking it in, holding it in my lungs as long as I can before I release it, slowly lift my head, and let my eyes open.

Angelina sits on the coffee table facing me, her fingers locked together tightly in front of her, leaning forward with her elbows rested on her knees, but she doesn't look at me. She stares at her hands as if they're the most interesting things in the world, or maybe she just *can't* look at me anymore after what she just witnessed.

"What was that?" Her question comes soft, barely above a whisper, almost like she's afraid to even ask it.

I release a heavy sigh. "Fuck."

This is the last conversation I want to be having with her, with anyone, but I can't just tell her to go now. Knowing Angie as well as I do, I know she wouldn't go anyway.

"Something I had hoped you would never see."

She nods slowly and finally glances up at me. "When was the last time you left this apartment?"

Jesus. She knows how to cut right to the issue, doesn't she?

I pinch the nape of my neck and try to think back.

You don't have to think.

You know exactly when it was—to the day, to the hour, to the minute.

I want to look away when I answer. I want to bury my face in my hands so I can't see her reaction, the one I know is coming. But I force myself to hold her gaze, to stay locked swimming in the Caribbean blue. "One year, eleven months, and thirteen days ago."

Her eyes widen slightly. "You haven't left here in almost two years?"

I shake my head and see the wheels churning in hers.

Those bow lips I pressed mine to only yesterday open and close a few times, and she finally manages to find the words she's looking for. "But you came to Nana's. You were at all the openings. The events. You were always with Luca and Byron. You weren't exactly chatty and interacting with everyone, but you *came*."

"That was a long time ago. Before..."

"So...what happened?"

I lean forward and rest my elbows on my knees, dropping my face into my palms. "I really don't want to be having this conversation with you, Angie."

If I have to tell her what triggered all this, I will never be able to face her again.

"Shit, I'm sorry, Jude." She releases a sigh. "I don't want to make you uncomfortable, asking things I shouldn't. I just don't know what I'm supposed to do here."

Getting into the shower with me practically naked was one way to deal with it. I never would have asked, wouldn't have recommended it under any circumstances, but her touch calmed me instantly, like a soothing balm spreading across my body. Just like she always has, Angie provided me that safety net, ensured I was protected.

Even though it could have been something so different, it was innocent. She took care of me...like I'm a child.

She shouldn't have to fucking do that.

"I can't." I shake my head. "I can't talk about this with you."

"Please, Jude." She reaches out and rests her hand on my leg, her touch searing me even through the fabric separating my skin from hers. "I want to help you, but I need to under-stand to do that."

I jerk my head up and lock my gaze with hers again. "No."

"I owe you a huge apology for the shit I gave you about bringing the coffee, about you not going to Sunday dinners and missing other stuff...I didn't realize you were going through this." She waits for me to say something, and when I don't, she pulls her hand from my leg. "Does *anyone* know?"

I stare at her and don't bother giving her the answer.

"Please, Jude." A single tear falls from the corner of her eye, and she swipes it away. "Talk to me."

It seems like such a simple ask.

People talk to each other every day, share their hopes and thoughts and dreams, discuss their nightmares and what haunts them in their sleep, but it's different when the person you're staring at has been the *only* woman you've ever wanted. The only one you dream about. The only one who has ever gotten your cock hard and made you believe there was a chance to find something resembling happiness.

"I can't."

Her soft brow furrows, her distress making her release a little frustrated sigh. "Why?"

Swallowing back the emotion clogging my throat, I look her directly in the eyes so she really hears me. "Because I never want to see you looking at me the way you are right now again."

She recoils like I've slapped her and shifts back on the coffee table, dropping her eyes back to her hands. Her bottom lip disappears under her teeth, and she shakes her head. "I don't know what to do—"

The buzzer sounds downstairs, and I flinch, placing my hands flat on the couch to push myself up and go handle whoever is at the door.

Angelina gets to her feet first. "That's probably Allie. I texted her."

I freeze. "You *what*?"

She gives me an apologetic look. "I didn't know what to do, Jude." With a sigh, she waves absently toward the corner I collapsed in when we got inside. "You were practically fucking cata*tonic*."

Her voice breaks on the final word, and she chokes back a sob and heads toward the door.

Fuck.

The whole thing scared the shit out of her, and I've been too absorbed in my own mental conflict to even think about how it's affected her.

She presses the buzzer but doesn't come back over by me, just leans against the kitchen counter, waiting for Allie. Seconds tick by, and I open my mouth a dozen times to apologize for being such a dick to her, but the condo door flies open, and Allie rushes in, a whirl of dark hair behind her.

Her worried gaze darts from Angelina to me. "Jude, are you all right? What the hell's going on?"

I wave a hand to stop her from completely flying off the handle. "I'm fine."

Sort of.

She races over to the couch and throws her arms around me, burying her face against my neck and squeezing me tightly. "What happened?"

I showed your sister another reason to stay very far away from me.

As if she needed another one...

Allie looks up over my shoulder at Angie. "You want to tell me?"

Angelina's sigh fills the air. "I'm going to go back to work."

I don't turn or even thank her.

If I tried, I would completely fall apart again. I just let Allie hold me as I think about how I fucked up everything even more and have no way to ever go back. How Angelina will never look at me the same way again.

13

ANGELINA

No matter how hard I try, it's impossible to tear my eyes away from the front window. I can't stop myself from peeking up to Jude's condo, looking for him, waiting to see his familiar blue eyes and mop of blond hair as he stares down at the street.

But no matter how many times I look up there when I should be getting the café ready to open this morning, he never appears. Nor does Allie, even though she spent the night with him last night.

Something that *shouldn't* bother me so much.

She stays over there all the time, and I never questioned it before. But now, I can't stop wondering if she sleeps in the bed with him or on the couch. If they snuggle.

No. Stop.

Even if they do, it's none of my fucking business.

If they can give each other some sense of peace and normalcy in their lives, if she could do something to help him last night, that's a good thing.

The only thing that matters.

It isn't about Allie.

It's always been you.

Jude's words ring in my head, the ones I haven't been able to stop thinking about since he said them. The ones I was so certain didn't mean anything. But even hearing them over and over again doesn't change the thing that feels an awful lot like jealousy creeping up.

That's fucked up, Angie.

So, I'm standing here, watching a window, when customers will begin coming in soon and I don't have anything ready.

I force myself to return to putting the baked goods into the display case, trying to create a mental list for myself of what I still need to make. My usual morning routine has been shot to pieces by my inability to concentrate on anything except what happened and wondering if Jude is okay.

My eyes drift to the window again just as the door at street level pushes open and Allie appears. She checks for traffic, then crosses and stumbles into the café, breathless and disheveled in the same clothes she showed up at Jude's in yesterday, her hair pulled back into a messy bun.

She immediately beelines for the counter, looking as exhausted as I feel.

Was she able to sleep? Because I sure wasn't.

I set down the now-empty tray. "Is he okay?"

She releases a heavy sigh and inclines her head toward the kitchen. I grab my coffee and the empty tray and follow her back there, where I should be in the first place, making sure everything gets in and out of the oven on time.

Half-finished trays of cookies and other pastries scatter the counters, and she scans the room and turns back to me. "I see you couldn't concentrate this morning."

I set down the empty tray and tighten my grip on the mug. "How can I after *that*?"

She drops her purse onto the small desk and lowers herself into my chair, dropping her head back and cracking her neck side to side. "How bad was he before I got there?"

I wince and lean against one of the metal counters. "I mean, I don't really have anything to compare it to, but it was pretty fucking bad, like the-day-we-met-him bad."

She winces. "Shit. Well, at least he didn't end up back in a closet."

"He..."

Shit. How much should I tell her?

This isn't something I can keep to myself. Not when he's such a major part of the family. Not when everyone loves him and only wants to help, especially Allie.

"He told me he hasn't left his condo in almost two years. Not for *anything*."

Allie flinches and rests her elbow on the desk, dropping her face into the palm.

"Did you know?"

She glances up at me. "I suspected, but no, I didn't know for sure."

"Allie, how could you not know your best friend hasn't left his goddamn place in two years? How is that even possible?"

Annoyance flashes in her Hawke-blue eyes, and she throws up her hands. "Because he hid it from me the same way he hid it from everyone." A faraway look takes over, like she's thinking back and trying to make sense of all of this the same way I have been. "He went to school. He came to all our family stuff. Even if he didn't want to be there, he *came*. And then one day, he told me he was dropping out of his master's program and was going to write full time." She shrugs. "I didn't think anything of it. His first book had already been signed by the publisher. He had a big check sitting in his bank account. Luca and Byron already bought him the apartment and the space for the bookstore, so he had a built-in business ready to go. I never suspected there

185

was more going on than him just concentrating on that career and thinking he didn't need a degree on a piece of paper."

"But you told me—" I stare into my coffee, trying to figure out if there's a way to ask this delicately. "You told me that he went out and hooked up with different girls all the time who he met on apps."

Something that always bothered me far more than I ever wanted to examine.

Allie plays with the strap on her purse, avoiding looking at me. "Because *he* wanted me to believe that. On nights I didn't stay there, he acted like he had taken a writing break and gone out." Her shoulders rise and fall. "I didn't have any way to disprove it."

"But you never questioned it?"

She finally looks at me again, and the pain there matches my own. "I did, eventually, when he literally wouldn't go *anywhere* with me. When he wanted me to bring him coffee every morning instead of coming over here like he used to." Allie shakes her head. "At first, I didn't think it was weird because he gets in these almost trances when he's writing."

I can definitely see that happening. Jude can be intense in a normal situation, but when he's writing words like the ones I saw on his computer, he must be in a completely other world.

Staring down into my coffee, I think back over the last few years and everything that's happened. "But, I mean, he's missed Nana's birthday parties. Thanksgivings and Christmases. He hasn't even met Jack or Viviana yet..."

Allie's lips twist almost wistfully. "I remember seeing him standing at the window, watching us when they made the announcement that she was pregnant. And Luca seemed, I don't know, pissed, upset, something, when he came over from Jude's to join everyone."

"I remember. Do you think they know?" I raise a brow. "They have to, right?"

Her lips turn down. "Shit, what if they don't?"

We stare at each other for a few minutes, neither one of us knowing what to say or what to do next.

I take a sip of my coffee and think about everything Luca and Byron have said about Jude lately. "I don't think they know. It's why he hasn't done the bookstore yet, and I don't think they'd be pushing it if they understood what was happening with him."

She nods slowly. "He won't even go downstairs in his own building..."

"Did he tell you anything more after I left?"

Allie climbs from the chair and starts pacing the kitchen. "No. Anytime I tried to bring it up, he'd redirect the conversation back to this." She points to her still-flat stomach. "I guess I'm an easy target now."

Christ. With everything that's going on with Jude, she and I haven't even gotten to sit down and have a conversation about that very big topic.

"So, he didn't say a word to you?"

She chews on her nail. "No, not about what happened, just that he didn't want to talk about it and that he was fine."

"He is most definitely *not* fine."

Tears well in my eyes again, picturing him in the corner. The way his body shook. How he almost scrubbed off his own skin in the damn shower.

"You think I don't know that?" Allie shakes her head, tears finally streaming from her eyes. "He's my best friend. Seeing him like that..."

"By the time you got there, he was so much better. You should have seen him when I found him outside the café. I almost called Aunt Nora or Skye or Pope."

It probably would have been better if I had.

Jude would have hated me for dragging them into it and letting someone else see him like that, but it would have meant he got *real* help. None of them, with all their medical training, could have walked away from *that,* not knowing he needed it.

"Why didn't you?"

"Because he asked me not to, and I didn't want to further upset him by going against his wishes. But believe me, my finger was hovering over that fucking dial button."

"How did you calm him down?"

Shit.

Allie definitely isn't hearing about my impromptu shower with a very naked and traumatized Jude.

I take a sip of my coffee and clear my throat. "He just needed somebody with him. That's all."

She nods slowly.

The chapters in Jude's first book that I read and what Byron told me about the contents rattle around in my head, and I stare down at my shoes, my discomfort at having to ask this almost making me swallow the question down. "Do you think this has anything to do with whatever happened to him before he came to live with Luca and Byron?"

We never talk about it.

In the fifteen years since they showed up on Christmas Day with the skinny, blond boy who wouldn't say a word and sat in the closet while we all celebrated, the Hawkes haven't pried into what brought him to Luca and Byron. All we ever needed to know was that he needed a home and they offered him one.

The closest I ever got to actually getting any specific information was the *one* thing Luca told me that day, that they had to protect him from his father.

Allie shrugs. "I don't know. He won't talk to me about it. But it must've been really bad because I know he has nightmares."

My spine stiffens. "Nightmares?"

She nods. "They don't seem as bad when I'm there, but every once in a while, if I show up early and he's asleep, I can hear him crying out through the door."

I lean back against the wall and drop my head on it. "Do you think we should talk to Luca and Byron or Aunt Nora? Pope? I don't know what to fucking do."

She twists her lips. "I don't know, either."

Lifting my head, I let my gaze drift down to her still-flat belly. "And Jude isn't the only thing we need to have a discussion about. You need to tell Mom and Landon that they're going to be grandparents."

Her entire face whitens. "I'm not going to do that for a little bit."

"What?"

"I'm just..." Allie shakes her head. "I need to figure some things out first."

"So, you expect me and Jude and Aunt Nora to keep this a secret for how long?"

She throws up her hands. "I don't know, just until I figure it out."

"Figure *what* out?"

My clipped tone makes her retreat a step, and I instantly regret it coming out that way. It's just the last few months, everything that happened with Satriano and Roselli, Falco Enterprises, and now all these new complications, it feels like things are piling on enough to suffocate me.

And keeping this from Mom and Landon for any length of time will only make it harder on everyone.

"I don't know." Allie shrugs. "All of it."

"Have you told the father yet?"

Her lips press together in a hard line, and she shakes her head. "It's only been one damn day since I looked at the results."

And now she'll try to use what's happening with Jude as a way to put off dealing with her own situation. It's classic Allie behavior —live recklessly and handle the fallout only when it becomes impossible to ignore any longer. But this isn't something that can be pushed onto the back burner while she attempts to make everyone focus their attention on another family member's issues.

"You need to tell him."

"I will, but I just need a little bit of time so that when Mom and Dad ask me what the hell my plan is, I have one and I don't look like a total moron who got knocked up and now doesn't know what to do about it—which is exactly what I did and where the hell I am at."

Tears stream down her face, and a sob slips from her lips.

"Oh, honey. It'll be okay." I set down my coffee, walk over to her, and pull her into my arms, tightening her in a hug that's probably a little too hard. But if I don't, she might try to run— another classic Allie move. "Everything will work out with you and this baby."

She buries her face against my shoulder, her tears soaking into my shirt. "What about Jude?"

"I don't have a fucking clue about that."

———

JUDE

Somehow, through some miracle, I've managed to avoid looking out that window today. Or maybe it's out of sheer fear that I might *actually* see her, that I might see that look in her eyes again.

That pity.

The thing *no one* ever wants to see from the person they love.

Angelina will never look at me the same again after seeing that. She'll never be able to, and I can't even blame her for it. Not when I can't even look at myself right now.

My feet pound on the treadmill, and sweat pours down my

bare chest and back. I can barely breathe at the pace I've set, but I won't stop pushing myself, not until I collapse.

It's the only way to run this out, to get rid of all this anger and frustration bottled up inside me after what happened yesterday. The only thing I can do to even *try* to release the tension and the pain.

Because I sure as fuck can't write right now.

All that would come out is word vomit.

I can't concentrate on that story, on that world, when it's based on my real one, which has been flipped upside down over the last few days. With everything out of sorts and such a jumbled mess, I won't be able to put anything on the page that isn't a mess, too.

The knock on the door finally pulls me from the trance my run is starting to put me in.

Shit.

Immediately, my gut twists.

What if it's Angie?

Allie would've just walked right in, and I wouldn't expect her back until after her shift ends later.

I would love to pretend I'm not here, ignore the door and just keep running, but if it is Angie, she'll know and won't go away until I open up for her.

"Fuck."

That doesn't leave me any option but to slam my palm down on the stop button, climb off the treadmill, and make my way to the door. I tug it open and let out a relieved breath when Byron offers me a tight smile.

He gives me a once-over. "I hope I'm not interrupting anything."

My chest heaves as I try to catch my breath, and I motion backward. "Just running. But I'm done."

Even if I wanted to, I couldn't make it much longer, no

matter how hard I pushed the limits of my cardio. I would have collapsed on that machine well before I hit mile eleven.

Byron raises a brow. "May I come in?"

Unlike Luca, who prefers to just barge in whenever he wants, Byron actually respects that this is my space, my home, even if they were the ones who bought it for me.

I step back from the door to let him enter, and he pats me on the shoulder despite what a sweaty mess I am.

"It's good to see you." He gives me a tight smile, but warmth radiates in his brown eyes like it has since the first day I met him. "It's been a while."

The pain in his words lances through my gut. It's my fault we haven't seen each other in at least a month. Because I always say *no* when they invite me over, or call to see if I'm going to come to Nana's for Sunday dinner, or to one of Atlas' fights, or to meet Isaac's girlfriend and daughter.

I've missed it all, and the guilt threatens to swallow me whole as I let the door close and follow him in, still trying to catch my breath and let my heart slow down to a normal rhythm.

Byron settles on one of the stools, then seems to think better of it and slides off to walk over to the window to look down the street.

"Did you just stop by to say hi or..."

Did Angelina tell them what happened?

What if everyone knows the whole fucking hot mess?

He glances over his shoulder and offers an apologetic look. "Luca asked that I come and talk to you."

"Shit." I wipe the sweat from my brow with my arm and yank a bottle of water out of the fridge. "So, you guys are doing the good cop, bad cop thing?"

A slow grin tilts his lips. "Would that make me the good cop?"

I smirk at him. "I don't think anyone would ever consider Luca the good cop."

We both laugh at that thought—Luca Abello, a *good* anything—and it releases a bit of tension from the air.

I chug half the water, finally able to breathe normally, even though my legs are shaking like Jell-O and the rest of my body hums and vibrates.

"Have you given any more thought to what you and he discussed the other night?"

I stretch my neck from side to side, trying to get it to pop. "I have."

Though far more time has been spent thinking about Allie's situation and my own with Angelina. The threat to her livelihood from those fuckers, Falco Enterprises, has weighed heavily on her, and I can't ignore the fact that I have the capability to do something that might help her ensure her business thrives when it could easily crumple under the competition.

"And have you come to any conclusions?"

Just that I'm a fucking wreck who's ruined the life you two tried to build for me, the one I had no right to.

They took me in, literally off the street, and gave me safety for the first time in my life. I never wanted for anything, and they never asked for anything in return until now. And all they're asking is that I do what I always told them I wanted to, what my *dream* has always been.

And I can't even do that.

"I don't know when I would be ready to open the bookstore..."

The mere *thought* of going down the hallway again, of descending those steps, of opening that door is enough to make bile rise in my throat. But I remember the joy I felt the day they bought this building and told me their plans for it. That I would finally have what I had always wanted. It was the first time I felt like I had a place that was truly *mine*.

I don't want to lose that any more than I want Angelina to see me differently now. "But I still want to do it. I don't want to give up on that dream."

He approaches slowly and stands on the other side of the counter, watching me carefully, as if he's searching for something I'm not willing to say. "I spoke with Isaac and Jack about it again."

"And?"

Isaac isn't the type to let anything go once he gets it in his head, and if Jack means as much to him as everyone says she does, then he will do anything to give her what *she* wants. Even if it means trampling over my dream to accomplish it.

Byron crosses his arms over his chest, still muscular and imposing, despite already hitting his sixties. "And what if there's a way to compromise?"

"What do you mean, *compromise*?"

He shrugs slightly. "It's a big space." His eyes move around the condo. "Same footprint as up here."

I nod slowly. "Yeah? What are you getting at?"

"What if we outfitted the place in a way that the back third could be a studio workspace for Jack and the front two-thirds could be both a bookstore and an art gallery where she could sell her pieces while you sold books?"

An image of what it might look like down there flashes in my head. The way I had always seen it, with floor-to-ceiling shelves and rolling ladders. Everything separated by genre. Featuring not just the popular books but the ones that touched something in me and deserved the spotlight.

I never considered anything resembling art in there, but the picture morphs even as I think about it.

"Is her stuff really good enough to sell?" I hold up a hand. "I don't ask that to sound like an asshole, but—"

"You haven't even met Jack."

I squeeze my eyes closed. "No." I release a breath and return

194

my gaze to him. "Which is why I ask. Although Allie has told me a lot about her, and Allie has seen her stuff. *She* thinks it's good."

"It is. Isaac's a smart businessman, Jude. He's not going to ask to do something like this if he didn't think they could make some money on it."

"Unlike the non-existent bookstore that's sitting empty underneath us right at this moment?"

Byron's gaze softens to the same one he always gave me when I was a child, when I had a meltdown or would lock myself away in my own head. "Look, Jude, we know you're going through something." He holds up a hand to stop me as I'm about to protest. "And you don't have to tell me anything. *Really*. Luca and I, of all people, know what it's like to keep things close to the chest to protect ourselves and even others, but we've tried to give you space to work through whatever it is, and...it's been a long time."

His shoulders rise and fall.

"We miss you. Everyone misses you. And now that we have this competition coming in down the street, we have to think very long and hard about what's best for the family. And that means putting something in downstairs. I'm not trying to take your dream away from you. I would never do that, but maybe we can just tweak that dream. Let her do what she needs to do downstairs, then when you are ready, you can do what you need to with her."

It isn't an unfair ask. In fact, it's a lot more than I thought they would offer. Given how forceful Isaac can be when he wants something accomplished, I figured he'd find a way to get Luca and Byron to hand over the keys without a second thought.

Maybe I underestimated the men who became my fathers, but I shouldn't have, not after everything they've done for me.

I owe this to them. I owe this to the Hawkes. It's frankly the least I can do, especially when it's only going to benefit Angelina.

"I think I could live with that."

Byron grins, then leans forward and rests his hand on top of mine on the counter, squeezing it softly. "Good. I'm going to tell Isaac to call you so that you can talk with him and Jack. We can have a crew here as early as next week sometime to get started."

I nod slowly, the thought of work actually happening downstairs starting to make my skin crawl slightly. "Okay."

He pulls his hand back. "I know Nana would really like to see you at Sunday dinner this week, if you think you can manage to find the time."

His gaze darts over to my laptop on the floor near the windows, then back to me with a hopeful half-smile.

Lying to him and Luca has been the hardest part of all of this. Constantly making excuses. Always sounding like I don't care about the Hawkes, the family that took them in and then accepted me with open arms with no questions asked. But the thing that might absolutely kill me is knowing Nana has been waiting for me for damn near two years to show my face at her dinner table.

Just thinking about going tightens my throat. "I'll see what I can do."

He gives me a hard smile, understanding it means I won't be there. "Well, hopefully, we'll see you then."

I down the rest of my water as Byron walks toward the door, knowing full well why he didn't try to hug me goodbye.

His hand tightens on the knob, but he pauses before he opens it. "You know, we're proud of you, Jude, no matter what. There's nothing you could do or say that will ever change that. So, if you want to talk about whatever is going on, our door is always open."

Fuck.

He opens the door, and it closes with a click behind him as tears start to well in my eyes.

This would be so much easier if I were part of any other family. If I had been dumped in the foster system and kicked out on my own at eighteen, I wouldn't have anyone who gave a damn. But instead, I'm letting everyone down.

14

JUDE

Thunder rumbles outside, close enough that it rattles the windows, and I look up from my computer to the black clouds billowing overhead. Rain pelts the glass, a sudden deluge that blankets the world in a cleansing shower that only reminds me of being in mine with Angelina.

What was she thinking?

Actually, I don't want to know. It would only depress me more and shove me deeper into the foul mood I've been in all day.

Typically, a stormy evening would be great for my writing mojo and get me in the perfect mood for an all-nighter, but I've been staring at the blinking cursor for so long without typing a single word that it feels like it might never flow easily again.

All the things I love and hate about life—including Angelina—have always been the source of all my creativity. Putting on paper the things I can never voice. The stuff that would always remain hidden, that *had* to. But now that I've been exposed, now that *she* has seen me, when things are *finally* out in the open, I'm too terrified of what other truths might come to light to write anything fictional anymore.

I set my laptop on the floor beside me in favor of watching the storm roll in. Each rumble of thunder, every crack of lightning shattering the sky, the raindrops pinging on the windows, they all slowly melt into another memory.

Mom stares out the window with me at the storm, a smile on her face for the first time in days. "I love the smell of rain, Jude. It reminds me that we each get a new chance every day to wake up and do something good with our life. A reminder that all sins wash away."

I've thought about those words so much over the years, wondered what she could have meant by them. At five, I didn't have a clue what she was talking about, and I didn't know to ask. I didn't know how important everything she ever said to me would become, how her words would follow me through years of what Dad put me through once she was gone. How I would cling to them like lifelines when I had no others...until I met the Hawkes.

Now I've driven them all away through my unwillingness to accept their embraces. My inability to let anyone in. The need to keep myself walled up to feel safe has only hurt the people who actually care.

But it's the way it needs to be.

Nothing, not even the most powerful storm off the Gulf, can wash away the taint marring my mind and body. The permanent scars and ugly truths that will forever live in me.

The very reasons Angelina should stay far away.

But even knowing that can't stop me from watching and waiting, wondering what she's thinking after what went down yesterday. It's all I've thought about all day, and it will be another sleepless night tonight, imagining all the horrible things likely running through her head about me.

Another rumble of thunder shakes the windows, this one

softer, the most intense part of the storm having passed over, and lightning flickers in the distance.

The café door swings open, and even through the rain and the darkness already settling over, Angie's gaze meeting mine heats my entire body.

Go home.

It would be better for both of us if we just went back to the way things were, where we kept this glass wall between us and pretended we were nothing more than forced family.

That's impossible, though.

Angelina cares too much. Feels too hard to just let what happened go without trying to *fix* it.

She'll learn fast that this isn't anything she can fix.

Instead of circling around the back of the building to where she parks every day, Angie bolts across the street toward my building, dodging the puddles forming near the curb.

Shit.

I thought I'd have more time to prepare for this, to figure out what to say about what she witnessed.

The buzzer doesn't sound, so Allie must have given her the key again, and the soft knock at the loft door confirms that.

Each step I take toward it feels like a damn mile and walking toward something I've fled from for so damn long. But I can't outrun this. I can't outrun her.

I shove my hand through my hair, trying to get it out of my eyes before I flip the lock and open the door. I've never wanted to disappear so badly, to crawl back into that damn dark closet corner and hide out until it all passes. But she isn't going away. Ang isn't going to *let* me hide.

She stands in the hall, her hair soaked and matted to her face, shirt clinging to her, her pebbled nipples straining against her lacy bra and T-shirt. Her jeans haven't fared much better, water dripping from them onto the tile in the hallway under her Chucks.

A sheepish smile tilts her lips. "Hi."

"Um...hi?"

Fucking smooooooth, Jude.

Real smooth.

"Can I...come in?"

I almost say no. It sits on the tip of my tongue, ready to leap off to prevent this woman from getting close to me again.

Anything she has to say isn't anything I want to hear right now, yet that pull, that deep yearning I always feel for her, makes me step back and let her enter.

The fresh scent of the rain mixes with the sugary-sweet one that is all Angelina as she moves right to the kitchen and turns to face me. "So, I've been doing some research online today."

I squeeze my eyes closed. "Please don't."

"And I talked to Pope."

My lids fly open. "You *what*?"

She holds up her hands, eyes wide and filled with guilt and concern. "I didn't tell him it was you. Okay? I just spoke in general terms and said I had a friend who was dealing with some agoraphobia."

Fucking hell...

If I *were* to go to anyone in the family about what's been going on, it would probably *be* Pope, since as an "adopted" member of the Hawke family, he's in the most similar position to understand the crushing weight of their expectations. But I didn't want him to know. I don't want *any* of them to.

"Why the hell did you do that?"

Angie releases a frustrated sigh, her gaze softening. "Because I want to *help* you, Jude."

"I don't want your help, Ang."

Her heart. Her love. Even an ounce of her affection. But *not* her *help* like I'm that same lost boy she met so long ago.

"Maybe you don't. Maybe you are happy to stay locked up in here by yourself for the rest of your life"—her voice breaks, and tears shimmer in her eyes—"but I'm not going to let that happen."

I'm terrified to ask the question, of what the answer might be. "Why not?"

She focuses her attention on the counter for a minute, running her hand over the smooth surface before she looks back over at me. "Because I care about you too much to do that."

My heart stops for a moment, and we stare at each other, neither of us breathing, neither of us moving, neither of us able to break the spell her words have cast.

Her tongue darts out over her lips, and she takes a step closer. "I want to try something."

"What's that?"

A dark brow arches. "Do you trust me?"

"Yes." I don't hesitate for even a second when I answer. I've trusted her from the moment we first met, the first time we touched. It was instant. A connection I've never been able to shake, a knowledge that no matter what, I *could* trust her. That she would always do anything in her power to protect me and ensure I was safe. "I've always trusted you, Ang."

"Then...come on."

She holds out her hand, and I stare at it, afraid to put mine in it, both because I know what I'll feel physically and because I don't know what she's going to do with me.

Another step brings her even closer. "Please."

Slowly, I lift my hand and set my palm on hers, the connection immediate and staggering. The same sharp crackle of energy pulses between us even as an instant sense of calm settles over me.

Her fingers tighten around mine, and she tugs me toward the front door.

I stop and pull her to a halt, my chest tightening. "What are you doing? I can't."

"Take a deep breath."

Tamping down my rising panic, I do what she commands.

She tightens her grip on me. "We're not leaving the building, okay?"

"What?"

The corner of her mouth twitches slightly. "Baby steps, and you'll be with me the whole time. Nothing's going to happen except you and me taking the stairs to the roof."

"The roof? But"—I glance at the darkness outside the windows—"it's still raining."

Her shoulders rise and fall. "So? I seem to remember you loving to run outside in the rain."

Holy hell.

"How do you know that?"

I've never told *anyone* about my love of running in the rain. How every time the angry skies opened, I would throw on my running gear and hit the street, relishing the cool drops pelting my skin, the fresh scent filling the air, the sense of God cleansing the world, enveloping me more and more with each step.

"I know you better than you think, Jude."

Right now, she *might* know me better than anyone, but she still doesn't know the truth. Still doesn't know everything.

Her blue eyes glow warmly as she waits for me to say something. "Will you go with me?"

I suck in a sharp breath, trying not to think about all the things that always keep me locked away in here. It's just the roof. My own building. Directly above us. No one else has access. It's *safe.*

She tightens her hand on mine. "We can always come right back in."

Fucking hell.

Instead of calming me, her reassurance only builds my

anger at myself because she shouldn't have to do it. I'm a grown-ass man she has to treat like a fucking child.

That anger alone is enough to make me want to prove to her that I can do this. "Okay."

She opens the door and steps out into the hallway, and I freeze inside the jamb.

Her thumb brushes across the top of my hand, sending a shudder down my spine. "It's thirty-two steps for me to the staircase. Less for you."

She fucking counted.

"Remember to *breathe.*"

Like that's so easy...

Angelina leads me down the hall.

One. Two. Three.

Her thumb brushes across my hand rhythmically, pulling attention from counting my steps and to the soft buzz the contract creates through my body.

We reach the stairs, and she turns to face me, still holding my hand. "Are you breathing?"

I nod. "Yes."

"Good." She motions up and takes the first step, waiting for me to follow. "Come on."

One by one, we take the steps up until we reach the solid metal door that separates us from the roof. She presses her hand on the bar that runs across it and pushes it out.

The refreshing scent of rain slams into me immediately, and I inhale deeply as she tugs my hand softly, urging me onto the flat expanse of the building's roof.

Heavy, wet drops still fall from the dark sky that's only lit by occasional flashes of lightning. Low rumbles of thunder in the distance indicate the direction of the storm's retreat after dumping the deluge on us.

A reminder that all sins wash away.

Angie turns to face me, raindrops rolling down her face and resoaking her. "Is this so bad, being up here with me?"

I shake my head and stare down into her eyes, unable to pull mine away. They hold so much hope, yet so much uncertainty I share. "No, but only because it's you with me."

Her brow furrows. "What do you mean?"

"Hell..." I rub the back of my neck with my free hand and look away. This would be an easy time to flee back to the loft, to avoid having to answer, but at this point, she already knows so much. I've already said things I can't take back. "You know why I was able to go to those family things? How I was able to tolerate it?" I return my gaze to her. "Because *you* were there."

She stiffens and swallows thickly. "But you went to school..."

I nod slowly. "And I spent most of the day counting down the hours when I could get back home or here to see you." All those days I raced home from campus rush through my head, seeming so damn long ago. "I worry about you leaving at night by yourself. If something were to happen, I couldn't—"

Her fingers squeeze around mine. "Nothing's going to happen to me."

The rain continues to fall, soaking through my shirt and chilling my skin despite the heat. "You can't say that, Ang. You have Falco just down the street and Roselli showing up at your goddam music night."

She flinches. "I know, but neither of them is stupid enough to do anything except maybe ask me out on a date."

It's my turn to stiffen, and a low growling sound I don't recognize comes from deep in my throat.

———

ANGELINA

Jude slides his free hand under my chin, gripping it tightly and tilting my face up to him, his jaw locked, muscles in his neck straining. "Cass asked you out?"

Shit.

I hadn't anticipated him reacting like this. "He didn't mean it." I try to wave it off with my free hand to dispel the rage I see simmering in Jude's gaze. "It was just a cruel *joke*."

One of his pale-blond brows rises. "A *joke*? Why do you think he didn't mean it?"

Why the hell would *he?*

This should be obvious to anyone who knows the Hawkes' situation with Falco Enterprises, to anyone who knows *me*. But some sort of switch seems to have flipped in Jude, something that lit up the green tinge of jealousy I see in his eyes.

"Because he works for the company trying to bury me, Jude. He wasn't being *serious*."

He grinds his jaw, his grip tightening slightly on my chin. "I'm pretty sure he was."

"Why do you say that?"

"You think I don't see what goes on?" He releases my chin and motions toward the street, where the Grind sits closed and dark. "I may be up here, but I can see everything that happens there." He leans closer, until the warmth of his breath flutters over my face, a sharp contrast to the cooling rain. "Cass has been watching you, and it isn't just because he's interested in taking down your business."

I shake my head vigorously, unable to accept it's even a possibility. "I don't think so."

Jude shifts even closer, his body aligning against mine, hard and unyielding. "I know what it looks like when a man is interested in a woman, Angelina, and Cass Whitaker is definitely interested in you." He grabs my chin again, forcing my head up and locking his fiery gaze with mine. "I don't like it one fucking bit."

A shudder rolls through me, and I have to clench my legs against the sudden throb between them. This is a whole different side of Jude. One I've certainly never seen. This Jude is jealous and possessive, and he's completely forgotten where we are or why he should be panicking.

I shouldn't ask the question working its way up my throat. Once I hear the answer, I'll have to deal with the consequences of it, but Jude's gaze blazes into me, searing my skin and raising heat to my cheeks. "Why not?"

"Why do you think, Angie?"

I try to dip my head because if I keep looking at him, I'm going to say or do something very stupid, but his grip on me keeps me in place, forcing me to see the passion blazing in his eyes. "Don't say things like that to me, Jude."

He shifts slightly, pressing his chest to mine harder, his growing cock pinned between us. "Why the hell not?"

Fuck.

The rain picks up slightly, from the heavy drizzle to a constant waterfall that raises goosebumps across my exposed skin. Or maybe it's the way Jude seems to be unraveling me so easily when I came over here to try to help *him*.

"You know why, Jude."

"No"—he drags his thumb over my lips, gripping my hip with his other large hand and squeezing the flesh there—"I don't."

"Because our parents are practically like siblings. Because—"

"We're *not* cousins, Angelina. We're *not* related."

"But I'm—"

"You're twelve years older than me." The corner of his mouth twitches into a half-grin. "Yeah, I get it, but trust me, this isn't a mommy-issue thing. It's a *you* thing."

A me thing.

It's the kind of thing every woman dreams of a man saying

to her, a declaration that goes straight to the core of what makes me *me*. The things that drive me, that make me tick, those are the things Jude sees and wants, but I can't let myself fall into this trap of believing any of this is real, that any of it can ever *happen*.

There's a reason I've pushed myself so hard with the business. A reason I'm there twenty hours some days. A reason I don't leave room for anything else in my life besides work and taking care of Allie...because I'm utterly terrified that if I let anyone else in, I'll get destroyed the way Mom was when Dad died.

I may have only been five, but I remember how she fell apart, the days she wouldn't get out of bed, the nights she cried herself to sleep, trying and failing to hide it from me. They live in my memory as clearly as the memories I have of Dad.

His smile. His laugh. Swimming with him at Nana's house. Our rides in his car. Him taking me to construction sites and showing me how to use all the different tools that fascinated me so much. The warmth of his strong arms wrapping around me when I cried.

I can't go through what Mom did. I can't handle a loss like that. I'm not strong enough.

And even if I were, what Jude wants isn't possible. It can never happen. He has to understand that. He has to know it as much as I do, even though my body clearly doesn't and craves to be like this with him, to feel his hard chest pressed to mine, his hands on my face, our lungs sharing the same air.

I try to tug out of his hold, but he grips my arm and pulls me back up against him.

"Don't leave, Ang." He loosens his hold on me, feathering his fingers along my jaw. "You said coming out here was a baby step, but you have to stop thinking about me like I'm a baby, like I'm a child, like I'm that little boy you met that night."

God knows I haven't been...

Not recently.

Not for a long time, if I'm being honest with myself.

It would have been impossible to ignore Jude, to not see how beautiful he is, how much he's grown as a person, and the type of man he's become. Even hiding away behind his invisible walls or these very real ones, he exudes an intelligence, an energy that screams to be seen.

He reaches out and captures my face in his hands, caressing me this time, gently nudging me to look at him instead of trying to force it like before. "I'm not a child anymore, Ang. I haven't been for a long fucking time. Since well before you met me, even. I may be fucked up in all sorts of ways, but I'm not a damn child you have to handle with kid gloves."

The pain in his words, the guilt, the embarrassment, it eats away at me like acid being poured over my heart.

I press my hands against his chest, clinging to the soaked material. "You're not fucked up, Jude."

He barks out a laugh into the storm and drags his thumb over my lips. "I am. I'm beyond fucked up. I'm more fucked up than even you realize. But it doesn't mean I don't know what I want."

I suck in a sharp breath. "What do you want?"

Jude's eyes burn in the night, blazing through the darkness up here, surrounded by the driving rain. "Do you really need me to answer that for you?"

The words I read the other night, the ones that reached deep into my soul and tugged at it, twisting me around and destroying what I thought I understood about him, come rushing back. "You didn't mean any of what you said before. It's just...the adrenaline of what happened the last few days. It's the—"

"Stop." He presses his thumb against my lips, silencing me. "Stop making excuses for how you feel." Anger tightens its grip on me, but it isn't directed at me, just the damn situation. "I know how hard you work, and I know why you do it." His jaw hardens. "Because you want to fill your life with something, anything other than the potential for love. Because you're afraid of what would happen if you ever lost it like your mom did. You put your entire soul into that café, and now, you're afraid you're going to lose it. That's what has you so rattled, not what I just said. It's the thought that someone might love you as much as your mom loved your dad. You don't know what to do with that."

His words strike at me as hard as Atlas's blows, and I struggle to pull in another breath.

"I'm done with that, Ang. Done with feeling guilty for wanting what I do or being afraid of taking it."

I know better than to ask again, to let it hang between us, filled with so much damn pressure and consequences. "What do you want?"

"You, Angie. I told you the other night, and I mean it—it's always been you. I've been in love with you since I was ten fucking years old."

"Don't say that."

He dips his head, hovering his mouth just over mine. "Stopping me from saying it isn't going to make it any less true, Angelina. I don't care if there are a thousand reasons not to do this. I'm going to do it, anyway."

Thunder rolls in the distance, and Jude presses his lips to mine before I have a chance to even contemplate the words he just said.

They move over mine, not slow, not sweet the way he kissed me the first time. This time is filled with a pent-up desperation, a passion, an aggression, and a need.

My fingers twist in his shirt as heat spreads between my legs and through my belly. I wrap my arms around his neck and drag him closer, needing the pressure of him pressing against me, the warmth he provides, the sense of rightness that consumes me when doing something so wrong.

He backs me to the roof door, devouring my mouth, kissing me fiercely, almost savagely, like he can't get enough of it. His cock hardens fully between us, rubbing against my pelvis, and I shift up onto my toes, trying to align it in exactly the right spot.

Lightning tears through the sky immediately overhead, lighting up the roof and crackling electricity in the air around us.

I moan into his mouth and twine my fingers in his hair, slipping my other hand down to cup him through his jeans. He stills instantly, his entire body going stiff.

He jerks his head back from me, eyes wide, hair wet and disheveled, plastered to his forehead and temples. That same fear that's lived in his eyes for the entire time I've known him returns, erasing the heat and desire that was once there.

"Jude, what's wrong?"

Shit.

Maybe he just realized exactly what I've been trying to tell him, that we shouldn't be doing this, that we *can't* do this. No one will understand, least of all Allie, and she doesn't need this kind of massive upheaval with everything else going on in her life right now.

He stares at me blankly for a moment, eyes unfocused, like he's lost somewhere else and not here with me at all anymore. Then he shakes his head, rubbing his palms into his eyes.

I take a step toward him, lifting my hand to grab him, but he drops his hands and seems to look right through me to the door behind.

Without a word, he brushes past me, tugs it open, and storms down the steps, his heavy footfalls echoing up the stairwell.

What the fuck just happened?

15

ANGELINA

J ust like most Sundays before dinner, Allie, Astrid, and Bishop tip their heads together over the Scrabble board, arguing about something that seems completely insignificant given everything else going on.

From over here, I can't hear the debate, but I typically give those wins to Astrid. There's a reason she's the teacher in the family. She knows the most obscure words and facts, and despite her rather laid-back and calm demeanor most of the time, when it comes to winning at a game, we all know to watch out for her competitive nature.

My gaze drifts to Allie, who watches Bishop and Astrid going at it, a smirk on her lips. It's nice to see, given how stressed we've all been, but it won't last. She has to tell Mom and Landon soon. Pregnancy isn't something you can hide forever, especially in this family.

I take a sip of my wine and scan the rest of Nana's living room. Aunt Nora's gaze meets mine from where she sits with Stone, Isaac, Jack, and Viviana. She glances toward Allie and gives me a knowing look, then raises an eyebrow and inclines her head toward where Mom and Landon stand, talking to Gabe and Skye.

Did she tell them?

The question goes unspoken, and I give a quick shake of my head to let her know we still can't say anything.

Nora offers a slight shrug and tight smile. She, of all people, understands what Allie is going through. It wasn't exactly perfect timing when she and Stone got pregnant with Isaac. But just like they did, Allie will figure it out. Maybe with the help of a few friendly nudges from Jude and me.

If he ever talks to me again.

I still can't figure out what the hell happened last night. The way he ran and locked himself back in his loft. Ignored me pounding on the door and my texts and calls after...

It was as if a flip had switched, but I have no idea what I did that caused it to happen. I was on the verge of doing something very stupid, something we would never be able to take back. Something I haven't been able to stop thinking about all damn day despite trying to distract myself with helping prep dinner and getting pulled into various discussions about those Falco fucks and Roselli's little visit.

How do you forget a kiss like that?

Uncle Savage comes from the kitchen, but instead of moving toward where Danika and Kennedy sit with Pope, Saint, and Caroline near the window, he approaches me with his brows raised. "I thought you'd be in a better mood, given that you finally managed to get Allie to show up." He glances over at her. "It's nice to have her back at Sunday dinner."

I nod and offer him a tight smile, then take a sip of my wine. "Yeah, it is."

His assessing gaze narrows on me, like he's seeing right through the façade I've tried to keep up all night that everything is okay. "Then why don't you look happy? Worried about the Falco Enterprises situation?"

My gut twists again, the same way it does every single time I think about it—especially now that we know their next move, which is far bigger than anyone could have seen coming. "I just don't understand it—why they have it out for us, why they are so damn intent on trying to ruin everything."

Over the last few years, they've mimicked every major business we have—the bars, the restaurants, the strip clubs. And now, not only are they targeting the Daily Grind, but Stone and Isaac unearthed the probable reason for Nancy and Cass' little coffee date—they're going after the Hawke Hotel before we even break ground.

Cass failed to stop it with his attack through the zoning board, so Falco Enterprises has taken the next major step. Opening a competing property of their own...directly across the street from the land we have earmarked for the Hawke Hotel.

Isaac and Stone are already at work trying to get an injunction to stop anything before it even gets started, but given the aggressive attacks Falco continues to direct our way, even if we manage to stop it, something else will only come at us from another side.

Savage sighs, rubbing his hand along the dark stubble spotted with gray on his jaw. "I wish I had an answer for you, Ang. Believe me. We've been trying to find one for the last few years since they showed up. But whoever's behind them, whoever has this vendetta against us, is good at covering their tracks." He reaches out and rests his hand on my free arm. "But they won't win. Hawkes always rise."

My foul mood can't stop the grin from pulling at my lips. "Hawkes always rise."

The saying that has been floating around in the family for thirty years seems to lift everyone's spirits, even in the darkest of times. And for some reason, hearing it from him, of all people, the one who had every reason to lose faith over the years, gives me a little bit of hope that things will work out—at least where the businesses and Allie are concerned.

Now, Jude, that's another story.

I sip my wine and drum my nails against the glass as I watch everyone talking, laughing, and having a great time while they wait for Nana to announce we're allowed to move to the table.

Savage continues to eye me, reading me easily, the same way he always does with everyone. "There's something else bothering you."

"Huh?" I glance over at him, doing my best to appear surprised by his statement. But there isn't any point in trying to lie to him. The man sees too much. "Just kind of disappointed we couldn't get Jude to join us, too."

His eyes soften. "I have a feeling that one's going to be a lot harder."

He has no idea...

Or maybe he does.

Given how much Savage seems to know about everything that goes on in this family, it wouldn't surprise me if he somehow already figured out what's been going on with Jude.

Looking back, I should have seen it. *Would* have if I hadn't been trying so hard *not* to focus on Jude. If I hadn't been fighting against that pull toward him so much that I wouldn't even glance his way for fear of what it could do to me.

My gaze drifts over to Luca and Byron near the fireplace, where they talk with Isaac and Jack, who have left Viviana to play with her grandmother, probably discussing the potential for opening the shop below Jude's place, which seems even more important now.

Luca's dark eyes meet mine, and he says something to them

before he approaches Savage and me. "What are you two talking about that has you looking so grim?"

Shit.

I force a tight smile, trying to fight the heat of a blush with my answer. "Your son."

He sighs and takes a sip of his bourbon, then leans back against the wall next to me and crosses his arms over his chest. "We were just talking about the bookstore/art gallery potential."

We've been too distracted by...other things...to even discuss the plan they presented him that would completely change the original idea for the store. "Did he agree to that?"

Luca scrunches up his face and holds out a hand, wiggling it side to side. "Sort of? Byron spoke with him, and he seemed receptive to the idea."

"Well, that's progress, right?"

It would require Jude to leave the loft, unless he was going to put one hundred percent of the planning and operation into Jack's hands, and I can't see him doing that when that shop was always his dream.

I can't really picture him willingly going downstairs to do what he would need to, either. At least, not yet.

Everything I read and Pope told me about agoraphobia suggests addressing it is a long, complicated road that never leads to a true cure. Cognitive behavioral therapy and medications can only do so much. And Jude isn't talking to anyone about this, not even me.

Savage watches Isaac lean in toward Jack and whisper something that makes a flush spread over her cheeks as he rubs his hand on her expanding belly. "It is progress, but none of us want Jude to feel like he's being boxed out. We all respect that it's his space, but we also have to do something with it before Falco gets that coffee shop open."

I don't want to betray Jude's confidence by saying anything

about what I know, but their hopefulness that he's going to be able to actually get that place up and going might be misplaced. "Are you guys ..." I glance between them. "Are you confident Jude's capable of doing this right now?"

How else do I ask it without revealing things I know he doesn't want to be public?

Luca and Savage exchange a look, and Luca takes another sip of his bourbon, considering his answer.

His jaw tightens as he stares into the glass. "Frankly, I'm not sure. When we bought the place, when he moved in, he was so excited about it, raring to go."

I nod. "I remember he was down there every day, measuring, sketching plans..."

Those memories of how he *used* to be come rushing back. Of him coming in every morning and setting up his laptop at the corner table so he could see the whole café and work until he had to head to class. Of the way his eyes followed me and I tried to avoid meeting them with my own because of the intensity they always held. Of how, even then, I knew Jude was something special, *someone* special, as more than just an adopted member of the Hawke family. And I need to figure out a way to get that back. To get *him* back without revealing something I shouldn't.

Gabe barks out a laugh at something Skye says to him, then leans in and presses a kiss on her cheek. His eye catches Savage's, and he raises a brow, concern darkening his green gaze. With everything going on, of course, he'd be wondering what we're discussing over here, especially if Savage is right and I haven't been hiding my mood very well.

Savage inclines his head toward the other side of the room, indicating Gabe should meet him over there, leaving me alone with Luca, one of the only people who might actually hold some of the answers I've been seeking about Jude.

"Do you think..." I meet Luca's hard gaze. "Do you think maybe something's going on with Jude...more than we realize?"

That's vague enough, right?

It opens the door for him to volunteer anything he knows, for him to give me any indication that Jude's struggle *isn't* as big of a secret as he seems to think it is.

Luca gives me a tight smile. "That boy has been through more than any one person should ever have to suffer. Byron said you read his book."

I nod slowly. "Part of it. To tell you the truth, I had a difficult time reading it, knowing that a lot of it's true."

"It isn't even the tip of the iceberg."

His comment mirrors what Byron told me the other night, and my stomach instantly sours. I open my mouth to ask how big that iceberg is when Nana's voice rings through the house.

"Dinner's ready!"

As if I could eat right now.

Everyone starts to file out of the living room toward the dining room, and the back sliding door opens. Coen and Atlas step through it, beers in hand, both looking tense. Atlas puts a hand on Coen's arm to stop him near the kitchen and leans in to say something that makes Coen jerk back and glare at him before he stalks away toward the crowd gathering in the dining room.

Atlas' eye catches mine, and I raise a brow.

"Everything okay?"

He waves me off with a tattooed hand. "Don't worry about it."

Under normal circumstances, I might try to delve a little deeper into what's going on with Coen. The youngest Hawke always seems to be drifting between jobs at the clubs and restaurants or on special projects for Savage or Gabe, aimless and not seeming to *want* to find a direction. But right now, there are far too many other things to worry about than Coen's listlessness and what was probably a petty argument with Atlas.

Luca doesn't make any move to head toward the table, so I don't, either, letting the rest of the family file past us to take their seats.

Nana bustles out of the kitchen with one of several trays of lasagna, her gaze narrowing on us. "You two aren't eating?"

I open my mouth to assure her we were just about to go in, but Luca places his free hand on my arm, stopping me.

He gives Nana a hard smile. "We're just discussing Jude. Give us a few."

"Oh..." Her reproachful look disappears, replaced by a depth of concern that slumps her shoulders slightly. "Okay, then."

There are very few things Nana will accept as excuses for missing Sunday dinner or being late to take our seats at the massive, custom-made table—Jude being one of them. She wants him here as badly as anyone.

Once she disappears into the dining room, Luca runs his hand back through his salt-and-pepper hair. "How much do you know about his life before he came to live with us?"

I shrug. "Not much, except what you told me when you brought him here that first time, that you were trying to protect him from his father."

Luca's jaw tightens, and a muscle there tics. He downs half his bourbon. "Yeah, well, it wasn't just his father."

"What do you mean?" The possibility makes me stiffen. "His mother, too?"

He shakes his head. "His mother was the one person who actually tried to protect him, so when she was gone, things got very bad."

"Where did she go?"

Luca downs the rest of this drink in one massive gulp. "She

died several years before we found Jude. He spent four years alone with his monster of a father, and the things he endured…" He shifts his weight, his shoulders stiffening, hand tightening around the glass. "It frankly surprises me he's done as well as he has. We did everything we could for him—took him to doctors, therapists, tried to get him to understand that what happened to him didn't have to define the rest of his life. I thought—" He closes his eyes and swallows thickly. "I thought he was doing well. I thought he had finally found a way to move on from the torture he endured, and then…it was like he took this massive leap backward and shut down again, shut us all out."

"Two years ago?"

His gaze darts to meet mine. "You noticed it, too?"

It would have been impossible not to see the change. He literally disappeared from the family, from the café, from everywhere but that damn window I couldn't stop looking at.

"Yes, do you think something triggered him? Something set him back?"

He nods. "I'm almost positive, but Byron and I are terrified of pushing him for an answer. We're afraid he'll regress even more and we'll lose him forever."

The emotion in his words brings tears to my eyes, and one falls before I can swipe it away.

We have to figure out a way to help him. Pushing him to the roof with me last night seemed to be an epic failure that only led to him locking me out again, but it seemed like a good idea at the time. A "baby step" in a space he could still feel safe, to experience something I know he always loved.

Yet, it backfired miserably.

Maybe the key is figuring out what triggered him in the first place, and given what Luca just said, one possibility races to the forefront.

"Could he have maybe…run into his father?"

Luca's already dark eyes go black, his jaw tightening so much that it probably cracks his teeth. "Impossible."

"How do you know that?"

He pushes off the wall and leans in close, locking his onyx eyes with mine. The pure hatred and determination in them send a shiver down my spine. "I made sure he would never hurt Jude again."

———

JUDE

They stood in the rain, both of them wanting. The pain of their longing gnawed away at them from the inside out. It had become a living, breathing thing, capable of hurting everyone around them as much as it did them.

BUZZ! BUZZ!

The buzzer drives me away from the scene where Rosalie finally gets everything she's been searching for, where the still-nameless hero in the story doesn't run away.

That world is so much easier, a place where the rain truly does wash away all sin and heal all scars, giving everyone a fresh start.

If only it were that simple in this *world.*

BUZZ!

Who would be here this late on a damn Sunday night?

I grab my phone and get to my feet, but I don't have any missed calls or messages from anyone. With the entire family tied up at Nana's, I wouldn't expect to hear from Allie until tomorrow anyway, but maybe she told her parents and wants to come talk to me about the fallout.

But Allie would just use her key...

A cold sweat breaks out over my skin as I look down at the

sidewalk. Angelina steps back from the door so I can see her and holds up what looks like a tinfoil-covered plate in her hand.

"Shit."

The single word hangs in the air like a grenade, and staring at her looking up at me with a hopeful half-smile, that's what it feels like, too.

I've tried not to think about what happened last night, how I completely blew my chance with her after making her cross that line she's always dancing along between what's wrong and what's right, what she wants and what she believes she deserves, the one that separates what she fears and what she craves.

That was it, Jude. Your chance. Maybe you're one *opportunity to show Angelina everything she is to you.*

And you fucking blew it.

I can't ignore her again tonight. I can't keep myself locked up in here and pretend like I did last night. I can't stand with my back to the door, listening to her begging me to let her in.

My heart can't handle that again.

Letting her in is the lesser of two evils, even though something tells me it will hurt just as much.

I run a hand back through my disheveled hair as I walk to the door and buzz her in, the list of her inevitable questions rattling through my head.

Why the fuck I pulled away...

Why I ran after I pushed her...

Why I didn't take what we both wanted...

Fuck.

Her soft wrap at the door makes me stiffen, and I take a fortifying breath and tug open the door.

She offers me the same half-smile she did from the street and holds up an apparent peace offering. "I brought you a plate from Nana's."

The day we met comes barreling back instantly.

Angelina opening that closet door and sliding two plates of food in for Allie and me...

The way my heart thundered against my rib cage every time she came back to check on us...

Her genuine smile lifting some of the anxiety I had felt since the day before when Luca and Byron had found me and told me I was going home with them....

The reassurance she gave me that everything was okay, that *I* would be okay eventually...

The thing that I have clung to for so many years.

That day changed everything. It was the start of my new life and my love for Angelina Matthews.

She watches me, so hopeful, plate extended out to me like a lifeline I so badly want to take, but something holds me back. The knowledge that I might not be capable of giving her all the things I want to. The confidence that if she really knew my whole past, she wouldn't want it anyway.

The corner of her mouth curls up. "I-I figured you must be missing Nana's lasagna." She nods toward the plate. "And I put a big piece of chicken parm in there for you, too. I know it's your favorite."

She knows my favorite food.

Why does that send hope flickering through my heart?

Her smile falters, and something dark overtakes her wet gaze. She's holding something back, and that evaporates my hope as quickly as it came. "Can I come in?"

Saying no would be easier. I could take the food and close the door on her and this *thing* I was stupid enough to attempt, but the part of me that's become addicted to her touch and the way she makes me feel every time we're in the same room makes me open the door farther and take a step back, allowing her inside.

She pauses next to me and looks up, now close enough that I can see the red rimming her eyes.

"What the hell, Ang?" I reach out and grab her arm, that instant connection crackling between us. "Are you okay?"

"Yeah, I-I guess so." She swallows thickly and brushes past me. "I'll put this in the kitchen."

"You guess so?" It isn't like Angie to completely brush off a question like that, and that makes me hustle after her, letting the door click closed behind me. "Did something happen at dinner?"

It's been two years since I've spent my Sunday evenings with the Hawke family, but I still vividly remember how those dinners can be. Thirty people crammed into Nana's house. Wine, bourbon, food, laughter. All of it slightly overwhelming.

Angie sets the plate on the counter and turns to face me. "No, nothing happened. Allie still hasn't told anyone and won't talk to me. She just keeps saying she needs some time."

I step around her, careful not to let my body brush against hers, and pull off the foil from the plate. The familiar scent of Nana's cooking hits me hard, and my eyes start to burn with tears I never would have expected from a damn plate of food. My stomach rumbles, reminding me I haven't eaten all day, but I can't imagine doing it now with Angie standing next to me, looking so upset over something.

"Did you just come here to bring me this plate of food?"

She stiffens slightly, shakes her head, and turns to face me. "No, it was just an excuse to come see you."

"You need an excuse to come see me?"

The corner of her mouth twitches. "I mean, I guess not..." She glances down at her hands, interlocking them in front of her. "I talked to Luca and Savage tonight."

"Okay..."

"About the bookstore." She lifts her gaze to meet mine. "Seems like they offered you a good compromise."

I nod slowly. "I think so."

It's the only option, really. The more I think about it, the more I see they're right. I can't leave the space empty forever. Not when the entire street is full of bustling Hawke businesses...and soon, a major competitor. It would be selfish to keep it for myself when I don't know if I'll ever be able to actually set foot in there again.

Angelina looks away again, out the front windows, fidgeting with the hem of her shirt.

She won't even look at me.

"What is it, Ang? You clearly have something you want to say, so say it."

"Luca said something tonight..." She trails off and bites her lip, glancing up at the ceiling, and when her gaze meets mine again, tears shimmer there. "About your dad and how you met him and Byron..."

Ice immediately rushes through my veins, the scent of the food that had been so mouthwatering only a moment ago now nauseating me.

Luca and Byron always promised never to reveal anything about my past, *nothing* about how they found me or what I was doing to anyone except Nora for medical treatment and Savage and Stone because they needed to help with the legal finagling and favors they needed to push through my adoption quickly.

Why would he tell Angelina anything?

"Jude, please don't be mad at him for saying something. I told him I was worried about you. We were discussing the bookstore—"

"What did *you* tell him?"

"I didn't tell him how long it's been since you've left this place, okay? I would *never* reveal that to anybody without your permission. But I was just trying to understand what might have happened, what might have triggered all this, so that I can help you."

"I don't want your goddamn help."

She takes a step closer, then seems to think better of it, abruptly stopping her approach. "Bullshit, are you telling me going up on the roof last night, being out in the fresh air, feeling the storm, the rain...that you didn't enjoy that? Being back out, being able to experience the world?"

"I was only able to *do* that because you were with me. Because, for some damn reason, since the day we met, you've been a safe place for me." I fist my hands on the counter. "You can't be with me all the time, Ang, even if I might want that."

She winces and closes her eyes. "Is what happened before Luca and Byron found you why you're so reluctant to go outside?"

"Fuck."

I push off the counter and shove my hands through my hair, regret for opening that damn door for her growing with each word she says.

This isn't a conversation I ever imagined having with Angelina, but I can't hide it from her forever.

Can I?

I can't pretend I'm a normal, healthy human being when I'm very clearly not. Angie may think she knows me after fifteen years, but she has no idea who I really am, *what* I really am, what happened to make me this way and prevent me from living life the way it should be lived.

"What did Luca tell you?"

"Nothing specific, just that what your dad did to you and made you do was likely an ongoing..."—she searches for the right word—"issue."

Issue.

I snort a sardonic laugh and move around the island in the opposite direction from her to stare out the windows at the quiet street below. "My father was a piece of shit. My mother... she tried, but she was too in love with him to ever leave, even when it was bad. When I was six"—I swallow through the sudden rock in my throat—"when I was six, I watched him beat her to death."

Angelina's gasp fills the loft, and I squeeze my eyes closed, unable to turn to see her reaction. Not wanting to.

"What? No. Oh my God, Jude—"

I hold up a hand to stop her from saying anything else, even as I can sense her approaching me. "I don't want your sympathy or your apology for something you had nothing to do with. I'm not telling you for that."

And truly, I wish I weren't telling her any of this at all. But there's only so long I can keep this hidden from her.

All my sins and scars will get laid on the table for her to see now, and ultimately, what she does with the knowledge will be her decision. I can't change how she'll see me after she knows it all, after all the secrets I've held so close to the chest have been revealed.

A car drives by on the street below slowly, like the driver is looking for something. Just like Dad did that night, searching for the perfect location...

"He made me help him dump her body to make it look like it had happened on the street and not in the shitty apartment we lived in at the time. I was too young to understand what he was doing other than throwing my mother away."

Angelina's soft sob behind me makes me wince, but I can't look at her when I tell her this. I can't bear to see the pity and disgust in her eyes once she knows the whole truth. I clench my eyes closed, keeping myself protected from her judgment.

"I don't really know what he did to her. All I know is he never got caught. He never went to jail. He never paid for it. He just kept on going like he had when she was alive. Snorting and shooting anything he could get his hands on. Violent and angry when he couldn't get his fix. That's why he had me..."

I can't say the words. I refuse to speak them to Angelina or anyone else. Even through all the damn counseling Luca and Byron forced on me as a kid, I never said the words, and I don't plan to *ever.*

Thinking them alone is enough to make my stomach turn, for the brutal memories that haunt my nightmares to come racing back during my waking hours.

"He had me...helping him make money. I didn't have a choice. After seeing what he did to my mom, I knew what he would do to me if I said no, if I tried to run."

I finally open my eyes again and catch a glimpse of her in the glass, standing a few feet behind me, arms wrapped protectively around herself like a shield against my words.

She has no idea how much worse it's about to get, but if I've come this far, I might as well reveal the entire brutal truth.

"Luca found me in the parking lot of The Steele Hawke Cage, where my father had left me to try to make money on Christmas Eve..."

16

JUDE

"What?"

Her soft question only holds confusion, none of the judgment I expect to hear in it. It's the only thing that allows me to keep moving forward with the story, to tell her what eventually brought that little boy to the Hawkes.

I scrub my hands over my face. The memory of Luca's dark eyes meeting mine, the way I cowered behind the dumpster, afraid of what he would do to me, is so vivid, it's as if it were yesterday and not fifteen years ago.

And my first impression of the man who would become my father figure makes bile rise in my throat. "I thought he was just like the other men I had met there outside the club. I assumed he wanted something from me..."

Angie releases another sob, trying and failing to stifle it, and her soft footsteps move closer, making me tense.

"He took me into his office and brought in another man."

"Byron?"

I nod, casting a quick glance at her over my shoulder. "They told me they owned the club, that I wasn't in trouble, that they were just trying to find out what was going on. Asked me how I got there."

It had been natural then, just as it is now, to shut down when someone asked me something like that, especially someone I don't know.

"At first, I didn't say a word. Wouldn't even tell them my name. I was too afraid. But then Byron sat next to me." A smile pulls at my lips, remembering the kind way he looked at me, the sense of calm and ease he carried with him even when he was a complete stranger. "He told me he had been kicked out of his house when he was young, and he could see I was as lost as he was back then and that I needed somebody to help me. He said they wanted to be those people. And I don't know." I shrug and watch her slowly complete her approach and stop next to me, eyes red and tear stains down her cheeks. "For some reason, I trusted him in that moment when I never trusted anyone else my entire life."

She gives me a sad smile. "Byron has that effect on people. That's why he was such a good bartender back when he spent his time behind it. People tend to open up to him."

I snort and push a hand through my hair, watching a plane fly over, lights bright against the dark backdrop of the sky. "Yeah, well, I told them everything. I still don't know why, but I did. And Byron said they would protect me." I glance at Angie. "Luca didn't say a word. Now I realize it's because he couldn't. Because he was so angry that he was afraid he would lose control. At the time, I thought they were full of shit." A humorless laugh slips from my lips. "I believed my dad was the most powerful person on the planet. He was my whole world, and after what I had seen him do, I really thought he was capable of hurting anyone."

And worse.

Mom wasn't his only victim. He had no qualms about resorting to physical violence to get anything he wanted or allowing others to use it against me to take what *they* wanted.

I just didn't understand who Luca was and what *he* was capable of yet.

Angie slowly reaches out, giving me all the time in the world to move away, but the moment her hand hits my cheek, all the anguish building in me with telling this story starts to melt away. That low buzz ripples through me, electrifying every part of me, awakening all the reasons this is so good with her.

I lean into her touch slightly, press a kiss to her palm, then pull her hand into mine. "Are you sure you want to hear all this?"

She doesn't hesitate for a moment with her nod. "Yes."

Releasing a heavy sigh, I stare back out at the Grind, the same view I've had for so long that looks so different tonight. Maybe because things will never be the same with Angelina after this.

"Byron took me back to their place, the most fucking beautiful home I'd ever seen. And then he called a bunch of people. Nora came and did a medical exam, drew blood to test for anything and everything."

Her hand tightens around mine, and I squeeze it back.

"All these clothes and a dozen different types of food showed up. It was like a dream, but I couldn't even enjoy it because I was so fucking terrified of what my father would do when he found me."

"So, what happened?"

"They put me in a guest room with a comfortable bed and five-hundred-count thread sheets, but I couldn't sleep at all. At some point in the middle of the night, my door opened, and I immediately panicked. I assumed they were coming for..."

I trail off because after everything I've been through with them over the years, thinking they would have ever done anything like that makes me feel like a fucking asshole. I'm sure they knew what I thought, but they never said a word about it, never pushed me or tried to convince me of anything before I was ready to accept it.

Almost as if she can read my mind, Angelina leans her head against my shoulder and squeezes my hand again. "Given what you had been through, it's a reasonable assumption. You can't feel bad about that."

"I know that logically, but it doesn't mean I won't always feel guilty for thinking it, even for a second, when I was ten."

Luca and Byron have been my protectors since the day they found me, and they've never asked for anything in return. They're selfless and loyal to the core, which makes disappointing them so much worse.

"That night, when Luca came in and sat on the edge of my bed, he told me that he had spoken with my father when he came looking for me and that everything was going to be okay. He said I could stay with them if I wanted to. That they had it all worked out. Then he got up and walked out and told me I could lock the bedroom door if it made me feel safer."

"Did you?"

"I jumped out of that bed to throw the lock so fast, all the covers went flying."

Ang offers a humorless laugh. "And the next day?"

"The next day was Christmas."

She lifts her head and looks at me. "Good God, Jude. No wonder you were hiding in a fucking closet."

"I thought my father was going to find me there, at Nana's, that he was going to hurt all of you because Luca and Byron had taken me. I still didn't understand what was happening. But then, the next day, Luca and Byron called someone they knew in the human services department, and she came over to their house and talked with me. She asked me the most important question I've ever answered in my life."

One of Angie's dark brows rises. "What was that?"

"Whether I wanted to stay with Luca and Byron."

Angie shakes her head. "How did the parish allow you to stay with them? They weren't certified foster parents..."

"No, but your family has enough power in this city to get things done." I shrug and rub my thumb over the soft skin on the top of her hand. "From my understanding, they got emergency certification so I could stay, then got the paperwork going to adopt me."

"Didn't they need your father's signature for that?"

I nod slowly. "Yes, and they got it."

"But how? Luca told me..." She bites back her words, her eyes wide like she's said something she shouldn't have.

Hell, I guess if the cat's out of the bag.

I had been avoiding mentioning *that* particular portion of this story to protect Luca and prevent any potential consequences for what he did to protect me, but the look in her eyes tells me he already told her. Or at least said something that led her down the right road.

Rubbing the back of my neck, I turn my focus back out the window. "At first, Luca told me my father had signed off. That they had spoken the night they found me. They said my father had left town and was never coming back. But I...I wasn't sleeping. I was so terrified. I was always looking over my shoulder, waiting for him to show up. Worried he was going to hurt Luca and Byron or the Hawkes if I was out with any of you. After a month, Luca finally sat me down and told me that he made *sure* my father would never hurt anyone again."

Angie shifts nervously beside me, glancing at me out of the corner of her eye like she shouldn't say what she's about to. "Did he tell you that he..."

Killed him.

In any other family, this conversation would be absurd, but

235

the Hawkes aren't above taking care of things permanently when it's the only appropriate resolution.

And where Dad was concerned, it was the right call. I've never felt one ounce of guilt over what Luca did. He made the world a safer place by pulling that trigger.

"Not in so many words, but even at ten, I understood what he was saying. I had already seen a lot of death, so I knew he wasn't coming back, and it helped. I was finally able to breathe again."

The tiniest smile pulls at her lips. "I remember you were much more active with the rest of the kids, especially Allie, after a little while with us."

Even Allie doesn't know any of this, though I think she's pieced a few things together over the years. The best thing about her is she never pushes me for more than I want to offer. Not the way Angelina does.

It should piss me off the way she probes, but the genuine interest and desire to know me better, to help, makes it impossible to say no to this woman, no matter how much I may want to.

"Allie will always be my best friend. It's more like we're twins than just friends, really. She's like my sister."

Angelina looks away, down toward the café, and presses her free hand against the glass. "That's what makes this so hard." She closes her eyes and drops her forehead against the glass. "What are we doing, Jude? None of this makes any sense."

The last thing I want to hear from her right now.

I turn her toward me, tilting her chin up. "Yes, it does. It's the only thing that *does* make sense."

She stares at me, so much confusion and fear floating through her eyes that it makes me wonder if she'll ever believe that as much as I do. "If it wasn't your dad, then what happened two years ago to make you lock yourself away in here?"

The question makes me stiffen. "What does that have to do with us?"

She pulls her head back and out of my hold, like she needs to put some distance between us. "Because if you and I can't be open and honest with each other about *everything*, then whatever's happening between us doesn't matter, anyway, right?"

Sometimes, I wish Angelina wasn't so damn smart. So insightful. So caring. She wants to fix everything for everyone, and she thinks she can fix me, too. She thinks she needs to.

"You don't want to know everything about my past, Ang. Trust me, no one wants to hear all the dark and dirty details. And you don't *need* to."

"Yes, I do." She reaches up and places her palm flat against my chest, directly over my thundering heart. "I have to know, Jude, if I want to *really* know you. You keep so much of yourself locked away from everyone, but if you can't let your walls down with me, then what are we even doing other than setting ourselves up for some major fucking heartbreak that will hurt more than just us?"

I lean into her touch, that same simmering heat spreading through my body that always does when we're this close. She's right, of course. Just like she always is. That if there is *any* hope of us ever having anything together, she does need to know it all. But it doesn't mean I can look at her when I say this.

Closing my eyes, I rest my hand over hers, threading our fingers together, the thudding of my heart vibrating through her hand into mine. "I was on campus, heading to class for my master's program." I swallow, the vision of that day flashing against my closed lids, trying not to let the panic of that day engulf me now. The way the world spun. My vision blurred. Everything felt off-kilter. My lungs wouldn't work. "And I saw one of the men who hurt me..."

That's all I can say.

It's all I'll ever say to her about the specifics.

ANGELINA

"Oh, God." I tighten my fingers around his, curling them against his chest. "Why was he on campus?"

He opens his eyes to meet mine, the pure fear still there. "He's a professor. I didn't figure it out until I searched the university site later."

My mouth falls open at the revelation. "Oh, my God. Did you tell anyone?"

"No." He shakes his head. "I almost passed out. I hid, making sure he didn't see me. And then I managed to stumble back to my car, and I just...came home and..."

Tears burn my eyes, blurring my vision. "And you never left again."

Now that I know what made him lock himself away up here, now that I have this insight into his past and his pain, everything that's happened in the last fifteen years since that day we met makes so much more sense.

It has all clicked into place, like a million puzzle pieces finally aligning to create a picture of Jude Abello-Harris I never expected to see. And it explains *everything*. All the things we saw and used as reasons to think the worst about him were all a direct result of the horrific abuse he suffered, his way of coping with what had been done to him by the man who was supposed to protect and love him.

Why he was always so afraid.

Why he wouldn't let anyone but Allie and me touch him.

Why he never let *anyone* in, even the two men who became his fathers.

I finally understand it.

All of it.

I finally understand *him*.

Jude *wants* all those things. He *wants* to be a part of the life he has in front of him, the one he watches pass by outside those windows. He just doesn't know how to do it anymore.

He can't move past the trauma and the fear, his body physically shutting down every time he makes an attempt. When he thought he finally had it figured out, was doing great in school, had this plan for the store, and had published his first book, life threw this bastard in his face again, taunting him with what he suffered by letting one of the people responsible go free.

And just like he was never able to believe in his safety until he knew his father was truly gone and no longer a threat, he won't be able to move on from this and try to get back to how things were if nothing is ever done about the man who caused this trauma.

"Jude, you need to tell someone. The police, your dads—"

He shakes his head, his jaw tightening as his skin pales. "No, because that means telling them that I haven't left the goddamn apartment in two years. It means proving to them that I'm the failure they already think I am, that everything they did for me was for nothing. All the time, the money, the care they put into me for fifteen years...and I'm still beyond fucked up."

That's really what he thinks?

The fact that he sees himself that way and believes Byron and Luca do shatters my already destroyed heart. For such an incredibly smart man, Jude doesn't seem to have any grasp on reality where his own life and the people who see him are concerned. Everything Jude sees is shadowed by this belief his piece-of-shit father drilled into him that he wasn't good for anything except helping to feed his addiction. He could never trust anyone, and now, he doesn't even trust himself.

I shake my head and take his face between my palms, forcing him to look at me when he tries to turn his head away. "You're not fucked up."

He barks out a laugh that has zero humor in it. "I'm the definition of fucked up, Angelina."

"Then, I'm fucked up, too."

His gaze softens. "You're far from fucked up. You're absolutely perfect."

"Ha, I'm far from it." Though, the way he's looking at me, combined with his words, sends a warmth through me that goes all the way to my soul. "You know I'm not still single at thirty-seven because I'm some sort of Playgirl who has so many men throwing themselves at me that I can't choose and won't settle down."

The corners of his mouth curl into a grin. "I don't believe for a second you don't have men chasing after you. What about Dan Roe or Cass Whitaker?"

"Cass is a jerk, and Dan flirts with *everyone*. It doesn't matter, anyway."

"It sure as hell does."

"No, it doesn't, Jude. That's my point." I drop my hands from him and take a step back. "I'm just as fucked up as you think you are. When my dad died..." I shove my hands through my hair and shake my head. "It destroyed my mom. I was only five, but I remember it so vividly. She was a shell. She couldn't get out of bed, could barely take care of me, and definitely couldn't take care of herself. Half the time, she didn't go to work, and when she did, she'd come home and crawl right back into bed. The rest of the family helped take care of me. They made sure I got to school on time when Mom didn't have it together. They cooked for me, they took me places Mom never would again, the places I used to go with her and Dad."

A sob threatens to climb up my throat, but I swallow it back.

Anytime I think about Dad, about the time immediately after his death, before Mom met Landon and he woke her up from the listless non-life she had been sleeping through, I lose my ability to think rationally. Because she wasn't. Her life was gone. It had ended the day of the fire, and not even her *daughter* could pull her out of the abyss of sorrow she was content to drown in.

That isn't anything I ever want to experience, nor the guilt she carries now for how she feels she failed me during that time.

"The older I got, the more I understood why it happened. Because she let him become her entire world. She loved him so much that she literally couldn't function without him. I will never allow myself to be like that, Jude, to love anyone so much that losing them would destroy me. I've pushed away every man I've ever been interested in as soon as things started to get serious because I couldn't *allow* that to happen. I couldn't grow attached to anyone." I throw up my hands. "And now look at me, pushing forty with nothing to show for my life."

His eyes widen, anger flashing in them as he takes a step toward me. "Nothing to show for your life?" He motions out across the street. "You have a thriving business. You have helped build Hawke Enterprises into what it is today. You took care of all of us when we were growing up and *continue* to, even right fucking now, with me. You've done more than anyone could have ever asked of you and then some."

I shrug, tears finally flowing freely down my cheeks. "Yet I'm still fucking terrified when I start to feel something for someone."

He takes another step toward me. One of his blond brows rises slowly. "For me?"

Shaking my head, I retreat a step. "Don't do that."

Jude advances slowly. "Don't do what?"

"Don't pretend you don't know."

"What don't I know, Angelina? Tell me."

With his blue eyes blazing, staring straight through me, after what he just revealed, the whole sordid truth that only makes me love him more, it's impossible to hold it back any longer. "You know I'm not just *starting* to feel something, Jude. There's *always* been a connection between us. Something I felt the moment I saw you in that damn closet with Allie that day. I've always been drawn to you, Jude. Back then, it was as a protector, wanting to calm the fear I saw in your eyes, wanting to make sure you were okay—"

He takes two more steps until his chest brushes mine. "And now?"

Hell.

If I had any hope of resisting this attraction to Jude, it disappeared the moment he told me everything. I understood he was strong, that he had suffered and come out of something truly horrible, but knowing the violent, horrific details only proves how incredible the man standing in front of me is. What he had to go through to grow from that scared little boy in the closet to who he is now utterly destroys me. I can't ever see him as that boy again, and if I'm being honest, I haven't in a very long time.

"Now, I just want to kiss you."

"Fucking hell, Angie."

He wraps his arms around my waist and drags me against him, crashing his lips on mine. All the reasons that should make both of us stop seem trivial compared to everything he's survived to even be standing here today. All the tension and longing, the fighting with ourselves, it was all only delaying *this* inevitable moment.

Jude kisses me like a dying man starved for the air in my lungs. Taking it from me and sucking it down into his chest, which vibrates appreciatively against mine. Heat spreads from between my legs out through my entire body, a searing, burning need that threatens to fully consume me.

He groans into my mouth and backs me against the window, the hard glass behind me finally breaking through the haze that clouds my brain.

I pull my mouth away from his and press against his chest

to keep him back for a second, glancing behind me. Anybody looking up from the street could see us, could watch what we're about to do.

We're completely exposed here, and while the thought of Jude taking me against the window sends a little thrill rolling through every fiber of my being, neither of us is ready to make this public.

His gaze follows mine, and his cock twitches between us.

Apparently, the thought of us against the windows excites him just as much as it does me.

He grips my chin and forces my face back to his, kissing me again as he spins me away from the cool glass to walk me backward toward the bedroom.

His hard cock presses against my belly, and with every step that we move closer to our final destination, my clit throbs hard, my pussy clenching desperately for him to fill me.

Jude Abello-Harris is a quagmire of complications. Bruised, battered, and broken, so damaged he doesn't think it's possible to ever repair him, but underneath all that, his true beauty shines.

An old soul lives inside him, one that has survived more in twenty-five short years than anyone could ever imagine. And he's come out on the other side. He has, until recently, found a way to process his trauma and keep living, and he will do it again. I won't let him fail.

It doesn't even matter that we shouldn't be doing this, that there are a thousand reasons not to.

I couldn't stop myself now, even if I tried.

17

ANGELINA

Jude's hands tighten around my waist as he reverses me into the bedroom until my legs hit his mattress. I start to fall back, but he uses his strong grip on me to keep me tight against him, his hard cock eagerly pressing against me.

I twine my hand around his neck, tangling my fingers in long, thick hair, returning his kiss frantically.

But he tears his head away and grips my chin tightly, staring so deeply into my eyes that it feels like I may drown in his. All the desperation and passion there matches my own, but something else lingers beneath all of that, a different type of fear, the same one I saw last night before he ended things so abruptly and ran from me.

He's not doing that again. I won't let him shut me out.

"Jude, what's wrong?"

Maybe he's second-guessing this. Maybe all the reasons we shouldn't be doing it are finally coming to the forefront of this mind, but instead of backing away, he brushes his finger over my lips softly.

"I've been dreaming about this moment for so long, Ang. I never thought it would happen, and now"—he swallows, his Adam's apple bobbing slowly as he finds his words—"I'm afraid I'm imagining all of it. That this is some wild dream that seems incredible but is going to morph into one of my nightmares again."

My heart breaks for what he's been through, for the fact that he has to worry about what happens when he closes his eyes at night, about what demons will attack him from deep in his past.

I press my palms flat against his chest, curling my fingers into the fabric of his T-shirt and tugging him gently. "It isn't a nightmare. I promise you that."

"What if I fuck this up?"

"Fuck this up, how?"

He glances away for a minute, almost like he's contemplating whether to finish that thought or not. When he turns back to me, determination fills his heated gaze. "I want this to be perfect for you, for us, and I don't know how to do that."

"What do you mean you don't know how to do that?"

The way he's already lit my body aflame with just his kiss tells me everything I need to know about how Jude and I will be together once we hit this mattress.

He starts to pull away, but I tug on his shirt, keeping him firmly in front of me.

"No, you're not running away. Talk to me."

Releasing a heavy sigh, he lowers his forehead to mine. "I couldn't do it with anyone else. Believe me"—he releases a little sardonic laugh—"I fucking tried. All through high school and college. Blondes. Redheads." He twirls a finger around my dark hair. "Even brunettes with stunning blue eyes. But when it came time to actually do the deed"—he drags his head back and locks his eyes for me—"I was never *up* for it. Only when I was dreaming or thinking about you."

Holy shit. Is he serious?

"You don't mean…"

Surely, I'm misunderstanding.

He grips my face almost harshly and drags me up against him even more, grinding his erection against my stomach. "I've never been inside a woman—not in a throat, not in a cunt, not in a damn ass—because you are the only one I ever wanted."

Jesus Christ…he's a virgin.

How the hell is Jude a virgin?

A man who looks like him, who talks like him, who has the mind of a fucking genius, who could walk down the street and have any woman he wants…has never had sex.

"Say something."

"Shit." I shake my head, still cradled in his strong hold. "I don't know what to say. I'm pretty fucking speechless."

He starts to slip back from me again, his entire body stiff, unease and embarrassment rolling off him in powerful waves.

"No, don't." I wrap my hand around his wrist and drag it back up to my face, pressing a kiss against his palm and then his wrist, up his tattooed arm, to his bicep, where I swirl my tongue over the ink there.

He groans and tightens his fingers on my hip.

"It doesn't matter, Jude. Christ, it's been so long since I have been with anyone that I'm practically a virgin, too."

The low chuckle that rumbles in his chess releases the tension my initial reaction created, and he tugs his arm from my hold and topples me down onto the bed.

His long, lean body presses me into the soft mattress as he captures my mouth with his again, moving over it slowly, savoring every taste. I groan and arch my hips into him, aligning my core along his hard length.

He hisses. "Christ, Ang, and I can feel how hot and wet you are, even through my fucking pants."

I grin against his lips and kiss him back, tangling my fingers in his hair and using it to keep him where I want him, not letting him pull away. His hips begin to roll against mine, both of us frantically searching for something we won't find if this keeps going.

Tugging my mouth free, I reach down and grip his hips, stopping him. "If you keep doing that, we're both going to come before we're ready. And neither of us wants to do it like this, right?"

He issues a low little growl of frustration and rises to his knees, staring down at me as he undoes the fly of his jeans and frees his long, hard cock.

Good God.

My pussy spasms just looking at it, at him, at how fucking beautiful and strong he is like this. He grips it in his hand and strokes it several times as his free one grazes up my bare leg, tickling the sensitive skin as he makes his way to the apex of my thighs.

He lifts the hem of my dress, his gaze burning across every inch of my exposed body. A slight grin tilts his lips as he slips his fingers under my thong to find my soaked core. "*Fuuuck,* Ang."

Something about the way that word rolls from his lips makes me clench my thighs around his hand, and he groans his approval and slides a finger inside me easily.

Dropping my head back, I squeeze around it. "Fuck."

A satisfied grin spreads across his lips. He curls it to find that perfect spot, then slowly thrusts in and out of me, dragging his fingertip along the inner walls in time with the way he works himself over.

Holy hell.

I grip the sheets beneath me, desperate for anything to hold me steady. He adjusts the angle of his hand to slide his thumb up over my clit, and he rolls it there in a way that has me bucking against his hand while his other one slowly strokes his straining cock.

Jude may not have had sex, but he definitely fooled around with enough women to know what he's doing. The heat of an impending orgasm already builds low in my belly, and I squirm under his ministrations, trying to find my release from everything that has kept us apart.

My unwillingness to see what was right in front of me. My refusal to believe I can have this, have *him*. My damn all-around stupidity.

But instead of bringing me over that edge, he freezes and stares down at me, his finger still inside me, leaving me hanging on the precipice. A need burns across his gaze, barely hiding the uncertainty still lingering beneath it.

He's still afraid he doesn't know what he's doing and won't do it right. His hesitation is going to inhibit him, hold him back. He needs to let go.

I push up onto my elbows and reach forward to wrap my hand around his cock, just above his own. He groans, and his eyes start to drift closed. I drag my palm along the length and rub it against the dot of pre-cum at the head.

"Fuck." He pulls his lip between his teeth and bites down, and damned if that isn't the sexiest thing I've ever seen.

Jude Abello-Harris on the edge of control.

Tightening my grip, I give a sharp tug. "Come here."

His eyes fly open. "What?"

I shift back on the bed until I'm resting on the pillows. "Come. Here."

He only hesitates for a moment before he tugs off his jeans and crawls toward me, a hint of unease in his gaze. It's the last thing I want to see there, the *wrong* thing he should be feeling with me.

But he keeps moving forward, straddling my chest, finally close enough for me to wrap my hand around him again and swirl my tongue across the head of his cock.

"Holy fuck!" He buries his hands in my hair, tightening them until a sharp burn dances across my scalp, letting his eyes drift closed as I lick again. "Fuck..."

I tear my mouth from him. "Open your eyes, Jude."

"What?" His eyes flutter open, and he stares down with a hooded lust-soaked gaze.

"Keep your eyes on me. I want you to know I'm the one you're with, that it's just you and me."

That might be the wrong thing to say because the blue in his eyes morphs into a dark sapphire, and he tightens his grip even more on my hair, angling my head up. "You're the only one I've dreamed about, thought about fucking my entire life. You're the only one who can get me hard. The only one I ever want to. Believe me, Angie, if I close my eyes, you're the one I'm seeing."

If I weren't already a melted puddle of goo, those words are enough to make the rush of arousal soak my thong and coat my inner thighs, and I lean forward and suck him all the way down to the back of my throat.

His body jerks. "Christ..." His nails score along my scalp, and he shoves slightly forward, pushing himself even deeper as he reaches back and slides his hand up between my legs again. "Fucking Heaven, Ang..."

———

JUDE

My FINGERS GLIDE easily into her wet core again, the feeling of her cunt tightening around them enough to make my balls seize up even before she sucks me back down.

250

Jesus fucking Christ.

I've fantasized about what it would be like to be with Angelina Matthews my entire life since joining this messed-up Hawke family, and nothing could have prepared me for this, for how good she feels under me, for how incredible her touch is, for how her fucking mouth feels like Heaven.

She suctions around my cock and moans; the vibration down my shaft drives my hips forward, plunging me deeper. Her little hum of approval massages the head of my cock against the deepest part of her throat.

"Fuck..." I grit my teeth and tighten my grip on her hair with one hand while I thrust in and out of her cunt with the other.

So fucking wet.

For *me.*

She squeezes around my fingers, and my cock twitches in her mouth. I draw my hips back and thrust forward, my hips moving of their own accord. Angelina drops her hand from around me and lets me fuck her mouth until I can't hold it back anymore.

"Fuck, I'm going to come."

A low moan of approval ripples along my length, and she glides her tongue around the head with each pass, flicking it at that spot just underneath that finally sends me barreling over the edge.

I drive deeper, and she groans and swallows me down as I come, unloading all the pent-up need and want I've had for her for fifteen years as her pussy tightens like a vise around my fingers.

Holy fuck.

White lights dance in my vision as I sag slightly, and she pulls back, letting my cock slip free from her throat. She grins up at me, her pink lips wet and plumped by how brutally I fucked her mouth.

Christ is that hot.

I finally regain the power of thought long enough to realize my hand stilled between her legs during my orgasm, and she hasn't come yet. A fucking tragedy. And definitely not at all how I wanted my first time with her to be.

Angelina deserves to be worshiped, to come a million times before I ever had the chance, but once she had her hand and her mouth on me, I was a fucking goner.

Selfish prick.

I should have anticipated it, known it would happen, since hers is the only touch I've ever been able to tolerate, the only one I've ever craved and dreamed about.

This was why.

Because she knew exactly what I needed and gave it to me without question.

I pull my hand from between her legs and lean down to press my lips to hers. The taste of my come still lingers on her tongue, and she mewls and twirls it with mine, rolling her body up against mine wantonly.

My mouth waters to taste her, to have her release coating my throat and filling my stomach the way mine does her, and I lift my wet fingers to my mouth and suck. Her eyes follow the move, and she clenches her thighs against mine, grinding her clit against my skin, seeking the friction I'm no longer giving her.

"You taste fucking magnificent, Ang." I kiss the corner of her lips softly. "But this isn't nearly enough for me."

I pull back, slowly shift down her body, and tug her thong down her legs, tossing it over my shoulder. She watches me intently, her breasts heaving, dress pushed up around her stomach, fully exposing her cunt to me.

It glistens in the light streaming in from the living room, shaved, pink, and swollen...and so fucking ready for me.

Reaching forward, I brush my thumb up and down her lips, and she bucks her hips against it. "You're shaved..."

For someone who hasn't had sex in so long, I fully expected her to be au natural, not perfectly bare.

She nods her head sharply. "Waxing. I've done it for years..." I slip my thumb into her, and she gasps. "Just in case."

I raise a brow at her. "In case you ever decided to come across the street and let me bury my face in your cunt?"

"Fuck, Jude..." She clenches her thighs around my hand. "You can't say things like that to me."

"Why the hell not?"

"Because..." She lifts her head and meets my gaze. "You're going to make me come just from talking, and I'd much rather do it on your face or cock."

Sweet mother of God...

My cock re-hardens instantly, and without preamble, I tug my hand out and plunge my tongue inside her. She gasps and arches her hips against my face, the flavor of her arousal glazing my tongue.

Good God, she tastes just like she always smells. Sweet. Tangy. Warm. Addicting.

Her fingers twist into my hair, and she shifts her position, trying to center my focus on the throbbing nub at the apex of her pussy. I keep thrusting into and sucking at her lips until her entire body trembles so violently it shakes the mattress under us.

I slip a finger inside her and curl, adding a come-hither motion as I suck her clit between my teeth and bite down gently.

Her hips bow up off the bed. "Jude!"

I lick the sensitive bud, then bite again, alternating the action until Angelina goes rigid and finally comes. Her pussy clamps around my fingers tightly, her body twisting, hands wrenching in the comforter.

Drinking her down feels like finally being filled for the first time, her release warming my throat and stomach, her beauty when she comes a masterpiece that will be burned in my brain until the day I fucking die.

She finally floats back to Earth, sagging heavily onto the mattress, and I shift back slowly, pressing kisses to her wet inner thighs as I go. I tug off my T-shirt and let it fall with the rest of the clothes while she lies, panting, the tops of her breasts and cheeks pink.

With her dress hiked up, her glistening cunt exposed to me, my cock twitches and aches to be inside her, to experience finally driving home into the woman I thought I could never have.

I crawl across the bed toward her and grab the hem of her dress. She shifts up enough to let me tug it up over her head, and I wait for her to settle back down on the pillows.

Only she doesn't. She pushes at my chest until I roll onto my back, then straddles my hips, her perfect breasts peeking out of the black lace bra barely containing them.

She reaches back and unhooks it, then lets it slide off her arms and tosses it behind her absently, without ever taking her eyes from mine. All the things I ever wanted to see in her gaze shine down on me now, and she spreads one hand firmly against my chest, then leans down and feathers her lips across mine.

"I want you to be able to see everything, to be able to watch me do this."

Jesus, the woman's trying to kill me, but at least I'll die getting my one dream.

She sits back and reaches between us to align my cock at her slick core, slowly lowering herself. Her hot, tight pussy grips every inch of my cock, and I grit my teeth against the desire to thrust my hips up and fully impale her.

I grip her hips, relishing the way the soft flesh gives under my fingertips as she moves slowly, deliberately, almost like she wants to torture me. With one hand still planted against my chest, she digs in her nails, bracing the other palm on my thigh and leaning back slightly.

From this angle, I can watch my cock disappearing inside her until she's finally fully seated on me and squeezes.

"Fuck." My hips buck, and I tighten my hands on her hips.

She rolls them and clamps down again, starting that low tingle at the base of my spine already.

Fuck, no.

I clench my jaw. I'm not coming again so soon. I will not embarrass myself like that. It's already been awful enough having to talk to her about my past, having to reveal everything on top of the fact that I was a damn virgin until this moment. Coming so fast would be the last and ultimate embarrassment I refuse to accept.

Whatever willpower I have left, I funnel into holding it back, trying to last long enough for Angelina to take what she needs and find her release again before I do mine.

She leans back and starts moving, pushing herself up and down, riding my cock like she's a damn rodeo cowgirl, clamping tightly on each ascent and gliding back easily on the glistening flesh. Watching myself disappear inside her unleashes something from deep in my soul I never knew was there.

I always knew I wanted Angelina. That she was somehow *it*. That this was always meant to be. Even though there were a thousand reasons for it never to work, somehow, I knew it would, that we would come to this at some point, that something would finally drive us together. Now that it has, I can't ever let her go. I can't ever lose this tiny slice of Heaven.

That reality slams into me harder than my orgasm did when I came down her throat, and I need to taste her again, need to have my mouth on her, need to kiss her until she can't breathe.

I push myself up and take her mouth in a bruising kiss. She groans and keeps moving. I kiss her sweet, swollen lips and across her cheek and neck to suck that spot at the back of her ear.

Angie gasps, and her pussy flutters along my length. A low, rumbled groan fills my chest, and my balls tighten. She redoubles her efforts, moving faster, grinding harder, pushing her clit against my pelvis with every thrust, and squeezing around me so tightly it will undoubtedly draw my orgasm out the next time she does it.

Wrapping her long, dark hair around my wrist, I tug on it hard until she stills for a second. "I'm not going to last if you do that again."

I issue her the warning to get her to slow down, to hold back, to make this last, but she gives me the most beautiful smile I've seen in my entire life, a challenge flashing in her ocean-blue gaze.

"Good. I want you to come undone. I want to feel you come inside me, Jude. I'm so damn close..."

Sweet fucking hell.

It's all she needs to say to open the floodgates, and I thrust into her, rolling my hips to meet her. She rocks against me, her mouth falling open on a silent gasp, and I drive up one more time. Her pussy ripples and clenches around me, the start of her release drawing out my own.

I empty myself deep inside her, and she continues to grind her hips and fuck me until she finally drops forward to my shoulder and shudders.

Our bodies entwined, arms and limbs twisted together, I collapse backward onto the bed, taking her with me. My heart thunders against hers, matching its rhythm perfectly. I press my lips against the damp skin just under her jaw, salty and sweet and still smelling of everything I associate with Angelina.

Her eyes flutter open and meet mine, and the corners of her mouth twitch.

"What?" I brush dark hair from her forehead out of her eyes.

"What, what?"

I drag a finger over her lips. "What's *that* for?"

"What's *what* for?"

"That little smirk."

She chuckles and shakes her head, burying her face against my chest. "Nothing."

"No." I push onto my elbow and capture her face, forcing her to look at me. "Not nothing. What was that little smirk?"

She starts giggling so hard she can't control herself, and I narrow my eyes on her.

"Not exactly the reaction a guy wants after *that*, Ang."

"No, no!" She presses her hand against my chest and kisses me gently, squeezing my semi-hard cock still buried inside her. "Not that, it's just...I just took your virginity."

When she says it like that, I can't help but bark out a laugh and join her in losing my shit, dropping back against the pillow with a groan and lowering my arm over my eyes. "Jesus. Fuck, that makes me sound so sordid *and* like I'm a total loser, doesn't it?"

She stills beside me. "What, having sex with me makes you a loser?"

I drop my arm and look at her. "No, that I was a twenty-five-year-old virgin."

Her lips twitch again, and I roll her onto her back, her hair fanned over the pillow like a halo.

"It was worth it, though, Ang. Waiting all this time for you..." I brush my lips against hers, wishing we never have to come out of this little bubble we've managed to create for the last hour. "Because this is how it was always supposed to be. I knew it that day you found me in the closet, just like I did today when I opened the door for you."

I'm helpless when it comes to my addiction to this woman. Helpless and totally fucked because we're going to have to tell Allie and the rest of the family, and the shit is going to hit the fan no matter how we try to do it.

18

ANGELINA

"Good morning." Allie breezes through the kitchen door, far cheerier than she should be at six in the morning, especially with her continued morning sickness, and barely glances at me, setting her purse on the desk and scanning the kitchen for whatever I need help with. Her eyes bounce over the half-finished trays. "You're not done yet?" Her gaze finally lands on me, moving from head to toe, and she narrows her eyes. "Weren't you wearing that last night at Nana's?"

Shit.

It was impossible to leave Jude's bed last night, not when it felt so right to be in his arms, under him, on top of him...I press my thighs together against the throb and soreness between them, reminders I'm sure to feel all day.

And when Allie texted me to say she wasn't going to be home after meeting up with a "friend," I pushed away my worry in favor of hoping she might be meeting with the father of that baby to tell him what's going on.

It made it a lot easier to stay wrapped up in Jude and forget the outside world that will complicate what we've found so much, but I haven't given much thought to an explanation for why I'm still wearing the dress I had on at family dinner.

I glance down and clear my throat. "Uh, yeah."

She moves around the counter toward me, leaning a hip against it and crossing her arms over her chest, brows raised. "Since when do you do the walk of shame into work?"

Kneading the dough for the fresh pretzels a little too aggressively, I scowl at her. "It is not the walk of shame."

She points at me, dragging her finger up and down over the now-rumpled fabric. "Um, yeah. Wearing yesterday's clothes to work is *absolutely* the walk of shame."

"No one else is going to notice."

She raises an eyebrow. "Uh, really? Because when I left Nana's last night, Isaac and Jack said something about stopping by today after they got done talking to Jude. And Isaac is *very* observant."

I freeze. "They're going over to talk to Jude today?"

One of her shoulders rises and falls. "Apparently, they're going to discuss some sort of agreement about the bookstore space so they both can use it."

Somehow, with all the bullshit happening around me, I forgot she hasn't been here for the ongoing discussions of the Falco fuckers down the street or the necessity of a compromise so we can compete. Discussions she *should* be a part of, as both a Hawke and the assistant manager of the Grind. Getting her information second or third-hand means she's been a step—or three—behind the last week.

I nod as I work on the dough. "That's what Luca and Savage told me last night, too. I just didn't realize they were going to talk to him today."

Her gaze narrows. "Why does it matter if it's today or tomorrow..."

Because if they ambush Jude and he has another meltdown, there won't be any way for him to hide what's happening with him anymore.

While getting his struggle out in the open might help him find more ways to address it, more people who will support him and work with him without judgment, it has to be on *his* terms, or he'll never accept it.

I force a smile at Allie. "It doesn't matter. I'm just glad it's happening soon, with you know what going on down the block."

She scowls and looks in the general direction of the new coffee shop. "I drove by it on my way in this morning."

"Really?"

She nods, chewing on her lip and drumming her fingers on the counter.

I lift one hand from the dough and circle it impatiently. "And?"

"And that handsome douchebag, Cassius Whitaker, was there talking to some of the construction workers."

Overseeing our demise to ensure it's speeding along, I'm sure.

"How did things look? Maybe there's a delay?"

She winces. "I wish I had good news for you, but if anything, they seem to be moving a lot faster than we anticipated. You know the building already had a kitchen in the back that Pete and Barb used to make sandwiches and other smaller snack items." Allie offers another shrug. "They probably are just updating the interior. Maybe a few new appliances. It wasn't a full gut-and-redo job."

"*Fuck.*" I close my eyes and lower my head, letting the muscles in the back of my neck stretch out to try to release the tension building there the longer we speak. "This *isn't* good."

Allie offers a sympathetic look. "Yeah, it's a good thing Isaac and Jack are getting the ball rolling with Jude."

"You really think he's on board with it?"

He and I haven't even discussed it, with *other* things occupying our time.

She chews on her lip again. "When I talked to him about it after he spoke with Luca and Byron, it seemed like he was. He understands that his inability to move on it could put us in jeopardy, and he would never do anything to hurt you or me."

That's true. More than she even realizes. Still, I think about how out of control he was when he tried to come over here and even when we were up on that roof before he bolted.

"Are you sure he's ready for that, Al? To be down there and working and..."

So much love and concern matching my own fills her gaze. "I don't know." She nudges my hip out of the way and takes over just as the timer buzzes on one of the ovens. "Go get that. I'll finish this." She glances over at me again. "And don't think you got out of explaining the outfit to me."

Jesus, she's like a dog with a damn bone.

"There's nothing to explain." I shrug and try to appear unconcerned with her comment as I keep my back to her and pull out the muffins, setting them on the counter. "I got together with a friend after I left Nana's last night. Crashed there after some wine."

"A *friend*, huh?"

The way she says *friend* makes me wince, but with my back to her, I can hide my reaction—at least for now. "Yep."

"And that's really all you're going to give me?"

I glance over my shoulder at her. "This from the one who's pregnant and won't tell anyone who the baby's daddy is?"

She cringes.

Shit. Maybe that was a bit harsh.

"Sorry, Al. I didn't mean for it to come out like that." I sigh and make my way back over to her, leaning against the counter while she starts shaping the dough. "All I'm saying is you have your reasons for not wanting everybody to know who it is, and I have mine."

Like the fact that you'll freak the fuck out and never understand that I'm sleeping with your best friend.

I squeeze my eyes closed and suck in a deep breath.

What are we going to do...hide it forever?

Forever.

Jesus.

It's been one fucking night. One night with Jude Abello-Harris, and already, words like "forever" are floating around my head. I'm fucking losing it.

But nothing about that felt casual.

How could it be with all the history between us?

"Hey!" Allie waves a floured hand in my face. "Are you listening to me?"

"Crap." I force a smile. "I'm so sorry. I'm tired. No, what did you say?"

She inclines her head toward the main café. "I said I just heard the bell jingle."

And I was too lost in my thoughts of Jude to pay attention to my damn business.

"I'll go see who it is." I hustle out of the kitchen and out toward the counter as Kennedy approaches the swinging door. "Hey!"

"Oh, hi!" She pulls to a stop at the counter. "I was just coming to look for you."

"What are you doing here?"

She's typically at the office with Gabe and Savage by now, an entire pot of black coffee in, tearing apart anyone who stands in her way. We only see her when she wants to bitch about something or needs to handle something on this side of town and needs another pick-me-up later in the day.

Kennedy rolls her eyes. "My dad and Uncle Gabe sent me to mediate this thing between Isaac and Jude."

"They need a mediator?"

Her laugh fills the empty shop. "Have you ever tried to negotiate anything with Isaac?"

I narrow my eyes on her. "I mean, I'm sure as kids."

"Yeah." She leans on the counter, examining her nails. "Well, you remember how difficult it was for him to budge on anything?"

Understatement.

After growing up on Uncle Stone's knee at the law office and even following his dad to court because Nora was busy with her residence and fellowships, Isaac easily stepped into the role of top Hawke arguer and eventually fixer of all things.

"Yeah, but shouldn't *he* be the mediator?"

Ken shorts and shakes her head, picking at the cuticle of one of her nails. "Okay. Multiply that by ten thousand now that he's an adult, and then by another ten thousand because *this* has to do with Jack, the mother of his children..."

And I can see where this could go downhill very fast, especially with the way Isaac always makes offhand comments about Jude, like he's an ungrateful leech who doesn't appreciate anything Luca or Byron have done for him.

My worry over the potential showdown today doubles. "And what do they think *you're* going to be able to do about the situation?"

"I can play the peacekeeper." She rises and shrugs. "I do it between Dad and Gabe all the damn time, not to mention the interventions I have to do in order to keep Hawke Enterprises running. When they want to tell off a vendor we really need a good relationship with, I'm the one who smiles pretty, puts on the sexy heels and cute dress, and heads out to try to smooth things over."

"Oh, I see." I raise a brow at her and smirk. "So, the only reason you have the CFO role is because you're hot."

She scowls at me, adjusting her tight suit coat and glancing down at the ample cleavage showing in her blouse. "You take that back."

"I'm just kidding." I pour a cup of black coffee for her as a peace offering and slide it to her. "I know how important you are to the business."

"You better"—she points a manicured finger at me—"because I'm trying to save your ass here."

"Any movement on the Falco space?" I motion back toward the kitchen. "Allie said she drove by on her way in and that it looks like they may be ready earlier than we thought."

Kennedy scowls and takes a sip of her coffee. "I did the same, and yeah, it looks like two weeks at most. I couldn't get inside, though."

"Why not?"

"I parked and got out and tried, but they have damn security."

Security?

"What do they need security for at a coffee shop?"

This street has always been quiet. No break-ins. No robberies of anyone on the street. Even cars parked overnight are fine the next morning. It's one of the reasons we chose to buy up all the properties along these few blocks to create the unofficial Hawke District.

She shakes her head. "I don't know. Maybe they don't trust us not to get violent trying to stop them?" A playful grin pulls at her lips but disappears quickly. "But guess whose car was sitting outside?"

I cross my arms over my chest. "Whitaker?"

She sneers. "That arrogant prick. He was probably cowering inside and didn't want to have to face me."

I bark out a laugh and nod. "Yeah, I'm sure that's exactly what happened."

"Anyway, thanks for the coffee." She raises the cup. "I need to get over there before Isaac starts making threats to Jude."

"Does...Jude know you're coming?"

She narrows her eyes at me. "What do you mean?"

"Oh, um, it's just I talked to him yesterday, and he didn't mention anything about meeting with Isaac and Jack."

Her shoulders rise and fall. "I don't know. They were all talking about it at dinner last night. I assume someone called him and told him they were coming."

I wince.

There's no fucking way anybody did that.

If they had, he would've mentioned something to me when I was there, or the call would have interrupted something... which means they're about to blindside him with a request to head downstairs to talk about the space.

———

JUDE

MY PHONE BUZZES with an incoming text, and I roll over and grab it from the nightstand. A grin tugs my lips up at Angie's name. She's only been gone an hour, but she's already messaging me. It makes me feel like less of an obsessive ass for thinking about her non-stop since she slipped out the door this morning.

ANGIE

You're about to have company.

JUDE

Allie with my coffee?

ANGIE

No, Isaac, Jack, and Kennedy.

What?

I jerk upright in bed, trying to clear the fog created by a full night and early morning of having incredible sex with the woman of my dreams.

JUDE

WHY?

ANGIE

They want to talk to you about the bookstore/studio situation.

"Fuck."

Instantly, the warm, fuzzy glow I've been basking in all morning gets replaced by that familiar vise wrapping around my ribcage and squeezing tightly.

I scrub my hands over my face and throw back the covers just as the buzzer sounds downstairs.

Couldn't have given me a little bit more warning than that, Ang?

I plod naked to the bathroom and glance at the shower, but if they're already here, there isn't any way I have time for that, which means I'm going to go meet with them smelling like sex with their cousin.

Holy hell is that fucked up.

Cringing, I splash cold water onto my face and run my wet hand through my hair to try to tame it. What a clusterfuck of a morning, and it's just starting.

I tug on a pair of jeans and a T-shirt as the buzzer sounds again. "Yeah, yeah, yeah. I'm coming."

Smoothing my hand over my hair again, I move toward the buzzer to let them in downstairs, then open the loft door and wait for them to come up. My phone buzzes again, and I glance down at it.

ISAAC

Meet us downstairs with the key.

Ice floods my veins, my vision darkening at the edges slightly.

I thought they came here to talk, not...

Of course, they want to see the space, Jude. Don't be a fucking idiot.

No one's been in there for years, and Jack has never seen it except from across the street or outside the dirty window.

Why wouldn't they want to meet down there?

My hand shakes as I move it over the screen to reply.

JUDE

Give me a minute.

Like a minute's going to change anything. Like a minute's going to tamp down the panic already constricting my chest.

My phone buzzes again.

ANGIE

You'll be okay. It's your building. Same building. You don't even have to go outside. It's no different than the roof.

It's no different than the roof.

It's no different than the roof.

I keep repeating that mantra over and over again as I tug on my shoes and grab the key for downstairs.

"It's no different than the roof."

It's a *hell* of a lot different than the roof because I'm not going to have Angie by my side, but I can't ignore them. I can't leave them standing down there, waiting for me indefinitely, and I don't want to have to explain why I'm not coming.

That would lead to far too many questions and more animosity from Isaac.

I inhale deeply and step out into the hall.

One, two, three, four...

Seventeen steps to the top of the stairwell.

I grip the hand railing, then look at the stairs that lead to the roof. "You made it up there with Angie. You can make it downstairs."

And I sound like a complete lunatic talking to myself right now.

This is okay.

This can be okay.

I cling to the metal railing and take each step tentatively, trying to ignore the way the entire narrow stairwell spins as I descend. My feet hit the landing, and I release the breath I was holding.

Halfway.

Making the turn, I find Isaac and Jack waiting by the locked door into the retail space, faces pressed close to the glass door. They turn to look toward me, and a bright smile lights Jack's face, her amber eyes twinkling with genuine excitement.

"Jude, it's so wonderful to finally meet you in person."

Shit.

One step down. Two. Three. Four. Five. Six. My feet hit the tile floor of the foyer, and I continue to cling to the handrail, forcing a smile as my entire body trembles.

Four, maybe five steps to them at the door.

I free my hand from its death grip on the metal and shift one foot toward them.

Jack opens her arms, rushing toward me. "Sorry. I'm a hugger."

She throws them around me before I have a chance to say anything or prepare myself, and Isaac's blue eyes flicker with amusement as he crosses his arms over his chest and leans against the wall next to the door, watching his pregnant girl-friend embrace me.

I awkwardly wrap my arms around her and pat her back. "Nice to meet you, too."

She pulls away, and her eyes drop from my face, over my T-shirt and jeans, then back up. "We didn't interrupt anything, did we?"

"Just writing."

Isaac snorts and pushes off the wall. "If you ask him, that's what he is always doing."

"I am." I try to fight a sneer at him. "It's my *job*."

"Yeah, yeah, yeah." He waves his hand and motions toward the door. "Can you unlock this thing so we can take a look?"

"Of course."

The quicker I let them in, the sooner I can get them out and go back upstairs. I fish the key out of my pocket, take the two remaining steps to the door, and crank open the lock, then hold the door for them to enter.

I stand, staring into the space for a minute, and glance back up at the stairwell. My chest tightens again, everything in me screaming to run back up before the world goes dark again.

But I can't leave them.

I can't.

A sharp knock on the street door makes my heart leap into my throat, and I whirl toward it.

Kennedy motions to the lock. "Let me in!"

Fucking hell.

I press my hand over my racing heart and stagger the few steps to the door to open it.

She brushes in with a grin. "Morning." She hesitates in front of me for a moment, then pushes up on her heeled toes to press a kiss to my cheek. "Good to see you. They're already inside?"

"Um...yeah."

Kennedy grins and pulls open the inner door, holding it for me. "You coming?"

Do I have a choice?

Isaac, Jack, *and* Kennedy are all waiting for me, expecting me to come in there and have an adult conversation about something that affects the entire family.

I can't fail in this, too.

Forcing a smile, I follow her, letting the door close behind me, wincing at the metal clank of the latch clicking into place.

Jack and Isaac stand in the middle of the vast, open space, and she spins slowly, one hand placed protectively over her growing stomach.

"This place is huge. Is your condo above it as big, Jude?"

I take a few more steps in the dust covering the floor. "Yeah. I have it broken into a couple of different spaces, though."

Isaac wraps his arm around her and ushers her toward the back. "I'm going to show her the area that could be her studio."

Kennedy starts to follow them, then glances back and catches me rubbing at my chest to try to loosen the tightness there. Each breath comes sharp and short. Darkness creeping in on the edges of my vision.

Shit, I can't do this here.

I can't be here.

"Jude?" Kennedy's voice cuts through the fog, "Are you all right?"

"Um, yeah, just haven't had my coffee yet this morning."

She holds up a to-go cup from the Grind. "You want mine? It's black."

"No." I shake my head, wobbling slightly and lowering my head to rub at my temple. "I'm good."

Isaac's heavy footsteps draw my head back up, and he narrows his eyes on me as he and Jack approach. "Jude. Are you okay? You look...a little pale."

For Isaac to be demonstrating any concern for me, I must really look like shit.

Get this done quickly. Get back upstairs.

I square my shoulders, shoving my hands into my pockets to try to look more casual and not on the verge of another total breakdown. "I'm okay."

Isaac gives me a look that tells me he doesn't quite believe me. "All right, well, Luca and Byron said you were on board

271

with this. Do you think there's enough space and a way to make this work for both of you?"

It wasn't what I envisioned three years ago, but so many things are changing. This might be one for the better.

Jack pulls out a sketch pad from her purse, her cheeks pinkening slightly. "I know we've never met before, and you haven't seen my stuff, but I brought you a few samples so you could see the kind of art that we'd be displaying for sale."

My hand shakes as I pull it from my pocket and hold it out to take it from her.

She glances back at Isaac in question. "Are you sure you're all right?"

I take the sketch pad and rub my temple with my free hand. "Yeah. I'm okay."

I'm not okay. Definitely not okay.

Kennedy's phone rings, and she digs in her purse, pulls it out, and scowls. "Look, I need to take this. Are you guys going to come to blows, or can everyone play nice so I can go do my real job but still tell Dad this is resolved?"

Isaac crosses his arms over his chest, but his gaze softens. "I think the three of us are good."

She doesn't even answer him, just puts the phone to her ear and hustles out the door. "If you're calling me and not my father, then—"

The rest of her conversation gets swallowed by the door closing, and I flip open the first page of the sketchpad and try to focus on the image in front of me.

A familiar one—the view from Isaac's condo. I haven't been there in years, but I'd know it anywhere. The river. The buildings. A boat on the water. "Wow. This is incredible."

"Thank you." Jack blushes slightly. "Would you be comfortable hanging something like this in your book space?"

I flip to the next page, to a portrait of Isaac.

Wow.

Even through my foggy vision, it's easy to see how good it is. How she managed to capture everything about him. His toughness shines through, yet something in the eyes screams loyalty and love. For her to have so accurately portrayed that with just a piece of paper and a charcoal pencil shows how much she really loves him.

The picture starts to blur the longer I look at it, that inky blackness creeping into the edges.

I stumble slightly.

Isaac's strong hand grips my bicep. "Jude?"

Jack pulls the sketchpad from me. "Jude, are you all right?"

The door behind me opens, and I try to take a breath.

"Oh, there you guys are!" Angie's voice hits me like a tidal wave of calm, enveloping me in a soothing balm that releases some of the tension. She rushes to my side and loops her arm through mine, nudging me. "Jude, I brought you your latte."

She holds out a travel cup in front of me, and that cinnamon and coffee scent of hers invades my lungs, helping me pull in air slowly.

"Th-th-thank you." I barely get the words out.

Angie presses it into my hand, letting her fingers brush over mine. "That's why I'm here—to make sure you get your caffeine fix."

Isaac's gaze flicks between us briefly before he clears his throat and scans the space again. "So, what are your thoughts, Jude? I know everyone would like to get the ball rolling as quickly as possible, given what's happening down the street."

Squeezing my arm, Angie looks up at me with her brows raised. "You told me you thought it was a great idea, right?"

Thank God for this fucking woman.

I nod. "Yeah, I think it's a great idea. We could even theme different displays around your artwork. Something like your New Orleans landscapes, along with the travel books or portraits with romance novels."

Jack laughs so hard that she practically doubles over.

Her boyfriend seems less amused. "You are *not* putting me near the romance novels."

She reaches over and pats my arm. "I *love* that idea. We're definitely doing that just to piss him off."

Isaac scowls. "Very funny."

Angie elbows me again. "So, we're good? Savage and Gabe are going to line up the contractors to come get started?

Isaac nods. "That's my understanding. We just need to get the plans together and approved through the city. Obviously, we'll try to push them through as fast as possible."

"Through Nancy?"

He glowers, rubbing at his jaw. "That normally would be who we would call when we need something done quickly. But given her friendship and apparent business partnership with Cass, I don't know if we've now lost that contact."

I barely hear his words. Blood continues to rush in my ears, adrenaline and fear coursing through my system.

"Well, if we're done here." Angie slips her arm out from mine. "I need to ask Jude about a couple of things upstairs. You two want to stay?"

Jack peeks back at Isaac, already making her way toward the door. "I think I've seen enough."

Isaac gives me a strange look, then clears his throat and holds out his hand. "Thank you for agreeing to this."

I switch my coffee to my left hand so I can take his, and when his palm hits mine, he squeezes.

Leaning in slightly, he checks to ensure Jack isn't in earshot. "I know how difficult this is for you. I can *see* how hard it is. I appreciate it."

Shit.

He walks out after Jack, leaving Angie and me alone, and I practically sag against her, my legs trembling so badly now that they'll barely keep me upright.

Angelina wraps her arm around me. "Jude, they're by the front windows. Keep walking to the door."

She helps me move to the wall, then pulls open the door and gets me over toward the stairwell. I drop onto the first step, and she takes the coffee from me and sets it between my feet as I bury my face in my hands.

Squatting in front of me, she checks behind her to ensure everyone has gone before returning her focus and placing her hand on my arm. "Are you okay?"

I take a deep breath and look up at her, staring into the eyes of the only person who's ever been able to calm the storm raging inside me. "I am now that you are here."

19

ANGELINA

My tentative knock sounds down Jude's hallway, and I stand, waiting for him to open the door, second-guessing this entire plan.

Maybe this isn't a good idea. Maybe it's pushing too far, asking too much, especially after what happened this morning with Isaac and Jack. But I can't help this need to try to make things better for him, to try to break him out of this mental prison he's locked himself in and the literal one he's created in his condo.

He sees it as a safe space, feels like it's the only place he can escape the threats in the outside world, and given everything that's happened to him, he isn't wrong.

The world sucks. Bad people do bad things, and good people get caught up in it and get hurt. Which seems like the understatement of the century when it comes to Jude and what he's suffered. But he can't keep living like this, and I can't keep watching him do it. Not when I know how much everyone else wants him back as a member of the family.

Though that in and of itself is going to create a massive issue we're going to have to deal with, sooner rather than later.

How the hell are we going to tell Allie?

Before I can come up with any answer, Jude swings open the door, and a slow grin spreads across his face. He rubs at his eyes and stretches his arms high above his head, his T-shirt riding up to expose those perfect washboard abs that make my fingers itch to touch them. "I wasn't expecting to see you tonight."

"I know."

I hadn't planned on coming. After Allie's comments about the walk of shame this morning, I had planned on spending the evening with her at our place, dispelling any possible suspicions on her part until Jude and I can work out what all *this* is and how to tell people. But she vanished again to see her "friend," and truthfully, I'm not so sure I could've stayed away from Jude even if I had tried.

Leaning in, I press my mouth to his, and he wraps his arms around me and drags me up against his hard, lean body. He glides his tongue along the seam of my lips, and I open for him. The warm, spicy flavor of bourbon fills my senses, and I issue a little groan of approval.

He drags his head back. "You said you needed to get home, spend some time with Allie."

"Did she say anything to you today when she came over after her shift?"

The door closes behind us, and Jude shakes his head. "No. I tried to get her to talk more about the baby and the father. But..."

"But she's still tight-lipped, even with you?"

He nods.

I sigh and drop my forehead to his. "She's not telling me anything, either. But she gave me shit for showing up this morning in the same dress I wore to Nana's last night."

He pulls back and fights a smirk.

"Don't you do that."

His blond brows rise. "What?"

"Don't you smirk at me." I poke my finger into his solid chest. "It's not funny, Jude. What are we going to tell people?"

He rubs at the back of his neck, his eyes drifting down over my simple black cotton dress to the basket in my hand. "What's that?"

I follow his gaze and hold it up. "Oh, I almost forgot my entire reason for coming over here."

He reaches for it, but I press my hand against his hard stomach and push him away.

"Nope. You have to come with me to see what's in it."

His eyes narrow on me, his entire body tensing immediately. "Come with you where?"

We haven't even left the condo, and already, fear fills his eyes. I grab his hand and find the skin cold and clammy. Panic has set in.

This was a bad idea.

It might be too much, too soon, but if no one ever pushes him, if he never tries to address any of the things keeping him locked in here, he's never going to get better.

I lean in and nuzzle my lips beneath his ear, his crisp scent invading my breath. "You trust me, don't you?"

He stiffens and turns his head slightly toward mine, his hand tightening on my waist. "Well, I did until you said that."

The slight hint of humor he's able to inject into this situation gives me hope that this might work out better than I feared. I press my lips against his neck, and he groans and leans into me, wrapping his arms firmly around me.

"We could just stay here."

I pull back and shake my head. "Nope. Come on."

He gives me a wary look, but I open the door and motion toward the hallway. That same dark fear fills his eyes again as

279

he stares down it, and I reach up and angle his face toward me.

"Keep your eyes on me. Count your steps. I'll be with you the whole time."

Jude sucks in a shaky, uneven breath. "I don't think I can. My whole body is still vibrating from this morning."

Dammit.

Leaving him to go back to the Grind earlier gutted me, but I can't be with him all the time—even if I may want to be.

"Which is exactly why this is going to be what you need tonight."

I hope.

I'm no fucking doctor. Far from it. I'm hanging everything on a prayer right now that what I'm doing isn't going to set him back. But everything I read said to start with small things.

Going places that elicit good memories. Counting your steps. Focusing on something other than your panic and fears. It can all help someone cope when they *do* have to go outside.

I just hope it works tonight.

I tug on his hand, urging him toward the door, and he pauses at the threshold. Every breath he takes seems to pain him, like his chest is tightening around his lungs.

"Breathe."

He nods and slips on his shoes, then steps out into the hallway, allowing me to lead him down the hall. With each step, his hand tightens on mine until it crushes my fingers, but I let him.

Whatever he needs to do this.

We hit the stairwell, and I motion up.

He raises a brow. "We're going to the roof again?"

I nod. "We're going to the roof again. No rain this time."

The corner of his mouth twitches. "I kind of liked you all wet."

"I bet you did."

Humor is good. It means he isn't locked away in his mental

jail completely. If the soft, funny, irresistibly charming side of Jude can still break free in a moment like this, then there's hope.

I tug him up the stairs, and this time, he takes them faster, with far less hesitation.

Another good sign.

We push out onto the roof, the metal door clanking back against the wall, and I suck in a deep breath of the hot, heavy summer air. A breeze blows across the open space, and Jude steps out behind me.

"What the..." His gaze darts all around the flat roof at the dozens of strands of lights hanging from wherever I could find to attach them to the picnic blanket spread out in the middle of it. "When did you have time to do all this?"

"I came over here right after we closed. You must have been deep in whatever you're working on not to have noticed me come across the street." I move us forward and set the basket on the blanket. "I was afraid you saw me come into the building and would know what I was up to."

He shakes his head and rubs his hands back through his hair. "Yeah. I only have a few chapters left. I was pretty into it for a while." A sheepish half-grin crosses his lips. "I don't normally miss you leaving."

"I know. I don't normally miss *you* miss *me* leaving."

He smirks and motions toward the basket. "What is it?"

"Late dinner. I figured you weren't eating."

His stomach growls loud enough for me to hear it, and he presses his hand flat against it. "You'd be right."

I don't want to sound like a mother hen nagging him, but it slips out before I can bite it back. "You have to take better care of yourself, Jude. You have to eat. You have to get fresh air. You have to not get so lost in other worlds trying to ignore this one."

His gaze darkens and hardens slightly, a muscle in his jaw ticcing.

Shit.

I've already ruined our night by saying something I never should have. Before he says a word, I hold up a hand. "Look, I'm sorry. I just..."

Am fucking this all up.

I close my eyes and suck in a breath, trying to figure out a way to say this. When I reopen them, he stands unmoved, waiting for me to continue, anger still present in his gaze. I spread my palms over his chest. "I care too much about you to see you hurting yourself."

He grits his teeth. "I'm not hurting myself, Ang. I'm fine."

I feather my fingertips over his cheek and shove them through his hair, tightening my grip. "You are most definitely not fine, Jude."

The comment should anger him more. It should make him pull away. It should stoke the fire of his resistance to anyone's helping him.

He drops his head and presses his lips to mine, kissing me deeply as he drags my body fully against his, his cock starting to harden between us. "I think I proved to you last night and this morning that I am more than okay."

As much as I enjoy having him pressed against me, his mouth moving over mine, the spread of heat between my legs, and the throb of my clit with every touch of his skilled hands, I force myself to drag my head back.

Jude is trying to distract me, to divert my attention from my concern, and I can't let him do that. If I don't get this off my chest, it will crush me.

"No, I meant"—I press my hands over his heart—"life. You can't stay locked up in your condo forever. You know it isn't healthy. You know exactly why it's happening. You're smart enough. You knew exactly what triggered you and what sent you on this path."

He takes a step back, then another, and turns and walks

over to the edge of the roof to stare down at the street. From up here, the lights along the shore twinkle off the water, and the entire city is spread out before us.

It would be insanely beautiful if I weren't so distracted by his retreat.

This is not going well.

But he seems...okay otherwise. Like his panic dissipated the moment we got up here.

That's a positive sign, right?

He shoves his hands into his pockets, looking every bit the broody, damaged man he is. "You're right, Angie. I *do* know that. But maybe I don't want everybody to know about this. Maybe I don't want the whole world to know my weaknesses. It's bad enough you do."

Tears burn in my eyes, and I approach him and wrap my arms around him from behind, pressing my face between his shoulder blades. "I know you, Jude. I knew you the moment I opened that closet door and my eyes met yours. I knew you were damaged. I knew you were broken. But I've never, for one minute, thought you were weak. And no one else will, either."

The Hawkes have all been through so much, suffered so many losses, and made it through struggles that would crush a weaker family. Jude is one of us, whether he wants to accept that or not, and it means no judgment from them. If they knew, it would actually make things easier because everyone would understand his behavior instead of thinking the worst.

"You don't have to tell the whole family the backstory. Luca and Byron have kept it from everyone for years. They've protected you in every way they can, and they will continue to do that. But you have to let them help you. You have to let *me* help you."

He turns in my arms and cradles my face in his palms, tilting it up toward him. "You *do* help me. You're the only thing that does."

JUDE

ANGIE BLINKS AWAY the tears filling her eyes, and they slide slowly down her cheeks. "But that's just as unhealthy as doing nothing about it, Jude. You can't rely on me to be the sole thing that can calm you down, the only way that you have to cope with this. That isn't right."

She isn't wrong about any of it. She isn't saying anything I haven't thought myself a hundred times, but it doesn't make the reality change. And the reality is, Angelina is my lifeline. She always has been.

I shake my head. "I don't care if you are the only person I ever see every day for the rest of my fucking life. I would be happy."

She swallows back a sob. "But *I* wouldn't be because I'd know how much you're missing out on, how many things I want to be able to do with you outside of this little protective bubble you've created for yourself." A tiny smile curls her lips even as more tears stream down her face. "And we can do that. We can work on it together. But you have to *want* to."

"I want you."

"You *have* me, Jude."

The moment those words leave her lips, I know it's true. This could never be something casual between us. It never was. All those years that led up to this, it was like we were waiting for each other, for me to be in this place, for her to need me as much as I do her.

I lower my head and kiss her again, and even though we've solved absolutely nothing, she doesn't pull away. Her tongue slips against mine, and I back her up until her shoulders hit the brick beside the roof door. All her lush curves align perfectly along my body, and I grind my hard cock against her stomach.

A moan tumbles from her pink lips, and my cock twitches, remembering what it felt like to be inside her when she made that noise last night. Feeling like I was home, like I had finally found the place I belong in this crazy, terrifying world.

She drags my head away from me, panting softly. "What about our picnic?"

I bury my hand in her hair and tug it sharply. "Fuck the picnic. It'll still be there when we're done."

Lust burns across her gaze, and I devour her again, groaning into her mouth, unable to get enough from her.

Every brush of Angelina's lips, every little mewl that slips from her throat, the way her nails score my skin as she frantically grips at me for purchase only makes me need her and want her more.

She may think I'm missing out on life, that I'm missing out on all the good things, but she's it. Angelina Matthews *is* the good thing in my life. And as long as she isn't going anywhere, I can survive anything.

But in this moment, it feels like if I don't get inside of her in the next five seconds, I might completely explode. Somehow, I've managed not to embarrass myself completely with this woman, and I hope to keep that streak alive.

She unbuttons my jeans and lowers the zipper, reaching her warm hand inside to cup my hard cock. I groan into her luscious mouth, pushing her even harder against the bricks as I tug down her thong and let it fall to the roof.

I grasp her thighs and lift as she works my pants down to my thighs and wraps her legs around my waist, aligning her wet heat perfectly to glide up and down along my length.

"Fuck, Ang." I drop my forehead to hers, our hearts beating rapidly against each other. "You have no idea how much I love you."

The words come out before I can stop them, before I can

even think about how fucking stupid it is to say that to her after the way she reacted the first time I said it.

But instead of retreating, instead of pulling away, she aligns my cock with her wet heat and kisses me deeply. "Show me how much."

Good God.

Angelina Matthews might just kill me.

Her passion. Her heart. Her desire to make everything better for everyone else while never thinking about herself and her needs.

Someone needs to take care of her if she won't do it herself.

And that someone is *me.*

It feels like this is what I was born for, to make Angie happy. To watch her unravel and release all the stress and tension of her day. To see her come apart in ecstasy.

I drag my hips back and drive into her, her wet heat clasping around me, pulling me even farther inside her. She clenches and swivels her hips, rolling them to meet each thrust. It spurs me to move faster, to fuck harder, plunging even deeper and slamming her back against the brick.

She lets out a sharp cry, and I still.

Her eyes fly open. "No, keep going."

A good cry, then.

One I could listen to forever and never get sick of hearing. It means she's letting loose, unleashing all the emotions she keeps bottled up inside while she's taking care of everyone else.

Her hands loop around my neck, and she tangles them in my hair at my nape as I set a rhythm of long, slow strokes.

I want to fuck her brains out. I want to barrel into her like the out-of-control lunatic I've always felt like when I'm around her, but I never want it to end. I want to savor every minute, every noise, every kiss, every time her nails scratch my neck and her pussy clenches around me. I want all of it to last forever.

If only that were possible.

But very real problems face us when we leave this roof.

The judgment we'll face when the Hawkes find out. When *Allie* discovers what we've been hiding. Not to mention Angie pushing me to come clean with everyone about my personal issues that I want to remain personal.

It can all wait, though. I won't dwell on any of the negatives when I'm buried deep inside her welcoming cunt.

I glide into her, rolling my hips up with a snap, trying to grind against her clit to give her the friction I've now learned she needs to be able to get off.

She takes my mouth again and wars with me for control of it, gasping against my lips. "Harder."

Fuck!

Angie doesn't know what she's asking for, doesn't know how badly I want to do that, how badly I want to destroy all the things standing in our way, how badly I want to fuck them into oblivion.

I draw back my hips and thrust into her again and again, each time bottoming out deep inside her. She moans and drops her head back against the brick, exposing the long, elegant column of her neck, and I lower my head and kiss my way up it along her jawline over to her ear.

The taste of her warm, damp skin makes my cock twitch inside her, and I nip at her earlobe and run my tongue along the edge.

She shudders against me, her cunt squeezing and rippling along my length. "Fuck, Jude. Yes, like that."

Learning what she wants, what she likes, what she needs, gives me this heady sense of power and control I've never had over anything in my life before.

Ang is at my mercy in this moment. The woman I've loved forever, the one who can reach a part of me I never thought anyone would be able to, is putty in my hands, relying on *me* to get her where she needs to be.

And it all started in that fucking closet.

I'm not going to let it end like that, hidden away.

I shift my head back and capture her face in my palm, forcing her to look at me as I roll my hips and thrust into her again. "I'll try for you."

Her eyes shimmer with unshed tears, and she leans forward and kisses me softly, gently, in complete juxtaposition with the way I'm fucking her. I slow my hips to match her tempo, long and sweet, savoring all of her.

"I love you, Jude. I don't care about what anyone is going to say. We'll figure it out. But I don't want to keep doing this and hiding with you. I don't want you to hide away from life anymore. I want you to live it with me."

I kiss her deeply, and my pace starts to increase until I'm slamming into her again, and she's rolling her hips to meet mine with each thrust. Her nails score my neck, and I tighten my grip on her hip and cheek, keeping her mouth exactly where I want it so I can devour her soul.

She starts to thrash her head back and forth, her neck muscles straining.

So close.

She is so damn close, and I need to take her there, need to feel her come apart, need to know that I'm the one who does that for her.

"Tell me what you need, Ang."

"I need...I can't..."

I pull my hand from her face and slide it between our bodies until my thumb finds her clit. She bucks wildly at the simple contact, and I roll the pad over it fast and hard, then pinch it.

Angie detonates, her mouth falling open, her eyes rolling

up into the back of her head, her body convulsing as I pin her to the wall and keep driving into her relentlessly.

Her pussy flutters on my cock, trying to drag out my orgasm. I grit my teeth and fight it for as long as I can until she finally starts to twitch and sag against me. She drags her lips across my neck and licks over the spot.

Sweet fuck.

I plunge into her one last time and spill myself deep into her core, slumping against her, keeping both of us upright with her body between me and the wall.

She presses light kisses along my collarbone, and we stand like this for a few moments, the warm summer air flowing around us, the breeze making her dark hair flutter against my face.

I pull back and brush it away, then lift her head so I can kiss her again. "Have I ever told you how fucking perfect you are?"

She grins at me and shakes her head. "I don't think so. But also, I'm not."

"You are."

She barks out a laugh and buries her face again. "Yeah, tell that to my mother."

"I'll tell anyone who asks. Hell, even if they don't."

Her light laughter floats through the air, and I spend a few seconds relishing in it, in the perfect moment before an explosion tears through the night air, knocking me off my balance and sending us both tumbling to the roof.

20

ANGELINA

Pain burns through my right arm and temple, and I struggle to take a breath, the wind knocked completely out of me by the force of whatever the hell that was and hitting the hard rooftop.

I groan and roll onto my back, rubbing at my arm, trying to clear the ringing from my ears. "What the fuck was that?"

Jude pushes up off the roof, his hand at his head, too, shaking it slightly. "I-I don't know. Are you all right?"

Aside from the splitting pain in my head, the ringing in my ears, and the ache in my arm, I seem okay. "I'm good. I think." The acrid smell of smoke hits me with my next inhale. "Oh, my God."

I struggle to my feet and rush to the edge of the roof overlooking the street. Flames leap from the front of the Grind, glass and wood and other debris strewn across the street.

"No." My heart sinks into my stomach. "No. No. No!"

Jude appears next to me, still rubbing at his head. "Holy fuck, it looks like a war zone."

"The café..." I turn and race toward the door to the stair-well, Jude hot on my heels, still trying to button his pants.

"No. Angie, you can't go over there."

"I have to try to stop it." I tug the door open before he can get to me and race down the stairs, his litany of "Fuck, fuck, fuck, fuck, fuck," behind me as his bare feet pound down each step.

I hit the landing and glance up at him.

He points at me, eyes wide. "Don't. Go to my place. We'll call 9-1-1 and everyone."

There isn't any time. If I don't do something, I'm going to lose everything I've worked so fucking hard for. My mind negates any potential danger with the thought that I might be able to stop it, to salvage something.

I ignore Jude's warning and keep flying down the steps.

He snarls and continues descending behind me. "Moth-erfucker."

His frustrated footsteps grow closer, his long legs eating up the distance far quicker than I can, but I keep making my way down to the first floor as he darts off toward his place to grab his phone.

Where the hell is mine?

The constant ringing in my ears makes it impossible to think clearly, and I shake my head again to try to clear it, an inky blackness creeping around the edges of my vision.

What the hell happened?

We were kissing, and then it was like the entire world exploded around us. A literal bomb blowing us sideways...

I hit the first floor, and the glass front door is blown inward, large shards scattered all along the hallway. Whatever happened was powerful enough to shatter all the panes on this side of the street, too.

"Oh, God. No. No. No." I weave through the mess, pieces crunching underneath my shoes, and step through where a pane of glass once stood, out into the fucking war zone that was once the quiet, quaint, little business district.

Thick black smoke billows up and out from the Grind, flames leaping and jumping wildly, like they're being fed by something inside, already engulfing the businesses on either side—a specialty butcher and the space Astrid uses to hold her tutoring sessions with the employees.

I take a few steps across the sidewalk to the street, and another blast sends flames barreling out of the now-destroyed storefront toward me, along with pieces of shrapnel from everything inside. Strong arms wrap around me from behind, jerking me back against a powerful chest, and we slam into the wall beside the destroyed windows of Jude's building.

His warm breath flutters in my hair, coming in heavy pants. "Jesus Christ, Ang. What the hell are you doing?"

He brings his phone to his ear and presses his lips against my neck, right behind my ear. "You're not going over there. I have 9-1-1 on the phone. You need to call Savage...call everybody."

I try to process his words, but all I hear is the roar of the inferno, the crackling of glass, the small explosions of anything flammable inside when the flames finally reach it.

It's all gone.

Everything.

"Yes. I'm still here. Okay. No, we won't go near it. We're across the street. There's damage to the buildings on this side, too. No, we own this whole side of the block and that side. No other owners to call. Okay. Thank you."

He ends the call and slips his phone into his pocket, wrapping both arms around me and fully cocooning me back against him. His familiar scent mixes with the sharp tang of smoke in the air. "I'm so sorry, Ang."

I can't form a response.

What the hell do I say as I watch my entire life's work burn?

"Who could have..." I shake my head, tears streaming down my face, blurring my vision. "How did this..."

"I don't know, Ang." He kisses that spot between my collarbone and neck again, letting his lips linger there as he gathers himself together. "Fuck, I'm going to call Savage and everyone."

Sirens sound in the distance, but it's too late for them to do anything. By the time I got out here, it was already too late.

Gone.

All of it.

In a fucking instant.

My stomach heaves, and I turn to the side and retch, emptying everything onto the sidewalk to join the rubble littering it.

"Shit." Jude squats next to me, pulling my hair back with one hand as he pulls out his phone with the other to make another call. He watches me intently, concern furrowing his brow as I retch again. "Uncle Savage, it's Jude." He swallows thickly. "The Grind just exploded."

Even with the phone to his ear, I can hear Savage's response. "*WHAT?*"

"It *exploded*. The whole thing is in flames, along with the butcher and Astrid's place. Shattered all the glass on my building, too, and a few on either side. Fire trucks are on their way. You all need to get everyone over here." He listens intently for a moment. "No. They're okay. No one was inside."

Thank God...

The thought of what could have happened if anyone were still there makes my stomach turn again, and I heave with nothing left to throw up.

Jude's other hand starts to rub between my shoulder blades softly. "Are you okay?"

I sob and wipe the back of my hand across my mouth. "No. How the fuck can I be okay?"

There isn't anything anyone can do now.

Hawke's Daily Grind is gone.

And every breath of acrid smoke carries with it the burning remnants of my dream. I finally can't bear to look at it anymore or to face it and breathe in the end of everything I worked for.

I turn, and Jude helps me stand to bury my forehead against his chest, letting him engulf me in his arms and press his lips into my hair.

"I'm so fucking sorry, Ang."

"Who would do this? Who would fucking do something like this?" My sobs fill the air around us, and even I can hear how unhinged they sound, how frantic, how on the edge of completely losing control. "It doesn't make any sense..."

He drags my head back, my cheeks between his palms, and forces me to look up at him as tears stream down my face. "You know we're going to find out what happened. No matter what, if someone did this, if it wasn't an accident, they're going to pay. The Hawkes don't let shit like this go."

I dart out my tongue to wet my dry lips and squeeze my eyes closed, my legs starting to tremble beneath me like I can barely hold myself up anymore. Only Jude's strong arms around me keep me upright as the firetrucks turn onto the street and come to a screeching halt in front of the shell of the café. Firefighters jump out, rushing around, attaching hoses as quickly as they can to the hydrants to spray water on a fire that's already taken its victim—my entire fucking livelihood, the only thing I ever had that was *mine*.

Jude presses his lips to mine softly and pulls my cheek against his chest, his other hand holding me steady at my lower back. "We'll fix it."

"It's gone, Jude. There's no fucking fixing that."

"Don't talk like that." He kisses the top of my hair, likely filled with ash that floats through the air around us. "We'll rebuild. You know the Hawkes are capable of anything."

I pull my head back, pure hatred and wrath filling my veins. "And apparently, so are Falco and Cassius Whitaker."

His eyes widen. "You think this is Falco?"

I motion back to the carnage, to the firefighters running around, trying to get control of it. Three police cars join the fray, and they start cordoning off both sides of the road to stop the very light traffic this time of night and control the scene. "Who the fuck else would do this to us? Who else would have the fucking balls?"

Something flashes in his eyes. "Roselli...he was just here."

"Fuck." I bite my lip, considering the possibility. "You're right. But why? I don't—"

"Hey!" He takes my face again and jerks it up harshly, effectively stopping my downward spiral. "This isn't the time to lose your shit. You keep it together, okay? It's not up to you to figure this out on your own. Especially now. Everyone will be here soon, and you know no one's going to stop until they get to the bottom of what happened."

I stare up into his pale-blue eyes, the love he has for me shining so strongly in them. The need to ensure I'm okay, to protect me in the only way he can. I don't know how I never saw it before. Mostly because I didn't want to see it because I was afraid of what it would mean, afraid that I could feel the same way about a man who's twelve years younger, who I fucking babysat, who, for all intents and purposes, is a member of the Hawke family.

But that's exactly why this works, exactly why Jude and I fit together so well, because we *know* each other. We know *every-thing*. Now, I know all his secrets, what haunts his nightmares and what he dreams about, and it only makes me love him more.

A car screeches to a stop down the street near the barricade, and we both whip our heads in that direction to find Saint and

Bishop climbing from their SUV, both of their gazes locked on the inferno.

"Fuck." I jerk away from Jude and shove my shaking hands back through my hair. "They got here fast."

Bishop rushes across the sidewalk, her eyes darting between the blaze and us, and pulls me into her arms. "Oh, my God. Angie, are you okay?"

I nod, even though I'm not at all okay, and a sob slips from my lips.

Saint approaches and wraps a massive arm around us, leaning in to whisper to me. "We're going to find out what happened, who's behind this."

I lift my head and look him dead in the eye. "It had to have been Falco or Roselli."

He presses his lips together in a firm line and stares up at the café. "Or it could've just been a gas leak or something else completely accidental."

"There was no gas leak." I shake my head and incline it toward the ruins. "I was just in there an hour ago, and everything was fine. I never smelled any gas."

Jude still leans against the brick next to the blown-out windows of what will be the bookstore and art gallery, staring into the flames which reflect back across his blue eyes. "I didn't smell anything, either. And I was outside just before it exploded."

He doesn't say anything else, doesn't explain what he was *doing* outside, and I release a heavy sigh of relief. There's too much to deal with at the moment to be answering questions about *us*.

Saint's gaze drifts over to him. "Are you all right?" He looks up at the shattered windows on Jude's loft. "Shit, it destroyed this side of the street, too."

Jude nods. "I'm fine. Nothing some new windows won't fix."

Saint pulls out his phone. "I'm going to go make calls to a

couple of our contractors, see if I can get them out here tonight to at least board all this up if they can't replace them right away."

Two more cars pull to a stop behind his, and Gabe, then Savage, exit one while Isaac and Stone exit the other, all eyes wide and pointed at what was once one of our most-profitable businesses.

"Holy shit." Isaac's words don't even come close to describing what we're seeing.

He walks over, and Bishop allows him to tug me out of her arms and into his. "I'm so sorry, Ang."

I lift my head. "Did somebody call Allie?"

He nods. "My mom is going to get her right now, and your parents are on their way. Everyone will be here soon." His gaze darts to Jude. "Luca and Byron are on their way, too."

Jude nods slowly and runs a hand through his hair. "It seems like it's going to be a long night."

———

JUDE

HAWKES CLAMOR in and out of the condo, half of them on cell phones, rattling off orders to various people, the other half, arms wrapped around each other, comforting one another and quietly whispering about the situation.

I stand in my usual spot with my back to the brick, next to the now-open windows, staring out at the remnants of the fire, finally almost under control. Only a few hot spots remain that the firefighters struggle to settle.

Almost five hours later, smoke still wisps from the ruins of the Grind and the buildings on either side of it. It could have been much worse. If the winds had been strong tonight, the flames could have carried much farther and destroyed The

Hawkes Nest just down the street or any number of our other businesses.

Though it's hard to feel *lucky,* seeing Angie's dream destroyed like this.

I watch Saint down on the street, talking with the fire chief, motioning toward the café in a heated exchange. The big man, who's always been our protector and head of security for all the Hawke operations for as long as I've been alive, doesn't look too happy with whatever he hears.

He turns to Bishop, who stands beside him with her arms crossed over her chest, tapping her foot and looking every bit as angry as her father, and says something that makes her scowl.

She turns back and marches toward my building, then appears in the condo a moment later, the door slamming behind her. Everyone turns to look at her, and she stalks across the wood floor directly to where Savage, Gabe, Stone, and Isaac huddle together, whispering.

Whatever she tells them stiffens all their backs, and they exchange pained and angry looks.

Shit.

My gaze immediately darts to the couch, where Angie and Allie sit wrapped in blankets, with Storm and Skye on either side of them, whispering to them reassuringly, though I don't know what the fuck they could be telling them that would make any of this okay.

All I want is to pull Ang into my arms, to hold her and let her know I have her, no matter what. That *somehow* things will work out...eventually. But I can't even do that. Not with everyone milling around and watching me like a hawk.

Most have never set foot in here, and many of them haven't seen me face to face in two damn years. I'm as much of an attraction to them as the destruction outside.

I close my eyes and rub my hand over my face. The stress of yesterday and what's happened since the blissful few moments we had up on that roof—before the world went to shit—are all finally catching up to me.

My body sags more against the wall, and I consider dropping onto my ass and not even bothering to try to stand anymore. I cough slightly, likely a response to the smoke we've all been inhaling for hours. Dropping my head back, I close my eyes and try to go back to the roof. To how it felt to hear Angie say those three little words to me that I never thought she'd ever say.

Heavy footsteps approach on the wood floor, and someone nudges something cool and wet against my arm.

"Looks like you could use this."

I open my eyes and accept the bottle of water from Luca. "Thanks."

Another cough rattles my chest, and I crank off the top and take two long swallows of it.

Luca narrows his gaze. "Are you all right? Did you get checked out? You and Angie must have inhaled a lot more smoke than any of us did."

"I'm fine."

The last thing I want is to be poked and prodded by more doctors. I've had enough of that for ten lifetimes.

He looks over to where Aunt Nora is talking with Coen. "Should I have Nora come?"

"No, Luca, really. If I need a damned doctor, I'll call her or Pope."

The harsh tone in my response makes him hold up his hands defensively. "Sorry. I'm just worried about you."

Fucking hell.

Nothing like being a total dick to the man who literally saved your life.

"No." I press my hand to my temple, clamping my eyes shut against the growing migraine forming there. "It's not that. I'm sorry. I'm just exhausted." I meet his gaze again, doing my best to soften mine to convey I'm being serious. "I appreciate you worrying about me."

He lets out a laugh, his eyes widening slightly. "Really? I don't think you've ever said that in fifteen years or given me any indication that it didn't just piss you off."

Well, fuck, if that isn't a guilt trip, I don't know what is.

I rub at the back of my neck and take another sip of water. "I do appreciate it, everything you and Byron have done for me. I am just really fucking bad at showing it."

My words seem to stun him for a moment. The unshakeable man who controlled a massive, violent criminal empire shifts uncomfortably in his thousand-dollar Italian loafers and looks away for a second, like he's trying to compose himself before he replies.

He clears his throat. "Well, I'm glad you feel that way." Visibly uncomfortable with the topic of conversation, he scans the street and the open window frames in front of us. "What time was the construction company going to be able to come over to put in new windows?"

"They said before noon."

"Good." He takes a step forward and glances down to the sidewalk that's already been cleared of debris by one of our teams. "Downstairs, too?"

I nod. "Yep."

"Fuck..." He shakes his head, his jaw hardening. "What a mess, huh?"

"You have no idea." The ache that's taken up residency in the center of my chest throbs again, and I rub at it with my free hand, glancing over at the woman I want so badly to help. "This is going to destroy Angie more than anyone even knows."

A familiar car pulls up outside, and Caroline climbs from the driver's seat, then rushes around to the passenger side.

I quickly scan the condo, where literally everyone else has

gathered to assess and address the situation and offer each other comfort in the middle of the fucking night. "Who's that?"

Luca stands on his tiptoes to look down. "Nana."

"Nana's coming?"

He waves his hand back to literally the entire Hawke family crammed around my space. "You think she wouldn't?"

It never crossed my mind that the matriarch of the family would make an appearance, but maybe I should have anticipated it. Antonia Hawke doesn't like to be left out of anything and doesn't let her age slow her down at all.

"She's never been to my place before."

Luca gives me a pointed look. "You haven't invited her."

"Shit"—I rub a hand over my stubbled cheek—"that's fair."

The old woman climbs from the passenger seat with a little bit of help she clearly doesn't want from Caroline, pushing her away slightly. "I can do it myself."

Her insistence carries up to the second floor through the open windows, and I can't help but smirk. Every bit as feisty as I remember her from the last time we saw each other in person.

She glances up, and a smile breaks out across her old lips as she waves to Luca and me. Her gaze drifts over to the wreckage across the street, and I can see her heart sink, the moment of joy at seeing me wiped away by knowing what's been lost.

With a deep sigh, she allows Caroline to lead her across the sidewalk, through what was the glass door, and disappears inside.

"What do you think about all this?" Luca motions to the café. "What's your take?"

"What do you mean?"

His dark brows draw low over his even darker eyes. "Son, you're here every day. You see everything that happens on this street and at that building. You need to tell me what you've observed. Did you see anything before the explosion?"

I gulp.

Only Angelina's fucking cunt wrapped around my dick.

Shifting slightly to hide the twitch of my cock at the thought, I scan the street. "I was working all night. I didn't see much of anything."

"And when did Angie come over?"

I jerk my head in his direction, brows raised. "What?"

He raises a brow in return. "Wasn't she here when the explosion happened?"

Shit.

We've been so busy dealing with the authorities and family showing up in droves that Angie and I haven't had a chance to discuss how we're answering these questions.

Motherfucking hell.

Any way I answer this, it's going to raise questions. Ones neither of us want to be addressing right now, with so many bigger things happening all around us.

The door opening gives me the reprieve I desperately need from the questioning, and Nana and Caroline enter, Saint hot on their heels, carrying several grocery bags that he must have retrieved from his wife's car.

Savage moves over to his mother, and she leans down to whisper something to him. He nods and motions to the couch, where Angie and Allie both sit, crying.

Nana walks over to them, and they both get up to give her a hug.

My heart shatters for all of them, for what they've lost, for what this is going to do to them. Then Nana turns, and her gaze locks with mine. She offers a sad smile and makes her way over slowly, almost tentatively.

She gives Luca a hug. "I know you're going to find out what happened."

"Of course, Nana."

He pats her on the back and leaves me alone with the

woman who's always treated me like a grandson, even when I couldn't even allow her to touch me.

Her old eyes, that still seem to see too much, travel over me from head to foot. "You've changed a lot in two years."

"Hi, Nana. It's good to see you." My focus automatically drifts over to the smoke curling from the burned-out building. "I wish it had been under different circumstances."

The old woman issues a long sigh, twisting her hands around the strap of the purse strung across her body as she looks at the carnage. "I agree; the circumstances are not ideal." She turns to face me. "Now, I know this is a huge ask, Jude, but it's been a very long time since I've seen my grandson. Can I hug you?"

The moment she says the words, tears well up in my eyes, and instead of flinching from her touch, like I have so many other times, like I have with everyone who's ever tried it, except for Angie and Allie, I take a step forward and pull the frail woman into my arms.

She issues a little *oomph* sound and laughs as she tightens her arms around me. "You're so tall, so muscular. You must work out a lot."

I laugh. "That's basically my whole life, Nana: writing, working out."

She pokes me in the stomach. "You could use a few extra pounds here. If you came to Sunday dinners, I could get you filled up."

"I know." I squeeze her shoulders. "I miss your cooking."

Her eyes narrow on me. "I saw Angie sneak away with a plate the other night."

I try to look stupid, raising a brow. "Oh, really?"

She purses her lips. "Yes, I wonder where she took it, since everyone was at dinner except you."

Shrugging, I step back from her before she delves too

deeply into her suspicions. "Perhaps leftovers for herself so she doesn't have to cook."

A knowing smirk spreads on Nana's face. "Possibly."

Angie approaches, almost as if she can hear us discussing her, the blanket still wrapped around her. Allie follows her, and the four of us stare out at the café.

I want to reach out and pull Allie and Angie into my sides, to hold both of them and offer them what little comfort I can, but I can't pile any more complications into tonight...or, I guess, early this morning.

Everything has been thrown into such disarray. The last thing we need now is a bunch of speculation about what's happening with the girls and me.

Nana glances over at us. "So, what do we all think? Those cunts Falco Enterprises or that douchebag Roselli?"

All of us whip our heads toward her, eyes wide. "Nana!"

Our chorus makes her chuckle. The Hawke matriarch never was one to mince words, but still, I wouldn't have expected that to come from her mouth so freely.

Angie wraps an arm around her grandmother's shoulder. "Nana, we don't know what's happening yet, and you can't talk like that."

She laughs again and motions backward to where all her kids and grandkids linger around the loft. "Oh, yeah? Why not? After ninety years on this planet, I think I've earned the right to say whatever I want, especially after everything we've all been through."

That's definitely true.

Who are we to criticize the woman and how she chooses to live her life, considering the way we all have?

Allie rests her head on Nana's shoulder. "I'm glad you're here, Nana."

Nana snorts. "Well, somebody had to cook for all of you."

Angie drops her arm. "What? No, Nana, you don't have to."

She waves a dismissive, wrinkled hand. "Caroline already grabbed everything I need before she picked me up. I'll get started now. Everyone must be hungry."

My stomach rumbles, reminding me that Angie and I never *did* get to our picnic, which is still sitting untouched on the blanket on the roof. "What are you making?"

She smiles at me and pokes my stomach again. "Lasagna and chicken parm, your favorites."

21

JUDE

Angie's dark brows draw low over her concerned blue eyes. "Are you sure you want to do this?" She tightens her grip on my hand and returns to staring across the street at the burned-out remains of Hawke's Daily Grind. "You don't have to come with me."

I grasp her chin, my finger and thumb gripping it tightly, and turn her head back to face me. "I *do* need to go with you. And the last thing you need to be worrying about right now is me. I'm okay. I'll *be* okay."

She releases a heavy breath and nods. I drop a quick kiss to her lips, then release her so we can both face what was her thriving business. Two days after the fire was finally extinguished, the smell of smoke still hangs in the air, along with the heavy weight of what was stolen from her.

All I want is to be able to absorb her pain. Cast some magic spell, like the ones they use in all the fantasy novels I've lost myself in over the years, to turn back time and fix it all in an instant.

There aren't even any words I can say to make this any easier. There never are in any of these types of circumstances. Even as someone who literally uses words for a living, I can't come up with a fucking thing to say to her.

The only thing I can offer her is a hand to hold and a shoulder to lean on as she takes her first steps into the wreckage. Now that the fire chief finally released the scene—still *insisting* the arson investigator says it was a gas leak—and said we could go back in, Angie didn't want to wait.

I've been dreading this moment, though.

Thoroughly.

Nothing good will come of seeing what the fire did, of what's been decimated by the flames, but she has to walk through it. She has to see it all for herself before she'll ever be able to move on and start to heal from all of this.

Any one of the Hawkes would've gone with her, would've held her hand and tried to comfort her, but it *should* be me. I should always be the one who's with her, who's trying to make things better for *her*, not the other way around.

Angie shouldn't be worrying about me when she's just lost everything. My issues seem minor compared to seeing so many years of her hard work reduced to nothing but ashes.

Things will never be the same; they never could be. Even if they rebuild, the memory of the destruction will always haunt her. The same way what was done to me will always be a demon on my back.

But not today.

Today isn't about what I need or what she can do for me. It's about giving her the only thing I can offer.

I squeeze her hand. "Let's go."

My chest tightens as we take the first few steps across the street, but I breathe through it and keep a tight grip on her small hand that trembles with the rest of her body.

Just across the street.

You can do that for her.

She's proven to me that I'm capable of so much more than I knew. Not just going up to the roof or down to the bookstore space. It didn't even strike me until much later what happened when that explosion hit—I stopped thinking about my own fears and worried about *her.*

I stood outside on that sidewalk with her for hours. I had *all* the Hawkes in my place, crammed together, filling it with the very type of chatter and noise that always sent me running from family gatherings to seek somewhere quiet. All that...I didn't have a single panic attack.

Somehow, I even hugged Nana without recoiling.

Caring about Angelina, wanting to protect her and be there for her, took me out of my own head, and it will again today as we do this.

It has to.

We reach the opposite curb and step up onto the charred sidewalk.

There isn't even a door anymore, nothing to open, the second floor they used for storage collapsing onto the first, leaving a mangled mess with only pockets that we can even step through.

Dust and ash float through the air, kicked up even more with each inch we advance, giving the entire place a hellish haze.

Angie covers her mouth with her free hand, and I do the same with mine.

Tears trickle down her cheeks as she scans around us.

Broken China. Chunks of wood and twisted metal that were the tables and chairs. The display cases crumbled into piles of broken and charred boards. Occasional peeks at things we can't identify at all.

"It's all gone."

Her words hang in the air with the ash, and she releases a sob that tears through the eerie silence.

I pull my hand from hers and slide my arm around her shoulders, drawing her closer and pressing my lips against her temple. "I'm so sorry, Ang."

It's worse than I even expected.

Everything utterly obliterated.

Though, given how powerful that first blast was and the few other smaller ones, I guess I should have known it would be like this. The blaze burned hot and long, nothing salvageable.

We'll have to tear down everything and rebuild. Something Savage and Gabe are already on top of, while Saint, Bishop, and Luca have already started investigating who could have been behind it.

No one believes the official cause—gas main explosion. Not for a fucking second.

Whoever did this either covered their tracks incredibly well or is powerful enough to have paid off whomever they needed to within the fire department to ensure that finding would come out no matter *what* the evidence showed.

But the Hawkes all know the truth.

We didn't smell gas that night out on the roof, and there was no indication of any issues an hour earlier when Angie left the building.

This was deliberate.

Pure and simple.

An attack on the Hawkes and everything they stand for.

The only question is...who's behind it?

It's what we've all been asking for the last two days, scouring for anything that might suggest where to point the finger. All it will take is one piece of evidence and the Hawkes will unleash their own firestorm on whomever is responsible.

I'd like to be a part of that hit squad, to look into the eyes of the man who did this to Angelina and fire a damn bullet right into his fucking balls.

I tighten my grip on her shoulder and halt her advance. "Are you sure you want to see anymore?"

Each step we take only seems to bring her more pain, to deepen her sorrow, and I can't bear to see her like this— completely destroyed.

She shakes her head as tears stream freely down her cheeks. "I don't know if I want to."

"I do." Allie's voice from behind us makes us turn back. She stands just inside where the door would've been, tears matching her sister's rolling down her cheeks.

Angie swipes at her cheeks. "I didn't know you were back."

Eventually, everyone had slowly filed out of my place and returned to their homes, started doing their part—whatever it may be—to help the situation, leaving me alone again.

Without Angelina and Alessandra right across the street.

Without my best friend and the love of my life here with me.

But it was the wrong time to tell Allie, and they needed to be together, to comfort one another.

Knowing they were both hurting while I was stuck here, watching the aftermath of the fire from my new windows, broke me apart even more than seeing Angie's face when she realized it was gone.

I raise my other arm, and Allie tucks herself under it.

We all stare toward where the small stage and bookshelves used to be in the back corner, now just a tangled mess of scorched wood and indistinguishable metal.

I suck in a long breath. "I know it looks bleak."

"Bleak?" Allie gazes up at me. "It looks like the apocalypse in here."

"I know, but we can rebuild." I raise a brow at her and

squeeze my arm around her. "Isn't that what we do? Always rise."

It seems so cavalier to say it, especially when I'm not technically a Hawke. When I wasn't part of the family when they suffered their string of tragedies, but it still draws a slight grin from Angie and Allie.

Allie releases a sigh. "We don't have any choice, right?"

Angie shrugs. "How fucking ironic..." She lets out a sob and clamps her hand over her mouth. "A fire took my dad from me and destroyed The Hawkeye Club THREE. It's what almost ended Stone and Nora's relationship and then what almost took my mom and Landon from me." She looks around. "And now, it's what took the Daily Grind."

Allie shakes her head, her jaw hardening. Anger flashes in her eyes. "No. What took the café was some fucking asshole with a vendetta against us that we are no part of. We've done nothing." She bites back a sob and pulls her bottom lip under her teeth. "There's no reason anyone would do this to us."

Footsteps crunch behind us, and I glance over my shoulder to find Byron and Luca approaching slowly.

Byron offers a sympathetic half-smile. "We're not interrupting, are we?"

Angie shakes her head. "Of course not. I'm glad you're here."

Luca steps up next to us, glancing at my arms around them. "How are you girls doing?"

They both fight back more tears and brush them away, though I don't know why they bother putting on a brave face for him. Luca has seen the worst of the worst, the type of things that haunt a man's dreams. There isn't anything you need to hide from him.

Byron stands at his side, waiting for the girls to say something. Of anyone in the family, he's the easiest to talk to, the one everyone is most open with, the one who seems to see through everyone's façades and straight to how they're really feeling. But when neither offers anything, he scans what's left of the café, a sad smile on his face.

"I have to say." He waves a hand. "Seeing all this...reminds me of some pretty bad memories."

Angie looks at him. "I was just saying the same thing."

He releases a heavy sigh and runs a hand through his salt-and-pepper hair. "I know you were only five and you never came to the wreckage of THREE. But..." He takes a second to gather himself. "But it was really hard being there, knowing we lost your father that way. Having to rebuild it..." His gaze moves to me. "But I'm glad you girls have each other and Jude and the rest of the family to support you through this."

I give him a tight smile. "Thanks, but I'm not doing much of anything."

His gaze narrows on me. "I beg to differ. You were the one with Angie when all this happened, weren't you?"

Shit.

Luca looks on silently even though Byron just touched on the same question he had the night the fire happened. They don't keep secrets from each other, so if Luca suspected something was going on between Angie and me, he would have told Byron.

Which leaves us in a very precarious situation.

I glance at Allie, who stares up at me with her brow furrowed in question.

"What does he mean you were with her?"

Fuck.

I pull my arms off the girls' shoulders and rub the back of my neck, looking to Angie, who offers a shrug, all her energy to fight drained by the last few days.

"Um, yeah. Angie and I were hanging out after she got done with work that night."

Allie narrows her eyes on me. "You were? But I thought you

313

were working all night. That's why I didn't come over—"

I hold up a hand to stop her before she goes off on a tangent. "I *was*. She brought me a late dinner, figuring I hadn't eaten."

She turns back to Angie. "And you didn't think to mention this to me? I would've stayed late with you and helped, and we all could have eaten together."

Angie reaches out and squeezes Allie's shoulder. "I know you would have, but you worked a long day, and you're..."

Her gaze immediately flicks to Byron and Luca.

Luca raises a dark brow. "Should we leave?"

Allie glances over her shoulder at him, then her gaze bounces over us in question. She wants to tell him, and ultimately, it's her decision, not something we can force her to do. "Well, if there's anyone in this family who can keep a secret, it's you."

Byron and Luca share a knowing smirk before Luca takes a step toward her, concern in his gaze.

"We are definitely good at keeping secrets when it's called for"—his gaze darts to me for a moment before returning to her—"but if this is something someone else should know and you're keeping it from them, I can't promise I won't do what's in your best interest by revealing it to say...your parents?"

Allie huffs and presses her hand flat over her belly. "It's not really something I can hide for long."

Byron's gaze drops to her hand, then back up, his mouth falling open. "You're pregnant?"

She nods.

A smile splits Luca's face, and he pulls her into his arms. *"Congratulazioni, mamma."*

She wraps her arms around him, burying her face in the chest of the man who has become like a true uncle to her and a father to me.

Byron nudges him out of the way for his own embrace, and

for the first time since she found out she's pregnant, a look of relief washes over Allie's face.

Keeping it a secret has been weighing heavily on her, and now that Luca and Byron know, I have a feeling it's going to open the floodgates for her to tell everyone else who should know.

Luca grins as Byron releases her. "Just remember, Allie, secrets are hard to keep in this family. If there's anyone else who needs to know, I suggest you do it quickly."

He glances between Angie and me.

Fuck.

ANGELINA

JUDE STIFFENS BESIDE ME, the tension rolling off him in waves. I don't know if he thought his answer earlier was going to be enough to appease everyone standing here, staring at us, or just isn't fully prepared to have this conversation with his fathers and Allie.

But maybe this is the time to come clean. Maybe this is the time to start introducing the idea that a few people have already referenced and made suggestions to recently.

I don't have the energy to hide it anymore, not when all I've wanted the last few days was to climb into bed with him and let him hold me instead of having to stay away.

There were so many times I almost came clean, almost unloaded the truth on Allie just to get the weight of it off my chest, but I didn't want to create a rift with her when everything else was already so fucked up.

Only the longer we keep this hidden, the more it's going to hurt her when it does get revealed.

"Yeah, so ..." I glance between Jude and Allie, and he nods, giving me the indication that he's behind me if I want to do this now. I swallow thickly and kick at a burned piece of wood. "I was over bringing Jude dinner as more than a friend."

Allie stiffens, her brow scrunching. "What?" Her confused gaze darts between us. "I don't understand..."

Yes, you do.

She just doesn't want to accept what we're telling her.

Jude wraps his arm around my shoulder again, pulling me in close. "It just happened, Al. It's not like it's been going on for a long time. But I—"

Allie's mouth falls open. "Holy shit. You two?"

She motions between us with a frantic flap of her hand while Byron and Luca offer knowing smirks. Apparently, we did a pretty bad job of hiding what was going on between us when everyone was over at Jude's place.

Luca wraps an arm around Allie. "Come now, *bambolotta*. You really never noticed anything going on between the two of them?"

Allie gapes. "No. I mean..." Her wide-eyed gaze darts between us again. "I knew you two had, like, an, I don't know, trusting thing. Jude always said he felt safe when you were around when we were growing up. But we're like ..."

She doesn't utter the word, but I know what she was going to say because I've said it to Jude myself—that we're *family*. And now I understand why he always got that pained expression when I did say it to him, when I used it as an excuse to keep my feelings for him bottled up deep inside me.

Jude looks at his best friend, begging her to understand. "Believe me, Al, this was not something either of us took lightly, and we know there are going to be some members of the family who are not exactly thrilled with the situation. But..." He looks down at me with so much love in his eyes that tears form in mine again. "We're together now."

Byron grins. "That's amazing. Congratulations."

Allie still looks dumbstruck. "Um, yeah..."

Um, yeah?

I'm not sure what I expected her reaction to be, but definitely something more than, *um, yeah...*

Maybe she just needs time to process this, to let it sink in, and then the three of us can sit down and really talk about it. Jude watches her with a pained expression, like her reaction hurts him even more than it does me.

And maybe it should.

She and I are family by blood. They're family and best friends by choice. Or maybe something stronger, like fate. I can't tell if she feels more betrayed by me or by him. But looking around, standing in the ashes of my life, Jude's strength at my side, I don't want to have any more secrets.

I just hope he doesn't, either.

"Jude?"

He glances down at me. "What?"

"You know, while we're talking about coming clean on things, is there anything else you maybe want to tell Byron and Luca?"

His brows fly up. "Really? Right now, right here?"

I shrug. "What better time than when my world is literally in ashes?"

Perhaps it isn't fair to put him on the spot like this, but the other night he said he wanted to *try*. That he would take the steps he was capable of to get his life back. And telling Luca and Byron the truth would be a major one.

His eyes drift closed for a moment, like he's gathering his strength to say the words he's been keeping inside for so long. He clears his throat and glances back toward his place. "Um, so I know I haven't been around much the last couple of years."

I tighten my hold on his waist, squeezing him to me and pressing my cheek to his chest, giving him the only thing I can in this moment that I know he's been dreading.

Byron and Luca both nod but let him continue.

"Well, I've been kind of having some issues with leaving the loft."

Luca's gaze softens. "We kind of figured it was something like that or that one of us did or said something to piss you off so badly that you didn't want to spend any time with any of us anymore. I can't say either would be a better alternative, but I'm kind of relieved it wasn't the latter."

Jude offers him a grin. "No, it had nothing to do with either of you, not with any of the Hawkes." He rubs the back of his neck, glancing down at me before his gaze darts over a still-stunned Allie and back to Luca and Byron. "I, uh..."

Shit.

I hadn't meant to force him into revealing things in front of Allie that he never wanted her to know. And now I've put him in the position of having to say things in front of her that she won't have any context for.

His body trembles, the nerves finally hitting him. "I ran into somebody from my past..."

Byron and Luca both stiffen, and Luca's hands fist at his sides.

They both know Jude can't be talking about his father, and it doesn't take a huge leap to figure out who he might be referring to without him even saying it.

Jude releases a huge rush of air, opening his eyes again to finally look at the men who have given him so much, who were willing to kill for him. "And it triggered some things I wasn't expecting."

Luca locks his jaw and issues a low growl. "Who was it?"

A shudder rolls through Jude's body, and he sags against me slightly, his eyes clenched. "One of the men I met outside the club..."

Byron staggers back a step, kicking a burned, twisted piece of metal that clanks as it rolls across the other debris.

Luca opens and closes his fists at his sides, his barely contained rage vibrating off him. "Where did you see him?"

Allie finally takes a step forward, her mouth hanging open. "Will someone tell me what the *hell* you're all talking about? I feel like I'm in the fucking pitch black about everything going on around here."

Jude scrubs his hand over his face and turns to her. "Shit. I'm sorry, Al. I-I promise I'll tell you someday. Okay? I just can't right now..."

She opens her mouth to object, but the look Luca gives her silences her immediately.

Allie has no idea what she's stepping into, what she's witnessing, and part of me longs to be able to tell her so she'll understand. But it's Jude's story to tell, should he choose to. His pain to share with her, not mine.

"*Piccolo guaio,* I need you to tell me who he is, where you saw him, a name..."

No one questions why Luca is looking for the information or what he plans to do with it once Jude reveals it.

It wouldn't be the first time he's killed for Jude, and if he could create a list of every single person who ever laid a hand on him, I'm sure he would work his way down it with a vicious efficiency that would leave everyone stunned.

I press up on my toes to bring my lips to Jude's ear. "You need to tell him. It's the right thing. He could be hurting someone else the way he did you. We need to end this."

Advocating to give someone a death sentence was never anything I even remotely considered myself capable of, but after hearing what Jude went through, what was done to him, I harbor zero remorse over pushing him to seek his own type of vengeance through the man more than willing to enact it for him.

Jude leans toward me, his eyes meeting mine as he hands

the man his death sentence. "Aaron Harper. He's a professor of anthropology at Tulane."

Byron steps between Luca and Jude and waits for Jude to look at him. "I'm so sorry, son."

Jude shakes his head. "You don't have anything to apologize for. You can't make my entire past disappear, no matter how badly you may want to."

Luca growls low again. "I sure as fuck can try." Unshed tears shine in the eyes of the man who has always been a solid rock, an unbreakable wall of protection for the family since he was brought into it. "This never should have happened. It's my fault. I should have..."—he winces—"tried harder to track them all down, to weed them out and ensure you'd never have to worry about anything like this happening. It's *my* fault, *piccolo guaio*. I promised to protect you, and I failed."

The sheer anguish in his words slices at my heart, and if it's eating away at me, it must be destroying Jude to see Luca like this.

"No." Jude slips out of my hold, advancing to stand in front of Luca. "You did everything you promised. You and Byron gave me a new life. You gave me safety I never had before. You can't protect me from *everything*. No one could." He shakes his head. "I just need to work through the things that are holding me back, try to find balance again."

Luca swipes away an errant tear and reaches out to clap his hand on Jude's shoulder, the first time I think I've ever seen them touch in all the years since they took him in. "I will take care of this, *piccolo guaio*. It might only be one small thing, but it's one I am happy to do for you. I only wish you had told us sooner so that..." He closes his eyes for a moment, then reopens them with a renewed regret. "So that we didn't lose so much time."

Fuck.

As if coming here wasn't emotionally charged enough, now

we've all laid everything out on the table and shattered any barriers we had built up around the harsh truths we've been living with.

Allie watches the scene unfold, her brow furrowed, but I can see the wheels turning in her head. Jude may not have told her about his past, but she knows enough, has picked up small pieces over the years.

His nightmares.

His unwillingness to be touched.

His inability to connect with anyone despite their reaching out to him.

And now she's heard him give a name.

It doesn't take a rocket scientist to put the pieces together, to see Luca and Byron's reactions to know what was done to Jude.

Allie slaps her hand over her mouth and sobs, and Jude turns to her and pulls her into his arms, pressing his lips close to her ear to murmur something meant only for her.

She nods against his chest, tightening her arms around him, and he presses a kiss to the top of her head and holds her for a long moment. Those two are definitely going to need to have a private conversation after this.

The fire may have burned down the café, but it also burned down the barriers we put up to keep our private struggles in, walls that *had* to come down for any of us to move on.

Allie pulls back from Jude, fear flashing in her gaze. "I have to tell you something."

He glances back at me and Byron and Luca. "Okay? What's wrong, Al?"

She opens her mouth to say something, but the rumble of an engine pulling up at the curb turns everyone's attention that way.

The sleek Maserati shines in the sun, and the driver's door opens as Cass Whitaker slips out.

That motherfucker.

22

JUDE

Anger flares in Angie's eyes, lighting up the blue with a blazing fire that mirrors the one that took her café from her. She storms around me before I can grab her and marches across the rubble toward where the front door once was.

Cass approaches, the first time I've seen the man looking so casual. In a pair of jeans and a tight-fitting T-shirt, he exposes a few tattoos I never would've expected on his arms, given his typical buttoned-up appearance.

He sees her coming and steps over the curb onto the sidewalk, waiting for her.

Angie points a finger at him as she steps out of the debris, barreling toward him like a bat out of hell. "You get the fuck out of here."

He holds up his hands, green eyes darting from her to the rest of us following her. "Look, I need to talk to you."

"No."

Luca and I reach her in time for me to put an arm across

her chest and hold her back from physically trying to strangle him while Byron keeps Allie close to the building, well back from what could become a very volatile situation very fast.

What the fuck is he doing here?

He had to know coming here would start something, yet he still showed his face. The man must have a death wish.

I glower at Cass, making it clear he isn't welcome. "You need to leave, *now*."

His eyes flicker over to me. "And who are you?" His gaze moves up and down me, then over Luca and Byron. "Jude, I presume?" He looks over at my building, where the new windows now make it appear as if nothing ever happened. A simple fix we won't be able to make to the Grind. "It's good you're here, too. All of you need to hear what I came to say— Falco Enterprises had *nothing* to do with this."

The air thickens around us, tension vibrating off everyone, stoked by his claim that not a single one of us believes for a damn second.

A heated rage I've never felt before boils in my blood. This guy thinks he can come here to try to cover his own ass while upsetting Angelina and Allie when they're already on the edge of losing it completely.

Motherfucking son of a bitch.

"Bullshit!" Angie tries to take a step forward, but I nudge her back and shift in front of her, effectively blocking her from going at Cass the way I know she wants to. "You fucking *liar!*"

She will have her hands around this man's throat in two point five seconds if I don't stop her, and the last thing we need is her facing criminal charges when everything else has already gone to shit.

I've never been one to be confrontational or to get involved in a fight, but after what he did to the girls, there's no way this fucker is getting close to either of them again.

Not on my fucking watch.

I shift toward him, puffing out my chest slightly, making use of the few inches and at least twenty pounds of muscle I have on the man. "You came onto the street already a threat to them. You've been showing up here, getting your coffee every morning, and taunting them with more vague threats. And from what I hear, you're schmoozing everyone down at City Hall to get what you need done as fast as possible to compete with the Grind. And now, it mysteriously explodes and burns the fuck down. You expect us to believe this is all just coincidence?"

Luca steps up beside me, arms over his chest, his dark eyes an almost black as he stares down Whitaker. "You must think we're fucking stupid."

Cass' eyes dart between the two of us and over the girls. "I know how it looks, believe me. That's why I wanted to come here to speak in person once things had cooled down." He winces. "Bad choice of words. I'm sorry. I just want to have a conversation with you. I would've gone to Isaac and Stone since I work with them in a professional capacity, but I thought it might be a *safer* option to come directly to the people affected."

"Affected?" Angie tries to shove me out of the way, but I turn to face her, pressing my body to hers to keep her back.

Dropping my head next to hers, I brush my lips to her ear. "Relax, Ang..."

I understand her ire and share it, but a physical confrontation on a public street doesn't do anyone any good and will only complicate things more.

Ignoring my warning, she continues to push against me, pointing a finger at Whitaker over my shoulder. "You destroyed my business. *All of it*. It's fucking gone." Tears stream down her face as she chokes on a sob. "This is all I've worked for my entire fucking life, and it's *gone*. It's exactly what you wanted, exactly why you put in your place just down the street."

Her heart beats wildly against mine, her face red with her anger. She's going to lose it. Everything has finally come to a boiling point, and Angelina is stuck in the middle of the fucking pot.

It's a state I recognize easily.

One I have been in more times than I care to count.

I wrap my arms around her, crushing her to me and nuzzling her neck, pressing my lips to it and murmuring what I hope are the right words to get her under control. "Baby, stop. I know you want to destroy him, make him pay, but this isn't the way...not like this. Not now. I need you to take a breath."

She fights against me for a few more seconds, pushing me, trying to get me to let her go until she finally sags and unleashes an anguished sob against my chest.

All the pain she's tried to hold back, kept contained to try to appear strong through it all, has finally detonated, her hatred for Cass Whitaker the catalyst for her own explosion.

Luca maintains his place at my back, keeping himself between Whitaker and the rest of us, but he doesn't say a word, just stares down the man who represents the greatest threat to Hawke Enterprises.

I glance over my shoulder at Cass, glaring at the audacity he has to come here and say something like that.

He throws up his hands. "You keep saying 'your,' but I need you, *all* the Hawkes, to understand something. I am *not* Falco Enterprises. I represent their *interests*. I do what they *pay me* to do, but none of this is *me*."

How can he say that with a fucking straight face?

Luca issues a sardonic snort, taking a half-step toward him. "You can hide behind your law degree, your expensive fucking suits, and your $500 an hour fees, but you're choosing to work for them, knowing what they're doing. Knowing they've been targeting us for years. That makes you just as bad as them. That makes you complicit."

Cass clearly knows who Luca is, and if he were smart and valued his life, he would back away slowly and then drive away quickly. Luca may be "retired" from the life, but everyone knows Luca isn't above taking a step back to what that required role when need be.

To protect me from Dad.

To eliminate threats lurking in the shadows.

Or those in plain sight.

Luca's reaction to my earlier revelation just proved to me what he's truly capable of and how much he cares. Far more than even I knew.

He won't let anything or anyone touch the Hawkes, and Cass Whitaker must know that.

Cass presses his lips together in a firm line, the reproach seemingly taking him down a peg. He pushes up on his toes to look over my shoulder at Angie again. "I'm sorry you feel that way, Angelina. I really did enjoy your coffee, and the croissants weren't half bad."

"Fuck you, Cass." Luca waves up and down the street. "If I ever see you near any of our properties again, here or anywhere else in New Orleans, I will have you permanently removed by whatever force necessary." He shrugs nonchalantly. "I will even enjoy doing it myself."

Back stiffening, Cass raises a brow. "Is that a threat?"

Luca shakes his head. "It's a promise, *stronzo*."

Cass snorts. "I knew you could never walk away from that life, Abello. Not from what you were born and bred to do. It's in your veins. In your *blood*."

Angie finally lifts her head, her fight renewed. She sneers at Cass over my shoulder, pushing against my chest again to try to get to him. "And you know what's in *ours*? Hawke blood. And you just pissed off a whole lot of us. You should be more careful about the enemies you make."

"I'm telling you—it wasn't Falco."

He keeps saying that, but the recent history doesn't lie. The long line of attacks against the Hawke businesses has been a constant thorn in our side, and it doesn't take a major leap to see Falco Enterprises resorting to more severe measures if they weren't succeeding through other avenues.

Isaac and Stone have looked into every angle, have searched high and low for any paperwork that would lead to who actually owns and operates Falco Enterprises, and they've come up with nothing. Even Gabe and Saint's less-than-legal channels have come up dry. Perhaps it's because whoever is behind it is powerful enough to keep themselves hidden forever until they've accomplished what they set out to do—destroy all of us and everything the Hawkes have built.

But I won't let that happen to Angelina, and the longer we have this standoff with Cass, the harder she trembles in my arms. The adrenaline coursing through her veins will only last so long, and when it's gone, she's going to crash.

Hard.

Luca sees her distress and pulls his gun, pointing it squarely at Cass, unconcerned with what anyone driving by might see. "We've asked you to leave nicely. You've failed to comply. I suggest you get back in your car and stay the fuck away from the girls and all the Hawkes if you hope to keep breathing."

He sure knows how to end a standoff.

His threat sends ice through my veins even when it isn't directed at me, and it hangs in the air along with the acrid smell of smoke.

Cass releases a resigned sigh and backs away toward his car, hands raised. He pauses when he reaches the still-open driver's side door. "Remember, I came to you peacefully. I'm being completely honest when I say this *wasn't* Falco. My client knows better than to come at the Hawkes this way."

He climbs in and drives away, tires squealing, and Angie finally fully collapses against me. I lift her easily into my arms, cradling her to my chest as she sobs and clings to my neck like a lifeline—what she's always been for me.

I glance over at Allie, where she stands stunned with Byron, his arm protectively around her shoulders.

Luca drops a hand on my arm. "I'll make sure Allie gets home safely."

Any other time, I would just bring her with me to my place, but her reaction earlier and the way she's staring at Angelina in my arms suggests the conversation we'll have won't be an easy one. That isn't anything Angie or I can handle right now.

Not after all this.

It will have to wait.

As much as it kills me to walk away from Allie, to leave things on such bad terms with my best friend, I have to.

I don't know how any of us are going to survive this.

————

ANGELINA

JUDE CARRIES me into his condo and lowers me to sit on the edge of the bed. He squats in front of me, tugs off my shoes, and grabs the hem of my shirt, pausing for a moment. "We need to get you out of these clothes. They smell like smoke."

I hadn't even noticed the scent hanging on them, too lost in the rush of adrenaline and utter despair that overwhelmed me out there.

Not waiting for a response from me, he pulls my shirt over my head, then works off my jeans, leaving me sitting in my thong and bra. His gaze rakes over me slowly, but there isn't anything sexual in it.

Worry.

Jude is worried about me, about what I might do next after

almost trying to kill Cass with my bare hands out there, then breaking down and collapsing in his arms.

He pushes to his feet and grabs a T-shirt from his drawer. With slow, tender hands, he gets it over my head and covers me, stopping to press a kiss to my lips before he steps back and strips down to his boxers.

Sheer exhaustion—mental and physical—hits me so hard that it feels like I might not ever be able to move again. Almost as if he senses it, he scoops me up into his arms again and settles me on the bed, crawling in next to me and tugging the covers up over us.

He brings my face against his chest, burying his into my hair and inhaling deeply. "Are you okay?"

Am I?

It's a stupid question, given everything that just happened out on the sidewalk, but his concern makes me grin against his warm skin and press a kiss over his heart. It has finally returned to its steady rhythm after thundering away wildly for so long during our confrontation with Cass.

I release a heavy sigh, some of the tension of the day melting away with it. "I don't think *okay* is the word, but I'm not in as bad of a place as I thought I would be."

For a moment there, rage blinded me, consumed me so completely that I was contemplating doing things I know I would have regretted. Only Jude's strong hold on me kept me grounded and reminded me that there was something else to fight for besides the physical building lying in ruins behind us.

If I had lashed out at Cass, I would have paid the price, potentially in a way that would prevent me from having *this*.

What the hell would I do without Jude?

The question hits me so squarely in the chest that I have to fight back a sob. It's only been a week, one damn week, since he came back into my life, and already, I can't imagine what it would be like to go back to the way things were.

Watching each other through the glass.

Pretending we didn't feel something more.

Keeping ourselves from being happy to avoid the complications of what getting that happiness could create.

Jude kisses the top of my head. "I guess that's something." He trails his fingers up and down my spine over the T-shirt. "It's okay to be scared and to be pissed off, and even not to know how you feel with all this. It's a lot for anyone to process, but especially for you after how you lost your dad."

Pulling back so I can see his face, I trace the thin lines along his brow and cheek. "You weren't here when all that went down, but I know you've heard the stories from other members of the family."

He nods. "It isn't anything I ever would've asked you about, but Allie's told me some things. So have others."

I drop my chin against his chest and stare at it rather than look at him. "New Orleans has always been home. We Hawkes have made a name for ourselves here. Savage built all this with Gabe, and then everyone else eventually joined the empire. Everyone stepped into their own roles, each as essential as the next. We've done everything the right way, tried to stay away from the world that took my father, yet somehow, we keep getting sucked back into it."

First, with Satriano coming after Jack, and now, this blatant attack on us.

Jude hums lightly. "Why do you think that is?"

I shrug, mulling over the answer. "Savage seems to think it's a curse."

His hand stills on my shoulder. "What do you mean?"

Unlike the rest of us, Jude didn't grow up hearing the family lore, being constantly reminded of how we got where we were. There are so many things, so many events that shaped the family and brought us to this point.

"When Savage started out after college, he borrowed money

from Luca's father, Dom Abello, to buy his first bar. And even though he paid it back very quickly, he always felt like it was making a deal with the devil, like it had opened the door to something he never should have delved into."

Jude stiffens under me, lifting my chin so my eyes meet his. "He doesn't seriously think that has anything to do with all the bad things that have happened over the years?"

I sigh and pull out of his hold, pressing my cheek against his chest and trailing my fingers over that little trail of hair across his abs. "I don't know. Sometimes, I wonder. Savage's accident. Gabe almost dying during the hurricane. My dad's death, then Mom and Landon almost dying in the fire..."

Just mentioning the turmoil over those few years makes tears pool in my eyes. All the uncertainty. The pain. It comes rushing back, the very memories that I've used for so long as an excuse to avoid the type of connection I've found with Jude.

"It was a lot, Ang, and you were just a child when it happened. I can see how it would be hard to process all of it."

I sniffle and wipe away my tears. "I didn't really understand it then, and I still don't know how so many bad things could happen to us so quickly."

"But a curse?" He runs his fingers through my hair slowly. "I believe in some pretty wild things, and I've written them into these fantasy worlds I create, but I don't think I believe in curses. Maybe bad luck? Strange coincidences?"

"It's just a coincidence that everything in my life gets burned and taken away from me?"

He shifts to force my face up to look at him, taking it between his palms and brushing his thumb reverently over my lips. "This. You and me, it's never going to burn away. You know that, right?"

I close my eyes and try to believe his words. "But what if it does? What if this is just, I don't know, years of weird tension and all the stressful situations we've been in the last couple of weeks? The adrenaline. The—"

"Stop. And open your eyes and look at me, Angelina."

My body trembles as I follow his command.

The pale blue I'm so used to looking into has darkened, a swirling tempest of so much emotion it threatens to drown me. "You know that's not true, Ang, and you're just saying that right now because you're scared of what's going to happen, of what our future's going to look like. But *this* isn't going to burn out. That would be impossible."

"But what about Allie?"

His gaze softens. "She wasn't exactly excited." He presses his lips together in a firm line, likely replaying her reaction. "But you and I will each talk with her. We'll explain. She'll come around because she loves both of us."

"Will she?" Uncertainty tightens my gut. "She's your best friend. And we hid it from her. Christ, she's the only person you've really talked to for fifteen years. The only person you'd ever let touch you—"

One of his pale brows rises. "I let *you* touch me."

That draws a smile from somewhere deep inside me, despite the seriousness of the conversation. "Yeah, you have. And I saw you hugged Nana the other day."

He nods slowly. "And Jack kind of threw her arms around me before I could stop her. But Nana...that woman..." A little mirthless laugh tumbles from his lips. "She's really something, isn't she?"

I nod. "She really is. She's been through a lot, raising the kids by herself after my grandfather died. But whatever strength she found has kept her alive and kicking at ninety."

Jude chuckles, the vibration shaking the bed and both of us, and he drags me up into his arms to bury my face against his neck, my entire body spread over his firm one.

Strong arms wrap around me, and he lowers his lips to my

forehead. "I think everything will work out. Allie will come around. Everyone else in the family will, too. I got the impression Nana, Luca, and Byron already knew something before I even said anything today."

"Really?"

He nods. "So maybe whatever was happening between us has been a little bit more obvious to other people than it was to us."

That brings up a question that's been rattling around in my head for the last several days. "What do you think would've happened if you and I had actually seen each other in the last two years? If you had kept coming into the café and hadn't locked yourself up in here?"

He stiffens under me, and I instantly regret asking. "Shit, I'm sorry, Jude. I never should have—"

"No, it's okay." He runs his fingers up and down my spine, relaxing under me again. "I think, eventually, something would've been a tipping point. I hate that it was Allie's situation, that we had to go through all that agony over wondering if she was okay and worrying about her to force us to see each other again. But I think this would've happened, anyway. Somehow."

"You do?"

He feathers his lips across my forehead, the motion so reverent that it makes my heart clench in my chest. "I do." His finger twirls around a strand of my hair. "My mom always said, 'Sometimes you're the windshield, and sometimes you're the bug.' Right now, it feels like you're the bug, but in reality, you're the windshield."

"That's the strangest analogy I think I've ever heard."

His chest vibrates with his laugh. "Yeah, but it's an apt one, isn't it?"

"I guess..."

If I understood at all what he's trying to say...

"It just means that bad things happen, Ang, and it can feel like life is crushing you, beating you down. But it won't always be that way. Look at all the things you've survived. Everything that's been thrown at you that only made you stronger. I believe in karma and in good things happening to good people. Like us finally ending up like *this*."

"You think this is karma?"

"I don't know." He shrugs. "Maybe God is paying me back and trying to make amends for all the awful things that happened to me before by giving me the only thing I've ever truly wanted."

Tears pool in my eyes at his words, and I lift my head and press a kiss to his cheek and then drift over to his lips, gliding my tongue along his slowly. He groans into my mouth and tugs me tighter against him, like he can't get me close enough.

I pull back and press my forehead to his, closing my eyes and just sharing our breaths. "Everything feels so out of control right now."

"I know, Ang. That's how I've felt for the last two years, except for when I'm with you. It's the only time things feel..."

I open my eyes and pull back to look at him. "Right?"

"Yeah, *right*. And that makes me believe that all of this will get sorted out. We'll get the café rebuilt. We'll figure out who is behind it, and you know full well that no one is going to let whoever did it get away with it."

I wish I could share his confidence, but seeing Cass today only made me less certain. "You really think they'll get to the bottom of it?"

"We all know it wasn't a gas explosion. No matter what the fire chief said. They missed something, or they've been paid off to say that. Those are the only two explanations. But you know your family and how relentless they are. They're not going to stop. You saw Luca today."

I nod, a smile pulling at my lips. "Yeah. Kind of reminded me of how he was when I was a kid. The *old* Luca."

"I don't think there is an old Luca and a new Luca. I think there's just Luca."

While I never thought about it that way, it makes sense. He may have left his role as the head of the family, but he can't change who he is at his core any more than any of us can.

"I think you're right."

Jude brings my lips to his, kissing me slowly, sweetly, pouring a thousand promises into one simple act. "And eventually, you're going to feel like the windshield and karma's going to come for whoever did this. Karma is going to come, and so are the Hawkes."

23

ANGELINA

The sound of a car pulling up to the curb behind me barely registers as I dig into the seemingly bottomless cavern of my purse for my keys.

Shit, how the hell did I lose them between parking the car and here?

Maybe because my brain seems to be as fried as the café. Everything that happened since our confrontation with Cass outside what's left of the Grind is a mere tangled blur of anger, tears, and confusion.

I barely recognized the person I became when that man set foot on the sidewalk. The blind rage. The utter despair. The gut-wrenching agony. All of it was just too much.

Falling asleep in Jude's arms and waking in them helped, but now I have to go in and have a very awkward conversation with Allie.

What the hell do I say?

It was hard enough looking her in the eye while telling her as we stood in the ruin of our business, but now I don't have the buffer of everyone else around us. Having Jude at my side would make it easier, but that felt like ganging up on her.

She's already on the defensive, feeling like we somehow lied to her, so putting her in the middle of us at the same time wouldn't be fair.

Which means facing her alone.

I finally get my hand on the keys, slipping my finger through the ring to pull them from the bottom of my bag. A car door opens behind me, and someone clears their throat. I glance back at the black sedan and the familiar man standing outside it.

Fuck.

All the blood in my veins instantly runs cold, dread coiling around my spine as Roselli's goon opens the back door of the vehicle.

Cristiano Roselli offers a sly grin and motions to the empty seat next to him. "Ms. Matthews, please join me."

My hand tightens on the keys, the only potential weapon available to me, and I peek at the apartment building door only inches from me.

How quickly can I get it unlocked and get inside?

The goon clears his throat again, drawing my attention back to him and his hand at his gun.

Fuck.

Not fast enough.

Roselli glances toward the building, then pats the seat again. "I suggest you get in before your sister looks out the window and sees you with me. Stress isn't good for someone in her condition"—he raises a heavy, dark brow—"is it?"

Holy shit.

How the hell does he know she's pregnant?

He sweeps his hand in a "welcome" motion. "Please. Join me."

Shit, shit, shit.

It isn't an invitation, no matter how much he might try to make it sound like one. It's an order, and if I make any attempt to thwart it, his muscle will ensure I get into that car, anyway.

But it doesn't mean I can't protect myself sitting next to Roselli.

I shift the keys in my hand so the sharp prongs stick out from between my knuckles, just like Saint always taught me.

Simple but effective.

Everything he and Bishop taught me about self-defense and what to do in these situations floods my brain, but none of it means anything when the man sitting in the car is Roselli.

I approach cautiously, and Roselli's goon reaches a meaty hand down to tug my keys out of mine before I even know what he's doing.

"Hey!"

He dangles them from the key ring in front of me, like someone toying with a damn cat. "You can have these back when we're done."

I glance up at our window on the second floor.

Part of me wants to see Allie's face and know that she's seen what's happening so she can call in the cavalry for help. But Roselli's right—there's been enough stress in the last few weeks.

She definitely doesn't need any more. It's better to just find out what Roselli wants. And hopefully walk away from this "meeting" with something that might be useful for us.

Sucking in a fortifying breath, I slide in, and his bodyguard closes the door, sealing me inside the plush sedan with one of the most dangerous men in the city.

We pull away from the curb before I can even get my seat-belt on, and I watch our building disappear as we turn the corner.

Don't let them take you to another location.

Shit.

They could be taking me anywhere, to do anything, and there's nothing I can do about it now that I've allowed them to get me in here.

Real smart, Ang.

But it isn't as if I really had a choice.

Roselli didn't just pop by because he was in the neighborhood. He sought me out for a reason, and a man like him doesn't take no for an answer. I would have ended up in here with him, one way or the other.

An awkward silence hangs in the tight space, my palms sweating as my heart races the farther we drive away from the apartment. "What do you want, Roselli?"

The handsome older man with the smooth accent and perfectly tailored suit shifts slightly to lean a shoulder against the door and face me. A slow grin spreads across his lips as he takes me in, his gaze roaming from my disheveled hair piled on the top of my head down over the clothes that still smell like smoke from walking through the rubble yesterday. "I thought it was time that you and I had a little chat."

"A little chat?" I raise a brow at him. "*A. Little. Chat?*"

It might be wiser to try to hide my disdain for him, considering I'm literally at his mercy right now, but I've never been very good at concealing my emotions. And each block that blurs past us as we move away from the relative safety of my apartment only ramps up the tension and my unease.

Though, he seems undeterred by my animosity, continuing to stare at me with appreciation and amusement in his eyes. "Yes, about the unfortunate incident at your café. I heard there was a fire."

"It wasn't a fire." I sneer at him, leaning closer even though I should be keeping my distance. "It was a goddam *explosion*."

One of his brows rises. "Gas main?"

"Fuck you, Roselli." I practically spit the words at him, my hands tightening into fists on my lap. "It was arson."

Roselli's muscle glances at me from his spot in the passenger seat—a silent warning that I better keep myself in control—and we take another turn. My gut clenches as the familiar route I take every morning continues to pass by outside my heavily tinted window.

He spreads his hands wide. "That's not what my friends in the fire department tell me."

Arrogant prick.

"Because you fucking paid them off to say that?" I laugh at his audacity, apparently completely forgetting my self-preservation instinct. "You think you aren't at the top of our list of suspects?"

I ask as he takes us back to the scene of his crime...

He chuckles low, shaking his head. "I assure you, Ms. Matthews, the last thing I would want to do is *firebomb* your café. I quite enjoy your espresso."

I scowl at him. "Is that why you forced me into your car? To tell me that you like my espresso?"

"No." He shakes his head and drums his fingers on the leather-wrapped door. "I had hoped we could talk when I swung by during music night, but things were a bit tense with some of your other family members there."

He was there to talk to me?

It doesn't make any sense. I'm not involved with anything having to do with Roselli or even any other parts of the Hawke businesses anymore. Once I opened Hawke's Daily Grind, it sucked in all my focus. Savage and Gabe, Luca, even Isaac and Stone might have to deal with him, handle any issues that may develop—like a rival mob boss coming into town to try to marry Isaac's girlfriend—but not *me*.

"What the hell did you want to talk to *me* about?"

Releasing an annoyed sigh, he looks out his window. "I find the men in your family to be"—he glances over with a smirk

—"a bit overbearing at times. I thought if we had a chat, we might actually be able to get somewhere."

"I think you should be talking to Kennedy."

He chuckles again. "Your cousin is quite the spitfire. I've heard some stories. I'm not sure I'd get anywhere with her, either."

He probably isn't wrong about that.

Kennedy may look like her mother and certainly inherited Danika's feistiness and drive, but she definitely got Savage's strength and unwillingness to back down from a challenge.

Which is exactly how she would see Roselli...

I cross my arms over my chest as we turn the final corner onto the street I left only a short time ago. My eyes immediately dart to Jude's place, hoping he'll somehow look down and see me even through the darkly tinted windows. "What makes you think you'd get anywhere with me?"

"Because you are the eldest, Angelina. You may have been young, but you were around for my predecessor." He pauses for a moment, something that almost resembles sympathy crossing over his hazel eyes. "You've also personally felt the sting of loss."

We pull to the curb in front of the remains of the café, his words echoing in my head. My eyes burn, staring at the charred, mangled piles, knowing what it should look like, that I should be in there, slinging coffee and schmoozing with customers instead of out here with this mobster. But I refuse to cry in front of Roselli, refuse to show any weakness when he already knows so much more than he should.

I turn my attention to him, looking him directly in the eye. "And you think having my father murdered by Dom Abello makes me more receptive to you, to your world and what you do?"

He shakes his head. "No. I think it makes you smart enough

to realize that fighting me on what I want is only going to put you in a truly terrible position."

Goosebumps pebble across my skin with his warning, and I shift uneasily, ready to grab the handle and bolt across the street to Jude.

"What *do* you want, Roselli?" I release an exasperated sigh. "First, you tell us that Satriano is in town and that it could pose an issue for you. Then, after we get rid of him, you show up and act like we owe *you* something. We did what you wanted. We got rid of the competition."

He looks out the window at what's left of the café. "I wish it were that simple, Angelina. But there's *always* competition."

"Who's your competition now?"

Luca typically keeps abreast of what goes on in that world, constantly listening for any rumblings or rumors. Tracing moves. Tracking anyone who might pose a threat. But it's been years since anyone has stepped up and tried to challenge Roselli.

Tearing his eyes from the carnage, Roselli focuses on me again, and we pull away from the curb, back onto the street, heading toward the construction happening at Falco's location, before I even have a chance to try the handle. "Another player has entered the arena. Someone who has remained"—he shrugs slightly—"shall I say, well concealed. But in order to ensure I don't lose power, I need allies."

"You think the Hawkes are going to ally with you?" I release a little laugh that draws a look from his front-seat goon. "You're fucking insane."

His gaze darkens. "You may not have a choice, Ms. Matthews. Falco Enterprises has been after your family for a while. I hear they're setting up their own hotel right near where you plan on breaking ground on yours."

The fact that he knows that before anything is even official makes my stomach turn. "That's the rumor."

343

We slowly drive past the new coffee shop, lettering already on the windows—Daily Grounds.

Those fucks are even copying my name...

"And what about when they find a new business partner, Ms. Matthews, one with unlimited resources, unlimited funds?"

That doesn't seem like a question, more like a warning of something that's already happened. "Who are they partnering with?"

He shrugs, but he knows more than he's saying. "There may be a new enemy coming for both of us. We all need to watch our backs and each others'."

I snort. "You did a real good job of that. My business is *gone.*" I try to bite it back, but I can't, even with him sitting a foot away from me. "And frankly, Mr. Roselli, I still don't believe you couldn't be behind the explosion."

"Explosions aren't my style, Ms. Matthews." He shifts closer, leaning across the middle seat between us. "I like to do things up close and personal."

A chill rolls through my body at his words.

He offers a lecherous smile. "I'd like you to have a conversation with the powers that be about my offer."

"And what exactly *is* your offer?"

The corner of his lips twitches into a half-grin. "That our truce become something more, a friendship. I scratch your back; you scratch mine. These unintended consequences that have arisen after you took out Satriano need to be remedied."

"It isn't our problem."

He retreats slightly as we make our way through the city again. "It is if the same people who are coming after me have teamed up with Falco."

"You think that's what's happening?"

He shrugs again, apparently unwilling to give me any information, while he sits here and asks for a *friendship.* "That's entirely unclear, Ms. Matthews. But what is clear is that some-body wants to fuck with the Hawkes and with me."

"What have they done to you?"

Shaking a finger at me, he grins. "I don't think discussing my business in any more detail with you would be wise."

We turn the corner and end up right in front of my building again, pulling to the curb. The doors unlock, the click trig-gering me to start to pull the handle.

"We have a lot in common, Ms. Matthews, your family and mine. We don't have to be enemies." He glances up at the apart-ment. "It truly is a shame about your shop, though. It was quite adorable, and you had excellent espresso."

"Can I go?"

He nods slowly, and I pop open the door.

"And Ms. Matthews?"

I turn back to him. "What?"

"Tell your sister congratulations."

The sense of dread sitting in the pit of my stomach doubles, threatening to make me heave right in his car. "How the hell do you know?"

His eyes twinkle with a mixture of danger and amusement. "The same way I knew Giacomina Marconi was in town. I have eyes and ears everywhere, Ms. Matthews. I could be useful for you, if you let me."

I slide out onto the sidewalk, my legs unsteady, heart hammering against my rib cage. His goon steps out and hands me my keys. I take them with a shaking hand and try to stick the key into the lock as Roselli's car squeals away from the curb.

It takes me three tries before I finally manage to flip the lock open and slip inside, tugging the door closed behind me.

I lean back against the glass, my knees threatening to give out.

What else does he know, and what is he holding back?

I have to call Savage.

I have to call everyone.

———

JUDE

LUCA'S EYES dart from the road to my death grip on the door handle for the millionth time since we left my place. "You're sure you're okay, *piccolo guaio?*"

For the tenth time, I swallow through the panic threatening to choke me and lie. "I'm fine."

It's just the first time I've been in a car in two fucking years.

The first time I've been on a road.

The first time I've been *anywhere* except my damn building or across the street.

The first time I've been somewhere without *her.*

My vision blurs even more, narrowing into a pinpoint of light, and I squeeze my eyes closed, trying not to think about where we are, instead concentrating on where we're *going* and *why.*

To Angie.

She needs me.

Repeating that over and over in my head doesn't stop my knee from bouncing wildly or my hand from gripping the handle on the car door so hard it feels like it might break right off.

Luca's hand rests on my knee, briefly stopping the nervous motion, and he squeezes it gently. "Just keep breathing."

I glance over at him and nod. "I am."

"No, you're not." He shakes his head, keeping his eyes on the road. "I can see you holding your breath every time I check on you."

"Fuck."

He pulls his hand away, tightening it on the wheel instead,

346

and my knee goes right back to its violent bouncing. "I can take you back. You don't have to—"

I whip my head toward him. "Yes, I do."

Roselli fucking *took* her. That bastard snatched her straight off the damn street in front of her apartment. If I stayed locked up in my place while everyone else dealt with the fallout of what just went down, if I weren't there for her, I would never be able to forgive myself.

She's been by my side every fucking step of the way since she saw me fall apart, and I can't hide away at my place, lost in my own damn fucked head when she just went through something like *that*.

Luca gives me a sharp nod of understanding and doesn't push it any further as we pull up in front of Angelina and Alessandra's place.

Christ, it's been forever since I've been here...

Literally years.

And now a fucking mobster is threatening them in their damn home.

How the fuck did this happen?

She wasn't even gone an hour...

My chest tightens, the breaths I've been forcing myself to take coming shorter, more strained. The tight space spins, windshield warping in front of me.

I squeeze the handle tighter.

No.

Hold it together.

Luca turns off the car. "Looks like Gabe and Savage are already here."

Someone pulls up behind us, the purring engine of a sports car replacing that constant whoosh in my ears, and he checks the rearview mirror, diligent as ever.

"And Stone and Isaac just arrived."

He climbs from the car and meets Stone and Isaac on the

sidewalk to my right. I watch them through pinpointed vision, shaking my head to try to clear the fuzziness.

They all scan the street cautiously, and Isaac glances into the car at me. He slowly approaches and opens my door.

Fresh air whips in on a light breeze, and I suck in a deep breath of it, letting the scent of the water and the restaurant just across the street fill my lungs.

Remember why you're doing this.

This is about Angie.

She needs you right now.

I let out my breath slowly, then glance up at him.

He raises a brow, hand resting on the top of the door. "You coming?"

"Yeah."

I didn't force myself down my steps, into Luca's car, and ride over here in the throes of a damn panic attack just to sit here with Angie upstairs. It may take every fucking ounce of willpower I have, but I am getting to her.

Isaac takes a step back, and I set my feet on the sidewalk and slide from the car, my entire body tense. The world around me spins, and I grip the top of the door to steady myself.

Sounds assault me from all sides.

Tires on pavement. Honking horns. People talking on their cell phones. A dog barking...

I take a step forward, releasing my death grip on the door, and shove it closed behind me. The weight sitting on the center of my chest increases with every step I take toward the door Luca holds open for me.

Visualizing the lobby, the stairs, the short walk down the upstairs hallway to their apartment helps me move forward, and Luca places a hand on my shoulder.

"You're good, *piccolo guaio.*"

It isn't a question this time.

It's a statement from a man who never says something he isn't one hundred percent sure is true.

Forgoing the elevator, Isaac and Stone ascend the steps, leaving Luca and me standing at the bottom, staring up.

"You're doing fine." He moves up on the first tread, waiting for me to do the same. "Roselli has a lot of fucking balls to come after Angelina..."

I nod, fingers wrapped around the banister as I take another step up. "He has to know what it would do, that it would set us off."

Luca glances my way. "But Roselli's smart. If he had come to one of us directly, I don't think anyone would've listened to him long enough to hear what he had to say."

I hate that he is right about that, but I also know exactly what he's doing. Keeping me talking means keeping me thinking about anything except my own panic.

Smart.

There's a reason he held his position, and it wasn't just because he was Dom's son. And the more I consider the reason we're here, the more I realize that Angie probably is the best person Roselli could have approached.

Besides Astrid, she's the most even keeled, the calmest, the one who always seems to be able to see the clarity of a situation when no one else can. She's one of the peacemakers in the family. If he had gone to Kennedy, we likely would have seen the fireworks lighting up the sky from anywhere in town.

We reach the top of the stairs without me even counting them, but the sudden silence closes in around me like a blinding fog. My legs wobble slightly. Luca's distraction worked for a while, but it won't last forever.

The door to their place stands open only a few feet away, and before I can even move toward it, Angelina rushes out and throws her arms around me. Even without being at the Grind for days, she still carries that cinnamon and sweetness scent that swallows me whole and instantly soothes the pain in my chest.

I crush her against me, letting the tension melt away with the press of her body to mine. "Fuck, babe. Are you okay?"

She tightens her grip around my neck, clinging to me the same way I do her. "I am now that you're here."

The same words I said to her only a few days ago—in my own moment of weakness and need.

I pull back and kiss her, gliding my lips over hers, needing to feel that she's okay despite her verbal assurances. She responds, moving her mouth with mine, issuing a little moan and digging her nails into my nape.

Someone clears their throat, and I pull back to find Allie leaning against the doorjamb, an annoyed glare focused on us.

Shit.

"You haven't talked to her?"

Angie shakes her head, glancing at her sister. "No."

That isn't going to make this any easier, but we can't avoid it forever.

I release Angie and follow her toward the apartment. She brushes past Allie, but I pause next to my best friend.

At least, I hope she still is.

Her blue eyes watch me suspiciously. All the trust that usually looks back at me has drained away, like she's staring at someone she doesn't even know anymore.

Any positive feelings I just got from having Angie in my arms vanish in an instant, replaced by the very real fear that it may not be possible to salvage this with Allie.

I lean down to drop a kiss on her forehead, but she pulls away.

My heart twists violently, all that anxiety rushing back. "Don't do that, Al."

She looks up. "Do what?"

"That." I lean closer, not wanting to draw attention to our conversation. "Pull away from me."

"I can do whatever I want, Jude. It seems you do."

Hell.

She's still pissed, and not being able to address and explain what happened between Angelina and me because we all have to sit in this room and discuss the Roselli situation is only going to make things worse.

But there's nothing I can do about it right now, no matter how badly I want to force Allie to listen.

I run a hand through my hair and make my way into the apartment that used to almost be a second home to me for a while. Allie and I spent so much time here after she moved in with Angie. But that all changed the same day I did...

Savage and Gabe already wait for us in the living room, talking with Isaac and Stone. Gabe's brow furrows when he sees me, but Luca waves off his question as everyone settles in for what is bound to be a very tense conversation.

Angie settles in the corner of the couch, and I sit on the arm of it, leaning back slightly so I don't crowd her but wanting to stay close. Needing to. Both for her and for me.

She rests her hand on my leg, and half a dozen pairs of eyes immediately go there.

Shit.

We will have a lot of explaining to do to a lot of people, but this isn't the time. They can all wonder and think whatever they want. I'm not about to hold back from comforting Angie right now just because we haven't had a chance to talk with anyone about what's going on between us.

Savage rests his elbows on his knees, his hands clasped together. "Tell us exactly what happened. Everything he said."

Angie begins to shake, her hand tightening on my leg. "He said he came to me because he knew none of you would listen."

Isaac snorts. "He's fucking right. Fucking balls on this guy. He's lucky we don't go over there and—"

Stone casts a glare his way, giving his son a look I wouldn't want directed at me. "Let her talk."

Isaac looks significantly reproached and holds up his hands. "Sorry."

Angie shifts nervously, glancing back at me before she continues. "He said there's a new player in town."

"What?" All the color drains from Luca's face, and he narrows his eyes on Angie. "Who?"

Gabe shakes his head. "That's impossible. One of us would've heard something from one of our sources."

I grab Angie's hand, interlocking our fingers and squeezing it tightly. This can't be easy, relaying what that man said to her, reliving the fear she felt sitting next to him.

Angie takes a deep breath and nods slowly. "That's what I thought, too, but he seemed to suggest they may be partnering with Falco."

"Falco?" Savage sits up straight. "What does one have to do with the other?"

Angie shrugs, her frustration at not knowing the answers to their questions tightening her shoulders. "He says he wants us all to partner. That if we watched each other's backs, we could protect each other."

Stone snarls, pushing off the wall he leans against. "Fat fucking chance of that. If anyone is here threatening him, it has nothing to do with us. And getting rid of him might not be the worst thing in the world."

Luca holds up a hand. "Now, wait a second. I put Roselli in place thirty years ago, gave him my entire territory. There's a reason I chose him, a reason his crew stepped up. It's because he's a very rational man, one who can be reasoned with. If there is someone challenging him, we don't know who or what they'd be. Roselli may be a nuisance, but he is a fairly *predictable* nuisance who doesn't cause problems for us."

Usually.

While what Luca says certainly makes sense, something's been niggling at the back of my head. And even though I probably have no business being part of this conversation, I can't not say it. "But what if Roselli was the one behind the attack on the café, and he did it specifically to set this up, to put us on edge so we'd be more liable to want to partner with him?"

Isaac nods slowly, rubbing a hand over his jaw. "I had the same thought."

Gabe pushes to his feet, pacing behind the couch, the frustration rolling off him in violent waves. "We know it wasn't a gas explosion. We can all agree on that."

Everyone nods.

"And Angie, you can't think of anyone else suspicious, anyone who's been hanging around the Grind, anything you might've seen to suggest that there is someone else who's been watching us or targeting you?"

She leans back in the chair, her shoulder against my thigh, and glances up at me. "Not that I've noticed. But Jude sees a lot, probably more than I do. I'm so busy taking care of customers, I probably wouldn't even see anything unusual."

Luca raises a brow at me. "Son, anything you can think of?"

"Shit." I run my free hand through my hair, trying to think back over the last few weeks and months. "I mean, there are so many people who come in and out of there every day. It would be impossible for me to keep track of them all."

Especially when I spend all my time watching Angie...

Gabe grips the back of the couch. "But no one leaps out at you?"

I rub at the back of my neck, squeezing my eyes closed as a thousand faces flash in front of them. "No, I wouldn't even know what to look for. It could be anyone, right?"

353

Luca nods slowly. "It's all right. It's a lot to ask."

Angelina looks around the room, her attention darting to Allie, who stayed by the door, her back pressed to the wall, listening intently but not interjecting anything. "That's not all he said. He...knew things."

Gabe freezes. "What do you mean?"

"He knew something about Allie that he shouldn't."

Allie's face goes white, and her hand drops to her stomach.

Savage gapes. "Are you...pregnant?"

She winces and pushes off the wall. "Yes. But guys, my parents don't even know. So how the hell did he find out?"

Isaac sneers, his back stiffening. "He knew about Jack because she was taken to the ER. He obviously has people working in the hospital. He's monitoring their systems for our names, for anything that might pop up and be useful."

Allie cringes. "Aunt Nora ran a blood test..."

Gabe approaches her, offering a tentative smile, likely because he can feel the uncertainty of the situation. "Congratulations."

She gives him a half smile. "Thank you. It wasn't exactly planned."

He pulls her into his arms. "Do we know the father?"

She tenses and slips out of his hug. "It isn't really important. I don't think he's going to be involved."

My heart sinks.

It's the first time she's said anything like that or suggested that she's even had a conversation with the father.

I catch her eye, and she shakes her head, indicating she doesn't want me to ask anything else, at least not with everyone else around.

Savage leans back and releases a sigh. "So, we have Roselli watching us. He knows things he shouldn't. He's looking for blackmail material, ways to try to force us to team up with him

354

against someone he *claims* is a threat to us both. What do we do?"

Gabe's gaze bounces from Savage to Luca, then over to Isaac and Stone. "We do what we always do: we dig. We'll see if there's any merit to his claim about someone else coming in, and we keep looking into the café fire for anything that points to who's behind it. We have to keep Falco and Roselli both at the top of that list. Neither of them can be trusted."

Luca nods. "Agreed."

Stone crosses his arms over his chest. "And in the meantime, no one goes anywhere alone." His gaze bounces from Allie to Angelina. "Especially you two."

I push to my feet, resting my hand on Angie's shoulder as I look at Allie.

My best friend won't even meet my eyes, but I won't let her anger cloud her ability to see how dangerous this is. I can't risk anything happening to either of my girls.

I'll protect them, even if one of them doesn't want it.

"I won't let either of them out of my sight."

24

JUDE

"You won't even look at me?"

Allie stands with her back to me, arms crossed protectively over her stomach. She stares down from the roof, from the exact same position I was in only a few nights ago, looking at the ruins of the café, her shoulders stiff, like she's ready for a fight.

It's the last thing I want—to *fight* with her.

After everything that's happened the last few weeks, I just want things to go back to the way they were with her—easy.

"Al, please." I approach her cautiously, not wanting to startle her or send her scurrying away. "Talk to me."

It was hard enough to get her to agree to even come back here with us when we all left their place. Nobody wanted to leave them there alone, and the girls definitely didn't want to go to Storm and Landon's house.

I can understand why, since she doesn't seem ready to tell them about her pregnancy, but she's made it abundantly clear she doesn't want to be here, either.

My best friend fucking hates me.

The one person I could always rely on, always turn to, who has helped me through the worst times of my life...and she won't even look at me.

I step up behind her cautiously and wrap my arms around her, resting my chin on her shoulder and looking at the carnage across the street. Even days later, it's hard to accept the new reality that what was once there is gone.

Allie stiffens at my touch, but she relaxes after a few seconds, leaning back against me like she usually does. "Why didn't you tell me?"

It sounds like such a simple question, one that I should be able to answer with a few words. But there are so many layers, so many facets to what happened and why.

Years' worth of feelings, of anguish, so many things I don't think I can put together, at least, not in a way she'll understand it.

But thinking back on it all, it's hard to imagine Allie didn't have any idea how I felt.

"To be honest, I'm surprised you didn't know."

She glances up at me. "How?"

I squeeze her gently. "Come on. Really?"

"I mean..." Brow furrowed, she returns her focus to the Grind. "I saw you watching the café all the time. Watching us. But I always thought it was just your way of staying connected. How you liked it. To keep everyone on the other side of the glass so you could get lost in...whatever you were writing. I didn't realize you were..."

"In love with your sister?"

She closes her eyes and sucks in a sharp breath. "God, that's weird to hear."

"I know." It still feels weird to say it to anyone else but Angelina. "But I've always felt that way."

358

Her lids flutter open, and she stares back up at me. "Always?"

I nod, hugging her close as fifteen years of memories with the Hawkes come rushing back all at once, starting with the most important one. "That day that you came and sat in the closet with me..."

Allie rests her hands over mine across her chest.

"...you became my best friend instantly. And then Angie showed up, and you told me I could trust her. For some reason, even though I had literally every reason not to trust *anyone*, especially adults, I knew I could. You became my best friend, but she became...I don't know how to explain it. I couldn't ever shake the feeling that she was mine, that I was hers, that we were...something."

"Oh, God"—Allie laughs, the sound light and airy, cracking the remaining tension holding her back—"you have no idea how sappy you sound right now."

I chuckle. "I know. But really, that's how I feel."

She pulls out of my hold and paces away, rubbing at her lower back, eyes following the strands of lights lit up here from my failed picnic with Angie. "Angie did all this for you?"

I shove my hands into my pockets and try to give her the space she obviously needs. "Yeah."

One of her dark brows rises. "And you're okay up here?"

I suck in a deep breath of the fresh night air, remembering what it felt like that first night in the rain, the first time I truly got to *enjoy* being out here. "I'm okay up here. And honestly, her pushing me to do it was the right thing, even though I didn't want to see it at the time."

Allie gives me a sad smile. "She's good for you, is what you're saying."

"She's the best thing for me. And as awful as it sounds, that"—I motion toward the café—"pushed me to face it even more. I don't know how I did it, how I went over there with her. Fuck, how I came to your place today when I couldn't even set foot out of my door."

Her gaze softens, the anger she's been holding starting to melt away. "Is it better now?"

I shake my head, even the thought of doing it again constricting my chest. "Not really. I mean, no, but...I don't know. Knowing she needs me, that I have to be there for her, helps me get through it in a way that nothing else ever could." And it feels like I'm failing miserably at explaining this to her. "Fuck, she isn't a *cure*. There isn't one. There never *will* be."

"Do you think when Luca..." She doesn't say the words, just kind of makes a gun motion with her hand. "It'll make a difference?"

Jesus.

In what family is casually discussing someone murdering someone else normal?

But that's the thing with the Hawkes.

They'll do *anything* for each other.

And Luca is going to do the one thing I've never been able to do—confront one of my abusers and give him what he deserves.

I shrug. "I don't know. It did when he told me my dad was gone."

Allie winces and approaches slowly. "You don't have to tell me everything, Jude. I have always understood that there were things in your past, and you don't need to rehash it with me for me to know how terrible it was, what was done to you." Tears shine in her gaze. "If Angelina can help tame those demons, then...I'm happy for you."

"Really?"

It's exactly what I wanted to hear, but if she doesn't mean it, if she's just saying it to try to lighten this tension between us and still harbors anger about the entire situation, then I can't just accept it and pretend everything is okay.

A tear trickles from her eye, and her bottom lip starts to quiver. "I am. It's weird as fucking hell, but I am. I just..."

"What?"

"I feel like I'm going to lose you now."

"Fuck, Al, you're never going to lose me." I tug her to me, letting her cry against my chest while I run my hands through her hair. "You're the other part of me. I swear to Christ, keeping it from you has been the hardest thing I've ever done."

She looks up at me with wet eyes. "Even harder than leaving your place?

"Ten times harder. You've always been my rock, and I don't want my relationship with Angie to change that. Will it?"

I hold my breath, waiting for her to reply.

Eventually, after what feels like an eternity, she shakes her head. "No, but you can't complain about your girlfriend to me when it's my sister, you know?"

I chuckle. "I don't know that I'll have anything to complain about where she's concerned."

She barks out a laugh and pulls away from me. "Then you don't know my sister very well. I've lived with her for a long time, and believe me, she has some pretty gross habits."

"Oh yeah? Like what?"

A true grin spreads across her face. "You'll find out."

I smirk. "Are we okay? Really, though?"

She releases a heavy sigh. "Yeah, we're okay. It's just a lot, you know? Finding out I'm pregnant, losing the café, and now this."

"I know, Al, but that's exactly why we all need each other now, right?"

She looks down at her stomach, feathering her fingers over the flat surface that won't be for much longer. "I need to tell my parents."

"We'll go with you. Or, at least, I'll try."

Her eyes snap up to mine. "You will?"

I nod. "Did the father really say he didn't want to be involved?"

Or did you just not tell him?

She chews on her bottom lip for a minute before she answers. "Yes."

The corner of her mouth twitches.

Lie.

Allie's lying again, and I don't have a fucking clue why.

But we finally just got to a good place, so I can't call her out, not without the risk of returning to another argument. Whatever reason she has for not telling the father, it had better be a good one because like Roselli proved today, it's impossible to keep secrets in this family or from a man like him.

"You should really go talk to your sister. She's been really upset. You two just need to talk. Hash it out. Tell her how you really feel."

"I feel like she's stealing my best friend."

I walk over to her and take her face in my hands. "She's not stealing anything. I love you, Al. I always will. Nothing's going to change that, especially not me loving your sister. Okay?"

She gives me a sharp nod, and I kiss her forehead.

"Now go talk to her, please, because I'm fucking starving, and I know she's not going to cook until all this is resolved."

A grin plays at her lips. "Is that why you insisted we come stay with you? So somebody will cook?"

"I can't just want the pleasure of your company?"

She pokes me in the stomach. "I'll go talk to her. And maybe I'll even help her in the kitchen."

That brings another belly laugh from deep in my gut. "You, help in the kitchen? Yeah, right."

"Hey, I know my way around a kitchen. I just choose not to be there."

It's my turn to point toward her stomach. "Once that one hits a certain age, you're going to have to start cooking for it, you know. You can't rely on your grandmother and your sister and your mom for the rest of your life."

"Don't I fucking know it." She lets out a huff. "You staying up here?"

I nod. "I'll give you guys some privacy."

And I could use a few minutes to decompress and think.

She heads for the door, then pauses to look back at me before slipping back down the stairs. I return to the side of the roof that overlooks the street.

Tomorrow, the crew will arrive to start tearing down what's left of Hawke's Daily Grind and the two buildings on either side that were too badly damaged to keep up, then it's going to be time to rebuild.

My eyes drift down the block to where Falco's coffee shop is going in. In only a matter of weeks, they'll be up and running, while it's going to take several months, if not longer, to get the Grind back up.

It's going to make what we're doing downstairs even more essential, and I refuse to let my own shit get in the way of it. I've spent years hiding away here, pushing everyone and everything away so I won't have to deal with the things I try to keep buried.

I can't keep doing it. Not if I want to keep Angelina.

My hands shake as I pull out my phone to dial Nora. She's the only one who might understand it all, who might be able to help.

She answers on the second ring. "Jude, are you all right?"

"I'm okay, Aunt Nora."

"Do you need something, dear?"

"Yeah." I suck in a deep breath, close my eyes, and say the words I never thought I would. "I need you to give me the name and number of a therapist or something."

A brief silence lingers on the line, and I hold my breath, waiting for her to say something, anything.

"I'm glad you called, Jude. Tell me what's going on, and I'll make sure I get you to the right person."

ANGELINA

THE LOFT DOOR CLICKS OPEN, and I freeze, my hand tightening around the wooden spoon mid-stir. All the anxiety and tension of waiting while they went up to the roof to talk coils inside me, threatening to snap the damn spoon in half.

Soft, hesitant footsteps approach me from behind, and I release a heavy whoosh of air from my lungs, loosening my grip slightly.

Allie, not Jude.

I keep stirring and glance over my shoulder at her, waiting for her to say something because I have no idea how to start a conversation about the fact that I'm now with her best friend and kept it from her.

Looking at it from the outside, I can completely understand her anger. The feeling of betrayal. While she was struggling with her own personal issues, Jude and I were hooking up—at least, that's the way she sees it.

But there's so much more to the story.

So much more I hope she lets me explain.

She stands at the edge of the island, twisting her hands in front of her, scanning the counters and the various ingredients I have spread across them for dinner. "Do you need some help?"

I close my eyes against the sting of tears her offer brings. "That would be great."

The tension between us is so thick we could cut it with the knife she picks up, and for a split-second, I wonder if she wants to use it on me, before she starts chopping the carrots laid out on the cutting board to my left.

Allie peeks at me from the corner of her eye while I stir the onions to keep them from burning. She doesn't know what to say, either.

We've had some doozies of fights over the years, but this feels different. Something neither of us is quite sure how to navigate. But if one of us doesn't say something, we're going to stand here in this awkward silence all night and nothing will ever get resolved.

I swallow through the lump in my throat and glance at her. "Is Jude still up on the roof?"

She nods slowly. "Yeah, he said he was going to stay up there for a little bit."

"He's...okay?"

Her hand freezes, and she slowly lowers the knife, setting it on the cutting board, staring down at the pieces she's sliced off. "He seems to be a lot better the more you two are together, actually."

I let my eyes drift over to her. "I can't believe he came to our place today."

"Me either." She leans her hip on the counter facing me. "He said that knowing you needed him helped him move past the mental block he's created, but he knows he needs to get some serious professional help."

"I know." The promise he made to me on that roof before my entire world blew up rings in my ears, one I hope he can keep. "He told me he'll try."

And really, that's all I can ask of him.

After all he's been through, the things he's pushed past to be there for me over the last few days, I can see a brief flash of light at the end of the tunnel.

"Good." She gives me a tight smile, then lifts the knife and returns to chopping. "I think he will."

Another long silence drags out between us, and the scent of the onions starting to caramelize fills the loft. I keep stirring, peeking at her from the corner of my eye, hoping she's going to broach the topic we're both dancing around so intently.

Things have never been this awkward between us before, and I finally break, unable to keep acting like there isn't this six-foot-two, blue-eyed, blond elephant in the room. "So...are we good?"

She tenses slightly. "Yep." The corner of her mouth twitches, and she slices at the carrot a little too aggressively, sending a round rolling from the board and onto the wood floor. "Good."

Shit.

"So...that's a no..."

Allie remains silent for a moment, continuing to chop without acknowledging me calling her out on her lie, long enough that I'm not sure she's going to respond at all. "I just don't know why you felt the need to lie to me."

The pain in her words slices at my chest, and I wince.

"I wasn't lying."

Her eyes widen. She whirls toward me, knife in her hand. "Then what the hell do you call it?"

I hold up my hands, wooden spoon in one. "Can you put that thing down while we're having this conversation, please?"

She scowls and tosses it back onto the cutting board. "The other day when I came into work, and you were wearing the same clothes..."

I cringe. "I told you, I stayed at a friend's."

"But you didn't mention that *friend* was Jude. *My* best friend. *Our* Jude."

Shit.

If the positions were reversed, I'd be pissed, too. I've never seen any two people as close as Jude and Allie have been since the day they met. And he's been keeping a lot from her, not just what's happened between us recently.

"I know, Al, but it just *happened*."

Her jaw drops, eyes widening. "Oh, you just tripped and fell on his dick?"

Ouch.

I scowl at her. "No, I mean this thing with him, it's—"

She glances into the pot. "Your onions are burning."

"Shit." I whirl back around and throw the spoon back into the pot, stirring them vigorously, but it's too late to salvage them. "Shit. Shit. Shit."

Tears fill my eyes, staring into the black mess. Another thing burned and ruined beyond repair.

I turn off the heat, grab the pot, and throw it into the sink, cranking on the water to try to get them off the bottom before they permanently stick to it. Pressing my hands against the counter, I drop my head, trying not to get frustrated with her.

Allie has every right to be upset about this, the way it was sprung on her. But she has the wrong idea about why we didn't tell her. "You know how hard this has been for Jude and me?"

"How long has it been going on?"

I turn off the water and stare out the window, straight ahead, where I used to be able to see the second floor of my building. "Not long." Turning back to her, I cross my arms over my chest. "Since you did your disappearing act."

She winces and mimics my stance.

"I started bringing him his coffee and—"

Her lips curl into a half-smile. "And you tripped and fell on his dick?"

I smirk at her. "No." *At least, not right away.*

Thinking back to that day when he opened the door and I stood face to face with him for the first time, the way my heart stalled in my chest, my breath rushing from my lungs when I looked into his eyes, I can't believe it was only two weeks ago.

"You know Jude and I hadn't been in the same room together in almost two years?"

She shakes her head. "I guess I never realized you'd never been over here."

I look around the loft, the four square walls where Jude has spent his life for so damn long, watching the world pass him by while the rest of us went about our days, completely unaware of the struggle he was going through. "Nope."

"Was that intentional?"

"What do you mean?"

Her shoulders rise and fall. "Were you avoiding him?"

Wincing, I stare at my bare feet rather than look at her when I admit it. "Kind of."

"I noticed, you know..."

I look back up at her, immediately seeing that her tense shoulders have relaxed. "Noticed what?"

"The way you two always danced around each other." She peeks up at me. "That there was something there."

"Really?"

"Yeah." She nods, getting a faraway look in her eyes. "It seemed like the older he got, the more I saw the looks he gave you. The way he watched you, the way you kept your distance from him but were always monitoring, checking to see that he was okay. I don't know. I thought it was...I mean, maybe I knew he had a crush on you, but I didn't know you felt the same way."

"Neither did I." I run a hand over my face, clenching my eyes closed. "God, Allie, I mean, I'm twelve years older than him. I obviously never saw him like that when he was a kid. I just..."

"Wanted to protect him?"

I nod. "But then he grew up and..."

Allie grins. "And he looks like *that*."

"Yeah, and he looks like *that*." But it isn't just about how

368

physically beautiful Jude Abello-Harris has become. He also has a beautiful, old soul that shines through in everything he says and does. "He's incredibly smart, kind, and caring, and I don't know, Al. I just...it feels right when we're together. The only thing that never did was that we kept it from you, even though it hasn't been that long."

Her lips twist down into a frown. "I wish you had just told me."

I look at her stomach. "You had a lot going on."

"I know." She sighs. "And I think I should go tell Mom and Dad tonight after we eat. I'll stay there so you and Jude can have some alone time."

"Really?"

She nods. "Really."

"So, we're all okay?" I ask the question full of hope that her answer will be yes because I'm not sure I would survive if she said we aren't. Being with Jude has changed everything, but if it means losing my relationship with Allie, I'm not sure I could handle it. "The three of us?"

Allie drops her hand to her stomach. "Four now, right?"

"I know you're terrified, but what Jude said is true. We're all here for you. If the father doesn't want to be involved, you know that's not going to change anything. We're all going to help. You're never going to be alone."

"I know that." She gives a little humorless laugh, shaking her head and staring up at the ceiling. "It just isn't how I thought this would go."

"How what would go?"

A tear rolls down her cheek. "Having a baby." Her lips tremble. "I thought it would be like Mom and Dad, you know? Or Mom and *your* dad. Fall in love, get married, have a baby."

I release a heavy sigh and walk over to her, resting my hands on her shoulders, giving them a gentle squeeze. "There are a lot of different ways to create a family. You, of all people, should know that. Look at what we have. Skye and Gabe have been together for thirty-plus years and have never gotten married. Saint and Caroline, Luca and Byron, they aren't genetically Hawkes, but would you ever say they aren't part of the family?"

"God, no." She sniffles. "Of course not."

"Exactly. Family isn't just blood, Al. It's our love for each other. It's what we're willing to do for each other that makes us family, and everyone will support you no matter what."

"Good." She sobs, tears flowing freely now. "Because I don't have a fucking clue what I'm doing."

I bark out a laugh and pull her to me, hugging her tightly. "I don't think any of us do. Hell, I don't even know what I'm going to do while we rebuild the Grind."

She pulls back. "Yes, you do. You're going to help Jude and Jack downstairs getting the bookstore and art gallery together."

"You too, right?"

"Of course." One corner of her mouth rises. "And we can even get an espresso machine or something in there while we wait for the Grind to reopen."

"That's actually not a bad idea."

"People love coffee and books, right?"

"Right."

The fact that we seem to have hashed things out lifts the weight that's been crushing me, but I can't help but worry about things with Jude. "And you and Jude are good?"

She smiles and nods. "We're good. I just made him promise that you weren't going to steal my best friend."

"I'm not going to be able to complain about my boyfriend to you, am I?"

A laugh floats from her lips, the sound so needed after the heavy conversation, and she returns to chopping the carrots. "That could make things a little awkward."

"A lot of things are about to get awkward. I am going to have to tell Mom and Landon about Jude."

She smirks at me.

I point my spoon at her. "Don't you give me that look. You're talking to them first, and yours is way bigger than mine."

Her smile falters. "Shit, you're right."

25

JUDE

For the first time in months, the words pour out of me, a cathartic tsunami sweeping over the page, spilling so fast that my fingers can barely keep up with my head.

The end of the story unfolds naturally, as if it were always meant to be this way and I just couldn't see it. Too blinded by my fear. By my insecurities. By my inability to move past the massive roadblocks I put up for myself—in life and in the damn book.

All the upheaval of the last few weeks and the continued uncertainty regarding this situation with Roselli and Falco Enterprises should have shut me down creatively, but instead, it feels like adrenaline has been injected straight into my veins.

And it's been like this since the moment I woke up, still dark outside, with Angelina wrapped in my arms. Her warm, soft body aligned perfectly with mine. Her sweet scent invading every breath. The absolute feeling of *rightness* that consumed me.

The perfect ending hit. One I hadn't planned. One I never

saw coming when I started the book. One I never *could* have seen when I was so blinded by all the things clouding my own head. And if I didn't get it out on paper immediately, it would have eaten me alive.

Even as my fingers fly across the keys, the drastic shift in the narrative continues to shake me to my core.

Everything has changed.

This was never meant to be a love story.

It was always a tragedy.

One man watching the world pass him by and one woman too afraid to fully live in it. But somehow, it has morphed. It has changed as I have. As *this* life altered so completely, so did the story I thought I knew when I started it months ago.

The first pale light of sunrise starts to creep in through the new windows, but I keep typing, desperately trying to put Rosalie's journey on the page, ensuring she gets the ending she deserves.

After everything that's happened, everything she's lost, I couldn't let Rosalie's story end the way I originally saw it. The bleak, dark future filled with loneliness and longing doesn't have to be her reality anymore.

It doesn't have to be anyone's...

At last, I type the final period, and a massive weight I didn't even realize I was carrying lifts off my shoulders, replaced with a sense of calm I don't know if I've ever felt.

"You know, in twenty years, you're going to regret sitting like that while you work."

Angie's voice breaking through the silence jerks my head toward it. She leans against the doorjamb to the bedroom, my T-shirt hanging off one shoulder and barely reaching mid-thigh.

"How long have you been standing there?"

She offers a little half-shrug and inclines her head toward the windows. "Since before there was any sun coming in those."

A sudden chill settles over me.

Angie has been watching...

It never bothered me before, when I used to go sit at the Grind at the back corner table and write for hours, but it feels different now—maybe because of the content.

She approaches slowly, her bare feet hardly making a sound on the wood floor, and stares down at me where I sit against the wall near the windows, the same place I've always watched her from. "Really, that must be terrible for your back."

I smirk at her. "I'm still young. My body can handle it."

A scowl twists her perfect lips, and she raises a dark eyebrow. "You making fun of my age now?"

It's impossible to fight my grin, and I hold out my hands and tug her toward me, then pull her palm to my lips to press a kiss there. "Absolutely not. You're a fucking goddess and always have been, when you were twenty-two or now at thirty-seven."

"Mm-hmm."

Her little playful hum tells me she really isn't mad at my joke, and the sudden need to have her pressed against me makes me push my computer onto the floor beside me and urge her to sit on my lap.

She straddles me, her knees on either side of my hips, and takes my face in her palms. "How long have you been sitting out here?"

"I don't know, four or five hours."

Her eyes widen slightly. "Good God. Did you sleep at all last night?"

I shake my head and press a kiss to the inside of her wrist. "No, not really. After you fell asleep, I just had to come finish it."

"You're done?"

I nod.

Her gaze drifts over to my laptop, and she pulls her bottom lip under her teeth. "Can I read it?"

Acid crawls up my throat, and I swallow it back, my skin getting tight and clammy at the thought of her reading words that weren't meant for her eyes.

She wasn't supposed to see it.

Wasn't supposed to know it was about her.

I never wanted her to know how I've always seen her—even when she couldn't see herself that way—or know about all the things I ever wanted for her in her life and thought I could never give her.

Almost as if she can sense my hesitation, she lowers her hands to my shoulders. "It's okay if you don't want me to. I get it."

The disappointment in her voice fucking kills me.

"It's not that I don't want you to. I just..." I drop my head back against the wall and close my eyes, searching for a way to explain it to her.

How do I tell the woman I am madly in love with that I'm afraid she'll think I'm a fucking stalker if she reads my damn book?

Her lips touch the base of my neck, and a shudder rolls through me, my cock twitching against her warm core settled over it. She kisses her way up my neck again, to my lips. "It's just what?"

I let my eyes open and meet hers again. "I'm afraid of what you'll think when you read it."

Her brow furrows. "What do you mean? What could I possibly read in there that's going to change anything between us or the way I feel about you?"

"You think you know everything. You think you understand exactly how I feel about you"—I take her face in my palms—"but you have no idea how obsessed with you I am, and I'm worried that once you see it on the page, you're going to run screaming from me."

A smile tilts her lips, and she leans in and kisses me again. "If I haven't run screaming already, do you really think I will now?" Her fingers tangle in the hair at my nape. "I've known you since you were ten years old, Jude. And yeah, there have been a lot of surprises, but nothing that would ever make me run. At the end of the day, family is all we have, isn't it?"

There's that word again—family.

For so long, I resented being a Hawke, hated the fact that the family took me under their wings, because all I ever did, all I've ever done, is disappoint them and hurt them by pushing them away, by acting like I didn't care about everything they had done for me, because I didn't know how to show it.

I couldn't make myself react the way I should when someone tried to hug me, offered me congratulations on something, or tried to strike up a conversation.

Everyone believes what they want about me, most of it probably not good. But after the last few days, I'm finally starting to feel like I am part of the family, like maybe this really is where I belong, even if it does complicate things tremendously for Angelina and me.

She feathers her fingertips over my brow. "What are you thinking about right now?"

How badly I let everything get out of control. How much I fucked up with everyone who tried to care about me. How badly I want to fix it all...

"Family."

"What about it?"

I meet her inquisitive and concerned gaze. "That some people are family from the instant you meet them. That Christmas at your nana's house, it was my first day of freedom, but it was also the most terrified I've ever been in my life. Until I met Allie..."

Angelina's eyes soften.

"Allie gave me a safe, quiet place. But you"—I shake my head—"when you opened that door and looked at me, I felt my whole world shift. It was like I was seeing true love, true caring,

377

true understanding in the eyes of another person for the first time. And she promised me that you were cool, remember?"

The corner of her lips twitch. "I am pretty cool."

"Yeah, you are." I feather a kiss to her forehead. "And you protected us. You kept that closet locked down. You kept us safe. You made sure we weren't bothered and that I would have the time and space I needed because you could see I couldn't handle the Hawkes that night. You've always protected me, Angie, even when you didn't know you were doing it. All those family dinners, all those events that overwhelmed me, I saw the way you redirected people when they came near me. I noticed how you always kept your eye on me, always made sure you knew where I was and that I was okay."

She pulls that lip under her teeth again and glances down, almost like she's embarrassed by my realization.

I tip up her chin. "Why are you doing that?"

She lets her lip go. "I don't know. I didn't even realize I was doing it most of the time. I just...felt like you were mine to protect."

Mine to protect.

"Shit, Ang, it should be the other way around. I should be the one protecting *you*. And that's what I'm worried about, that you're going to read this book, you're going to see how fucking ass-backward all this is, and realize you can do so much better than me."

She tenses, and her lips press into a hard line. "Fuck you for even saying that, Jude."

I rock my hips up against hers, so she can feel how hard I am just from her straddling me. "I think you've already done that."

"Very funny." She slaps at my shoulder playfully, and her eyes dart to the computer again. "Now...can I please read it?"

It's a losing battle.

If I say no, she's going to think I don't trust her and wonder

378

what could be in there that I don't want her to see, but if I say yes, then she'll see it *all*.

The years of watching her. Wanting her. The *true* depth of my need for her.

I release a heavy sigh and lean forward to press my lips to hers. "Okay, but you have to promise me something."

"What's that?"

"That you won't hate me when you're done."

She nuzzles my cheek, releasing a heavy breath as she presses her hand over my heart. "I could never hate you, Jude."

I hope she's right.

———

ANGELINA

There were only so many ways to say I love you, and Rosalie had tried them all, screaming them into the dark void of her world, hoping someone would hear them and respond.

But all she ever heard was silence. That heavy, deafening sound that weighed down on her, that she carried around on her shoulders every moment of every day. While she cared for everyone else and worked to ensure their happiness, she was suffocating under its weight.

Until she finally got her response, but it didn't come in the words she had anticipated. It came in a single look. Given from across a street. Through a pane of glass that kept them apart as much as life itself did.

The look told her there were no words in existence strong enough to describe the way he felt about her. Nothing deep enough to make her understand how completely she was his world, how she was the

glue that held everything together and made life worth living.
When their eyes locked, she knew she had finally found her answer.

I STARE at the screen for a few seconds, the words blurring through the tears as my mind struggles to grasp what I just spent my day reading.

Holy shit.

This whole time, I thought I understood what was happening with Jude. I thought all the years of wondering, all the time we spent dancing around each other, all the tension and anticipation, and then the adrenaline of everything that's happened had all culminated in this explosive coming together. Something that might not have ever happened if not for the perfect alignment of events.

Allie's disappearing game...

Falco moving against us again...

Roselli showing up with his threats...

If none of them occurred, if we hadn't been pushed together, I'm not sure we ever would have found our way to each other.

But he's *always* seen it.

He's *always* known.

When he said he *sees* me. He really means he *sees* me. He sees past the walls *I* put up that rival his own. He sees through the smiles that hide my pain. He sees all the things I've tried so hard to conceal. And he has been able to since that very first day.

Page after page, a love story unfolded.

A hauntingly beautiful, traumatic, heart-wrenching tragedy of a woman who fought love and a man who only ever wanted it from one person.

He wrote *our* story, and he did it *before* we were even together. Almost as if he were writing the future on the page, willing it into existence through each letter and word he typed.

I set down the computer on the couch beside me and swipe at tears streaming from my eyes. The windows overlooking the street make up the entire wall in front of me—Jude's perch.

Where he apparently saw *everything.*

I glance behind me to the kitchen, where Jude leans against the counter, rubbing his damp hair with a towel, watching me closely. After lifting weights and then running for what felt like twenty miles while I read today, I was shocked he didn't collapse. But he seemed to need it. A distraction from his nerves about me reading this.

His gaze meets mine, and one of his blond brows rises. "Well?"

I slowly climb to my feet and approach him. "I literally can't process what I just read. I need some time."

"Oh." His face falls slightly, regret darkening his gaze. "Okay."

It isn't the answer he's looking for, but I can't even put what I'm thinking into words at this moment. And I don't want to say the wrong thing.

I turn away from him and walk to the bedroom, stripping off his T-shirt I slept in, intending to take a long, hot shower and try to decompress, but he wraps his arms around me from behind, stopping me in my tracks.

He nuzzles my nape, tugging me against him tightly. "You're not mad, are you?"

I rest my hands over his on my stomach. "God, no. That's the furthest from what I am. I'm just kind of...stunned."

Warm lips flutter against my ear. "Stunned, how?"

I turn my head slightly until I can look at him out of the corner of my eye. "Because that's the single most beautiful thing I think I've ever read."

His breath catches, and he squeezes his eyes closed and presses his forehead against my temple. "Oh, thank God."

"Why? What did you think?"

He pulls his head back. "That letting you read that might have ruined this."

I shake my head. "Nothing could do that."

"Thank fuck." Jude pushes my hair over my shoulder and kisses his way down the back of my neck, sending a shiver down my spine. "You have no idea how terrified I've been all day. How much I thought I had fucked up everything by letting you see how completely and utterly obsessed I am with you."

Hell...

Maybe I should be more worried about how wholly fixated the man in that story is on Rosalie. Maybe it *isn't* healthy for two human beings to be so completely wrapped up in each other.

It's the very thing I've fought against so hard for so long.

Wanting someone so much.

Needing them so much.

But my body heats at his simple touch, and being in his arms instantly melts away any reservations.

Pressing his hard body against me, Jude nudges me forward. "Climb on the bed. Lie flat. Turn your head to the side."

What the hell is he doing?

It doesn't matter. At this moment, after reading *that*, I'd do *anything* Jude asks of me.

I climb on the bed and sprawl out, peeking up at him as he tugs off his shirt and shoves down his gray sweatpants, exposing his perfect rippling abs leading down to his already hard cock.

The familiar dull throb starts between my legs, and I press my thighs together to try to ease it. Jude climbs onto the bed, softly dragging his hands from my ankles to my ass as he works his way up.

He nudges my legs wide, and my body vibrates in anticipation. But instead of diving right in, he braces his arms on either side of me and leans down, kissing me softly from my temple all the way down my cheek, across to my lips.

His tongue glides along the seam, demanding entrance, and I open for him, groaning into his mouth and clutching the comforter under me.

"Lie still."

Oh geez. What the hell is he going to do?

He moves his lips down the column of my neck before concentrating on each shoulder blade. Soft, sensual kisses of pure reverence move down my spine. Alternating with little flicks of his tongue that explore every dip and valley.

Fire scorches across my skin, followed immediately by goosebumps as he drags his fingertips over the places his lips just left. I twitch under him, and my clit throbs hard enough to make me groan in frustration.

Moisture pools between my legs, but with Jude straddling the back of my knees, I'm pinned to the mattress, helpless to do anything about the need surging through my entire being.

"I would do this every day, you know." His murmur buzzes against my skin. "Spend all day worshiping you, kissing you, adoring your body."

"That doesn't sound too bad."

He chuckles, the vibration sending a little zing straight between my legs, making me groan again. "I would hope not."

His lips reach the little divot above my ass, and he slowly spreads the cheeks apart and kisses all over them, then nudges my legs open even wider and works his way down my inner thighs, avoiding the spot I want him the most.

I twitch, my back arching to try to get him to my pussy, and he presses a palm against my spine, holding me in place. Making his way up and down my legs, he drags his tongue in the most sensitive spots, kissing softly in others until my entire body vibrates like a goddamn drum.

He finally starts to work his way back up, and I'm a quivering mess.

Then it's there, the flick of his tongue across my wet cunt, and my whole body bucks back, bowing toward him. He pushes me down again, keeping me prone so he can eat at me relentlessly.

His tongue probes in and out, like he's trying to devour all of me all at once, then it slips up around my asshole.

"Fuck!" I clench instinctively, and he groans and slides a finger inside my cunt. Thrusting in and out softly, he uses his mouth to explore a place no one else ever has.

Jesus Christ.

Jude is full of surprises, more than any man I've ever met in my entire life. Some bad, some good, some undefinable.

If this is the result of his obsession. If this is what it feels like to be loved by Jude Abello-Harris, then I have zero complaints.

He drags his head back and presses his entire body along mine. Hard and warm. Soft and strong. He aligns his cock with my slick opening and pushes in slowly, so I can feel every exquisite inch.

Fuuuuck.

His hands settle over mine on the mattress, and he twines our fingers as he rolls back his hips and plunges in softly again. "Christ, Ang, your cunt is my favorite place on the fucking planet."

I groan at the weight of his body on top of me. The feel of his cock stretching me wide, completing me. Of him filling that void I've always felt in my life. The one I never let myself even acknowledge before. Where I let a man become something to me, let him mean everything. To actually love another human being enough to know that if I lost him, it would destroy me.

Tears leak from my eyes, and he stills, dragging his tongue along the path they left on my cheek.

"What's wrong?"

I shake my head. "Nothing. I'm just really fucking happy."

He grins against my damp skin and starts his slow rhythm again. "Good. Me too."

Every thrust cements him farther inside my body and heart, ensuring that no matter who or what may try to separate us, may try to attack our relationship or the family, nothing will ever drive us apart.

Not again.

We've wasted so much time dancing around each other, worrying so much about what everyone else would think, how everyone else would feel, talking ourselves out of doing what we want without giving any credence to how we felt about each other.

But now that we have, there's no going back.

We're a runaway train, and until the track ends, we're going to keep rushing toward our future.

I roll my hips back to meet each one of his thrusts, and the slow, sweet glide starts to build the orgasm deep in my belly quickly. Sensing how close I am, he slides his hand under my body to let his fingers find my clit. The first contact makes me buck and clench around him, and when he swirls his fingertips around it, my release washes over me.

My body twitches as he pumps into my cunt, his hand tightening on mine in the comforter, the other continuing to work over my clit to drag out my ecstasy. He groans against my ear and empties himself inside me quietly before completely collapsing onto his side and rolling me with him.

His arms wrap around me, and he holds me tight.

Jude says I protect him and that it should be the other way around, but he has no idea what he's done for me. I'm finally starting to believe what he said, that everything will be okay.

We'll fix the Grind.

We'll deal with the situation with Falco Enterprises and Roselli.

We'll help Allie raise that child.

Anything that comes at us, we'll face it together.

And he doesn't even have to say the words because I see it in his eyes, just like I always could, even through those panes of glass.

EPILOGUE
THREE WEEKS LATER

ANGELINA

I f anyone had told me that we could get this place ready to open in three weeks, I would have told them they were fucking crazy. The list of what needed to get done was daunting, but somehow, the Hawkes pulled it off.

Gorgeous custom-built bookshelves line the walls, broken only by spaces specifically designed to display Jack's art. Books from every genre fill the shelves, meticulously organized by Jude's exacting eye.

It shouldn't surprise me what this family is capable of when they put their minds, money, and effort into something, and after what happened to the Grind, getting Hawke's Novel Idea up and running before the new coffee shop opened down the street became the top priority.

Naturally, my eyes drift through the front windows and across the street to the framing finally going up.

That fix isn't so quick.

Neither is working through the issues that made Jude lock himself away from the world for so long.

I glance over to the register area, where he leans over the counter, flipping through a stack of printed pages and scribbling furiously at the edges.

Each time we come down here, it gets a little easier, and when he manages to focus on something else—like edits on his book—it's easy to forget the level of panic being in this space used to cause.

I won't take it for granted, though.

Especially not when customers will start coming in tomorrow when we open, and there's no way to know how that change will affect him.

But Allie and I will be here, ready to do whatever it takes to make sure this business is successful and Jude has all the support he needs to keep taking baby steps.

I grab the empty box that contained the last of the books for the shelf in front of me, tuck it under my arm, and make my way over to him, pausing on the other side of the counter and waiting until he finally lifts his head, his eyes trailing over my breasts and finally up to meet my eyes.

A slow grin spreads across his lips. "Hey."

"Hey, yourself."

He rises to his full height and stretches, cracking his back.

I can't fight the smug smile at his wince. "I told you that you were going to regret it..."

He smirks and leans across the counter to brush his lips over mine. "Maybe when I'm your age."

"Very funny."

He quickly scans the shop. "Shit. Are you done?"

I nod as I take in my handiwork. "Yep. While you've had your head buried in these pages, I managed to sort and unbox the last shipment. And since Jack and Isaac got everything hung earlier, we're officially ready to open tomorrow."

His hand goes to the center of his chest, and he starts

rubbing at it, a sure sign his anxiety is starting to ramp up again.

"Why don't you look happy?"

"I am. I'm just a little..." He shrugs and gives me a half-smile. "I don't know. I felt like this would never happen. That I fucked it up so badly that we'd never get here."

Even now, his guilt over keeping everyone in the dark about what was going on still eats away at him.

I press my hand over his, stilling the nervous motion of his fingers. "But we did get here. Together. It's a really good thing."

So are the meetings he's been having with Dr. Cochran. Nora's recommendation for a therapist who could help Jude deal with his childhood trauma and agoraphobia issues has been a godsend.

It's a long, incredibly bumpy road that will probably never be smooth, but he's taking steps down it. He's making progress. He's *trying*, and that's really all we can ask for.

I bite back telling him how proud of him I am because I know he gets sick of hearing it. Instead, I hold up the box. "I'm going to go throw this into the storage room, and then we can head out."

He smirks. "Okay."

Heading toward the back, I keep an eye on him and the odd look he's giving me. His focus drops to my ass, and I put a little extra swing in my hips as I throw open the storage room door and step in.

I only make it three steps in before I sense movement behind me and turn to find Jude leaning his tall frame against the jamb. Mischief and desire dance in his eyes, and his lips tilt into a slow grin.

Oh no. I know that look all too well.

"Don't look at me like that, Jude."

He takes a step in and nudges the door closed with his foot. "Why not?"

I retreat a step, then another. "Because we have to be at Nana's in an hour."

He grins as he finally reaches me and cages me against the wall with his arms. "An hour is plenty of time."

Hell...

My body heats instantly, and I squirm against him, trying to shift out from underneath his arm.

"I'm sweaty and disgusting from working all day. I need time to shower and get cleaned up."

His hand lashes out to grab me and keep me up against the wall, palm pressed flat over my hip. He curls his fingers into the flesh there, the contact enough to send that little electric spark skittering through me.

He lowers his head, brushing his lips against my ear. "I promise to clean you up afterward."

Good fucking God.

The man is insatiable, and normally, I wouldn't complain, but it's Jude's first time going to Nana's for Sunday dinner in two years. His first time being around the entire family since everyone came to his place the night of the fire.

It's a big deal, one he should mentally be preparing himself for.

I lock eyes with him, trying my best to convey how serious I am. "We should really get you prepared to go."

His lips move over mine slowly as he grinds his hard cock against my stomach. "You know what would help relax me and make sure I was in the best possible mental state before we leave?"

"Oh, Jesus." I push against his chest, but he doesn't budge. "That's not fair, Jude."

"What's not fair?"

I glower at him. "You know."

He slides his hand past the waistband of my yoga pants and cups me between my legs, no doubt feeling how wet I already am through my thong. "What's not fair is you pretending you don't want me to fuck your brains out right now."

"Jude!"

One of his brows wings up in mock innocence. "What?"

"You know what it does to me when you talk like that."

"I know." He nips at my bottom lip. "Why do you think I said it?"

"The front door isn't even locked."

His shoulder rises and falls casually. "We aren't open yet. No one's coming in."

"You don't know that. Someone could walk right in off the street and steal something."

He slips my thong to the side and drags his finger through the moisture pooling between my legs. "Let them take it."

His finger slides inside me, and I gasp. He catches the sound in his mouth, thrusting up as my pussy clenches around the digit.

"Oh, God."

If I had any chance of resisting him, it was gone the second he put his hands on me. I don't know if it'll always be like this with him, but I sure as hell hope so.

The man lights me up from the inside out, sets my entire body on fire, and I am more than willing to burn with him just to feel this kind of heat.

I unzip his jeans, shoving them down to free his cock, and when I finally get my hand around his length, he groans into my mouth, kissing me frantically, feverishly, as if it's our first time and our last all rolled into one.

His thumb finds my clit and circles around it, making me buck on his hand, and I tighten mine around his shaft.

He tears his mouth from mine, his eyes blazing the same way my body does. "Turn around."

Fuck, yes.

I spin in his arms, and he presses my chest against the wall and tugs my pants and thong to my knees. His large hand caresses my ass, and then it's gone, only to come back and smack against it hard, the sharp sting of pain making me yelp. But his soft touch soothes it immediately as he pushes my hair over my shoulder and kisses up the length of my neck.

Warm breath flutters against my ear, and he sucks the lobe in and bites softly. "I'm going to fuck you hard, and I'm going to make you come at least twice. I don't want you to be able to walk into dinner tonight. I want to have to carry you."

My legs tremble in anticipation, and he grasps my hips and pulls them out and back, positioning me at exactly the right angle to take him. He bends his knees, drags the head of his cock through my arousal, and then shoves up into me in one harsh thrust.

"Fuck!" I rock forward against the wall, my body pinned between him and it, the pressure of his weight the only thing keeping me upright.

His hand tightens on my hip, and he pushes into me again, plunging himself so deep that it steals my breath. My head spins, and I scratch at the wall, desperate to cling to something. His lips find that spot behind my ear, and he sucks and licks there, making my pussy spasm and clench along his length.

With every thrust, every drive of his hips, I lose myself more and more to Jude Abello-Harris.

All the things we worried about, all the reasons we used to convince ourselves to stay away and that what we were feeling wasn't real, have finally disappeared, replaced by the passion we both know will never fizzle out.

I roll my hips back to meet his, and my body heats, the brilliant flame starting at my core and racing out, reaching for that precipice I know is right there. He slides one hand down my stomach to find my clit and rolls his finger there in time with his hips, then pinches it, setting off an orgasm that leaves my legs faltering and my vision going black. He barrels into me over and over again, finally crying out his release and burying his face into my hair.

I tremble between him and the wall, his hand at my hip keeping me upright.

"That was one."

"Oh, God, I don't know if I can handle another one..."

But his cock is still hard, and his hand is still positioned between my legs. He starts to roll his finger over my clit again, doing that thing with his hips that drags the head of his cock in exactly the right spot inside me.

My first orgasm has barely ebbed, and already, he's building another one. I twitch against him, his hot breath fanning over me. My body throbs, my blood rushing in my ears.

This one comes slowly, a soft, gradual build that trickles down through my limbs like a waterfall until I sag to the wall.

He grins against my cheek and kisses his way to my lips, tilting my head back toward him to take my mouth at the angle he wants. I clench around his cock, and he groans, his grip on my chin tightening.

"Hello?" the voice calling out makes us both freeze.

Jude jerks back from me, his cock sliding out. "Shit."

Still encompassed in the post-orgasmic haze, I laugh and sink against the wall. "I told you someone could come in."

He tugs up his jeans and tucks his wet, still-hard cock into them, scowling at me. I burst out laughing, pressing my hand over my mouth as I reach down and try to right my underwear and pants. He runs a hand back over his hair, though it doesn't do any good since it's always disheveled and out of control.

Pausing to ensure I'm covered, Jude opens the door and steps out. "Hi. Sorry. Can I help you?"

"Yes. Are you guys open yet?"

The familiar voice floats to me.

Damon?

I adjust my shirt, trying to get my breathing under control

as I make my way out of the supply closet to find them standing near the counter.

Damon's eyes meet mine, and he grins. "Angelina, it's been a long time."

"Damon, it's so nice to see you."

He scans the store and holds out a hand. "This place is quite impressive. I wanted to swing by as soon as you were open."

Jude looks between the two of us, his eyes darkening slightly with a hint of jealousy. He crosses his arms over his chest. "We open tomorrow."

Damon offers me a half-grin. "Then I guess I'll come back tomorrow."

"No, no, no." I nudge Jude to the side. "You can look around now if you want to. Jude, this is Damon, one of my regulars. I'm sure you've seen him out on the sidewalk with his morning paper."

Jude nods slowly, his jaw tight, so damn jealous, even though he just had his dick inside me and made me come twice. "Yeah. Sure."

I elbow Jude in the ribs. "Be nice."

He leans down to bring his lips to my ear. "Sell him some books and art, but remember what's dripping from between your legs."

———

JUDE

ANGELINA JABS her elbow into my ribs for the second time in the last hour. "Lose the scowl."

I jerk to a stop outside Nana's house, rubbing at my side. "What?"

"Lose the scowl, or everyone's going to think it's because you don't want to be here instead of you just being jealous."

394

Smartass.

I glare at her. "I'm not jealous."

Ang rolls her eyes. "Yes, you are." She pushes up on her tiptoes and presses her lips against mine. "He's just a customer, a very loyal one, I might add, who bought four books today before we're even open and will be the first one back on the sidewalk having his coffee every morning when The Grind opens. So, *stop* it."

I issue a low growl and tug her up against me. "I don't like it."

She shoves against my chest slightly, but I don't budge. "I don't care if you like it, Jude. It's the way it is, unless you're going to keep me locked away in your loft forever, like Rapunzel."

"Hey, now." I grin against her lips. "That sounds like a great idea."

Her laugh fills the summer night air, and she swats at my shoulder. "Come on. We have to go in. Nana's waiting. So is everyone else."

Everyone's waiting for me...

I suck in a heavy breath and release it slowly, trying to work through the slight tightness already trying to encroach on my chest.

She raises her eyebrows at me. "You're good?"

I nod. "So far, so good."

Over the last few weeks, I've done my best to try to push myself—to spend more time on the roof and in the bookstore, to take longer walks around the neighborhood with Allie or Angie, and each time, the same panic has started to overwhelm me to varying degrees.

Dr. Cochran assured me what I was feeling was understandable, given everything I've been through, and that it wasn't something I could get over in a matter of days, weeks, months, or even years.

A work in progress.

That's what she called me, and tonight, I really want to believe that things are getting better because if I walk in there and can't stay, it will destroy Nana.

But staring at her house now, with Angelina's arm looped through mine, a sense of calm settles over me. A resignation. A peace I typically only get at the loft when I'm wrapped around Ang.

We walk arm and arm up to the door, and she opens it and walks in without even knocking. Even though I've been here hundreds of times over the years, being with her sends me back to that day, what this place looked like, lit up and ready for Christmas, the feeling of walking in with Luca and Byron and not knowing what the hell was going on, of being that little lost boy with no family, no hope, terrified.

Angie closes the door behind us and tightens her grip on me. "You're good?"

I raise a brow. "Are you going to keep asking me that all night?"

"Do I have to?"

It's a fair question. She's only trying to do her best to help me. But sometimes, my ego gets in the way, and I hate the fact that she has to do it.

She presses up on her toes again, bringing her lips to my ear. "You know I love you no matter what. If we need to go, we need to go."

My jaw tightens, and she presses a kiss there, then slips her arm free of mine and walks into the living room to our right.

"Hey, everybody."

A chorus of "hellos" goes up, and Luca appears in the foyer, brows raised.

"You made it."

I nod slowly as I approach him. "I made it."

He shifts closer, glancing over his shoulder to ensure no one else is around. "How are you doing?"

I hate answering the question.

I hate that I have to.

I hate that everyone now knows why I haven't been around.

But at the same time, them knowing has opened doors I thought were long closed. No one looks at me like I'm an ungrateful interloper. That's progress.

"I'm good."

A hell of a lot better since he took care of the reason I ended up locked away in the loft in the first place. Even two weeks later, the rush of relief I felt when he showed up and said, "It's done," still fills my chest.

Two words were all it took for me to realize this family truly *will* do anything for each other.

"Is that my Jude?" Nana's voice carries through the foyer, my heart warming instantly. She rushes from the kitchen but pulls herself up short in front of me. "Can I?"

The hope in her voice makes me fight back tears. I nod, and before I even know what's happening, she throws her arms around me, crushing her small frame to mine.

Luca smiles at me and returns to the living room, leaving me alone with the sweet old woman who always tried to give me what I needed, even when I didn't know what it was.

She pulls back and looks up at me. "I'm so happy to have you home."

"Me, too, Nana."

"You let me know if you need to go. I've already got an extra pan of lasagna and chicken parm for you to take."

I chuckle at her and give her an extra squeeze as I wrap my arm around her shoulder and walk her back to the kitchen. "I think I'll be okay, Nana."

She pauses in the opening to the dining room and motions to the table. "Your seat's been waiting for you."

I scan the long table where somehow we manage to fit almost two dozen people every Sunday, and my eyes linger on the chair I always used—next to Allie with Luca on the other side. "Same spot?"

She squeezes my arm. "Of course. I would never let anyone else sit in it."

"Even when I wasn't here?"

Her lips curl. "I knew you'd be back, eventually."

She had a lot more confidence than I did.

Some days, I still don't know how I do it. Some days I can't. But Dr. Cochran was right about a lot of things. The biggest was that I have a massive support system I need to rely on instead of cutting them out for my own pride.

I drop Nana in the kitchen and wander toward the sliding glass doors that lead to the backyard, where Pope, Isaac, Coen, and Atlas sit around the table with a deck of cards.

Isaac glances up at me. "Well, look who decided to show up."

I could be offended by his comment, but his slow grin makes me smile back. The fact that he is comfortable giving me shit after all the tension that's existed between us in the past is a good sign for our professional working relationship now that his wife is technically my business partner.

Stepping out onto the patio, I inhale the fresh air, watching the lights in the pool flicker under the blue water.

"You want to play?" Pope raises a brow. "Coen's losing all his money, and I think he's about to quit."

Coen tosses his cards onto the table and leans back in a huff, arms crossed over his chest. "You guys all cheat."

Pope chuckles and pulls the pile of bills from the center of the table toward him. "I don't have to cheat to beat you. You suck at poker."

I grin and lean back against the house. "Nana would kill you if she knew you were gambling."

Atlas smirks. "Why do you think we're playing outside? She almost busted us last week in the dining room."

"Smart."

It feels like starting over from scratch with them, like I have to learn who each of them is again after so long. But Allie and Angie were both right. The Hawkes have never judged me, never made this any harder than it needs to be. Even without going into the gory details of my awful childhood, everyone has accepted my unique *issues* and how they'll continue to affect my interactions with them. Maybe it helped shed some light on my inability to connect with them when we were younger.

The door slides open, and Angie slips out with two glasses of wine, handing me one.

"Thank you."

She scans the table and laughs. "Are you guys taking Coen's money again?"

He scowls at her while Pope and Isaac chuckle.

Isaac smacks his brother's arm. "Something like that."

She takes my hand and tugs me out into the yard toward the pool. "We'll be back."

Atlas grins at us. "Don't get into too much trouble."

It isn't nearly as weird as we thought it would be—us being together.

The few initial strange looks and off-handed comments have quickly morphed into an easy acceptance—which I firmly believe has more to do with the fact that being with Angie romantically has gotten me to "return" to the family.

It makes it easier for everyone to just accept it and let us be happy. Plus, there are far bigger things to worry about than two people who love each other wanting to be together.

Angie kicks off her sandals and settles at the edge of the pool, dropping her bare feet into the water. I take off my shoes, roll up my jeans, and submerge my feet beside hers.

She drops her head against my shoulder and releases a heavy sigh. "This is good, right?"

I nod as I stare at the water. "This is good."

Really.

Only a matter of months ago, I never could have thought any of this was possible.

Being here.

Being with Angelina.

So much has changed so fast, and there is still so much left to do. So many things left hanging and unresolved.

I glance back toward the house. "Is Allie here yet?"

Ang shakes her head. "No, but I texted her, and she said she's on her way."

"You think she was with him?"

She takes a sip of her wine, swishing her feet back and forth. "I don't know. If she is..." She trails off. "She's going to start showing soon."

"I know." I take a drink of my wine, staring down into the water, trying to figure out what the hell Allie is doing. "You know she hasn't told him."

"I know." She turns her head to look at me. "And she's still lying to us, saying she did. Should we be more worried than we are?"

I snort. "I'm plenty worried. I don't like her lying to us about this."

"Me, either. We have enough to worry about."

Like her competition already poaching the café's clients while we rebuild.

Roselli's "request" for an alliance that we still haven't agreed to.

And the mysterious danger he referenced.

No amount of digging has been able to come up with any answer about who could be behind the attacks on his businesses or any evidence that anyone has partnered with Falco, as Roselli suggested.

It's left everyone on edge, like waiting for the other shoe to drop when the first one already destroyed something so major when it came down.

She leans against my arm. "Why'd you tense up?"

I glance down at her and press a kiss to her forehead. "I was just thinking that there are a lot of unknowns right now."

She nods. "There are. But we'll handle all of them together, right?"

"Right."

I take her face in my palm and bring her lips to mine, brushing a kiss across them.

This is it.

The moment I've waited twenty-five years for.

Sitting here with Angelina, enjoying great wine while a house full of people who love and support us wait to enjoy an incredible family dinner, it *finally* feels like I'm the windshield.

———

KENNEDY

STRANGLING Cassius Whitaker with my bare hands better not break a fucking nail. I just had this manicure done...

———

I HOPE you enjoyed *Reticent Hawke*. Delve further into the Hawke Family world with Cass and Kennedy's enemies to lovers story, in *Relentless Hawke*!

Get your copy: books2read.com/RelentlessHawke

To stay up to date on news, sales, and releases from Gwyn, join her newsletter here: www.gwynmcnamee.com/newsletter

ACKNOWLEDGMENTS

Thank you to everyone who helped me bring this angsty and emotional story to the page - Renee, Tabatha, Patricia, Stephie, and Caoimhe, you are all rockstars!

A special thanks to Jessica Call and Cassandra Lang for sharing their personal experiences with agoraphobia and beta reading Reticent Hawke to ensure Jude's story was told in the proper way.

ABOUT THE AUTHOR

Gwyn McNamee is an attorney, writer, wife, and mother (to one human baby and two fur babies). Originally from the Midwest, Gwyn relocated to her husband's home town of Las Vegas in 2015 and is enjoying her respite from the cold and snow. Gwyn has been writing down her crazy stories and ideas for years and finally decided to share them with the world. She loves to write stories with a bit of suspense and action mingled with romance and heat.

When she isn't either writing or voraciously devouring any books she can get her hands on, Gwyn is busy adding to her tattoo collection, golfing, and stirring up trouble with her perfect mix of sweetness and sarcasm (usually while wearing heels).

Gwyn loves to hear from her readers. Here is where you can find her:

Website: http://www.gwynmcnamee.com/

Facebook: https://www.facebook.com/AuthorGwynMcNamee/

FB Reader Group: https://www.facebook.com/groups/1667380963540655/

Newsletter: www.gwynmcnamee.com/newsletter

Twitter: https://twitter.com/GwynMcNamee

Instagram: https://www.instagram.com/gwynmcnamee

Bookbub: https://www.bookbub.com/authors/gwynmcnamee

Tiktok: https://www.tiktok.com/@authorgwynmcnamee

OTHER WORKS BY GWYN MCNAMEE

Billionaires of New Orleans:

The Hawke Family Series

Savage Collision **(The Hawke Family - Book One)**

He's everything she didn't know she wanted. She's everything he thought he could never have.

The last thing I expect when I walk into The Hawkeye Club is to fall head over heels in lust. It's supposed to be a rescue mission. I have to get my baby sister off the pole, into some clothes, and out of the grasp of the pussy peddler who somehow manipulated her into stripping. But the moment I see Savage Hawke and verbally spar with him, my ability to remain rational flies out the window and my libido takes center stage. I've never wanted a relationship—my time is better spent focusing on taking down the scum running this city—but what I want and what I need are apparently two different things.

Danika Eriksson storms into my office in her high heels and on her high horse. Her holier-than-thou attitude and accusations should offend me, but instead, I can't get her out of my head or my heart. Her incomparable drive, take-no prisoners attitude, and blatant honesty captivate me and hold me prisoner. I should steer clear, but my self-preservation instinct is apparently dead—which is exactly what our relationship will be once she knows everything. It's only a matter of time.

The truth doesn't always set you free. Sometimes, it just royally screws you.

AVAILABLE AT ALL RETAILERS:

books2read.com/SavageCollision

Tortured Skye (**The Hawke Family - Book Two**)

She's always been off-limits. He's always just out of reach.

Falling in love with Gabe Anderson was as easy as breathing. Fighting my feelings for my brother's best friend was agonizingly hard. I never imagined giving in to my desire for him would cause such a destructive ripple effect. That kiss was my grasp at a lifeline—something, anything to hold me steady in my crumbling life. Now, I have to suffer with the fallout while trying to convince him it's all worth the consequences.

Guilt overwhelms me—over what I've done, the lives I've taken, and more than anything, over my feelings for Skye Hawke. Craving my best friend's little sister is insanely self-destructive. It never should have happened, but since the moment she kissed me, I haven't been able to get her out of my mind. If I take what I want, I risk losing everything. If I don't, I'll lose her and a piece of myself. The raging storm threatening to rain down on the city is nothing compared to the one that will come from my decision.

Love can be torture, but sometimes, love is the only thing that can save you.

AVAILABLE AT ALL RETAILERS:

Books2read.com/Tortured-Skye

Stone Sober (**The Hawke Family - Book Three**)

She's innocent and sweet. He's dark and depraved.

Stone Hawke is precisely the kind of man women are warned about—handsome, intelligent, arrogant, and intricately entangled with some dangerous people. I should stay away, but he manages to strip my soul bare with just a look and dominates my thoughts. Bad decisions are in my past. My life is (mostly) on track, even if it is no longer the one to medical school. I can't allow myself to cave to the fierce pull and ardent attraction I feel toward the youngest Hawke.

Nora Eriksson is off-limits, and not just because she's my brother's employee and sister-in-law. Despite the fact she's stripping at The Hawkeye Club, she has an innocent and pure heart. Normally, the only thing that appeals to me about innocence is the opportunity to taint it. But not when it comes to Nora. I can't expose her to the filth permeating my life. There are too many things I can't control, things completely out of my hands. She doesn't deserve any of it, but the power she holds over me is stronger than any addiction.

The hardest battles we fight are often with ourselves, but only through defeating our own demons can we find true peace.

AVAILABLE AT ALL RETAILERS:

books2read.com/StoneSober

Building Storm (The Hawke Family - Book Four)

She hasn't been living. He's looking for a way to forget it all.

My life went up in flames. All I'm left with is my daughter and ashes. The simple act of breathing is so excruciating, there are days I wish I could stop altogether. So I have no business being at the party, and I definitely shouldn't be in the arms of the handsome stranger. When his lips meet mine, he breathes life into me for the first time since the day the inferno disintegrated my world. But loving again isn't in the cards, and there are even greater dangers to face than trying to keep Landon McCabe out of my heart.

Running is my only option. I have to get away from Chicago and the betrayal that shattered my world. I need a new life-one without attachments. The vibrancy of New Orleans convinces me it's possible to start over. Yet in all the excitement of a new city, it's Storm Hawke's dark, sad beauty that draws me in. She isn't looking for love, and we both need a hot, sweaty release without feelings getting involved. But even the best laid plans fail, and life can leave you burned.

Love can build, and love can destroy. But in the end, love is what raises you from the ashes.

AVAILABLE AT ALL RETAILERS:

books2read.com/BuildingStorm

Tainted Saint (The Hawke Family - Book Five)

He's searching for absolution. She wants her happily ever after.

Solomon Clarke goes by Saint, though he's anything but. After lusting for him from afar, the masquerade party affords me the anonymity to pursue that attraction without worrying about the fall-out of hooking-up with the bouncer from the Hawkeye Club. From the second he lays his eyes and hands on me, I'm helpless to resist him. Even burying myself in a dangerous investigation can't erase the memory of our combustible connection and one night together. The only problem... he has no idea who I am.

Caroline Brooks thinks I don't see her watching me, the way her eyes rake over me with appreciation. But I've noticed, and the party is the perfect opportunity to unleash the desire I've kept reined in for so damn long. It also sets off a series of events no one sees coming. Events that leave those I love hurting because of my failures. While the guilt eats away at my soul, Caroline continues to weigh on my heart. That woman may be the death of me, but oh, what a way to go.

Life isn't always clean, and sometimes, it takes a saint to do the dirty work.

AVAILABLE AT ALL RETAILERS:

books2read.com/TaintedSaint

Steele Resolve (The Hawke Family - Book Six)

For one man, power is king. For the other, loyalty reigns.

Mob boss Luca "Steele" Abello isn't just dangerous—he's lethal. A master manipulator, liar, and user, no one should trust a word that comes out of his mouth. Yet, I can't get him out of my head. The time we spent together before I knew his true identity is seared into my brain. His touch. His voice. They haunt my every waking hour and occupy my dreams. So does my guilt. I'm literally sleeping with the enemy and betraying the only family I've ever had. When I come clean, it will be the end of me.

Byron Harris is a distraction I can't afford. I never should have let it go beyond that first night, but I couldn't stay away. Even when I learned who he was, when the *only* option was to end things, I kept going back, risking his life and mine to continue our indiscretion. The truth of what I am could get us both killed, but being with the man who's such an integral part of the Hawke family is even more terrifying. The only people I've ever cared about are on opposing sides, and I'm the rift that could end their friendship forever.

Love is a battlefield isn't just a saying. For some, it's a reality.

AVAILABLE AT ALL RETAILERS:

books2read.com/SteeleResolve

You can find information on the rest of Gwyn's books on her website:

www.gwynmcnamee.com

www.ingramcontent.com/pod-product-compliance
Lightning Source LLC
Chambersburg PA
CBHW072020020726
47501CB00006B/1887